Manhunt
In The
Capital

Manhunt
In The
Capital

Rob Shumaker

Also by Rob Shumaker

Thunder in the Capital

Showdown in the Capital

Chaos in the Capital

D-Day in the Capital

Fallout in the Capital

Phantom in the Capital

Blackout in the Capital

The Way Out

Acknowledgments

A special thanks to Mom and Dad for offering their editorial assistance and the opportunity to visit many of the places that found their way into this book. Thanks also to Special Agent Dave for his law-enforcement insight.

" . . . proclaim liberty throughout the land to all its inhabitants."

Leviticus 25:10

CHAPTER 1

Georgetown University – Washington, D.C.

"I hate America!"

The hostile man behind the lecture hall microphone, venom dripping out of every pore, pounded the podium with such force his Styrofoam cup of black coffee almost fell to the floor.

Those seated in the hall were not shocked at the statement. Not one of the students was taken aback. There were no audible gasps, no twitches of conscience as if they had simply misheard the man ranting and raving in front of them. None of them rolled their eyes thinking the man was emotionally disturbed or simply out of control. They simply sat back and enjoyed the show.

Of course, they had been hearing the same vitriol the entire semester, some even all their lives. And, what's more, they all agreed with the man.

The class was called "Diversity in Thought: American History Revisited." It was a three-hour course under the multi-cultural studies program and its intent was to indoctrinate young twentysomethings in the politically correct world of America bashing. It was a crash course designed to foment as much anger as possible so graduates could hit the ground running in the progressive transformation of American society as community organizers, academics, bureaucrats, and if they so chose, as parents. The syllabus promised lively discussions and required hands-on activism. The readings started out with the slaughter of the Indians, then the ravages of slavery, then the oppression of women, then the war on illegal immigrants. On and on it went, demonizing the American system but conveniently leaving out the past historical failings of other countries and the boundless opportunity that awaits every free American. To Professor Alicia Alton-Mosby, the head of the leftist multi-cultural wing, her students were victims and they needed to be reminded of it every day.

The administrators were none too pleased about the lectures but too afraid to do anything about them. Along with using her race and gender as weapons, Professor Alton-Mosby had angrily waved the First Amendment at them on multiple occasions, and the higher-ups relented so as not to be branded as politically incorrect. She had once protested for the removal of the crucifixes from the university classrooms and called in her good friend Art Brennan for help to make it happen. He felt right at home amongst her students.

"I should clarify," Art Brennan continued, pausing just long enough to catch his breath. Despite his profession as a lawyer, the rancor burning inside of Brennan spewed forth in some sort of Baptist minister's hell-fire sermon on the evils of the United States. He was loud and abrasive, and his sentences usually ended with exclamation points.

"I hate the America every citizen has been told to love and cherish since they were forced against their will to pledge allegiance to the flag in kindergarten!" he huffed, his delivery ramping up for a raging peroration. "The America that people claim to be the greatest country in the world, the beacon of freedom for all mankind. All that ridiculous patriotic malarkey!"

Heads nodded. Smiles appeared. One boisterous male in the back of the hall shouted, "Amen, brother," which was followed up with laughter and clapping from his like-minded comrades. Those in the class liked what they were hearing.

Every Monday at ten, the class welcomed a "renowned scholar," "celebrated academic," or just some "enlightened" mind as a guest lecturer, but only if he or she could rant and rave and sufficiently foam at the mouth enough to make sure the students were properly educated on the evils of the United States of America. While Arthur J. Brennan was neither a "scholar" nor an "academic," his anti-America diatribes were well thought of enough in faculty lounges and progressive party circles to qualify as being "enlightened." He was a frequent contributor to MSNBC roundtables, and his provocative nature meant his bombastic quotes made the political columns of the *New York Times* on a weekly basis. As a pseudo-celebrity, the professor could always count on the firebrand Brennan stirring the pot and exciting the crowd. At least three different recordings of the lecture would find their way to YouTube before lunchtime.

Art Brennan was the pugnacious head of the ultra-liberal Civil Liberties Alliance, an organization intent on fanning the flames of class warfare and racial strife. He loudly claimed blacks were treated worse now than in slave times, and he warned Hispanics that they would soon be rounded up and sent back to Mexico. It didn't matter that the accusations weren't true – it was the seriousness of the charges and their constant repetition that made the mind-numbed listener nod in agreement. In turn, the CLA brought in millions of dollars in donations from foreign and domestic sources to promote its agenda and expand its reach throughout the globe. The money would also go toward supporting America's enemies – anarchists, terrorists – whenever the ne'er-do-wells found themselves on the wrong side of the law and in need of legal representation.

Bald with a fat face, the only time Brennan could keep his mouth shut was when he put a cigar in it. He managed to reach five-foot-eight when he wore his black loafers, but he made up for his short stature with a bulldog ferociousness that tore into the jugular of anyone who crossed him. Brennan focused most of his rage for those in the Republican Party and "their" Constitution, which he found restricted Government's ultimate right to remedy past wrongs with cradle-to-grave support by kindhearted Washington bureaucrats who lovingly dreamed of that nonexistent world utopia.

And no one took the brunt of Brennan's belligerent rants more than President Anthony Schumacher.

"What we see today with the current administration is nothing more than a continuation of the trampling of human rights that has marred this country since it was founded. The President says he is fighting terrorism to make our country safer," Brennan said into the microphone, pointing his finger toward the gathered throng. "I, on the other hand, believe his war on terror is actually a war on Islam, a tyrannical war on the Muslim community."

President Schumacher had come to office under a dark cloud of turmoil – assuming the Presidency after President Ronald Fisher tried to have him killed before taking his own life in an Oval Office suicide. As the country's chief executive, Schumacher rounded up terrorists while dodging assassination attempts on himself and his family. After winning his first election as President, he kept the American homeland safe and engineered a robust economic recovery. But, alas, some in the world continued to look for ways to bring America to its knees. Less than a year into his first full term, Russian operatives hatched a plan to hold the

President against his will during a meeting with the Italian Prime Minister in Rome and then transport him to the International Criminal Court for trial on charges of war crimes. The plan failed but only after a daring raid by an elite team of FBI agents.

With President Schumacher's rise to power and his overwhelming support by a large majority of Americans, Brennan had grown increasingly radical over the last several years. He had increased his stature throughout the leftist world with his legal representation of terrorist thugs and 9/11 planners. He was always willing to further the cause that America was the problem in the world and needed to be taken down a notch. When the guilty verdicts came down, it drove him deeper and deeper into his own personal hellhole. He drank more and lashed out at his CLA attorneys, secretaries, janitors, just about anyone who had the unfortunate luck to cross paths with him. Driven by rage, he passed information on from one of his clients, a CIA mole, to the Russian Embassy in London. That information was used in the plot to take the President hostage. Brennan had kept his hands clean of any involvement, but he was about to go off the deep end. He could not fathom another two years of that "evil" President Schumacher with the possibility of another four in a second term.

Something needed to be done to keep that from happening. He just didn't know what that something was. Not yet anyway.

"I want to thank Professor Alton-Mosby for inviting me to speak with you today," Brennan said in his concluding remarks. "The Civil Liberties Alliance is committed to fostering human rights throughout the world and promoting social justice and equality here and abroad. We are always looking for bright young minds at the CLA, and I hope you will consider supporting our organization in the future. Thank you very much."

The students rose from their seats and gave Brennan a standing ovation, and he soaked up the applause as it cascaded down into the well of the lecture hall. He nodded his head in appreciation and mouthed the words "thank you" as the students gathered their belongings and scattered to their next classes. Brennan thought it had gone well. A few stragglers stayed behind to shake his hand and tell him they agreed with everything he said. They told him his speech was a home run. Together with such fawning praise, Brennan's raging inferno inside his heart and mind told him his cause was right and it was only a matter of time before

Americans would see the world as he did and change the country for the better. It might take time but the time for action was now.

As Brennan exited the building, the August sunshine hit his bald dome. He reached into his suit coat for his sunglasses and headed for the parking lot. It wasn't long before someone wanted one last word with him.

"Mr. Brennan," a male voice came from behind him. It was not a shout, and it was not timid. The voice had a purpose behind it.

Brennan stopped and turned around, thinking yet another admirer wanted to congratulate him on a wonderful speech, maybe even ask for an autograph. "Yes?"

The man, three inches taller than Brennan, stepped up. "Mr. Brennan," he said behind his pair of reflective sunglasses. "My name is Hakim."

Brennan extended a hand to the stranger. "Nice to meet you, Hakim."

The man put a firm grip on Brennan's hand and made sure it lasted long enough to get Brennan's attention. "I just heard your speech and I was wondering if I might have a moment of your time."

Brennan looked down at the Rolex on his left wrist. He had allotted an hour for the speech, and his schedule had several meetings for the afternoon followed by a TV appearance on *Hardball* that evening. He was hoping for a quick bite to eat before returning to the office. The war on President Schumacher did not allow for much down time. Brennan ate, drank, and slept thinking about furthering the CLA cause. "I'm in a bit of a hurry," he said.

The man nodded and held up his palms as if he knew Brennan was a busy man. But the man knew what he had to say would cause Brennan to clear his slate for the rest of the day. "It won't take but a few minutes."

Brennan still wasn't convinced. "You are welcome to set up an appointment if you want," he offered, hoping the young man would take the hint. He didn't want to waste time on a student. "Or drop me an e-mail."

Hakim stopped Brennan from giving any further suggestions. Hakim had the plan Brennan wanted. He leaned in closer. He spoke in a whisper, but the tone had a forceful punch to it. "Mr. Brennan, it's about the destruction of the United States of America as we know it."

Brennan's head drew back slightly. The man could see Brennan's eyes squinting behind his sunglasses. He was definitely trying to size up the man in front of him, maybe discover whether he knew him or had met him before. Brennan was definitely intrigued. *A believer*, he thought to himself. Maybe an admirer whom he had stoked the anti-American fire and enlightened in only a single hour-long session. He tried to peer through the man's sunglasses but it was no use – he only saw himself in the mirror-like finish. He thought it couldn't hurt to hear the man out.

"I'm listening."

The man looked past Brennan and scanned the quad. It was obvious the man was searching for anyone who might be watching him or snooping in on their conversation. Students walked briskly to class, white ear buds indicating they were oblivious to the outside world around them. Brennan took notice and checked his surroundings to his left and then his right.

"Can I buy you lunch?" the man asked, pointing over to the café on the corner.

Brennan looked at his watch again but disregarded the time. "Sure," he said. "I could go for a quick bite."

The man named Hakim opened the door for Brennan and followed him inside. There was no line at the counter. Brennan ordered a tuna on rye and an iced tea, while his companion went with the side salad and a cup of decaf. The man paid with cash and put the change in the tip jar. The man pointed to a spot in the back, away from the windows and semi-private from the lunch crowd that were taking their orders to go.

Before Brennan quashed his hunger pangs, he started the conversation with a question. "I apologize, but my mind must be playing tricks on me today. What was your name again?"

"Hakim."

The sunglasses had come off, and the man's dark eyes were on full display. He looked Middle Eastern, around thirty years of age. No beard. The jet-black hair looked like it had been professionally cut and styled. He did not look out of place on campus.

"Are you a student here?" Brennan asked, taking a bite out of his sandwich.

"Yes," Hakim said, taking a sip of his coffee. He did not come off looking like a student. He had no backpack or computer bag with him. His shirt was white and the slacks were dark. There was no evidence of any allegiance to the Hoyas. Not even a bulldog cap.

"And your major?"

"Arab studies," Hakim said, "with a minor in performing arts."

Brennan found it an odd combination, but to each his own. He took another bite indicating he had no more questions.

Hakim al-Rashid had been at the university for three years. But he had been groomed to be a terrorist since the day he was born. Now thirty, he moved to the United States with his mother when he was ten years old. His father had been killed shortly after he was born, and he spent his formative years in the mosques of Riyadh at the feet of militant imams. Ingratiated in the strict Islamic Wahhabi sect, he had learned to hate America with every fiber of his being. While some of his friends had already martyred themselves in their quest for jihad, al-Rashid had much grander plans. Something more than just killing an infidel U.S. soldier invading a foreign land. He wanted to take the fight to all of America.

And he wanted it to be a grand production. He had enjoyed the performing arts and found the theater the perfect proving ground for his eventual plan. He truly believed the world would be his stage. He had a flair for the dramatic and relished the role of the bad guy. He had a secret admiration for John Wilkes Booth, and dreamed that someday his name would forever be remembered in the history books. But it wouldn't just be a jump to the stage after inflicting a mortal wound on one man, he wanted multiple victims to punish the United States for its sins.

He was patient, meticulous, and strong-willed. And it was time to put the final touches on his starring role.

"So you heard my lecture?" Brennan asked.

Al-Rashid had, but he was not interested in discussing the finer points of Brennan's speech. "Mr. Brennan, I need your help."

Brennan took another bite of sandwich as he thought over the statement. Once the tuna was down, he asked, "What kind of help? If you need a lawyer for some legal work, I think it would be better to discuss this in the office."

Al-Rashid put up his right hand. Brennan obviously didn't get it. He was going to have to spell it out. "Mr. Brennan, I am an associate of Mr. Hasni al-Masra."

Brennan swallowed his tuna hard, and it caused him to cough slightly. He reached for his iced tea. Hasni al-Masra was a disciple of Muqtada Abdulla, the terrorist mastermind that Brennan had unsuccessfully defended as a client. After being found guilty, Abdulla

16

was put to death by the U.S. Government. Since that time, al-Masra had called for worldwide jihad to avenge his leader's "murder" and bring the infidel Americans to their knees. He had been on the FBI's Most Wanted List for the past six months for the murder of U.S. nationals outside the United States, and his call for martyrs was greeted with great enthusiasm in the volatile streets of the Middle East.

While Brennan was obviously intrigued, he wasn't stupid. He was a deeply suspicious man, and his paranoia grew by the day. He wouldn't put it past the FBI or some other henchmen of the Schumacher Administration to try and entrap him to shut him up once and for all.

"Hakim," Brennan said. "Anyone can come in here and tell me that they are a close personal friend of Hasni al-Masra. His name is well known. He is public enemy number one in the U.S. But your statement doesn't make it so. And I would be a fool to believe you, a stranger, based solely on your own word." He looked around the room, the paranoia kicking in. He again looked over the man seated across the table. Nothing stood out to indicate an undercover informant was in his presence.

Al-Rashid nodded. He did know al-Masra, although they had never spoken. Their line of communication was always carefully planned and executed. He glanced over his shoulder. The students chatting at the surrounding tables indicated they were not interested in what the two men were discussing. "I understand completely, Mr. Brennan. But I think what I am about to tell you will show you that I am not merely an acquaintance of al-Masra or just some wannabe follower who likes his Internet postings and plans to wage war on the U.S. all by his lonesome."

"Go on."

"Things are about to happen around the world," al-Rashid said, lowering his voice as he leaned in toward Brennan. The ominous tone indicated he was to be taken seriously. "Al-Masra has called for global jihad, and it will take place within the next week."

Brennan's eyes widened slightly, and he nodded his head up and down. He was trying to take it all in, to try and put the pieces of the puzzle together. But since he didn't even know the picture on the puzzle box, he was still dubious. Anyone could say jihad is just right around the corner. People claim to know when the world is going to end too. It wasn't hard to make stuff up.

Al-Rashid took notice. "Mr. Brennan, I can tell that you have your doubts. I can understand that."

Brennan agreed. "You can imagine what I must be thinking. Some guy stops me on the sidewalk and tells me out of the clear blue that calls for violent jihad will be answered in the near future," Brennan said. He was beginning to wonder if this was just a waste of time. Maybe "Hakim," if that was even his real name, was some crackpot looking to get his jollies by yanking Brennan's chain. "What does this have to do with me?"

"We need your help," al-Rashid said for the second time, although this time it was "we" not just "I." "The plan for jihad in America has hit a snag because of President Schumacher's FBI. But there is a plan. And we need someone to act as the middle man."

Brennan licked his suddenly dry lips. He had passed on information from imprisoned terrorists and reprobates before, and if he could help further along the destruction of the Schumacher Administration he was on board.

"Your work as an attorney will offer us the cover we need to put the pieces of the puzzle into place. A lawyer-client relationship provides the secrecy to implement the plan. The Constitution will protect our rights at the same time we work to destroy America as we know it."

"How do I know you're not working for the wrong side?" Brennan asked. "How do I know you're not an undercover FBI agent? There are a lot of people in the current administration who would like nothing better than to screw me over. Silence me for good so they can further their murderous agenda on the people of the world."

Al-Rashid nodded. "Allah would not permit me to lie to you, Mr. Brennan." He then took a piece of paper out of his shirt pocket. With a pen in his left hand, he scribbled down several words on the paper, and Brennan noticed that his hand did not shake as he wrote. "I did not come here expecting you to jump on board immediately. Only a fool would do that."

"Don't get me wrong," Brennan said, trying not to offend. "I have a feeling you and I are on the same page. But you can see where I am coming from."

Al-Rashid nodded and then leaned in closer. "As I said, the attacks will take place overseas within the next week." With his hand covering the scrap of paper, he slid it over for Brennan to see. "These are the places where the attacks will occur." He cupped his hand so only

Brennan's eyes could see what was written. Brennan leaned forward and squinted his eyes in the low light of the café. He read the words and looked up at al-Rashid, who covered the paper and took it back.

"And?" Brennan asked.

"Once they occur, I hope you will see that I am serious about my plan here in America. That I can be trusted. I will contact you shortly thereafter to see if you would like to join my cause."

Brennan sat back. He didn't have to do anything now. He could just sit and wait. Plus, he could do his own investigation, maybe call his contacts across the world to see if al-Rashid was really who he said he was and whether he was an associate of al-Masra.

"Hakim, I would like to take you on as a client," Brennan said, something he had told to clients a thousand times over the years. He passed over his card. "Feel free to give me a call when you are ready to discuss further legal avenues."

"Thank you, Mr. Brennan. Your offer of support is greatly appreciated."

Both men stood and shook hands. Brennan felt a rush through his body, like he was back in the game, back on the playing field where he could make some changes. The wheels in his mind were spinning rapidly. He would be very interested in what the next few days would bring. When the two men exited the café, they said their goodbyes and went in opposite directions.

And the FBI's cameras captured decent snapshots of both of them.

CHAPTER 2

The White House – Washington, D.C.

"'Congress shall make no law . . . ,'" William Cogdon said as he sat on the couch in the Oval Office. It was half past six in the morning, and the President's chief of staff had been up since 4 a.m., his usual time, and arrived at the White House thirty minutes later after getting a ride from the Hay-Adams hotel across the street from Lafayette Park. His dark suit coat was still on and his white dress shirt for the most part was tucked in. His red tie was loose, however. It would be gone once he left the Oval Office. He wouldn't make any of D.C.'s best-dressed lists, but that was of no concern to him. His mind focused solely on politics. The man was a political dynamo, always thinking, always plotting strategy in service to his boss, President Anthony Schumacher.

As chief of staff to the President of the United States, the 64-year-old William "Wiley" Cogdon controlled the flow of information that made its way into the Oval Office. Although the job did not require Senate confirmation, the chief of staff did have the rank of a cabinet member and anyone wanting to have a word with President Schumacher had to go through the gatekeeper Cogdon first. With a political mind that was second to none, Cogdon never forgot he was upholding a long tradition of distinguished White House chiefs of staff like Alexander Haig, Dick Cheney, Donald Rumsfeld, and James Baker.

Fueled by generous amounts of Red Bull and coffee, Cogdon had been with the President since their days as lawyers in the small town of Silver Creek, Indiana. They had a general practice, the Law Offices of Cogdon & Schumacher, with Cogdon taking civil matters while his partner focused on criminal cases. Despite their semi-lucrative association, Cogdon was always looking to move up in life – to get out of Silver Creek and save the world. And he thought the best way was grasping on to the coattails of Anthony J. Schumacher.

It had been Cogdon's idea that Counselor Schumacher become Congressman Schumacher. The determined Cogdon ran the winning campaign and became the chief of staff to Indiana's newest member of Congress. For nearly six congressional terms, they worked to reduce the national debt and keep America safe from terrorists. From Capitol Hill, Cogdon followed Schumacher to the Office of Vice President of the United States and then ran the President's election campaign that resulted in a fifty-state landslide. Cogdon was on top of the political world.

The long journey, however, was not without its bumps in the road. Cogdon had kicked his drinking habit and proclivity for scantily clad hookers after publicly embarrassing himself and then-Congressman Schumacher with a one-night stand that almost ended in the Congressman's murder. After focusing his time and energies solely on the Schumacher political juggernaut, he sat at the elbow of power only to be exposed to VX nerve gas in a failed assassination attempt on the President on Election Day. He recovered only to take a blow to the head by Russian operatives in the kidnapping attempt on the President while in Rome. He was able to laugh off the two brushes with death, thinking it was simply bad luck or being in the wrong place at the wrong time.

Now a year later, fully healed and generously caffeinated, he was redoubling his efforts to make sure President Schumacher enjoyed a second term when the next election came around in three short years.

"'Congress shall make no law respecting an establishment of religion, or prohibiting the free exercise thereof,'" Cogdon said aloud, "'or abridging the freedom of speech.'" Half sprawled across the couch, he let the words waft through the air like a cigar aficionado admiring a good puff.

The President of the United States sat behind his desk – the famed Resolute Desk used by numerous Presidents throughout the years – and perused the morning papers. The desk fit his style perfectly – solid, stately, historical. And he hoped he could continue using it for another few years.

President Schumacher arrived in the Oval Office at 6:30 a.m. every weekday morning. You could set your watch by his arrival. He was a stickler for punctuality, and he expected others to be on time as well. But even at the early hour of 7 a.m., and with the first meeting still an hour away, the only occupants of the office were the longtime friends from Indiana.

"So now we're back to the Bill of Rights again," the President said as he checked the pitching matchups for the Cardinals game later on that evening.

Cogdon read American history like his life depended on it. He bled red, white, and blue. Any free time was spent studying the Declaration, the Constitution, anything by or about Lincoln. This then led to frequent discussions about the Founding Documents or the men who help create and protect the heritage of America since it was founded. Cogdon's inquisitive mind was like a "word-of-the-day" calendar – what could he learn today that he didn't know yesterday. And how could he use it to President Schumacher's advantage.

Cogdon often thought out loud, and the President would engage when he felt like it. But he always listened to what Cogdon had to say. Eight years younger than Cogdon, he had learned a great deal during their nearly thirty years of knowing each other. The chief of staff rolled off the couch and moved to a chair in front of the President's desk.

"You know what we ought to do," Cogdon said, the first of his daily brilliant ideas to come out of his mouth.

Uh oh, the President thought to himself. Here we go with today's installment. "What's that?"

"The Constitution was ratified on September 17, 1787," Cogdon said, looking at the pocket-sized copy he carried with him wherever he went. It was well worn – with dog-ears, scribbled notations, and highlights on seemingly every page. "September 17th is right around the corner. Why don't we make a special trip to Philadelphia to mark the anniversary?"

The President closed his sports page and looked over at Cogdon. He was a great admirer of the Founding Documents. He once told a reporter his favorite place in Washington was the National Archives, and he never stopped marveling at this grand experiment known as the United States of America. He liked Cogdon's idea. "What should we do? A speech?"

Now Cogdon's mind was humming at full song. "We could do a speech," he said. That was a fine idea, but he wanted something bigger. "I think we ought to just read the whole thing."

The President's eyebrows lifted slightly toward the ceiling. He pulled his own personal copy of the Constitution from his jacket pocket and started flipping through the pages. "You want me to go to Philadelphia and read the entire Constitution." *The entire thing*, he thought to himself.

"That would be some scintillating television."

Cogdon heard the concern. "Not just you," he said, his idea becoming grander by the minute. "We'll get dignitaries to read individual parts of it. You'll read the Preamble, and maybe the Speaker of the House can read Article I, sections one and two, dealing with the legislative branch. Members of Congress can follow him and then Cabinet secretaries." He then began flipping through the pages, reading clause after clause. "The Postmaster General could read the part of Article I, section eight, dealing with the establishment of 'Post Offices and post Roads.' The poet laureate of the United States could note that Congress has the right to secure 'for limited Times to Authors and Inventors the exclusive Right to their respective Writings and Discoveries.' The Treasury Secretary could read about the right of Congress to 'coin Money' or the Secretary of the Navy can mention Congress's power 'To provide and maintain a Navy.'"

The President was following right along.

"Maybe we could even get a Supreme Court Justice to show up to read Article III!"

The President sat back in his high-backed leather chair and rocked it back and forth a few times. "I don't know if we could get a Supreme Court Justice to show up at a political event," he responded, thinking it through.

"No politics," Cogdon said, promising. "It will be a celebration of the Constitution. An American celebration. Justices take an oath to support the Constitution so I can't see any conflict of interest."

The President was nodding his head in agreement. He kind of liked the idea.

Cogdon continued. "We'll call it the 'Celebration of the Constitution.'" He checked the calendar on his iPhone. "It's a Tuesday. Kids will be in school. We'll encourage readings throughout the country. Broadcast it over the Internet. I bet the cable news networks would even cover it live."

"Would we read the Bill of Rights?" the President wondered. "The first ten amendments weren't ratified until December 15, 1791."

Cogdon thought for a second, scratching his chin as he contemplated the statement. The President had a point. "I say we read them. They are amendments to the Constitution so they should be part of the celebration."

"I like it," the President said. "Let's do it."

Cogdon pumped his fist. "Yes!" Another fabulous idea – one that would be nothing but positive for the President's poll numbers. But his mind kept churning. They would hold similar events on July 4th for the Declaration, September 14th for the Star-Spangled Banner, November 19th for the Gettysburg Address. The President could lay a wreath, offer a few remarks, recite the patriotic words, and rekindle the red-white-and-blue fire that has fueled the hearts and minds of Americans throughout the centuries. Cogdon had wielded yet another masterstroke as a political genius.

A knock on the door of the Oval Office was followed by a parade of individuals right on time for the morning national security meeting.

"Uh oh," the President said, looking over at Cogdon. "Fun time is over. Looks like it's time for me to get back to work."

Cogdon practically jumped out of his seat. Although he would normally hover in the background of the morning security briefing just in case the President needed his brilliant mind, he wanted to get to work on his grand Philadelphia extravaganza. "I'm going to see if I can start lining people up." He turned quickly back to the President. "Maybe we could even get Lee Greenwood to show up too!" he gushed.

"Make it happen," the President replied.

A man on a mission, Cogdon hurried out of the Oval Office as the members of the President's national security team took their seats on the couches. This was the most important time of the President's day – focusing his energies on his number one job – the safety and security of the American people. Not one to simply read the national security issues in a daily memo, the President wanted to look the experts in the eyes and get the information he needed straight from the source. The President took his spot in a chair next to the fireplace. The couches were filled with Carl A. Harnacke, the President's National Security Adviser; Central Intelligence Director William Parker; Bradley Michaelson, the Secretary of Homeland Security; and Tyrone Stubblefield, the Director of the Federal Bureau of Investigation.

"Director Parker," the President started off, "I read the PDB this morning and it worries me."

The CIA was in charge of siphoning through massive amounts of intelligence data collected throughout every corner of the world. With help from the Defense Department, the National Security Agency, and the Director of National Intelligence, the CIA compiles every threat in every corner of the world and puts it in a nice neat folder labeled the President's Daily Brief. It never reported that the world was one big happy family.

"Worried because . . . ?" Director Parker wondered.

"There doesn't seem to be much going on," the President said, holding the PDB in the air. He wondered if the CIA was missing something.

"Everything seems quiet," Parker responded. He could feel the stares from his compatriots. A lot of what they did depended on the intelligence provided by the CIA.

"Too quiet if you ask me," the President said. "Quiet worries me. I expect to see terrorist threats *ad nauseam*. That way I know you know what the bad guys in this world are up to. Quiet tells me the terrorists are regrouping or a plot is afoot."

"I can assure you, Mr. President, that the CIA is working diligently to snuff out any plots. We are working our sources, gaining new footholds in dangerous lands, and providing you with the best intelligence we can offer. We have heard nothing in the way of chatter to indicate there is any type of plan for jihad here in the U.S. or against Americans overseas. Obviously, that assessment can change on a daily basis. But we are doing our utmost to track down any leads and root out all terrorist activity."

The President nodded his head. He didn't mean to question Director Parker's competence or that of the CIA. He just had a bad feeling about something. "I know you're doing your best. I have full confidence in you, Bill." He then turned to the man sitting at his right hand. "And what does the FBI know?"

In closeness to the President, Tyrone Stubblefield stood only behind the First Lady and Cogdon himself. The two went all the way back to their days as new agent trainees at the FBI Academy. They became fast friends and their friendship remained strong as both climbed the ladders of success – Schumacher as a Congressman, Vice President, and then President, and Stubblefield as Special Agent in Charge of the D.C. field office, Deputy Director of the FBI, and then the first African-American Director of the foremost law-enforcement agency in the world.

Not one to sit still behind his desk in his seventh-floor office, Director Stubblefield had put his life on the line on multiple occasions in defense of the United States of America. He shot dead a broken arrow of a Supreme Court Justice who tried to detonate a bomb strapped to his chest in an assassination attempt during the President's State of the Union address. While leading a team of FBI agents across the southern border to save Democratic Vice Presidential nominee General T.D. Graham from the clutches of Mexican drug cartels and al-Qaeda terrorists, he was shot twice during the rescue attempt. His latest act of heroism involved rescuing the President of the United States from Russian and Pakistani operatives in the daring raid of the Italian Prime Minister's residence in Rome. He seemed to always be in the right place at the right time.

And the President placed an enormous amount of trust in the six-foot-four lawman.

"Mr. President, we are following several leads," Director Stubblefield said, opening his own folder with the FBI seal on the cover. "Based on our undercover operation, we think we might have another home-grown terrorist looking to blow up a skyscraper in New York City. He is on our radar."

"Another one?" the President asked. "We captured a guy who tried to set off a bomb in downtown Chicago not too long ago, didn't we?"

"Yes, sir. He tried to set off an explosive at the start of the Chicago Marathon."

"And there was another guy in Oregon and one in Springfield. There were also plots involving the Brooklyn Bridge and the Federal Reserve in New York City."

"And the New York Stock Exchange," Stubblefield added.

The President started shaking his head like he just couldn't understand what made these terrorists tick. "It seems to me that they would catch on after a while. Maybe search for another line of business."

"I agree," Stubblefield said. "I don't know why they do it. They must think they are smarter than the last guy and too experienced to not know an undercover FBI agent or confidential informant when they meet him. As I was saying, we have several agents posing as radical Islamists on the Internet. I have also contacted the Attorney General on a matter involving a Muslim school and mosque in Virginia. We believe it may be a funding source for foreign terrorists. We're still looking at the financial and tax records but it might be a front to raise money to send overseas for jihadist training. I'll keep you posted on that. Other than that, we have also heard some talk about a few rabble rousers here in the U.S. looking to cause trouble."

"Terrorists?" the President asked.

"Actually, no," Stubblefield said. "They are your typical cranks. The types that like to cause trouble to draw attention to their causes. There's a guy who claims he has an offensive movie about Islam and the Prophet Mohammad. There's another guy, a pastor of some sort, who has threatened to burn the Koran."

"And offend a billion Muslims in the process," the President interjected.

"Unfortunately, yes." Stubblefield looked up from his folder. "Probably just attention seekers. Snake-oil salesmen looking for donations or their fifteen minutes of fame."

The President looked to the ceiling and raised his arms high. "Why can't we all just get along?" he asked in mock frustration. At least it helped lighten the mood of the tense situation.

"We'll keep an eye on it, Mr. President. Obviously, we don't want to infringe on the First Amendment, but I think it is our duty to watch it. Because if a movie comes out or a Koran gets torched, it could have serious security implications here and around the world."

"All right," the President said, "keep me posted."

When the meeting concluded, the national security leaders headed back to their respective offices scattered across the D.C. area to continue their work at protecting the United States. Director Stubblefield hung back for a moment.

"Are we still on for dinner tonight?" the President asked.

"Yes, Tina and I are looking forward to it, sir," Stubblefield said. "I'll see you at seven."

"Okay," the President said as he headed back to his desk. "Oh, by the way," he said, stopping his friend at the door. "Wiley might be contacting you about something."

"What's that crazy son-of-a-gun up to now?"

"He's planning a celebration of the Constitution in Philadelphia in mid-September. He's hoping to round up some big names to read portions of the Constitution at a public event. He might want you to read a clause or two."

"I'll be happy to do it," Stubblefield said, his mind running through the possibilities. "Tell him I want to read the Second Amendment."

The President smiled. "Spoken like a true FBI agent. I'll let him know. See you tonight."

CHAPTER 3

Munich, Germany

The cigarette smoke hung heavy near the ceiling of the dilapidated apartment's kitchen. The walls that had once been painted white were now a dull gray from the cigarette tar and lack of adequate ventilation. The occupants didn't care. The apartment offered them a place to wash, and eat, and lay their heads on the soiled mattresses on the floor. But they didn't complain.

Allah would provide them a place in paradise in the near future.

Mahmud Basra had rented the rattrap near downtown Munich for six months. The landlord/owner was a ninety-year-old woman who didn't care what the occupants did with the place as long as they paid the rent. What they did inside or what company they kept was not her concern.

Basra was an ideal tenant, keeping mostly to himself and paying his bills on time. He was an engineer by trade, and Munich and all of Germany offered bountiful opportunities for engineers of all nationalities to work on bridge work, skyscraper construction, and automobile manufacturing. He was 45 years old, unmarried, and without children. But, with four million Muslims in Germany, he was not without members of his religious ilk. He worked from eight to five at a local engineering firm but did not socialize with others in his office. His nights and weekends were spent praying – and planning and plotting. Those in the firm who knew him best would describe him as an intense worker – one who expected perfection out of himself and everyone around him. At times, he could be brooding, at other times downright hostile. Fearing a verbal explosion, some of his co-workers had learned to tiptoe around the office when Basra was in "one of his moods." A native of Saudi Arabia, he had mentioned to co-workers that he hoped to someday transfer to the firm's office in Dusseldorf or maybe even immigrate to the United States.

But he knew he wouldn't be long for this world.

Mahmud Basra had been trained at an engineering school in Riyadh but fell into the clutches of radical Islam after the killing of Bin Laden in Pakistan. It was then that he realized he could no longer sit on the sidelines and watch his radicalized brothers fight the good fight alone. It was time for him to take the fight to the enemy – the United States of America. He was not alone in his quest for jihad. Radical leaders in numerous Saudi Arabia schools instructed young men in the art of terrorism over the course of several years. They taught them about different cultures, how to blend into their new surroundings, wherever that may be.

Like so many young Muslims, Basra pledged himself as a martyr for the cause and set his life's course on jihad. It didn't take long for him to see his studies could help bring down the bridges and skyscrapers his fellow engineers were constructing. He dreamed big and worked his way to the top of the terrorist ladder. Now, Basra was the head of the Crescent Brotherhood, and it would not be long before it became as synonymous with terrorist groups like al-Qaeda, Hezbollah, and Islamic Jihad.

The Crescent Brotherhood had also become more practical. Gone were the days of plots for nuclear weapons or dirty bombs. Such lofty thoughts of mass casualties were great in theory but hard to pull off. The risk/reward ratio was too high. An operation to purchase nuclear or biological weapons would require a state-sponsor of terror, like Iran or Syria, and any attempt at buying such a hot property would inevitably bring the attention of the infidel spy agencies. Moreover, even if such a weapon were deployed, it would be met with such swift retribution that it would set back the course of jihad fifty years. The Brotherhood's plan, on the other hand, believed smaller attacks across the world would bring more destruction, more chaos, than one simple dirty bomb. Basra, the terrorist CEO, favored lean strike forces that would unleash its deadly terror and then slip away into the darkness. The hit-and-hide attacks would paralyze the industrialized world, cripple commerce, and force Western authorities to scatter their resources over the entire globe in search of the culprits. The evil plan called for death by a thousand cuts. The infidels would slowly bleed to death, and the Brotherhood would ultimately crush them and take over the world.

Within the last two weeks, Mahmoud Basra had been joined by four men – two from Saudi Arabia and the others from Iraq and Turkey. As the Brotherhood's "Deputy Commanders," they each had coordinated teams of five men for jihad around the world. The training had been completed, and the teams were in place waiting for the call to action.

The five men sat around the kitchen table, the ashtray in the middle full of butts and ashes. It was Friday night, and Basra had finished his day at the firm. He had scheduled a two-week vacation – Barcelona, he told his co-workers – but he knew he wouldn't be going back. The four deputy commanders would soon rejoin their teams, but the weekend meeting was needed to make sure all the pieces of the puzzle were in place.

Mahmoud, the engineer, ran the show like a corporate board meeting. He would ask the questions and he expected his underlings to give him the answers. And he had better hear what he wanted to hear. Behind his back, he was known as "the boss," and it was not used in deference to his leadership skills.

"Where are we in Madrid?" Basra asked.

Abdel Ramadi was the youngest of the group at the age of thirty-five, but what he lacked in years he made up in braggadocio. With arrogant self-assuredness, he had promised results from the first day he had been recruited for jihad. Unfortunately, Ramadi may have been a better soldier than a leader of his team.

"We are a little behind," Ramadi said sheepishly, the young braggart almost too embarrassed to look his older comrades in the eyes.

Nostrils slightly flaring, Basra glared at the man. He didn't like being behind. He was a stickler for staying on schedule. That's how he ran his ship. And if someone wasn't pulling his weight, Basra would throw the man overboard without a second thought and get someone who could get the job done.

"What do you mean you are a 'little behind?'" he growled. The operation was nearing execution stage. Being "behind" was not acceptable.

Ramadi looked at his boss and gave the excuse he had given a thousand times before. "I need more money," he demanded.

Basra slammed the table. He was tired of the excuses. "You have been provided with enough money! That is all I ever hear from you! More money! More money!" He pounded the table after each mention of more money. "Your comrades do not complain about money! Perhaps you should stop spending money on women and alcohol!"

The other men glared at Ramadi. How dare he squander the

Brotherhood's money on such frivolous and sinful vices. Clearly he was not ready, they thought. He had boyish good looks, which made him look ten years younger. This did not help create a lot of trust amongst the Brotherhood's Deputy Commanders because the man who fashioned himself a playboy was known to stray from the plan on occasion. Perhaps they should not have entrusted such a dangerous operation to a mere "kid."

"I have not wasted any money on alcohol!" Ramadi shot back. He would not offend Allah with illicit drink. He conveniently left out any mention of women. The deep pockets of Saudi Arabia and other Middle Eastern oil fiefdoms funding the operation did not require the collection of receipts for expenditures, and Ramadi found the prostitutes of Madrid a nice bonus for his men while they waited for their bevy of virgins in the afterlife.

"He is going to blow the whole operation," Anwar bin Hajj, the man in charge of the London operation, sniped.

"I will do no such thing!" Ramadi shot back. Snarling in anger, he looked ready to fight for his honor. "We are ready to proceed!"

Bin Hajj shook his head in disbelief. "That's not what I hear."

Unlike Basra and Ramadi, bin Hajj was not an educated man in the sense of a university education. He had grown up in Iraq during the oppressive regime of Saddam Hussein. His father ran an air conditioner repair shop, and the family had lived in cramped quarters above the store. Despite desperate pleas from relatives and repeated warnings by the United States, bin Hajj's father refused to move his family out of Baghdad during the first Gulf War. When U.S. bombs obliterated the neighboring block of buildings housing Saddam's intelligence agency, bin Hajj's home crumbled with the rest. He was the only one of his family to survive.

And now he vowed to return the favor to the United States.

At age fifty-two, he was the oldest of the group. He had worked to sabotage U.S. reconstruction efforts in Iraq, blowing up oil refineries and electrical substations, before settling in Yemen where he set up his shingle as jihadist for hire. It didn't take him long to find work. Given his age, bin Hajj had been given the London operation – the most difficult in Europe to pull off given the security structure in place. But he could not keep his nose out of other people's business. He fancied himself as Vice President of the Crescent Brotherhood, just one step below Basra.

"I talked to Shahid just two days ago," bin Hajj hissed at Ramadi. "He says your operation is in chaos. That you have spent more time bedding women than focusing on the plan."

Ramadi thought he now had a way to come back. "You are not to talk to members of my team! Who is the one who is going to blow the operation when you are calling my team and discussing specifics!?"

Bin Hajj jumped up from his seat and slammed both hands on the table. "Someone has to baby-sit you so you don't screw it up!"

Ramadi was not going to take much more from the old man. "We are ready!"

"You are a liar!"

Ramadi took one step to his left to confront bin Hajj when a fuming Basra grabbed him by the arm. "Sit down!" He had to say it again to get it through the man's head. "Sit down! Both of you sit down!"

What Basra had hoped would be a calm conversation on the progress of their plan for jihad had turned into a screaming match that was starting to piss him off. The two combatants had followed orders and returned to their seats around the table. But they glared at each other with righteous passion – their eyes indicating the fight would commence at a later time. Basra decided he would deal with the young Ramadi later.

Those seated at the kitchen table froze when a man appeared in the doorway and stood against the wall. No one had heard him come in. No one had even heard the door open or footsteps in the hall. It was as if the ghost of a man had walked through the walls and taken up position in their presence.

The man's name was Ahmed Yassar. He offered no greetings to his brothers, made no other sound. He just stood, ramrod straight, all six feet of him, his legs slightly apart. His left wrist was covered by his right hand, which had a crescent moon tattooed in green on top. Every man looked at him. And no one dared ask where he had been.

Yassar was the Crescent Brotherhood's most lethal weapon. At forty-two, Yassar looked to be at least ten years younger. The hair was all dark, no gray creeping in, and cropped close. A Saudi native and a second cousin of one of the kingdom's crown princes, he had been educated in the finest schools and mastered three languages. Trained by the Saudi police, he had become one of the best snipers in the country. He had worked on the force for fifteen years and even earned several commendations for his work. But, like so many other Muslim extremists, something was missing in his life. He had helped protect U.S. Presidents as they traveled to meet King Fahd, but he grew disillusioned with American leaders' dictates to his country in their love for Saudi oil. He began to hate the U.S., like so many of his countrymen. He wanted the United States out of Saudi Arabia, out of the Middle East, and out of power in the world.

Yassar told his commanders he needed a break from his duties – a pilgrimage perhaps to refresh his batteries. Given his relationship with the crown prince, his superiors had no choice but to oblige. They would welcome him back at any time, they told him. Angry and filled with a burning desire to exact retribution on the U.S., Yassar contacted his long-time friend, Mahmud Basra, in Munich. Basra didn't have to twist any arms. Yassar was on board after their first phone call.

Basra was overjoyed at his friend's decision to join the jihadist cause. It provided him with a great opportunity. As with many wanna-be terrorists, the violent jihadist background keeps most men from traveling outside of terror hot spots around the world. They might be able to walk safely in the dusty streets of Kandahar or Jalalabad, but passing through customs in London or New York would result in certain and, most likely, immediate arrest.

Yassar, on the other hand, had no terrorist background, no red flags on his passport that would alert the authorities to his presence. His royal family connections, not to mention his service with the Saudi police force, would bring a nod and a thank you at the customs counter. He would be one of Basra's few opportunities to get an experienced killer into the U.S. And they could do it right under the Americans' noses.

Basra gave Yassar a quick nod. Things had spiraled out of control in the kitchen, but the killer's presence had brought the Brotherhood back into focus.

"Where are we in America?" Basra asked as he checked off the next item on his agenda.

All eyes turned to Khalid Mukhtar, the chain smoker at the end of the table. He had said nothing during the meeting, and only offered quiet greetings when he arrived. Like Yassar, he was a man of few words. He took a sip of water, seemingly to increase the tension in the room as the others waited to hear what he had to say.

"We are on schedule," he said.

Mukhtar was born in Turkey but moved with his family to France when he was young. Educated in Paris, he slowly became a fixture in the burgeoning Muslim community. He could have been a politician given his ability to press the flesh and listen to the concerns of locals. But he too had fallen prey to the radical Islamists.

There is no stock version of a jihadist. They can come in all shapes and sizes. Some have beards, others like the clean-shaven look. Some smoke, while others like their lungs to be clear. Some, like Ramadi, can fly off the handle at the drop of a hat. Mukhtar, however, was the docile terrorist. He was five-ten with a nicely trimmed dark beard, and in a shirt and tie he could pull off the look of a university professor. He was learned, a good manager of people, and had a face that masked a hatred of the Great Satan. Blowing a final cloud of smoke toward the ceiling, he smashed the end of his cigarette in the tray.

"The team has scouted out their designated areas. I talked to Hakim the other day. He is preparing for the grand finale and promises it will be spectacular. He is also working on an angle that might provide us with even greater cover. We will have multiple sniper units throughout the United States." He pointed over his shoulder to the motionless Yassar, exhibit A if you will, standing behind him. "Once the word is given, we will paralyze the entire country." He was very matter-of-fact, ticking off operational details off the top of his head and the results that would surely follow. "We will distract the infidels, spread their law-enforcement authorities thin, and then decimate them with explosives at the point of maximum effectiveness. It will be a glorious bloodbath," he said. "We are continuing to get everything together."

Basra nodded. He liked the professionalism he was hearing. "We still have some time. You won't start the operation until the other attacks have taken place."

"Yes," Mukhtar agreed. "And when we do strike, it will be better than 9/11 because it will be nonstop, not just one day, but day after day after day. Before long we will raise the flag of Allah over the White House like we did at their infidel embassy in Cairo."

If the novice Ramadi had said it, the statement would be seen as grossly overconfident. But not when made by Mukhtar. Those around the table believed what he said. He had worked on the 9/11 plot in New York City and the 7/7 attacks in London.

"We're just waiting to get the go-ahead," Mukhtar said.

Basra nodded again. It will be soon. "As soon as we get a sign from Allah."

Near Atlanta, Georgia

The long dirt road filled with potholes brought curses from the TV cameramen driving their coifed and manicured reporters to the hinterlands to report on the big news of the day. The occupants bounced around inside – their seatbelts the only thing keeping them from banging their heads on the ceiling. The dusty one-lane road had never seen this much traffic – ten vans each with a satellite attached to the roof to broadcast live from wherever a story broke. Two vans would need shock repair by the time they were returned to the station later on that afternoon. The dust rising from the traffic snaked for a good mile as it escaped from the surrounding trees. It was as if a bunch of backwoods rednecks had sent out a call that there was free beer and grits and the charge was on.

"I can't believe they sent us out to the middle of nowhere to cover this freakin' idiot," Chet Varner said to the cameraman/driver in the seat next to him.

"We ought to get hazard pay for this," the driver said, as the right tire of the van took a direct hit from a pothole the size of a dorm-room refrigerator. "Oh, man! There goes the front axle!"

After a two-mile jaunt through the rugged terrain, the caravan of media types came to an opening in the trees and found a lonely double-wide trailer sitting in the middle of a blanket of green grass. The silver trailer basked in the sunshine – like a Taj Mahal of white trash in the middle of nowhere.

"This is it?" Varner huffed, looking out the front windshield. "We came all the way out here to see some religious hick's trailer?"

The "religious hick" was waiting outside for his invited guests to arrive. His name was Carson Levitt. A white male in his mid-forties, he was clean shaven and wore a dark business suit. His glasses were not in style, more of an '80s look, and his comb over looked several decades behind the times. He stood next to a folding table with a single book sitting on top. The media vans took up positions one right next to each other and came to a much-needed stop. One van appeared to be venting something from the engine compartment, while another was leaking radiator fluid onto the dust beneath it. The reporters opened their doors and stepped their polished loafers and high heels gently down into the Georgian dirt. One female reporter refused to go out in her $500 Jimmy Choos and switched to a pair of Nikes that she kept in the van for just this type of emergency.

"Gather around everybody," Levitt said, waving a welcoming arm. "Thanks for coming."

A few grumbles could be heard from the assembled throng. A few mumbled to themselves that Brokaw or Rather would never have been sent out to the boondocks like this.

"Let me know when you're ready to get started."

Levitt was a virtual unknown in these parts. A quick check by some investigative reporters uncovered nothing. They didn't know his background, where he was from, or how long he had been in the area. But the promises he made prevented the media from simply ignoring him. They couldn't take the chance that something big would happen and let their competitor get the story while they twiddled their thumbs back at the station.

"Could you spell your name please?" Varner asked. He being the dean of the group, he decided to take charge and get the job done so they could get the hell out of there and back to civilization.

"C-a-r-s-o-n L-e-v-i-t-t," he said graciously.

"Do you have a title?"

"I go by Reverend Levitt."

The reporters scratched notes on their pads and waited for Varner to fire again. "And can you tell us a little bit about what type of church you head?"

"I am the leader of the Worldwide Church of Believers," Reverend Levitt said proudly.

"Worldwide Church of Believers?"

"Yes, the Worldwide Church of Believers," Reverend Levitt said again.

"And where is your church?" Varner asked. He wondered why they couldn't have had the interview at the church – one situated on paved streets with a Starbucks in a local strip mall nearby.

Reverend Levitt smiled and pointed behind him. "It's right here."

Snickers could be heard throughout the media. Even the cameramen couldn't keep from smiling at the double-wide parish behind Levitt.

Reverend Levitt looked at this watch. He wanted to get started so he could make the top-of-the-hour news. "Are you ready to go?"

Varner looked around. The cameramen gave him a thumbs-up. Sound technicians positioned the microphones on the makeshift podium while others hoisted the boom mikes into the air. When the red lights came on, Reverend Levitt gave his sermon to the world.

"Ladies and gentlemen!" he belted loudly and unnecessarily like he was some crazed carnival barker. The welcoming smile turned to a menacing snarl. "The world is on fire! And soon judgment day will bring hell-fire to this earth! The war on God must be stopped! And the evil Muslims across this world must end their jihad or risk spending all eternity in the pit of hell with the devil!"

Reporters were scribbling as fast as they could. Some even thought this might be good – the ratings could go through the roof. Maybe coming all the way out here wasn't so bad after all.

"The Muslims say they are for peace! But that is a lie! Just like their religion is a lie! I am here today to call for a new crusade! A war on Islam! And I will start this war tomorrow with the burning of this here Koran!" Reverend Levitt yelled as he picked up the book from the table. "I will set fire to these lies tomorrow and every day thereafter until those dirty dogs admit to the fallacy of their religion!"

Reverend Levitt ranted and raved for a good ten minutes. Banners across the bottom of the screen scrolled his promise to burn a Koran over and over again. The man came off as an obnoxious jerk. Just about as vile as those Westboro types that parade up and down outside of military funerals with their "God Hates Fags" signs.

Varner could feel his pulse pounding harder every second. This might be his big break. A religious nut job calling for his own holy war against Muslims would make news the world over. Mention would be made of the Swedish cartoons and the Mohammed movie that had previously set the world aflame. Varner told himself to get it right, to make sure he was fair but not too fair such that a viewer might think he was siding with this idiot. Varner knew the dusty highway he came in on could lead to the bright lights and big city of network news. He pulled out a compact from his jacket pocket, opened it, and used the mirror to make sure every hair was in place.

"I will see you all tomorrow at high noon!" Reverend Levitt blasted into the microphones. "Thank you all for coming!"

Levitt spun around in his black dress shoes and made a beeline for his double-wide. The reporters stood stunned. They thought they would get a question-and-answer session. *Oh well*, they thought. They would just rerun the clip and tell the world what they had just heard.

"Let's go to Chet Varner who is live on the scene," the anchor in the studio said.

"Connie," Varner said in a serious tone into his microphone, "I can tell you I have never seen anything like this. In a venomous attack, Reverend Carson Levitt, head pastor of the Worldwide Church of Believers, called for like-minded believers to join forces and engage Muslims in a holy crusade. Reverend Levitt promised to burn a Koran tomorrow and, quote, every day thereafter until those dirty dogs admit to the fallacy of their religion, unquote."

Varner mentioned the possible ramifications of Levitt's inflammatory plan to burn the Koran and he promised to stay on top of the story. "This could become a worldwide powder keg, Connie, and Channel 5 will be here when any news breaks. Back to you."

"Okay," Connie said, her tone sounding as if she feared for Varner's safety in the dusty jungles of Georgia. "Thank you. Chet Varner reporting live from rural Atlanta on this very troubling story. Stay tuned to Channel 5 News at Six for an update."

CHAPTER 4

Venice, Italy

The train from Rome to Venice had taken just under four hours. The sun had yet to peek over the horizon when Karim Haqani boarded the train in Rome. He wore khaki pants and a dark polo shirt – nothing that would draw attention to himself. He carried a backpack that contained maps of Venice and a cell phone that he was to use only once he arrived at his final destination. He had taken his seat in first class and closed his eyes as the train rolled away from the station. He would miss the sights of the Italian countryside as he used the time to silently pray, but he didn't mind.

The man's calmness betrayed his itinerary for the day. He looked at his digital watch. Within the next five hours, he would be dead.

And that is just the way he wanted it.

Karim Haqani was a member of a five-man team set to bring jihad to his designated spot in the world. There were four other teams spread out around the globe ready to rain holy fire down on the infidels. It was to be the start of a glorious battle plan that would cripple the economies of the industrialized world and create havoc through governments across the globe. At thirty years of age, Haqani had played soccer as a youth, and his slim athletic build made him an ideal candidate for a suicide mission. He could run, wield a gun, and do the heavy lifting that a terrorist could be called on to do in the heat of the moment.

When the train stopped in Florence, Haqani saw his fellow terrorist enter the first-class car and take his seat at the opposite end. Both men shared the same m.o., *i.e.*, martyrdom operation. Seated facing each other, they did not acknowledge their like-minded jihadist other than with a quick nod. Haqani managed to suppress the smile that was about to cross his face. There were no police around, and the tourists on the train were too busy with their phones and their newspapers to take notice. The plan was coming together nicely.

After leaving the station, the train attendant had rumbled the beverage cart down the aisle and offered snacks and beverages to the passengers. When Haqani asked for water, the attendant asked whether he wanted it "with or without gas." Haqani finally showed some emotion. "Without," he said with a smile. As he took his sip, he inwardly laughed at the question. Shortly he would be pouring the proverbial gasoline on the fire. He gave a slight raise of his glass of water to the man at the end of the car. The man reciprocated.

"Ladies and gentlemen," the conductor said in English over the intercom. He had given the same spiel in Italian, French, and German. "We are now arriving at our final stop in Venice. Please remember to take all your belongings as you leave the train. Thank you for traveling with *Trenitalia*."

Haqani grabbed his backpack from under the seat in front of him and headed down the steps of the car. His cohort exited at the other end. Shakespeare had *The Merchant of Venice*. These two men were merchants of death, and no one around them knew the mayhem they were about to inflict on Venice, Italy. The two men did not meet up on the platform – the plan did not call for it. Instead, they walked separately amongst the tourists lugging their wheeled suitcases down the steps of the train station.

Haqani stopped outside the station to take in the view. The water buses, or *vaporetti*, crisscrossed the Grand Canal ferrying passengers from side to side. The tourists hauled their luggage on board as the *vaporetto* crew herded as many onto the boat as allowed. Haqani walked over to the ticket counter and paid five euros for an unlimited amount of rides on the water buses for the next twenty-four hours. He wouldn't need another day's worth. He looked at his watch again. Just two hours to go. Time to get moving.

The air felt good as Haqani watched Venice pass him by. He had never been to the city made famous by its winding canals. He pulled out his cell phone and, looking to blend in with the other tourists, he took a picture of a gondola floating slowly by – a young couple enjoying the ride on their honeymoon. The *vaporetto* crossed the canal back and forth to the various stops – *Piazzale Roma*, *Ferrovia*, and *San Toma*.

"Next stop *San Marco*," the driver announced over the intercom.

As the water bus approached the dock, the driver threw the engine into reverse and slowed the boat enough that the crewman manning the exit could throw a rope around the pillar and knot it tight. After the boat lurched to a stop, the crewman unhinged the sliding door.

"*San Marco*," the man announced, sounding thoroughly bored with his job. Get 'em off, get 'em on, and head to the next stop.

The San Marco stop teemed with people. The tourists who had already dropped off their luggage at their hotels carried only their cameras and shopping bags. Even to the oblivious tourist, the presence of various members of the Italian military was readily noticeable. They were unarmed but fully decked out in their finest dress uniforms – blues, whites, and olives. Today was a big day. The Piazza San Marco was to play host to the swearing-in of the 500 newest members of the Italian military. Recent graduates stood tall in their spiffy uniforms – posing for pictures with fathers, mothers, husbands and wives, snapping off salutes to superiors as they prepared for the ceremony an hour away. School children in matching white shirts and alternating red, green, and white hats had the day off from classes so they could partake in the festivities, wave their miniature Italian flags, and enjoy the pageantry.

It would be a day they would never forget.

Sitting on the north side of the lagoon, the Piazza San Marco is the main public square in Venice and is framed by the Doge's Palace on the south and the *Basilica Cattedrale Patriarcale di San Marco*, otherwise known as St. Mark's to the English speaking types, on the east. On the north side of the Piazza sits a wall of buildings housing shops selling Murano glass figurines, Ferrari apparel, and gelato. Narrow streets allow pedestrians to make their way into the inner parts of Venice for still more shopping and eating.

Haqani walked up the gangway, his eyes hidden behind his sunglasses. Per orders, Haqani's fellow terrorist would arrive on the next boat. Although Haqani had not been nervous on the trip north, the presence of such a large contingent of military did raise his pulse a few notches. He knew they would be there, that's why the date was chosen, but seeing them all in person gave him his first cause for concern. He told himself to be strong.

Haqani walked to the edge of the lagoon and leaned on a railing. He took another picture of a tall ship in the distance – members of the Italian navy in their dress whites standing in formation from bow to stern. After another look at his watch, Haqani punched in the number to make the call.

"I am at the Piazza San Marco," he said to the man on the other end.

"I am ready for the hand-off."

"Walk east and up the stairs over the canal," the man instructed. Haqani did not know where the man was taking the call, but he knew the man was the team leader. Three other phone calls would be made to the leader and each caller would be directed to the appropriate target. "Once you reach the other side, you will see a woman in dark pants and a white shawl draped over her shoulders standing by the railing near the lagoon. She is carrying a white bag. Go up to her, kiss her on both cheeks, and offer to hold the bag. You know what to do after that."

Once the instructions were complete, Haqani hung up the phone.

The crush of the growing crowd made it a slow walk. A line of tourists five deep snaked around the eastern and southern parts of St Mark's, some looking to view the interior of the cathedral and the others trying to make their way to find a good spot to watch the proceedings. Haqani could hear the thumping of the drums from the military bands playing behind him as they marched into formation into the Piazza. He walked up the steps, shuffled sideways past the tourists taking pictures of the Bridge of Sighs, and down the other side. It took a couple of glances to find the woman in the crowd.

He walked up to her slowly, his eyes scanning every face that passed him. "*Buon giorno*," Haqani said softly to the women.

"*Buon giorno*," the woman said in return. She smiled like she was happy to see him.

He gave her a kiss on both cheeks and looked down at the bag at her side. "Can I give you a hand with your bag?"

The woman looked down at the white bag with the handles. Emblazoned on the outside in large red letters were the words "Authentic Murano Glass – Not Made in China." Below the name of the local glass dealer were the words "Fragile – Do Not Drop." There were hundreds of the same bags in and around Venice. The glass ornaments and figurines from the nearby stop of Murano were must-have items for tourists to show-off to their jealous friends back home.

The woman handed the bag to Haqani. She then lightly grabbed him by the arms indicating kisses good-bye were in order. Although public displays of affection with a woman he did not know were verboten in his world, he played the part to blend in.

"May Allah be with you," she whispered into his ear.

The two stepped away from the railing and back into the horde of people heading to the Piazza. Haqani walked up the steps with the woman by his side but she would not walk down with him. Her job done, she simply faded away. The determined terrorist, with nothing but jihad on his mind, did not look back in hopes of seeing the woman one last time.

The clock tower on the north side of the Piazza indicated it was fifteen minutes before eleven. The crowd had thickened in the ten minutes he had spent looking for the woman. Police barricades had cut the Piazzetta, the smaller piazza between the lagoon and the Piazza San Marco, in half. Tourists standing in line for St. Mark's watched the parade of bands from the east side, while the military members in formation marched on the west side.

Haqani took up his position behind a barricade on the southern edge of the Piazzetta and to the side of a television scaffold. His heart rate was starting to quicken, and he reached up to wipe the sweat forming on his brow.

Now was not the time to show any nerves, he told himself. Ten feet in front of him stood two armed Italian Carabinieri in their dark blue berets and tactical riot gear outfits. The officer on his right had a 40mm single shot gas gun strapped to his back. The officer on his left had a PR24 collapsible baton on his right hip and a pair of handcuffs on the left. Their hands were empty, like they weren't expecting trouble. The two officers would be Haqani's second and third targets.

Remembering his training, he took out his cell phone and took a picture of the bell tower of St. Mark's. He then switched to video and scanned the entire Piazzetta and out to the lagoon. A push of a couple of buttons and the video would be sent to the other members of the team.

At five minutes to eleven, Haqani noticed a large vessel with the Italian flag idling up to the dock. It was no simple water bus ferrying passengers to San Marco. The white ship had "Guardia Costeria" painted in red letters on the side. It was the VIP's secure mode of transportation.

Haqani punched in the preprogrammed number and held the phone to his ear. "Stand by," he said softly.

"*Allahu akbar*," came from the other end.

"*Allahu akbar*," Haqani whispered twice.

While the bulk of the crowd was to the north of Haqani, a few tourist stragglers stopped at the barricade next to him. He looked them over. They were all women of small stature with hands full of shopping bags, some even like his bag from Murano. They would pose no threat to Haqani. He forced himself not to make any sudden movements. His eyes caught a glimpse of a man twenty-five yards to the north in the line with the tourists. He wore the same sunglasses and carried the same white bag purportedly full of Murano glass.

The suits came up the gangway first – half wearing sunglasses, the others preferring a more natural view. All of them had flesh-colored radio receivers in their ears. Once firmly on dry land, the group was met by high-ranking military men in their white uniforms and chests full of medals. Introductions were made and a four-person golf cart was readied. With the VIP seated under the canopy in the back and a general to his left and one in front of him, the driver took the entourage slowly forward. It would be a slow ride to the east then a left-hand turn north into the Piazzetta.

Haqani placed the bag at his feet. The four-inch wide and ten-inch long box inside was open on the top. Haqani's left hand pointed his cell phone at the oncoming parade of security agents surrounding the golf cart. He counted eight suits but they were not in tight formation around the man they were protecting. The Carabinieri officers in front of Haqani weren't even looking his direction. One had his hands behind his back watching the approaching caravan. Haqani saw no security on the top of St. Mark's or the Doge's Palace.

Haqani was solely focused on his job. This was his moment. The one he had trained for, prayed for, and dreamt about for the last year. It all came down to this.

Everything seemed to be going in slow motion. He saw every detail. The still photographer taking pictures across the way. The military honor guard saluting as the golf cart puttered by. As Haqani's right hand went down into the bag, he felt a tapping on his left arm. Startled, he shook like he had seen a ghost.

"Sorry," the English-speaking woman next to him said. She noticed how jumpy the man was, but she had something important to ask. "Who is that?" she asked pointing at the golf cart proceeding slowly across the walkway.

With sweat rolling down the side of his face, his mouth without an ounce of moisture, he could do nothing more than grunt and shrug his shoulders.

Undeterred the woman turned to her left and asked the woman

standing next to her. "Who is that man in the golf cart?"

The woman in the red dress spoke Italian but she understood the English. "*El Presidente*," she announced proudly.

As the golf cart began its slow turn to the left, the security agents turned their sights to the north. The Carabinieri officers raised their right hands to salute their country's leader. It was the perfect opportunity for Haqani. He thrust his right hand into the bag and pulled out an AK-47 with a fifty-round magazine. It was a seamless move and one that shot a surge of adrenaline through his body.

"Allahu akbar!"

Shots rang out, the sounds echoing off the buildings surrounding the Piazzetta. Haqani fired in the direction of the golf cart, bullets striking multiple targets. Security agents scrambled to return fire. The women next to him fainted to the ground. Haqani sprayed the expanse in front of him, the AK-47 blasting away as he moved it left and right. As the suits not hit by the barrage of bullets sprung into action, Haqani took out the two Carabinieri officers who had turned around and raised their weapons to stop him.

In amongst the screams of horror from those in the crowd, Haqani could hear shots being fired on the eastern edge of the Piazzetta by the man who had joined him on the train in Florence. Still more shots rang out on the north end of the Piazza. *It was working!* he told himself. Tourists were caught in the rain of bullets and fell to the ground.

"Get down! Get down!" people yelled in ten different languages. Husbands covered wives, men shielded children.

"Get out of here! Go north!"

The shots continued before a Carabinieri officer stepped from behind a pillar and fired three shots at Haqani, one bullet catching him in the shoulder and two more in the chest. He staggered to the side before falling to the ground and landing on top of the English-speaking woman who was screaming at the top of her lungs. She managed to roll out from under him as the blood started to pour through his polo shirt.

The wounded Haqani knew he had been hit badly. It had been expected. There was no thought of a bulletproof vest, and there had been no escape plan. He was going to die in Venice, Italy. He knew the end was near. But he fought the urge to simply close his eyes and die. He grunted and gasped for breath. Looking north, a mad rush had ensued. The tourists, the school children, the locals pushed and shoved their way for an opening to safety. Haqani could see the crowd stampeding toward the narrow streets hoping to save themselves. When one would fall, those behind would simply climb over them. Ten would die from suffocation in the heap of human bodies. The screams from those in the crushed mass of humanity would haunt the survivors for all eternity.

Haqani could hear the police approaching – the shouting and the yelling added to the chaos. People were begging for help, blood flowing into the Piazzetta. Haqani could feel his body about to shut down and the twitching started. But he fought hard to hold on to see it through. As a Carabinieri officer pointed his weapon at him, Haqani's eyes started to close.

The explosion that followed opened them wide for the final time. The blast shook the Venetian ground. It was followed by another and then another. The bombs strapped to the chests of the remaining three terrorists had detonated on separate streets leading away from the Piazza. They had waited for the moment when hundreds of frightened tourists and locals had sought to evacuate from the carnage and were funneled into the narrow corridors. The resultant death traps were pure slaughter. The sirens from police and fire boats could be heard making their way through the lagoon to San Marco.

With the explosions echoing in his ears and the smell of death in his nostrils, Haqani took his last breath and expired.

London, England

The woman seated in the packed subway car of the London Underground wore a Muslim headdress and sunglasses. The white ear buds were connected to her cell phone, which she held in her hand. In her lap sat a large Harrod's bag with a box inside.

"Next stop," the speaker squawked to those on the Tube. "Westminster."

It was almost 10 a.m. in London, an hour earlier than the eastern cities of Paris and Rome. The sidewalks outside of the Tube stop were teeming with tourists snapping pictures of Parliament and Big Ben. The morning fog had burned off and the sun was glistening off the dewy leaves of the trees in the park. Barges floated down the Thames at a leisurely rate. The London Eye wheeled around giving riders a bird's-eye view of the city – including views of Buckingham Palace, Parliament, and the Millennium Bridge.

"Mind the gap," the subway intercom warned.

The Tube riders stepped carefully onto the platform and passed others looking to herd their way on board.

The woman in the sunglasses clutched the handle of her Harrod's bag and headed down the east pedestrian tunnel for the exit closest to the Thames. The bulk of the other riders took the closest southern route and exited in the shadow of Big Ben. Upon her exit, she looked skyward at the sun peeking through the clouds. Her watch indicated she was right on schedule.

She walked to the stairwell below street level at the corner of Bridge Street and Victoria Embankment. Tourists posed for pictures with Thomas Thornycroft's statue of Boadicea and her daughters along with Big Ben in the background. Still more stared at the London Eye across the Thames.

"Hello," Anwar bin Hajj said softly into her ear.

She turned around, slightly startled. She was waiting for him but had not seen him approach. "Hello."

Bin Hajj kissed her on both cheeks. The woman reached into the bag and pulled out a small digital camera. In turn, bin Hajj grabbed the bag, turned around, backed up two steps, and stood tall.

"Smile," the woman said, snapping his picture.

They looked like any other tourist couple enjoying the sights and sounds of London. They came from all over the world, and a picture with the Clock Tower housing Big Ben in the background was a must-have memento. The two blended in nicely, but a British security agent had both of them on the closed-circuit television at that very moment.

The British Government had installed more surveillance cameras per capita than any other country in the world and used them to their utmost advantage. Cameras caught people walking to work, riding the Tube, eating in restaurants, standing in line, running down the Mall. Just about every public act was recorded. Some private moments were also taped, logged, and saved for future use. No one could hide from the U.K. Government's prying eyes. And the Brit authorities had no qualms with using it.

On July 7, 2005, four Islamist terrorists were recorded in the London Underground and a double-decker bus prior to blowing themselves up and killing 52 civilians. The 7/7 attacks were the deadliest act of terror on British soil since the bombing of Pan Am Flight 103 over Lockerbie,

Scotland, in 1988 killed 270 people. The security cameras helped the authorities uncover who the terrorists were and their mode of operation. Since that time, numerous operations had been thwarted with the help of the cameras peering into the lives of Londoners and tourists alike.

But this day, the camera operator moved on and focused on another man as he walked across the bridge.

"Have a good day," the woman said into bin Hajj's ear. "May Allah be with you."

The two walked up the stairs to street level and went in different directions – the woman went east across the Thames, while bin Hajj waited for the signal and headed south across the four lanes of traffic.

Once on the opposite sidewalk, he didn't need to check his watch or look at the Great Clock. The 13-ton Great Bell known as Big Ben told him the hour had arrived. He pulled out his phone and dialed the number. "Stand by," he said to the man on the other end of the line.

"*Allahu akbar*," the man said.

"*Allahu akbar*," bin Hajj whispered back.

He stepped toward the concrete bridge railing and waited. His ears picked up the faint sound of sirens from the east. To his right, the noise grew louder with every second. To his left, the eleventh-hour strikes of Big Ben told him they were right on schedule. He went ahead and smiled. It was okay to let a little emotion show. He knew what was going on.

The high-pitched whine of a speeding motor cycle could be heard coming over the bridge. Trailing thirty feet behind were two London Metropolitan police vehicles, both at full song with their sirens, chasing down the miscreant. Bin Hajj watched the cyclist blow through the stoplight and continue on the north side of Big Ben, the police hot on the man's tail. The eyes of hundreds of people on the sidewalks followed the high-speed chase toward the west. Some even got a blurry video on their cell phones. None of them was looking at the terrorist standing on the south side of the street.

Bin Hajj reached into the bag and pulled out the AK-47. "*Allahu akbar!*"

Bin Hajj gunned down those on the south side of the walk and methodically moved the barrel northward in a slow arc catching victims crossing the street and then those on the north side. Screams of horror echoed off the walls of Parliament and the shops across the street. People ran anywhere they could find an open space. Pandemonium set in. As a double-decker bus rounded the corner to head east, the driver took a shot to the head. Bin Hajj then let loose on the bus like he was in a shooting gallery.

With the river to the south, he had no concern about someone coming up behind him. After he had emptied the fifty-round magazine, he reached into the bag and pulled out a spare. He slapped it in and sprayed those unfortunate enough to have been walking west toward him on the bridge. A candied nut vendor found his only avenue of escape was to dive over the side of the bridge into the murky depths of the Thames.

With the second magazine nearly empty, he turned back to the west hoping to catch anyone he might have missed. But two bullets to his chest stopped him from doing any further damage. He staggered a few steps and fell backward. Two Uzi-toting London policemen were running in his direction and looking to end the carnage right then and there.

Bin Hajj could feel the blood running down the side of his body. His hand could no longer grip the gun. He knew he was dying. But he waited. He wanted to hear the explosion. The London attack would be on par with the one in Venice. That was the plan. The same glorious and deadly plan. He struggled to keep breathing, the blood starting to pool in his mouth. He coughed it out and it splattered in his own face. Still, he tried to hold on.

But he would breathe his last before he heard any more.

CHAPTER 5

The White House – Washington, D.C.

"Mr. President," Wiley Cogdon whispered in the President's ear.

It was 5:30 a.m., and the President of the United States was soundly asleep in his bed in his second-floor bedroom in the White House. He didn't flinch at the man's voice in his ear. It would be another ten minutes before the alarm went off, but his chief of staff felt he couldn't wait any longer.

"Mr. President," Cogdon whispered louder, bending down closer toward his boss. This time he gave a couple of light taps to the President's shoulder.

Cogdon had risen at his usual time of 4 a.m. after turning out the lights around midnight. Four hours of sleep was all he needed to kick-start the day in the job he relished. While the Secret Service didn't particularly like the hours he kept, they dutifully drove him from his residence at the Hay-Adams across Lafayette Square just north of the White House.

In contrast to Cogdon's restlessness and ability to work on little sleep, the President liked to get seven to eight hours per night. Although he was a sound sleeper, his internal body clock often woke him without the alarm.

Today, it appeared to Cogdon that the President wanted to get in every last minute of shut-eye. Thus, the taps turned into a firm shake of the shoulder.

"Mr. President."

The President's eyes slowly began to open when he was startled by the cherubic face of his balding chief of staff staring down at him in the low light of the presidential bedroom.

"Jeez!" the President blurted out, the bed shaking in his fright. He had never grown accustomed to Cogdon's late night or early morning intrusions into the bedroom. The First Lady woke as well, but seeing it was just Cogdon, she rolled over and went back to sleep.

Now seeing his boss awake, Cogdon wasted no time. "Sir, we have a problem."

The President blinked his eyes and took a breath. "I kind of figured that," he whispered, trying not to disturb his wife. "You never wake me to give me good news. What time is it?"

Cogdon looked over at the digital clock on the nightstand. "It's five-thirty, sir. There have been multiple terrorist attacks across Europe this morning."

The President's eyes blinked one more time then focused squarely on Cogdon. "How bad?"

Cogdon told him there had been four terrorist attacks in as many cities. "At least 380 deaths that we know of so far."

President Schumacher took the covers off, threw his legs out of the bed, and sat up. He took a deep breath. *Time to go to work*, he thought.

"I have called the national security team to meet at 6 a.m.," Cogdon said.

The President nodded. "Good. I'm going to get a quick shower and shave and I'll meet you down in the Situation Room."

"Yes, sir."

With Cogdon heading for the door, the President pushed his tired body out of bed and headed for the bathroom. It never took the President long to get ready for the day. He could usually be prepared to go in thirty minutes. He shaved, took a quick shower, and put on a dark blue business suit. He grabbed a bagel and a caffeinated Diet Coke from the First Family's private kitchen and headed quickly for the elevator.

"Morning, Mac," the President said to Mac Clark, the head of his Secret Service security detail, eating as he went.

"Morning, sir."

"Apparently the world is on fire yet again, Mac."

"Yes, sir, that is what I hear."

Mac Clark was no stranger to the fires of the world. He had served two tours of duty as a Marine in Afghanistan before joining the Secret Service. With his slim athletic build, tight jaw, and closely cropped hair, Clark was the prototypical security agent. He definitely looked the part and acted it as well. He had risen through the ranks and led his first detail guarding Vice President Jackson for the past two years. Although he had hoped to someday lead the presidential detail, it came about under difficult circumstances.

In the botched attempt to capture President Schumacher in Rome a year earlier, six members of his Secret Service detail, including his lead agent, Michael Craig, were killed in an attack by Russian and Pakistani terrorists. Craig had been with the President since his first days as Vice President, and the loss hurt the First Family greatly. President Schumacher had great appreciation for the Secret Service, he being a former federal law-enforcement agent, and took it upon himself after the attack to make sure his agents were spending time with their families and decompressing from the strains of such a demanding job – one where the history of the world could hinge on their success or failure.

Agent Clark raised his hand microphone to his mouth. "Shadow is on the move."

The President had finished his bagel by the time the elevator doors opened on the first floor of the White House. He and Agent Clark stepped outside and walked along the Colonnade framing the Rose Garden. The crisp September air indicated fall was just around the corner. The President loved this hour of the day – the quietness of the morning, the absence of car horns and police sirens. It usually presented the only peaceful moments of the day in the nation's capital. The two men rounded the corner and entered the Oval Office, an hour earlier than usual. The President grabbed a folder from his desk and proceeded down to the Situation Room in the basement of the West Wing.

The Marine guarding the door to the Situation Room opened it and those inside rose from their seats around the conference table.

"Good morning everyone," the President said in a serious manner, ready to get down to business. "Take your seats."

At the end of the table, the President took the high-backed leather chair underneath the presidential seal on the wall and sat down. The table had six black leather chairs on both sides and each one was taken. The wall to the left of the President consisted of two TV screens and three digital clocks noting the local time, the President's time (which given his current position was the same as the local time), and the Zulu/UTC time in red numbers. A six-foot-wide TV screen occupying the wall opposite the President showed various states of chaos – bodies strewn on the ground, fires burning, emergency vehicles hurrying here and there. The President grabbed another Diet Coke sitting in a bowl of ice and popped open the top. The bagels had gone untouched but every other person in the room had a cup of coffee in front of them.

Some were already on their third cup.

Seated around the table were Joint Chiefs Chairman Hugh Cummins, Secretary of State Mike Arnold, Secretary of Defense William Javits, National Security Adviser Carl Harnacke, CIA Director Bill Parker, Homeland Security Secretary Brad Michaelson, and FBI Director Ty Stubblefield. In the corner of the room, Cogdon stood ready with pen and notepad in hand.

"Director Parker, what happened?" the President asked.

"Mr. President," Director Parker said, straightening his stack of highly-classified intelligence documents and grabbing the TV remote. "There have been four terrorist attacks across Europe this morning. The first and most deadly attack occurred in Venice, Italy, at approximately 11 a.m. Italian time, a little after 5 a.m. here in D.C. Two terrorists opened fire with automatic weapons on the Italian President as he prepared to enter an open-air military swearing-in ceremony."

Director Parker clicked the remote and the screen with the test pattern blinked to life. "This is the only footage we have of the aftermath."

"Was President Baldini hit?" the President asked.

Director Parker nodded. "He was hit. It is believed to be a shoulder wound. He is in surgery right now, but the doctors seem to think he is going to make it. The same cannot be said of General Giancarlo Palladino, the highest-ranking member of the Italian Army, who was shot in the head and killed, along with several security agents and military leaders."

"My God," the President exclaimed. "How could the terrorists get that close?"

Director Stubblefield spoke up. "Mr. President, as you know, the Italian President is more of a figurehead in Italy. The Prime Minister is the mover and shaker in the country. That said, President Baldini has been known to have lax security. I just got off the phone with Director Defoe at the Secret Service, he said he has repeatedly warned the Italians about the lack of security. He was afraid something like this would happen."

Director Parker readily agreed. "Sir, they had President Baldini in an open-air golf cart. I could have run faster than that thing. There are only a handful of entrances to the Piazza where the attack happened. No metal detectors at any checkpoints. There were no snipers. They didn't even remove the trash cans or run the canines through. We think that is why the terrorists chose Venice rather than Rome. They knew it would be a soft target."

The President nodded. "And you said this attack was the most deadly."

"Yes, sir. At least 280 are confirmed dead. Once the shooting started, the crowd that had assembled to watch the swearing-in ceremony panicked and looked for a way out. They funneled down narrow streets where they were either trampled or killed by three explosive devices. It was absolute mayhem according to my Italian sources. We are not sure if suicide vests were used or whether the bombs had been planted in anticipation of the escape paths."

The President interrupted. "Do we know who's behind the attack?"

"We are virtually certain it's al-Qaeda. It's possible it could be a splinter group, but given the size and scope of the operations, it is most likely Muslim extremists."

"I thought Islam was a religion of peace," the President wondered.

"It is, so long as everyone adheres to it."

The President opened his folder and started scribbling down his notes. Venice, 280 dead, al-Qaeda. "And what about the other attacks?"

Secretary of State Mike Arnold thought he had something to add. "I wonder if this has anything to do with that idiot threatening to burn the Koran yesterday."

"I don't think he actually burned it," Director Javits reported. "He was just making threats."

The President didn't want to worry about what might have sparked the attack. "Bill, what happened after Venice?"

"Shortly after the initial attack in Venice," Director Parker said, "attacks followed in London, Brussels, and Madrid. There are believed to be sixty dead in the London attack, which followed a similar pattern of automatic-weapons fire followed up by the detonation of explosives. The attack could have been much worse but one terrorist on a motorcycle failed to make a turn and fell off the bike before he could detonate a device just west of Parliament. We're looking at about twenty dead each in Brussels and Madrid and scores wounded."

The President wrote down the cities and the numbers. He took a sip of Diet Coke and turned to Director Michaelson. "Brad, do you know of any plots here in the U.S.?"

The Homeland Security secretary cleared his throat. "We have nothing that would indicate a credible threat of a terrorist attack planned for this country at this time."

"Ty?"

"Nothing that would indicate an imminent attack on American soil."

The President nodded and then started in with the orders. "Let's put all federal law-enforcement agencies on high alert. General, do what you have to do to ratchet up security at our foreign installations." General Cummins nodded as the President continued. "Mike, get on the phone to your comrades to express our condolences for the loss of life and our commitment to fighting the evils of terrorism. I will call the leaders of Italy, England, Belgium, and Spain myself. Let's keep our eyes open and do what we need to keep this country safe."

Once the President rose from his seat and started for the Oval Office, the others filed out of the Situation Room. Before he headed upstairs, Director Stubblefield reached for his phone. He wasn't content to wait until he got back to the office down Pennsylvania Avenue. He dialed the number and only had to wait one ring.

"Schiffer, Stubblefield," the Director said. There were no exchanges of pleasantries. It was focused directness. "Have you seen the news?"

"Yes," Schiffer said. "I am watching it right now."

FBI Special Agent D.A. "Duke" Schiffer was Director Stubblefield's go-to guy when he wanted action. Schiffer led the FBI's top-secret "Phantom team," a five-member counter-terrorism unit that prided itself on stealth, agility, and, if necessary, lethality. With Director Stubblefield actually taking part, the Phantom team had led the operation to rescue President Schumacher in Rome. While Stubblefield had a number of Deputy Directors and Assistant Deputies at his disposal, Agent Schiffer was the man to get the job done.

Stubblefield didn't need to make any small talk or exclaim at the carnage halfway around the world. He had a country to protect. "Get the Phantom team ready."

"Yes, sir."

"I want the team on full alert. Make sure you have a chopper on standby just in case."

Schiffer didn't need to be told twice. "I'm on it."

CHAPTER 6

Office of the Civil Liberties Alliance – Washington, D.C.

The surly Art Brennan stomped into his office at 8 a.m. He had tossed and turned all night, the product of that "S.O.B" in the White House. He didn't know how much more he could take of the Schumacher Administration. Something needed to be done. Accustomed to seeing her boss in a foul mood, Brennan's secretary didn't even say hello as he walked in the door. Neither did he.

"Hold my calls," he snapped as he barreled into his office and slammed the door.

Like clockwork, Brennan headed straight for the liquor cabinet and found his morning scotch. He desperately hoped it would get rid of his pounding headache. His life was falling apart. The biggest donors to the CLA were questioning whether they were getting any bang for their buck – or more specifically – their millions of bucks. *The Republicans are going to annihilate us in the next election!*, they screamed at him. What the hell was he going to do about it!? Moreover, some of the moderate Democrats on whose support he could readily count were distancing themselves from him after his latest round of televised tirades. The vitriol, the vile insults toward the President, all of them had started to mount, and some wondered about his sanity. The CLA had changed its mission from defending the rights of the poor and innocent to all-out warfare against the United States of America. Two Democrats had even gone so far as to return five-figure CLA donations, fearing their opponents would allege they were in bed with that scum Brennan and agreed with everything he had to say. His friends were jumping ship and silently hoping he'd go down with it. The only thing Brennan knew to do was fight like a bulldog.

Brennan took a drink before he sunk down into his leather chair behind his desk. His bloodshot and glassy eyes were heavy from the lack of sleep. He tried to sit still hoping the pain would go away.

His closed eyes shot open when he heard the phone ring. And ring, and ring. His secretary had left her post to walk across the hall to complain and moan about her boss to the other secretaries in the Democratic Party think tank that shared the fifth floor with the CLA. For therapeutic purposes, she made the trip on a daily basis.

Brennan looked at the blinking light on his phone, the annoying ringing still filling his ears. "Isn't anyone going to answer the freakin' phone!" he shouted through the office wall. "Worthless wench," he whispered to himself. "I should have fired her years ago."

Brennan grabbed the handset. "Hello?" he grunted rudely, like he hated to have been bothered by the intrusion.

The man on the other end was slightly taken aback at the greeting. He expected a polite secretary who would extend a warm welcome before directing the call to the proper place.

"Is this Art Brennan?"

Brennan stuffed his morning cigar in his big mouth. "Yeah, who is this?"

The man cleared his throat. "Mr. Brennan, my name is Hakim. We met the other day at Georgetown University after your lecture."

Brennan did not respond. He had totally forgotten about the man he had lunch with after his lecture. He tried to picture the man's face but came up empty. He did remember meeting with a man and vaguely recalled their conversation.

"Do you remember me?"

"Yes, I remember you," Brennan said, his angry tone becoming noticeably softer.

"Mr. Brennan, I hope you recall the conversation we had, and the possibility of you providing legal representation to me and my group."

"Yes, I remember." Brennan was still searching his brain. He recalled Hakim telling him something big was about to happen, but Brennan had not wanted to jump on board until he could confirm the man was not some nut or government agent trying to entrap him. He hadn't asked around about the man's background or credentials like he wanted. "You said some things were going to happen to show me I should take you on as a client."

"Yes, I did."

The clueless Brennan had not even turned on his TV that morning. He could barely find the button to start his computer. Usually, his secretary did it for him before he made it to the office. "Well, I'm still waiting."

Al-Rashid was slightly dismayed. The world was on fire, four European cities were aflame, and Brennan didn't even know it. He was completely clueless on the news of the day. "Mr. Brennan, have you checked the TV this morning?"

"No, I haven't. I just walked into the office."

"Perhaps you should do so," al-Rashid said. His tone indicated Brennan ought to do a better job of keeping up to speed on world events. "I will call you back in ten minutes." Al-Rashid then hung up.

Brennan looked at the phone, somewhat put off by the man, a prospective client, hanging up on him. Unable to find the remote control to his TV, he walked over and turned it on. When the picture finally came into view, Brennan's jaw dropped. Each of CNN's four reporters took up their own quadrant of the screen and the background in each was a mix of fire, smoke, and blood in the streets of Europe. Brennan's eyes widened when he looked at the locations of the reporters – London, Venice, Brussels, and Madrid – the same cities al-Rashid had written down on the note and passed over to Brennan during their lunch. Brennan bent down to turn up the volume on the TV.

"Let's get a live update from Venice," Constance Rose, the CNN anchor, announced. "Maria Florentino is on the scene. Maria, what's the latest?"

Maria Florentino was CNN's Italian correspondent and had been in Venice to cover the military swearing-in ceremonies. She looked half-stunned, shell-shocked at the turn of events she had witnessed a short time earlier. She put her finger to the earpiece in her left ear, straining to hear what was said. She thought the explosion that happened directly behind her might have rendered her deaf in her right ear. Her white blouse had specks of blood on it but it wasn't hers. It was the blood of the BBC correspondent who was standing next to her when the attack started. He did not survive. But being a reporter, Florentino dutifully picked up her microphone after the attack ended and gave her report in the world's newest war zone. With her noticeable Italian accent, she rattled off what she knew. "Constance, I can tell you that it is mass carnage here in Venice."

The sun was now overhead and it beat down on the open Piazza as emergency workers tended to the victims. Triage tents sprouted like an open-air market, and boats were lined up in the lagoon ready to take away the injured to the hospitals that were almost filled to capacity. What had started out as a beautiful day in Venice had turned into a nightmare that no one would ever forget.

Florentino pointed over her shoulder to one of the side streets north of the Piazza. "As you can see behind me, emergency crews are desperately searching for survivors of the bombing that took place just over two hours ago. The rescue operation has been hampered by a wall that has collapsed and trapped those who had been unable to flee to safety." She then looked at the notes on her notepad. "As your viewers now know, the President of Italy, Donatello Baldini, was shot by suspected terrorists. I can tell you President Baldini is still in surgery at this hour, but we have received word that he is expected to survive. Constance, if we get more information, we will bring it to you as soon as we can."

Back at the CNN studio in Washington, D.C., Rose thanked Florentino for her report and then went live to the three reporters covering similar scenes across Europe. The pictures showed cars on fire, fire trucks blocking streets, and crying women wailing in four different languages.

"For those of you who may have just turned on the TV," Rose said glumly as the clock ticked near the bottom of the hour, "terror has reached the streets of Europe this morning. Terror attacks have been reported in Venice, London, Brussels, and Madrid. At least 380 people are confirmed dead and it is feared the number could go much higher as the day goes on. The President of the United States has issued a statement condemning the attacks and offered support to our allies who have been impacted by quote, these acts of madness, unquote. President Schumacher has also offered U.S. military help to Italy, England, Belgium, and Spain in the rescue efforts. Law-enforcement authorities in this country have been put on high alert as a result of the attacks."

The voice of one of the CNN producers filled Rose's ear. She put a finger to her earpiece to make sure she got it all. Another producer off screen handed her a piece of paper.

"We have just received word from our CNN office in London that the Crescent Brotherhood," Rose said slowly to make sure everyone heard it, "has taken responsibility for these terrorist attacks. The Crescent Brotherhood, an offshoot of al-Qaeda, has issued a statement praising the attacks and promising quote, the war on the infidels has begun in Europe and soon blood will run in the streets of the devil's playground, the United States of America, unquote." Rose's demeanor grew more somber by the minute. "Obviously, the war on terror has taken a new and violent turn. We'll go live to our correspondents after this break."

Even with the commercial running, Brennan didn't hear the phone ringing on his desk. He was still transfixed on the screen even though it only showed an elderly gentleman telling the world that his new denture cream gave him a new lease on life. Brennan's mind kept visualizing the note that had been passed over to him at lunch. Finally, he snapped out of his trance. With his heart beating faster, he picked up the phone.

"Hello?"

Hakim al-Rashid did not even introduce himself this time. "I take it you have seen the news?"

"Yes, I have," Brennan said seriously.

"I was hoping we could meet some time this afternoon."

For a split second, Brennan wondered if he wanted to go down this road. A road that was fraught with danger. But his massive ego quickly beat back any qualms of conscience. He was a lawyer, and he knew he could always hide behind the right to counsel and the privilege attorneys and clients share so they can speak freely and openly about anything without fear of the conversations being used against them. No matter how vile and sick a person could be in the eyes of Americans, he was entitled to be represented by an attorney. Child molesters had lawyers, wife beaters had lawyers, even terrorists had lawyers. Brennan told himself he could shield himself under the protections of the Constitution – the Constitution he so derided on a daily basis.

"Yes, this afternoon would be fine," Brennan said, the confidence back in his voice. "I can see you in my office to discuss your legal matters."

"No," al-Rashid said directly. "I don't want to meet in your office. Meet me at the Burger King on Sixth Street in Arlington at two o'clock."

Brennan looked at his watch. He didn't find the need to check his calendar. He'd be there. "Okay. I'll see you then."

CHAPTER 7

Arlington, Virginia

Art Brennan decided against having his CLA driver take him from his office in downtown D.C. to Arlington. He wasn't for sure why the need for secrecy – maybe it was his paranoid conscience that made him do it – but he felt he should go alone. It would just be him – no witnesses to offer their recollections of any meeting. Moreover, he often met with clients outside of the office so it was no big deal. At least that is what he told himself. He didn't tell his secretary where he was going, and she didn't care to ask. She could take messages with the best of them. Plus, it would give her time to scroll through the D.C. job listings on the Internet in hopes of finding new employment and finally leave the boss from hell.

At five minutes until two, Brennan drove his black Cadillac into the Burger King parking lot. The midday lunch crowd had come and gone with their flame-broiled Whoppers, large fries, and big Cokes. Brennan looked at the cars in the nearly empty lot. A few beaters on the end probably belonged to the employees, at least those who didn't take the bus. Brennan wanted to see what Hakim al-Rashid was driving but nothing stood out in his mind. He pulled the Cadillac into a spot and checked his watch. He was just a few minutes early. He grabbed a yellow legal pad from the backseat and placed it inside his briefcase. He turned around and tried to see if al-Rashid was already inside. He hardly remembered what the man looked like. He only saw one man at a table. The man had gray hair, most likely a retiree with nothing better to do than waste away an afternoon at Burger King, and he was fully engrossed in his newspaper and large beverage.

Brennan decided to go inside. He grabbed his briefcase, shut the door, and pressed the key fob twice to indicate the Cadillac was locked and armed. He walked inside and took a booth near the window. He was not accustomed to such surroundings. He usually dined at pricey D.C. establishments with white table cloths and fancy foods, and all of it was paid for on the CLA's credit card. He swiped a smattering of seeds from the last occupant's Whopper bun with the back of his hand. He felt the need for a hand sanitizer. Having none, he wiped his hands on a napkin and then looked at his wrist. His watch read two o'clock.

"Can I help you?"

Brennan was opening his briefcase when the question was asked but he didn't hear it. Too many things were going on in his head for him to pay much attention to his surroundings. He started rummaging around for his notepad.

"Excuse me. Can I help you?"

The pointed question came from the large black woman behind the counter. The tag affixed to the uniform covering her buxom chest indicated her name was Precious. Unfortunately for anyone in the vicinity, Precious was not in a good mood. Two customers had berated her within the last hour because they didn't get what they ordered. She had to stand there and take it even though it was the fault of the cooks in the back who couldn't read that the Whoppers with cheese weren't supposed to have any mayo and onions on them. What's worse, her shift should have ended an hour ago, but some tattooed teenage employee called in sick for the second time this week and the assistant manager told Precious he needed her to work a double shift. She silently cursed the man as well as that lazy teenager, who was probably just too stoned to come to work again. "Stupid, pothead," she kept repeating to herself. Since the assistant manager was crunching his numbers in the back office and there was hardly anyone else in the building during the afternoon lull, Precious decided it was her turn to lay down the law from behind the counter.

"Sir," she said in Brennan's direction. She looked around again and saw no higher-ups in the vicinity. She raised her voice. "Hey! You with the bald head!" she bellowed from behind the counter. Finally, she had Brennan's attention. He turned around in his seat. "Yeah you," she said, pointing at him. "This is a restaurant not a rest stop. You need to order something or leave." She gestured her thumb toward the door just in case Brennan didn't get the verbal message. Even if she was only going to get paid minimum wage, she would make sure the business made some money while she was working.

Brennan looked around and realized the intimidating woman was indeed talking to him. He then realized nobody would be coming around to take his order. He looked around again but still no Hakim. Precious continued to give him an evil glare, like she was two seconds away from jumping the counter and throwing him out of the establishment. Given her size, she could no doubt do it. Not wanting to pick a fight with the woman – he would have demanded to see the manager on any other day – Brennan left the booth and walked toward the counter.

"I'll take a Pepsi."

"We don't have Pepsi," Precious snapped.

Brennan seemed flustered, like he just wanted to order and sit back down. "I'll take a Coke then."

"That's it?" Precious shot back. He didn't want anything to eat. What the hell was wrong with this guy? He could have just gone to the 7-11 if he wanted a soda.

"Yeah."

"Well, what size do you want?" Hurry up, she seemed to say. She had people in the drive-thru waiting and ready to yell and scream at her if their fries were cold.

Brennan started looking at the menu board but gave up quickly. "I don't care. Just give me the biggest one."

Precious grabbed the large cup and punched in the order on the register. "Two twenty five," she said.

Brennan opened his wallet and handed over his CLA plastic.

"We don't take no American Express," Precious huffed, looking at Brennan's card.

Brennan grabbed a five-dollar bill and gave it to her. She gave him his change. Neither one said thank you. Brennan took the cup and went to the machine. He filled the cup with ice and looked at the screen. He had never seen one of the new drink dispensers – the ones with the touch screen and the single button that offers the consumer a million different choices of soda. He stood there and pushed and pushed and pushed but no liquid came out. The man's inability to master the contraption made Precious' day. She snickered loudly but didn't dare offer any help. She was content to watch the man struggle with modern-day technology. After a few more presses of the button, Brennan gave up and went to the tea dispenser on the counter. Once he had full cup, he turned around and saw the man he was to meet standing behind him.

"Hakim," Brennan said. "Nice to see you again."

The two men met near the condiments and shook hands. Brennan then extended a hand and ushered them over to the table. Precious didn't ask al-Rashid if he wanted to order. She was too occupied at the moment. Her large rear end was filling up the opening to the drive-up as she handed out a bag full of Whoppers and fries.

Before the two men started talking, Brennan looked around the restaurant. There was still only the man at the far end reading the News section of the *USA Today*. Otherwise, the place was empty of patrons.

Brennan grabbed a pen out of his suit coat and clicked it for action. "Now, what can I help you with?"

Al-Rashid leaned in closer and never spoke more than a whisper. He again told Brennan he was an associate of Hasni al-Masra, the leader of the Crescent Brotherhood. The European terror attacks had been the handiwork of al-Masra and the Brotherhood, and it was al-Rashid's responsibility to oversee the jihad that had been planned for American soil. Brennan did not write any of the information down on his legal pad. It was too explosive, but given its serious nature, he wouldn't forget a word.

"Are you planning similar attacks here in the U.S.?" Brennan wondered quietly.

Al-Rashid nodded.

Brennan remembered the details of the attack that occurred in Venice involving the Italian leader. Brennan had his concerns. "Are you going after the President?" he asked. The frown indicated what he thought of such an attempt and he did not wait for an answer. "I don't think that's a good idea." The terrorists he had represented had tried to assassinate the most powerful man in the world on a number of occasions but the only result was instant death at the hand of the U.S. military or a similar fate at the end of a needle provided by the Bureau of Prisons. "The President is well protected," he said, stating the obvious. "An assassination attempt will not succeed. And another thing, it will only increase his support among the American people." Something Brennan wanted less of, not more.

Al-Rashid and the leaders of the Brotherhood, however, were not stupid. They knew going after the President had little chance of success.

"We have plans on a much smaller scale," al-Rashid said. "But of a longer duration. Not only will it bring America to its knees it will cripple the Schumacher Administration. The U.S. Government will be unable to respond effectively, and once we list our demands, the American people will demand the President resign to save the country."

Brennan smiled. He liked what he was hearing. *It was the answer to all his problems*, he thought. "Okay," he said, taking his mental notes. "That sounds good. What do you need from me?"

"I need you to be my middleman," al-Rashid said. "We will need money to execute the plan, and I need you to accept funds and disburse them when I tell you."

"Why can't you just use a bank?"

"I can't afford to have the FBI snooping around my bank accounts. Money will be transferred in and out quickly – sometimes large amounts. I don't want to set off any red flags."

"Okay."

"If you are my attorney, the Feds won't give it a second look. Given your . . .," al-Rashid said, his eyes looking at the ceiling and his mind searching for the right words, "let's say, combative style, it offers us cover to set the plan in motion. The Government doesn't want you to be ranting and raving and raising holy hell while it tries to fight the war on terror. You would be too much of a distraction. If you take to the cameras and tell the American people how the Schumacher Administration is trampling on the rights of its citizens, snooping where it shouldn't be, the Government will be handcuffed. It will give us the opportunity we need to get the ball rolling."

Brennan nodded his head. The man sitting across the table from him spoke his language. He obviously had heard Brennan's lecture. They stopped talking as Precious waddled by to wipe down the tables. She sneered at Brennan – the man just gave off a bad vibe. At the far booth at the other end of the building, she asked the lone man, whom she referred to as "Honey," if he needed anything. He thanked her but declined the offer. He went back to reading the Sports section.

Once Precious was out of hearing range back behind the counter, al-Rashid said, "Once we have the pieces in place, we won't need you any longer."

"Until they catch you and charge you with every crime they can think of."

Al-Rashid smiled contently. Brennan still didn't understand who he really was. He was not just some courier making sure packages get to their desired destination or money finds its way to the intended recipient. His youthful appearance worked against him in that sense. He was mature beyond his years. And, more importantly, he was a committed terrorist. And soon he would be dead. "Mr. Brennan, al-Qaeda has a saying that 'we love death more than you love life.'" He stopped briefly to let the terrorist mantra sink in. "I am not long for this world. I will soon join my fellow martyrs in a much holier place."

Brennan finally started to get it. "I understand. I think I can be of service to you," he said. "I would like to be your attorney."

Al-Rashid smiled again. "Thank you, Mr. Brennan."

Brennan opened up his briefcase and pulled out a retainer agreement. That way it would be official, and the authorities couldn't go snooping around lest they violate the attorney-client privilege. Al-Rashid signed his name, or the name he went by, and shook hands with Brennan. The meeting was over.

"I will be contacting you shortly," al-Rashid said, sliding out of the booth.

Brennan scooted his fat body along the bench and extricated himself from the booth. "I will look forward to hearing from you."

The two men walked out of the building. Brennan went to his Cadillac and al-Rashid went in the opposite direction. Brennan turned around to see what al-Rashid was driving but he had walked around the other side of the Burger King and disappeared into the concrete jungles of greater Arlington. Brennan shrugged and headed back to the offices of the Civil Liberties Alliance.

And the only customer left inside the Burger King folded up his *USA Today*. He expertly managed the drink dispenser and filled his cup full of caffeine free Diet Coke.

"See you later, Precious," the man said, waving as he headed for the door.

"Bye, honey," Precious said, the first smile of the day crossing her face. "You have a good evening now."

The man crossed the street and got into his car. It was time for him to return to his office at the Federal Bureau of Investigation.

CHAPTER 8

Arlington, Virginia

The tree-lined street had little traffic as it ended in a cul-de-sac. There were no McDonald's or Starbucks within at least a mile and that is the way the locals liked it. It was a quiet oasis in the bustling metropolis that seemed to ever expand from the heart of the nation's capital. The solitude and serenity of the area provided a welcome respite from the day-to-day grind of Beltway traffic, and the Mercedes and BMWs that backed out of the well-maintained homes indicated the wealth of the residents. It was the home to doctors, lawyers, and other white-collar professionals.

It was also home to the Islamic Studies Center.

The Center had originated back in the early '90s as a Muslim outreach center, where Muslims in the area could come together, pray, and otherwise enjoy the company of others in the faith. It was funded by generous donations from Saudi princes looking to spread their wealth and their religion into the United States. By the end of the decade, the Center had transformed itself into a private educational academy, giving Muslim families a place to send their children to learn about Islam. It was a first-rate educational opportunity with boys and girls learning, laughing, and playing sports on the manicured lawns. Entry into the Center was tightly controlled, and admission into the academy required applications, testing, and lots of money. American Muslims all talked about wanting to visit the Center and still more dreamed of sending their kids to study behind its greenery-shrouded fences. It was the place to be.

But then came 9/11.

After the terrorist attacks, a number of families took their kids out of the academy and moved – some to other parts of the U.S. and others back to Saudi Arabia. More and more regulars decided not to show up at group gatherings – some fearful of being branded jihadists or terrorist sympathizers. The shrinking of the base meant the moderates were replaced by their virulent brethren, whose increasing hostility toward the

United States made the center a hotbed for radical Islamists. The academy curriculum also took on a more violent ideology. Textbooks urged readers to rise up against the infidels, calling it their duty in life. Young girls were placed into segregated classrooms where they were told to cover up and shut up. Sharia was the law of this land.

The current head of the Academy was a man by the name of Yousef Ibrahim. He had immigrated to the United States from Saudi Arabia in 1980 and had been at the Academy for over 25 years. His thinning hair, what was left of it was dyed black, looked awkward above his fat face and full beard. He dressed in white and black and spent a good portion of his time at the Saudi Embassy in Washington wining and dining with visiting dignitaries. There, he could demand more money for his school as well as get instructions from the homeland.

And now the FBI was on to him.

Three years ago, the FBI opened an investigation into the goings-on of the Academy. The Feds had been tipped off by an undercover informant that the serenity of the Academy's campus betrayed the hell-fire teachings on the inside. The FBI decided to proceed cautiously, not wanting to infringe on a religious group's right to practice their faith. But something very troubling was going on, and the FBI could not take the chance of letting questionable activity become criminal.

Informants with hidden cameras and microphones were sent in to infiltrate the Center's inner circle. The rise of YouTube and Facebook provided a treasure trove of information coming from the inside – anti-American speeches, radical postings praising terrorist activity overseas, the slamming of U.S. occupation of foreign lands. Anti-Semitic propaganda filled the hearts and minds of all believers. But it wasn't just instruction going on, those inside practiced their beliefs with deadly consequences. One female suspected of adultery within the Center's walls mysteriously vanished. A former member who had converted from Islam to Christianity had not been heard by his family on the outside in several years.

After a three-year investigation, it was time for the FBI to go in.

The five government-issue sedans pulled to a quiet stop in the Center's circle drive surrounding the fountain gurgling in the middle. Ten FBI agents exited their vehicles. The Kevlar helmets and body armor were still stashed at the office. Instead, it was khakis for everyone. Each agent had pulled on his dark jacket with "FBI" emblazoned in

yellow on the back. Their handguns were holstered on their hips opposite
their badges. Their weapon of choice at the moment was the piece of
paper Special Agent Wallace Jones held in his right hand.

Jones led the charge into the front door. The interior floors were
Italian marble, buffed to a high gloss. The walls were white and
decorated with the portraits of various Saudi benefactors, sans smiles,
who had graciously donated millions of dollars to the Center's cause
over the years. The FBI entourage stopped at the front desk.

The woman seated behind the counter looked at Jones and then the
rest of the men behind him. She knew this could not be good. She
scooted her chair closer, and her right knee hit the panic button
underneath the desk. "Can I help you?"

Agent Jones cleared his throat. "I am Special Agent Jones, FBI," he
said, holding his credentials in his left hand. "We would like to speak
with Mr. Ibrahim."

The woman knew Ibrahim's schedule, and these men were definitely
not on it. She wasn't really sure what she should do, so she decided to
stall for time. "Does he know what this is in regards to?"

Jones shook his head once. "He might, although I highly doubt it. We
don't have an appointment. If you could just show us the way to his
office, I would appreciate it."

"Sir," the woman said politely and with respect. "I'm not authorized
to send you back to Mr. Ibrahim's office."

Agent Jones nodded his head. He understood the woman's
predicament. He was not looking to jam anyone up, and he certainly did
not want to cause a scene.

They went round and round for five minutes before Ibrahim looked
out the peephole behind the closed door at the end of the hallway. He
had received his secretary's call via the panic button, and the closed-
circuit television in his office showed the FBI agents waiting patiently
for him. He knew what they wanted. They were going to arrest him for
bogus terrorism charges based on his supposed affiliation with radical
groups in Saudi Arabia. He knew this day would come sooner or later,
and he had planned an all-out assault on the FBI and the Schumacher
Administration when it did. The only thing he had to do before he
confronted the badged thugs out front was make two phone calls. And
it wouldn't take long for his cavalry to show up outside the Center's
front gate. The last thing he did was enter the side office where his

assistant was nervously biting his nails as he too watched the proceedings on the surveillance cameras.

"Get the video camera," Ibrahim whispered over to the young man.

When the assistant indicated the video camera was running, Ibrahim told him it was time to confront the men out front. He marched out, his chest pumped up, brimming with confidence.

"What is going on?" Ibrahim said in a calm voice. He had rehearsed the meeting many times over the last year.

Special Agent Jones stepped to the side of the secretary's desk. He noticed the assistant videographer behind Ibrahim and pointed at the young man. "Would you turn that camera off please?"

"I don't understand what is going on, sir," Ibrahim pleaded, obviously the victim of some terrible misunderstanding.

Agent Jones did not respond to Ibrahim. "Sir, would please turn off the camera." Now it was no longer a request.

The assistant's hand was shaking badly, and the video would no doubt suffer the same fate. Ten men with guns stood twenty feet in front of him, and he silently wondered if they would use them if he didn't comply with the request.

"Sir," Ibrahim pleaded. "I don't understand what this is all about. I don't even know who you are or why you are here." He played the role of victim well.

Agent Jones could see what was happening, and he wasn't going to be a pawn in Ibrahim's game. The FBI did not engage in any shenanigans when it came to these situations. He held up his badge for Ibrahim and the cameraman to see. "Special Agent Jones, FBI," he said.

Ibrahim quickly went next, trying to get the high ground and play to the camera. "Sir, I don't know why you would intrude on our peaceful Center. It is very rude of you to do so. We have done nothing wrong. We have rights too, you know."

Agent Jones stopped him. He had had enough. He looked down at the piece of paper in his right hand. "Mr. Ibrahim, I have a warrant here for your arrest."

"Arrest?" Ibrahim asked in feigned shock. "I have done nothing wrong. On what charges are you arresting me?" He made sure to get out of the way of the camera so it would record the moment when the FBI falsely arrested him on charges of conspiring with terrorists.

"You are being arrested on charges of tax evasion," Agent Jones said.

"Tax evasion!" Ibrahim shot out. That was what they were here for? Ibrahim looked like he had just crapped his pants. He thought they were going to make an example of him and string him up on false charges of supporting terrorism. He was going to be a martyr for the cause as a victim of the U.S. war on Islam. But not anymore. He gave a quick look to his assistant. "Turn off the camera," he whispered under his breath.

The cameraman gave his boss a look as if he didn't hear what had been said.

"Turn off the camera," Ibrahim said louder.

The cameraman complied and backed away. He wondered if he could run and hide but he stayed silent and still for the moment.

"Mr. Ibrahim, I have warrant for your arrest on charges of tax evasion. I also have a warrant to search any and all documents, including but not limited to, tax records and computer files that may pertain to the violation of the Internal Revenue Code." Jones took a step closer. "If you would come with me, I would appreciate it. Then my men here will need to search your office and your records department."

Ibrahim stood stunned. He had accountants who had cooked the books for years, but they had promised him that the U.S. Government would never find out, and even if it did, the Feds would never come after him because of his Muslim connections. *It would be too politically damaging for any presidential administration to target Muslims*, he thought and was told. So he lived high on the hog, well maybe not on the hog, but lavishly like his Saudi countrymen with their desert palaces and fancy imports.

Ibrahim had nothing to say. He just stepped forward.

"Mr. Ibrahim, I am going to have to place you in handcuffs," Jones said. "It is standard procedure for anyone we take in. Do you understand?"

Ibrahim nodded. He couldn't stop thinking about his five luxury cars and ten-bedroom mansion that he had enjoyed for so long. He wondered if the Feds would confiscate his property and auction it off like they do with those big-time drug dealers. He turned around and let Agent Jones close the cold steel around his wrists.

"Do you have anything on you that I need to know about?" Agent Jones asked as he prepared to frisk his new catch.

"No," Ibrahim said softly.

Once content that Ibrahim wasn't carrying any contraband on him, Agent Jones and two other agents escorted Ibrahim out of the building. Once outside in the bright sunshine, the agents saw the cavalry that Ibrahim had called in. Lined up alongside the Center's main drive were five satellite trucks from the various networks, and the cameras were on their tripods and rolling.

The anchor back at CNN Center tried to put a story to the pictures the viewers were seeing on their screens. "We have breaking news this hour coming from Arlington, Virginia. This is a live shot outside the Islamic Studies Center in Arlington, where FBI agents have just arrested the Center's director, Yousef Ibrahim, on suspicion of tax evasion. It is believed that Ibrahim has failed to pay tens of millions of dollars in taxes over the last five years."

The live shot then played the tape of Ibrahim being walked out by Agent Jones, now in sunglasses, and placed in the backseat of a sedan. The video was looped several times so the viewer could get a good look at the top of the suspected tax cheat's head, he being too ashamed to show his face to the cameras. Back to live action, the video showed FBI agents hauling boxes of materials and computer hard drives from inside the Center.

What Ibrahim had thought would be the media riding to his rescue over trumped-up terrorism charges turned out to be a colossal embarrassment for him and the Center. He had thought his false arrest would lead to even more money heading his direction, and a night in the lockup might actually increase his wealth even more. But he highly doubted it now.

While Ibrahim's first phone call had been to a friend at CNN, his second call went to his attorney. They had planned on this day for years. Both knew it would come some day, and Ibrahim had paid a large sum of money to have his attorney on standby should that day come.

Art Brennan was riding to the rescue.

Once Ibrahim had been driven out of the Center's gates, the TV cameras turned to the pit-bull Brennan. Dressed in his usual dark blue suit, he had his CLA driver haul ass down from D.C. On the way, he received word from inside the Center that the FBI had picked up Ibrahim on suspicion of tax evasion. While this was not what Brennan was expecting, he would only need to make a slight shift in the gears to get his point across like he had planned.

"Mr. Brennan, any comment on Ibrahim's arrest?" asked one reporter.

Any comment? If there happened to be a TV camera in the area, Brennan would find it and go to work defending his client. He lived for these moments, and he was ready to fight. The comments would come fast and furious.

Brennan cleared his throat. He started off calmly and stated the standard attorney line. "My client is innocent until proven guilty in a court of law. Mr. Ibrahim is a law-abiding citizen of this country and has done absolutely nothing wrong. He is one-hundred percent not guilty and he will be totally vindicated."

One female reporter in the back knew Brennan well. She had been granted numerous jailhouse interviews with Brennan's clients over the years so she knew how he worked. All she had to do was throw Brennan a little red meat and Brennan's animalistic instincts would tear into it.

"Mr. Brennan, do you think Mr. Ibrahim's arrest has anything to do with his connections with Islamic extremist groups in the Middle East?" she asked.

Brennan had to bite down on his lip to ward off a smile. He had been waiting for the softball and was now ready to swat it out of the park.

"I think it has everything to do with Mr. Ibrahim's contacts in the Middle East. And I might add that those groups are not extremists, they are the allies of the U.S. like Saudi Arabia, Kuwait, and Qatar." Brennan was just starting to get lathered up. "This arrest is nothing but a witch-hunt against Muslim Americans by the Schumacher Administration!" Here come the exclamation points. "President Schumacher and his henchmen at the FBI have trampled on the rights of Muslim Americans ever since he took office! He and his FBI have illegally wiretapped mosques! They have ransacked homes in the dark of night! They have engaged in racial and religious profiling!" The cameras caught Brennan's spit flying from his mouth as he raged on. "This is an all-out war on Muslims in this country! And this President's violation of their rights must be stopped! The unlawful war on terror must end! The immoral occupation of foreign lands must cease immediately!"

The reporters stood back and took in the show. They had become accustomed to Brennan's rants over the years. Some scratched down his diatribe on their notebooks, but others were simply content to watch the fire-breathing Brennan spew forth his vitriol and then watch the tape and write their stories later.

"My client is innocent!" the red-faced Brennan yelled again, trying to wrap it up. "And I look forward to embarrassing the Schumacher Administration, the FBI, and the U.S. Government in a court of law! There, the American people will see, once and for all, how criminal their executive branch really is! Thank you very much!"

Brennan then pushed through the microphones and reporters in a huff as he hiked back to his waiting CLA limo. The show was over for the reporters, but for Brennan, it was just starting.

CHAPTER 9

Great Falls National Park – Great Falls, Virginia

The four men dressed in business attire sat two to a van in the parking lot of Great Falls National Park located just outside the Capital Beltway in Fairfax County, Virginia. It was almost two in the afternoon, but they were not on a long lunch break. Despite their suits and ties, they had been lugging boxes into and out of the vans all morning. Now they were watching and waiting.

Abdel Ramadi and Hassan Jahdari sat in the van to the left of that occupied by Omar Faran and Ahmed Yassar. Ramadi looked out his side mirror and saw no traffic. A check of the rearview mirror with the evergreen air fresheners dangling beneath showed nothing either. The two vans had been in their current position for ten minutes, and those inside were simply waiting to see if they had been followed or maybe someone was snooping around in their business. The park was nearly empty, no one looking to view the falls of the Potomac River or take to the hiking trails. The September day, while sunny, was cool with a strong breeze. The picnic baskets were definitely not out, and the locals looking to get in some kayaking wouldn't be around until the weekend.

The four men had been instructed to meet at the park by Hakim al-Rashid, who was in charge of coordinating the terror teams in the United States. He would not be arriving to meet them, thinking it best that he stay away just in case U.S. law-enforcement agents were following him.

Content that no one was on to them, Ramadi got out of the van. He had arrived in the United States the previous week on a tourist visa for his "long-awaited trip to America," he told the customs agent. He even smiled when he said it. But he was burning with fire on the inside. He was coming to America to kill.

Ramadi had been the Crescent Brotherhood's Deputy Commander for the Madrid operation only to be yanked out of his position by Mahmud Basra just days before the planned attack. The decision was brought about by the highly contentious meeting in Munich. Something about failing Allah was the reason for the ouster – the women and the booze finally catching up with him. Needless to say, Ramadi was not happy. He had trained his men to the best of his abilities, and now he was out as leader and relegated to being a terrorist grunt. It pissed him off and he fought Basra hard trying to get him to reconsider. But Basra could not take the risk that the operation in Madrid would be exposed. So he sent Ramadi to the United States since he was still off the radar screens of U.S. security watchlists. That was one of the few things Ramadi had going for him. Otherwise, he would have been forced to the sidelines. Now in America, Ramadi was to meet up with a man in Virginia and do what he was told. No questions asked.

Despite the cloud cover, Ramadi covered his eyes with his dark shades. The four terrorists were obsessed with surveillance cameras. They knew many-a-terror operation had been foiled by Big Brother looking down from above. Even though nothing indicated the park was teeming with security cameras, and definitely not the trees in the distance, the three other men in the van refused to get out and kept their sunglasses on too.

"I just received a text from Hakim," Ramadi said to the others at the windows in between the two vans. "We are to start tomorrow night."

Hakim al-Rashid had been waiting for the appropriate time to start the American operation. It finally came today. While in Munich, Basra had been scanning U.S. media outlets and came across the story about the arrest of Yousef Ibrahim. The arrest of a Muslim brother provided the perfect reason to start the attacks. Just like that idiot in Georgia who threatened to burn the Koran, the arrest of Ibrahim would once again show America's war on Islam. Basra e-mailed the link of the story to al-Rashid and asked if he had "seen the news." That was the signal, the green light for jihad.

"Hassan and I will travel to Baltimore this evening and scout out a couple of places," Ramadi said confidently, the deputy commander in him coming to the surface. He then looked at Faran in the driver's seat of the van. "You and Ahmed can look for locations in Alexandria and in D.C."

"Okay," Faran, the youngest and most inexperienced of the group, said, taking his orders like a good soldier.

The sniper Yassar had no expression and said nothing. He just stared straight out the front of the van.

Hassan Jahdari, the sniper in Ramadi's van, pointed over at Faran. "If you choose a location in D.C., make sure it is in the slums. There will be less police around."

Faran nodded. *He could do that,* he thought.

"Remember your training," Ramadi, the second youngest in the group, reminded him. "Don't do anything to raise any suspicion. Don't drive above the speed limit. And make sure you wear your seat belt."

Faran nodded again and then ran his right hand up and down his shoulder strap of his seat belt to show Ramadi he had already remembered to follow the rules of the road. Yassar, himself buckled in, said nothing in the passenger seat. It looked like he might be sleeping, perhaps meditating behind his dark shades.

"Get some rest tonight," Ramadi said to Faran and Yassar. "Tomorrow the war on America begins."

Georgetown, Washington, D.C.
"Son of a bitch!"

Art Brennan had just entered his townhouse to find the place in a state of disarray, like an F-5 tornado had gone through the place, backed up, and then gone through again for a second round of mayhem. Papers littered the floor, shelves of books had been pulled down, furniture overturned and scattered about the place. Brennan was never a tidy person to begin with, but even this went beyond what was normal. He lived alone, as two of his previous wives had left him shortly after their marriages began, and he spent the better part of his life at the office or on the road. The tables and chairs were usually stacked with piles of legal filings and other documents.

It was a tony place, paid for with a handsome salary he paid himself as the head of the Civil Liberties Alliance. It had four bedrooms in its three levels. It even had a small garage, whereas most of the Georgetown riffraff had to park on the street. Brennan once threw a party at the place, but it was not well received because it was not decorated to the approval of the snobby D.C. social doyennes. The swanky neighborhood was a quiet one, and Brennan even had a Democrat senator living across the street. But best of all it was safe. Break-ins and burglaries were extremely rare. Except for today it seemed.

Brennan had just arrived back from his TV rant in support of Yousef Ibrahim down at the Islamic Studies Center. He hadn't been home since early this morning, and he remembered locking the front door before he left through the garage. He started tiptoeing around, trying not to step on something that might be hidden underneath the piles of books and papers littering the floor. He stepped over to the end table next to the couch. The cordless phone still had its dinosaur of a land line plugged into the wall. Whatever the thieves were looking for, they didn't find the need to take 20th century telephone technology with them when they left.

Brennan picked up the receiver, waited for the dial tone, and punched in the numbers.

"D.C. Metro Police, what is your emergency?"

"Yes, I want to report a break-in," Brennan said with indignation in his voice. While many people who come home to find the place in disarray would be scared out of their minds, Brennan just acted pissed – like it was a big inconvenience. *Somebody was going to pay*, he told himself.

"Okay, sir," the dispatcher responded. "And you are located on 34th Street in Georgetown?"

"Yes, you need to send some cops over here right now," Brennan barked.

"Sir, is there anyone else there with you?"

"No! Listen to me, you idiot! Just send the police over here!" Brennan was starting to get warmed up. "It's probably those miscreant Feds who did this!"

"Excuse me, sir?"

Brennan continued on, his face turning red as he yelled into the phone. "It's that ingrate President Schumacher and his FBI! They ransacked my whole house! Those sons-a-bitches!"

The dispatcher didn't know what to make of the man on the other end of the line. First, she thought she had a burglary victim on the phone. Now she was wondering if the guy might be a crazed lunatic. Maybe one of those black helicopter kooks that call every so often and claim the U.S. Government is conducting experiments on them in their basement.

"Sir, if this is a practical joke, I must tell you that is against the law," the dispatcher said with some authority in her voice. She turned in a lady recently who called 9-1-1 because the local McDonald's didn't put any ketchup on her hamburger. She'd turn the current nut case on the line over to the police if she had to.

"No, this is not a joke, you stupid idiot! Somebody broke into my house and trashed the place. And if you don't get the police here in five minutes or less, I am going to sue you and every other idiot down there too!"

The dispatcher put Brennan on hold and made the call. She alerted the D.C. Metro Police about the possible burglary. She also warned the responding officers to beware of an irate man who claims to be the homeowner. The line was dead when the dispatcher returned to Brennan.

Formed in 1861 at the request of President Lincoln, the Metropolitan Police Department of the District of Columbia is one of the largest police departments in the United States. Split into seven districts, the motto of the D.C. Metro Police is *Justitia Omnibus*, or Justice for All. And today, Art Brennan was looking for a little justice of his own.

The white Ford Crown Victoria squad car arrived in four minutes – the officer being on routine patrol just a few blocks down. Brennan, shaking his head, met the officer on the front steps.

"What seems to be the trouble, sir?" Officer Greg Dockery asked as another squad car pulled to a stop. He was six-four and thin as a rail. The single chevron indicated he was a patrol officer – first class. He definitely was new to the force because the donuts and idleness of patrol work had not set in around his waist line. His partner was off today, so a backup officer wouldn't be too far behind.

"I had a break-in," Brennan said in disgust, waving Officer Dockery inside. "Look at this. It's a total mess!"

Officer Dockery gave a quick scan of the living-room destruction. He had been to one break-in before but that was at a local tattoo parlor. He tried not to disturb any evidence as he made it through the foyer. "You mind if I look around?"

"Go ahead."

The officer gave the place a good once over, just to make sure the burglar wasn't hiding in the closet or under the bed. Once the investigative sweep was over, Officer Dockery took a notepad out of his breast pocket and turned to the fourth page. He was still on his first notepad. He clicked the top of his pen and made a notation before turning his eyes on Brennan.

"You're Art Brennan, aren't you?" Officer Dockery asked, looking down at the small man in front of him.

Brennan gave a single nod of his head. "Yeah."

Officer Dockery nodded and smiled. "I thought that was you. I've seen you on TV a lot." The officer came off as a little starstruck with the pseudo-celebrity in front of him. He would definitely be telling the folks back home who he met today. It would be even bigger news than the deputy director of the Commerce Department he pulled over for speeding last week. "Can you tell me how you discovered the break-in?"

"I just returned home about ten minutes ago. Parked the car in the driveway. Unlocked the front door and walked in to find the place in disarray."

Officer Dockery scratched the info down on his notepad. "What time did you leave this morning?"

"It had to be a little after six a.m."

"So it was still dark outside?"

What kind of a question was that? Brennan snorted. Yes, genius. "Of course, it was dark outside. They probably broke in after seeing me leave."

While Officer Dockery dutifully took down the details, his sergeant entered the residence and conducted a quick scan to see where the hoodlums might have entered. With three chevrons on her shoulder, Sergeant Gail Swanson had been on the force for twenty years, and the bulk she carried upstairs was mainly the result of the bulletproof vest she was wearing. Her tanned and lean face indicated she spent her downtime running to stay in shape.

Even in the relatively peaceful second district of D.C., Sergeant Swanson had seen a thousand break-ins over the years and she figured this one would be a routine investigation. She found the point of entry on her way through the kitchen to the garage. She looked at it from every angle, and something didn't feel right. She grabbed her cell-phone camera and took a picture of the door and the splintered remains. She made a mental note to talk to the detectives and then returned to the living room. "Looks like they busted in the back door from the garage. The door frame is splintered. He or they might have kicked it in or used a sledge hammer."

"Or a battering ram," Brennan huffed.

"Excuse me?" Officer Dockery asked, like he missed something.

"I bet it was those Government scumbags," Brennan shot out. "They've been hounding me ever since that piece-of-crap Schumacher got into the Oval Office. The guy's a menace. I'm going to sue those criminals the first chance I get."

Officer Dockery wasn't sure what to write – Schumacher, menace, lawsuit. Sergeant Swanson, however, wasn't buying Brennan's spiel. Unlike the rookie, Swanson knew Brennan and was not the least bit impressed. Georgetown was teeming with the rich and powerful, and most of them thought their station in life allowed them to berate and lecture anyone with a badge. She not only knew him from TV but the courtroom as well. And she couldn't stand the loudmouth prick. He obviously didn't remember her, but when she was a rookie cop she withstood a blistering cross-examination from Brennan after she testified to arresting his client for drug possession. She never forgot his condescending attitude as he attempted to embarrass her on the stand and taint her in the eyes of the jury.

"You got any idea who might have done this?" she asked.

Brennan snickered in contempt. "I just told you! It's probably those Fed thugs!"

Officer Dockery wrote it down again. He even added the exclamation points.

"Anybody else?" Sergeant Swanson asked, wondering if Brennan had a real human being in mind. "Have you seen anybody suspicious around here lately?"

"No, nothing," Brennan responded.

"Well, I'll let Officer Dockery get a list of what's missing," Swanson said, heading for the door. "We'll see what happens."

Brennan didn't want to deal with it. He was tired and in his typical foul mood. "Yeah. I won't hold my breath!" he shouted loud enough so Sergeant Swanson could hear it on the sidewalk. "Idiot," he muttered under his breath before adding. "No-good pigs."

"What was that?" Officer Dockery asked. The rookie really needed to have his hearing checked.

"Nothing."

"Okay, let's get started on that inventory of what's missing."

CHAPTER 10

Baltimore, Maryland

A tired Maureen Jackson sat at the bus stop waiting for the eight-thirty special to arrive and take her home for the day. The growing darkness meant the headlights of the vehicles heading toward home were turned on and illuminating the roadway. The African-American woman had put in a ten-hour day behind her desk, and she was in hurry to get home to her eleven-year-old son. As a single mom, she did her best to keep her son on schedule, and the list of chores she left for him when he returned home from school helped keep him out of trouble. He was supposed to be finishing his homework and getting washed up for dinner, which would be served a few minutes late tonight. She wasn't worried though, the bus would be here within five minutes. Soon she would be home.

Jackson had voted for Democrats most of her life. She had skipped a few elections here and there, but she proudly voted for Obama in '08 and again four years later. She voted in the last election but didn't check any ovals for President of the United States. She had her reasons, although she made sure to keep it to herself. The economy was humming right along, and Jackson was finally getting to enjoy the ride. Gone were the days of working two minimum-wage jobs just to keep her head above water. The economic policies of President Schumacher helped create scores of jobs across the U.S., and Jackson, as one of the millions of beneficiaries, was able to secure a secretarial job at a downtown Baltimore law firm. Still, Jackson could not bring herself to vote for the Republican candidate. As a sort of a nod of thanks to President Schumacher, however, she decided against giving her vote to the Democrat.

Jackson now made a decent wage, had health care for her and her son, and a small but growing 401(k). The dark business suit with pink blouse had been a recent splurge to make sure she presented herself well to the firm's clients. The rest of her paycheck had gone toward a down payment on a house in the "burbs," as she liked to call it, although it was still within the city limits of Baltimore. She didn't care, it was her home. And if offered a safe place for her and her son to lay their heads at night, in contrast to the high-crime high-rise they had been in for almost a decade. Next on her wish list – she dreamed of buying a used car so she wouldn't have to sit and wait for the bus every day.

She looked at her watch again. The bus couldn't be more than three minutes away.

The white van drove slowly past Jackson sitting at the bus stop and made a right at the corner. It went down the street and pulled into an open parking space. The driver got out and fed the meter with a quarter – just enough for twenty minutes. He didn't expect to stay long.

Abdel Ramadi wore dark jeans and a black button down shirt. He blended in nicely with the night. The disgruntled Ramadi could not believe his current situation. He still could not get over his humiliating demotion. He was a Deputy Commander in the Crescent Brotherhood, not some freaking chauffeur for the man in the back. Someone was going to pay in his mind. First the Americans, and then he would decide later who came second.

Ramadi got back into the driver's seat of the van. The evergreen air fresheners swung from the rearview mirror as Ramadi quietly closed the door. He had purchased the air fresheners to mask the scent of the two men who practically spent their whole day inside the van. Neither cared much for personal hygiene, and the interior of the van was beginning to stink.

The van had a body wrap on the sides indicating it was used in the delivery business. It was a fake name, and "Express Line Shipping" would be out of business by the end of the night. He turned off the engine and quickly glanced out the side windows. He hunched down in his seat and tried to get a good view out of his side mirror, which was full of the woman sitting at the bus stop.

"All clear," Ramadi reported.

"Where?" the man asked.

Ramadi looked in the side mirror. "That black woman at the bus stop."

Hassan Jahdari squinted his eyes in the low light and found his target. The woman was checking her watch and looking to the east, no doubt wondering where her bus was. Jahdari did not come to the United

States on a student visa. He snuck in ten years ago when the southern border was a whole lot more porous than it is now. He had been smuggled inside the United States with five other terrorists, all of whom had jihad on their mind. Four of those men had already been arrested for various crimes. Three were deported and one was serving ten years in the federal penitentiary. Jahdari, however, had found a job as a gardener at the Islamic Studies Center and lived in a dorm room. He rarely left the Center grounds because he knew he could not be discovered by law-enforcement authorities. If he was arrested and fingerprinted, it would mostly assuredly show him not as Hassan Jahdari but Yaman al-Sahaf.

And Yaman al-Sahaf was a very wanted man.

Al-Sahaf had spent the early years after 9/11 in the mountains of Afghanistan hiding from U.S. bombers with his fellow Taliban and al-Qaeda fighters. When U.S. ground troops arrived, he did his best to take them out one by one. A trained sniper, he had been lionized by his fellow terrorists who watched with glee his every kill. With the right weapon, he could hit a target a mile away. U.S. troops nicknamed him "the bastard," shortly after his third kill. But then, all of a sudden after his tenth victim was shot in the head, "the bastard's" killing stopped. He seemed to have vanished into thin air. The U.S. military presumed he was a victim of a B-52 bombing strike, but his wanted poster still hung in military installations across the globe.

Hassan Jahdari had his rifle resting on a bipod in the back of the van. A six-by-ten-inch piece had been cut out from behind the license plate between the bumper and the window and provided the necessary shooting space for Jahdari. The license plate was attached to a bottom hinge and connected to two loose springs on each side. All Jahdari needed to do was push a metal bar forward to lower the plate and pull it back to raise it.

Ramadi scanned the surrounding area. The area was dark and several of the streetlights were out. Traffic had thinned. They had checked the area earlier in the day, and the boarded up buildings meant there would be few people milling around. Ramadi checked for any security cameras but didn't see any. They were far enough away from downtown that surveillance cameras hadn't made it into the budget just yet. He made the call. "I think everything is clear."

Jahdari took a deep breath. He had done this what seemed like a thousand times before. The perspiration was a product of his cramped quarters and not any nervousness on his part. He put the woman in the cross hairs of his telescopic sight. He gave no thought to who she was, what she did for a living, or where she was headed. He did not care. She was not a woman to him. She was the enemy – the living, breathing embodiment of everything that was wrong with the Great Satan known as America. She should have no rights, he believed. She should not even be allowed to show her face in public. This was his opportunity for payback. He squeezed the trigger and let the bullet fly.

The round struck Maureen Jackson right between the eyes. Her head jerked back and then fell forward onto her chest. She felt nothing in the last second of her life.

Ramadi squinted his eyes in the side mirror. He couldn't see what happened. The novice terrorist thought the woman's head would explode or she would crumble to a heap on the sidewalk. He turned around in his seat. "Did you get her?" he asked anxiously.

Jahdari gritted his teeth. What kind of an idiot asks a question like that? Especially of him. The man was a trained killer. *Of course he got her*, he thought to himself. "Yes," he whispered calmly as he raised the license plate back into position. "Let's get going."

Ramadi did what he was told. He put the van into gear and slowly drove away.

The eight-thirty bus pulled to a stop ten minutes late. There had been a cyclist who needed to remove his bike from the carrier attached to the front of the bus at an earlier stop. Then the bus driver had to lower the bus at the next stop to let a man in a wheelchair get off. Now the driver was trying to pick up the pace so his boss wouldn't dock his bonus for on-time deliveries and pick-ups.

The driver, an African-American by the name of Max, pulled to a stop and opened the door. Max recognized the woman as one who had frequented his bus on a daily basis. He always noticed the nicely dressed woman walk in and out of the bus every day. He kept reminding himself to ask her name some time. He was fifty-two and single. He guessed the woman was forty-two, no older than forty-five, and he noticed she wore no wedding ring. She was a bit plump around the edges but he liked plump. Maybe today was the day to ask her out.

"Hey! Lady!" he shouted from the driver's seat before suddenly remembering his manners. "Ma'am! . . . . Ma'am! . . . You gonna get on my bus or not!?"

Maureen Jackson sat slightly slumped on the bench. She looked like she was sleeping. Max gave a couple of taps on the horn of the bus. He could tell the ten passengers in the back were itching to get moving. They were now late just like Max was. Just go, they screamed to themselves. She'll catch a later bus. But Max was concerned. It wasn't the nicest area in the world, definitely not the safest. And a nice plump and single woman shouldn't be out all by her lonesome at this time of night. He decided to make a quick passenger safety check.

Max left his seat and stepped off the bus. Given the darkness of the night, he couldn't see the blood running down onto Jackson's black business attire. "Ma'am," he said as he approached. "You gonna get on the bus?"

With no response, he reached his hand out and gave her a light tap on the shoulder. Still no response. He bent down on one knee and saw the woman he hoped to ask out on a date with a hole in her head. "Oh, God!"

Max almost tumbled backwards. "Oh, God!" He righted himself and hurried back into the bus. He grabbed the CB. "Unit number nine to dispatch," he stammered.

The bus dispatch downtown had noticed Max was running late, and they were already getting calls. The GPS on the bus indicated it had been stopped for a whole minute. "Go ahead nine, what's the problem?"

"I need the police at Seventh and McHenry," he said. "A woman has been shot at the bus stop."

Alexandria, Virginia

Joaquin Salazar unscrewed the gas cap and went to work filling up his pickup for tomorrow's day of work. It had been a long hard day, and he was dead tired. And he had to get home by ten so his wife could start her shift as the night housekeeper at the local Holiday Inn. His stop at the gas station was a daily occurrence, which was a good thing because it meant he was working.

Joaquin, Joe to his friends, was a jack-of-all-trades type of guy. The decal on the side door read "Joe's Handyman Service." He was part carpenter, part painter, and an exceptional yard man. The bed of his truck was filled to the brim with buckets, brushes, tool bags, a plunger, a Lawn Boy, and a Weed Eater, whatever he needed whenever he needed it. Today, it had been the landscaping, and his blue jeans were caked with dried mud and grass stains. The lines on his hands were still filled with dirt. It would take a good long shower to wash it all off.

Joaquin had immigrated to the U.S. from Mexico twenty years ago. He stood in line, filled out the forms, took the tests, learned English, and promised to be a good American citizen. And by all accounts, he had done so. He and his wife were raising two kids, paying their taxes, and continuing to dream the American dream. The handyman service put food on the table and money in the bank. For the past two years, Salazar had hoped to buy a second truck and expand his business, maybe hire a full-time employee instead of the part-timers when he needed them. That was the plan. His plan at least. His wife, of course, had a plan too.

Rosita Salazar had folded linens, made beds, and scrubbed toilets and bathtubs for just about as long as she and her husband were American citizens. It was mostly a thankless job. Travelers were too busy checking in or checking out to notice the maids. They worked quietly, except when the vacuum was running, and quickly to make sure the guests had a clean place to lay their weary heads. But she wanted something different. She wanted more. She wanted what her parents had back home in Mexico.

She wanted to open a family restaurant.

That was her dream. It would be Mexican fare – why would she try anything else? With tacos, burritos, and nachos at decent prices so the whole family could enjoy a night out at a nice restaurant. There would be checkered tablecloths and candles on the tables, sombreros for the servers, maybe they could even bring in a mariachi band on Friday nights. It would be a fun and inviting place – with lots of big smiles and great food.

Joaquin and Rosita had discussed their plans over one of the few dinners they were able to share together in their busy schedules. The spiffy new pickup truck was put out on the table as a possibility. Joaquin gave the pros – more job opportunities meant more money for the family. He didn't see any cons and didn't mention any. Rosita placed another helping of refried beans on her husband's plate. He loved them, and she scooted a bag of tortilla chips over his way. She knew how to win over her man. She talked about her restaurant idea – they would never go hungry, she joked. And the kids could work there someday and the family would be together more often. She happened to mention a nice corner building she found. It had good foot traffic with other local businesses in the area. It even had a parking lot!

Joaquin was slowly succumbing to his wife's presentation, crumbling under every mouth-watering possibility. He loved her cooking, and he knew others would love it too. He thought she would be a great restauranteur. And who knows, he thought, if they were successful it might help him get that second truck. The decision had been made last week. Tomorrow, they would meet with the realtor and then the loan officer at the bank. And within another three months, their bigger and better American dreams would be closer to coming true.

The El Camino turned the corner and pulled into an open parking space. The two terrorists had returned the van to the rental agency and opted for the old clunker of an El Camino. It was two tone in color, three if you count the reddish rust on the passenger side door, with a top layer of gray and bottom shade of black. It was one step away from the car crusher at the junkyard, but it did not look out of place in this rough section of Alexandria. Omar Faran hunched down in his seat and tried to get a good view out of his side mirror, which was full of a man filling up his pickup truck at the gas station. There was no one else at the gas pumps, and the lone attendant on duty inside was watching a small TV behind the counter. Other than the surveillance camera in the office, the attendant would have no view of the south side of the lot because of the wall behind her.

Omar Faran had been in the United States for two years on a student visa. He had performed satisfactorily in his classes at the University of Maryland, good enough for his academic counselors not to pry into his personal life and start asking questions. Per the instructions of his handlers in his native Saudi Arabia, he was told to blend in, not cause any suspicion, and be ready when the call for jihad came. Now that his visa was about to expire, it was time for him to wrap up his life in the United States.

Faran grabbed the walkie-talkie from the passenger seat and reported what he saw. "There is a man at the gas station," he said to the man on the other end.

As if by magic or remote control, the tailgate of the El Camino slowly lowered itself. It was not magic nor was it by remote. It was lowered without a sound with a rope by the man on the receiving end of Faran's message.

Ahmed Yassar had modified the El Camino with a plywood shelf covering the back bed. The top was covered by assorted junk, just enough not to raise any suspicion. Underneath was just enough room for the master sniper to lie prone with his weapon.

Yassar said nothing. And he didn't need to be told what to do. Yassar was already adjusting the sight on his new Russian-made Dragunov sniper rifle, which had recently come into his possession through a middleman acting on behalf of the Crescent Brotherhood. He couldn't bring his own weapon into the United States, but the "Dragon" gun, as he liked to call it, would do just fine. It had a range of 1,300 meters, a ten-round magazine, and a flash suppressor. Plenty of gun to get the job done.

Faran looked in the side mirror. He heard nothing coming from the El Camino's bed. He wondered if he should radio the sniper again. He was scared of the man, and his nervousness turned his mouth dry. They had barely shared ten words since they were introduced. Faran's handlers instructed him to do whatever the trained killer told him to do. Faran was simply the driver, and Yassar would make the decision on when and where to kill.

What was taking him so long? Faran wondered to himself. They should have been gone by now. He took the chance to ask the next question, hoping it wouldn't get him killed. "Do you want me to find another spot?"

Yassar readied himself. He said nothing. He had already told Faran once not to talk to him when he was preparing for the shot but it did not distract him. He just went through his routine like he had practiced a thousand times over the years. The man at the gas station had gone inside to pay for his fuel and was exiting the building. He walked around the back of his pickup and put his wallet in his back pocket. He reached up but his hand never touched the door handle.

The shot echoed through the El Camino's rusted metal, startling Faran in the front seat. He shook but didn't yelp. His eyes hurried to the mirror. There he saw a man lying motionless on the ground next to his truck. Faran sat there, frozen in fright.

"Go," Yassar whispered angrily into his radio, wondering why the El Camino wasn't moving. What the hell was the idiot driver waiting for? "Go!"

Faran's shaking right hand turned the ignition key. Once in gear, he slammed on the accelerator and the El Camino took off like a dragster on the starting line.

"Not so fast! You idiot!" came from the back.

Once Faran remembered his training and calmed down, he released the pressure on the gas pedal and kept the van within the speed limit. He glanced into the rearview mirror, noticing the tailgate was back in its proper position. After five minutes of driving, Yassar radioed that he wanted out so Faran pulled over. Yassar got out and took his spot in the right front passenger seat. Faran, afraid to even look at the man, thought Yassar might knife him but the man only buckled his seat belt.

They drove for five miles in total silence. Faran finally couldn't take it any longer. He felt the need to apologize. "I am sorry for what happened back there."

Yassar stared into the darkness out the side window, glancing at the mirror every so often to see if anyone was following them. "Next time," he said ominously. "Be better prepared."

Faran's still shaking hands gripped the wheel and he swallowed what little moisture was left in his throat. "Yes, sir."

It would be another ten minutes before anyone happened by the gas station. A police officer on routine patrol stopped and went inside to buy a cup of coffee. After he chatted up the attendant, he left and drove around to exit the parking lot. There he found the deceased Joaquin with a hole the size of a fist in his head, brain matter splattered throughout the bed of the truck.

"Dispatch, 128," the officer said into his radio.

"128, Dispatch. Go ahead."

"I have a shooting victim at the gas station on the corner of Fifth and Monroe," he said, before suddenly realizing he might be the next on the hit list. He moved behind a pump pillar and reported. "One male victim. I am going to need backup to cordon off the area."

"Roger that. I will send them your way. Do you need an ambulance?'

"No," he said, stopping short of saying he needed a body bag. "Wake up the coroner."

CHAPTER 11

Washington, D.C.

People in the Baltimore/D.C. metro area awoke to find four dead bodies filling up their TV screens. Two were dead in Baltimore, one in Alexandria, Virginia, and the other in the Anacostia section of the nation's capital. On any other day, the carnage would barely be given a second look. Both Baltimore and D.C. had some of the most dangerous streets in all of America. With a healthy collection of gang-bangers and drug dealers protecting their turfs and peddling their illicit wares, nightly shootings were a common occurrence.

But these killings were not your run-of-the-mill murders. The three blacks, two males and one female, and the one Hispanic male were not gang members and they weren't making a late night crack run. All of the victims had been shot once in the head from what appeared to be a good distance away. There were no robberies, they all had their wallets or purses with them. There was no evidence of any struggles with anyone, no scratches or bruising. It all appeared to be random.

And it wouldn't take long for the panicked frenzy to start.

Most in and around Washington had not forgotten about the Beltway sniper attacks in the fall of 2002. Just a year after 9/11, the whole area was paralyzed when one man and his young cohort terrorized the region. Ten were killed by a sniper's bullet and three others were injured in the three-week killing spree. Citizens risked their lives just to go to the grocery store. School children were kept inside lest one of them be picked off by a shooter hiding in the trees. Businesses closed early. People were afraid to venture out of their houses. Reports of suspicious vehicles strained police dispatch centers. Most residents hunkered down, fearing the worst. Anyone could be the next victim. And now it was happening again.

FBI Headquarters – Washington, D.C.

FBI Director Ty Stubblefield was standing in the conference room just off his seventh floor office at the Hoover FBI Building on Pennsylvania Avenue. His massive chest jutted out of his open suit jacket, his hands on his hips as he stared at the map on the TV on the wall. Red circles dotted the location of the shootings. He had taken part in the FBI's investigation of the Beltway sniper, and he worried it could be even worse this time.

The door to the conference room opened and a handful of FBI higher-ups took their places around the table. It was 9 a.m. Time for the morning national security briefing the Director held every morning once he returned from the President's briefing at the White House. But today was different. Dead bodies were showing up on the streets of the United States, and the FBI had to figure out what happened. Thus, everyone around the table was on edge.

Two FBI profilers sat perched in the corner like vultures waiting for someone to drop a morsel of information that they could use to feed their starving brains and uncover the clue to catch the killer or killers. Two other profilers were analyzing the crime scenes, the neighborhoods, and the victims' wounds to develop a profile on the perpetrators.

Stubblefield still had his eyes focused on the red dots, his back to the men and women who had taken their seats.

"Is this a crime spree or terrorism?" he asked out loud as he turned around. The stern look on his face made the listeners wonder if the question was asked of them or if the Director was just thinking out loud.

Deputy Director Pete Knowland leaned back in his chair and twirled the blue ballpoint pen in his right hand. "Terrorism," he said. "No one could have shot two people in Baltimore and made it south in time to kill the victim in D.C. and the other in Virginia."

"Same m.o. in each case?" Stubblefield asked.

Knowland nodded his head. "Yes, sniper shots to the head. These were professional shots, not done by amateurs."

"Surveillance?"

"Unfortunately, the areas around the shootings did not have surveillance cameras. Obviously that could be a reason the locations were selected. We might be able to pick up some vehicles at the closest cameras around the times of the shootings."

"Ballistics?" Stubblefield asked turning to Sally Crawford, the head of the FBI crime lab.

"Nothing yet," she said. "We're working as fast as we can."

"Once we get the information, let's make the rounds of the gun shops. Start asking questions. Any suspicious activities? That sort of thing."

Those in charge of the field investigation nodded their heads. They would spread the word.

"Have we heard from anyone claiming responsibility?"

Knowland shook his head. "Nothing has come in yet. No one in the media has come forward with anything."

Stubblefield nodded his head and started pacing around the table. "The Beltway sniper left a Tarot card at the scene of one of the shootings, didn't he?"

"That's right," Knowland said. "It was the 'Death' card. And someone had written 'Call Me God' on it. But, so far, our agents on the scene have not found any evidence that would show any similarity."

When the door to the conference room opened, Director Stubblefield took notice of David Connor, the Bureau's informational technology guru, walk in with a piece of paper in his right hand.

"Director," Connor said, handing Stubblefield the sheet of paper. "This just came in."

Stubblefield read over the contents once. He then read it out loud for all to hear.

To the Infidel Americans:
We have brought jihad to your shores once again. Just like our brothers did on 9/11, we have killed the infidel devils and we will continue to do so, one by one, until the annihilation of the Great Satan is complete. Your evil lifestyles will be punished, and our noble acts will be praised. You must release our brothers in Guantanamo Bay from their illegal detentions and stop your war on our brother Yousef Ibrahim. We will not stop until our demands are met. Allahu akbar.

Stubblefield indicated the statement was signed by the Crescent Brotherhood and handed the sheet over to Knowland, who read it again to himself before passing it around the table. The profilers hurriedly jotted down notes on their legal pads, practically giddy at the arrival of a new clue.

"Where did it come from?" Stubblefield asked of Connor.

"It originated in Nigeria," he said to the surprised looks of those around the table.

"So it could just be some wacko in Africa taking a break from sending out his bogus lottery schemes," Knowland said.

Connor nodded. "It's possible. But terrorist groups have been known to employ spammers in foreign lands to send out their messages in hopes of not getting caught or at least put a layer of protection in between."

"And?" Director Stubblefield asked. That was all he needed to ask.

"We're working on it to find out who the sender is and who might be the sender to the sender."

"Has the media gotten hold of it?"

Connor nodded. The cat was out of the bag. "Whoever sent it, sent it to us and every major media outlet in the country."

"Is Ibrahim still in custody?" Stubblefield asked of Knowland.

"No, he's out on bail. We're still looking into any terrorist connections he might have with his friends over in Saudi Arabia. But, so far, it's just tax evasion."

After a minute of contemplation, Stubblefield stood at the head of the table behind the high-backed leather chair. "All right. Let's stay on it. All hands on deck. Let's coordinate with the ATF, the Secret Service, the Department of Homeland Security, and the local police agencies. Route everything through the Joint Terrorism Task Force and get the information out as quickly as we can. I want these terrorists caught ASAP."

CHAPTER 12

Washington, D.C.

"Mr. Cogdon, thank you for joining us," said Jonathan Barnes, the anchor of NBC's *Meet the Press*, across the table from the President's chief of staff. The dapper Barnes had been the main political man at NBC for the past five years following a stint as White House correspondent, and his well-established liberalism was part of the reason for his fourth place spot in the ratings. His head of gray hair was combed over, fittingly to the left, and the pinstriped blue suit looked a little too flashy for Sunday morning. A coffee mug of water sat to his left with a mass of papers and notes spread out before him.

"Jon, thanks for having me back on," Cogdon responded.

William "Wiley" Cogdon was on national TV once again. It had been awhile. The Schumacher Administration had plenty of beautiful and well-groomed mouthpieces who could be sent out at all hours of the day and toe the company line. The President's press secretary, Kimberly Carmi, was a frequent guest on the Sunday news shows and had made the lists of D.C.'s best-dressed and best-looking for three straight years. She always represented the Schumacher Administration in a positive light.

It was a bit of a risk to send Cogdon out to act as the Administration's spokesman on this particular weekend. NBC was not known for being fair and impartial in its coverage of the President, and Cogdon had called them out about it on many occasions. Moreover, the conservative Cogdon was known to have a few deficiencies in the PR department. He oftentimes didn't come off well when the cameras were rolling. He once dropped an f-bomb in a particularly heated exchange with a Democratic congresswoman who had lied about the President's service in Congress. With his distaste for Democrats, he gladly delegated the role of congressional liaison to his deputies.

Cogdon was also known to get in the face of reporters and tell them how wrong they were on what they thought was right for America. He and Barnes had almost come to blows after one of Barnes' infamous hit pieces struck a raw nerve. While the libs in the media tried to be respectful to the President, they showed nothing but contempt for his right-hand man.

Conservatives, on the other hand, loved Cogdon. They cheered him when he appeared on stage at campaign stops with the President, although he was often oblivious to the cheers as he hovered in the background with his eyes glued on his iPhone. Print articles were routinely followed with positive comments from conservative readers whenever he made a statement to the newspapers. He was the embodiment of Dick Cheney and Karl Rove combined, pulling the strings and wielding the power in the White House. Angry libs caustically referred to him as Boss Cogdon or Darth Cogdon. A faux Twitter account labeled him the "Chief Ass Kicker" of the Schumacher Administration and tweets would invariably lampoon liberals and political correctness in mocking derision. There was even a list of "Wiley Cogdon Facts," a la Chuck Norris, that told the world of Cogdon's conservative political prowess. Cogdon loved them, with his favorite being: "When Wiley Cogdon eats breakfast, he has a double helping of liberals with extra hot sauce."

Given his high poll numbers, President Schumacher gave the go-ahead for Cogdon to step out of the shadows and get back in front of the cameras. Plus, the President wanted all his non-political people working on the sniper attacks. They would make appearances later in the day at various press conferences. The President's only advice to Cogdon – to make sure he wore a tie.

"Mr. Cogdon," Barnes said. "Last night, the D.C. area was hit with the sixth sniper attack in the last week. Six Americans are now dead. What is the Schumacher Administration doing to stop the killings?"

Cogdon nodded at the question. The glare of the stage lights shined off his bald head. He had a nice trim from the White House barber, who was done in a matter of minutes given Cogdon only had a thin ring of white hair around his chrome dome. His red tie was on but loose at the knot, like it had been strangling him prior to the show. At least the viewers would know it wasn't a clip-on. His dark suit coat didn't show any wrinkles in it either. He looked presentable.

"Jon, I can tell you President Schumacher is actively engaged with the investigation to capture the killers. As we speak, the President is meeting with the Director of Homeland Security and the Director of the FBI to make sure that all necessary information is funneled to the proper authorities so we can catch the terrorists. The FBI is also pursuing multiple leads in the United States and in Europe to hunt down those behind the attacks and bring them to justice."

Barnes listened to the question and asked his follow-up. "You said terrorists. You are calling this terrorism?"

Cogdon called it like he saw it. "This is definitely terrorism. Whether it is of a domestic variety or some foreign cell that has infiltrated the United States, it is terrorism and we are taking every measure possible, here and overseas, to find out who is committing the acts as well as find out who might be coordinating the attacks."

Barnes pointed his pen at Cogdon. He wanted to get down deeper to determine why the attacks were taking place. Let the grilling begin. "Is the Schumacher Administration partly at fault here for their uncompromising war on terror?"

Cogdon was not taken aback by the question. He expected it from the lib Barnes. Cogdon told himself to remain calm. "The Schumacher Administration is determined to keep the American people safe and, as the President has said, we will go to the ends of the earth to keep this country safe from the evils of Islamic extremists."

"Shouldn't the President do more outreach to Muslims around the world?" Barnes asked, his tone indicating his belief that the President was the problem and hadn't done enough the appease those who hate Americans.

"The Schumacher Administration has great relations with peaceful Muslims around world, it is the terrorists we are after."

"The 'terrorists', as you call them, Mr. Cogdon, demanded the release of Yousef Ibrahim, the head of the Islamic Studies Center in Arlington, Virginia. Will the President release him?"

The camera caught Cogdon shaking his head and rolling his eyes. "Mr. Ibrahim is not in custody, Jon. You know that."

"The second demand letter from the so-called terrorists mentioned Reverend Levitt in Georgia and his threat to burn the Koran. Will the President seek to arrest Reverend Levitt and others who want to do harm to the religions of others in hopes of preventing violence?"

Cogdon started to wonder how much longer he had to sit here and listen to this. He regretted offering to be spokesman for the day. He reached into his suit coat, pulled out his pocket copy of the Constitution, and flipped through the pages. "'Congress shall make no law . . . abridging the freedom of speech.' The First Amendment is not the problem, Jon."

"But they are inciting violence, Mr. Cogdon."

Cogdon shook his head. "No, Jon. They are expressing their own personal views. However warped those views are, they deserve protection. If we were to arrest or silence people because we disagree with what they say, we would have put you in jail a long time ago."

Barnes gasped at the statement, his mouth wide open like he had been sucker punched in the solar plexus. Did the Schumacher Administration just threaten to arrest a member of the press? Barnes thought so. He sounded offended as he stammered on but he had to end the segment and move to commercial. He would have to lambast Cogdon some other time.

When the red light went off, Cogdon pushed back his chair and started rummaging around for the wireless microphone clipped to his belt. He snapped off the mouthpiece attached to his lapel and threw it down on the table. "Now I remember why I hated coming on these shows," he shot out across the table. "You're an idiot. Nothing but a liberal idiot."

Barnes rose from his seat and pointed a finger toward Cogdon. He started yelling at him as he walked off stage, calling him a "political whore" and a danger to the country. Cogdon ignored him and kept walking. He exhibited enough self-restraint to keep his middle finger hidden. Barnes' rant went on nearly the entire commercial break and viewers clearly noticed his red face when he introduced his next guest to the program.

"We are back," a flummoxed Barnes said, almost out of breath. "Joining us now is Art Brennan, the head of the Civil Liberties Alliance here in Washington, D.C. Mr. Brennan, welcome back to the program."

"Thank you, Jonathan. It's an honor to be here," Brennan said before a smile crossed his face. "I wish I could say it was an honor to follow your prior guest."

Barnes made a snide comment under his breath. It was loud enough that the close captioning caught parts of it – something about the devil and the smell of sulphur. Barnes and Brennan reminisced like they were old friends chatting at the bar, nothing like the tension between Barnes and Cogdon. Brennan even appeared to be in a good mood, maybe it was the early morning or maybe it was the scotch he had for breakfast. Or it could be because Barnes told him he would serve up the softballs and give him twenty minutes of mostly uninterrupted air time.

"Given the terror attacks that have paralyzed the eastern seaboard and the endless wars on terror overseas, do you believe the Schumacher Administration is a danger to this country?"

Like some barrel-chested, beer-league softball player, Brennan was ready to swat it out of the park. "Absolutely. The President has engaged in a war on Islam ever since he moved into the White House. He has killed countless Muslims around the world just because they disagree with us."

He made no mention of the fact that those killed were terrorists.

"And I believe they are rounding up Muslims in places like Yemen and Pakistan and shipping them to CIA black sites and killing them."

"Really?" Barnes asked, like he hadn't heard that one before. He didn't ask a follow-up to clarify, he just let it hang out there for the bloggers and conspiracy theorists to run with later on. He shuffled some papers around and looked at his notes.

"That's right. I have talked to hundreds, no thousands, of people in the U.S. Government who are very much concerned with what is going on." He just made up the number. Nobody would know he was lying through his teeth. "It can't go on."

"You have become a much sought-after spokesman for the Muslim community here in D.C. Haven't you?"

Brennan nodded, appreciative of the praise. "There are a lot of victims of the Administration's policies here," Brennan said before adding, "and across the country and world. Somebody has to step up and look out for the oppressed. That's what we do at the Civil Liberties Alliance."

"Art, you recently wrote an article for the *New York Times* that it is time for America to change its ways so it can fit in with the rest of the world. Explain."

Brennan was nodding his head. Barnes had told him he would be asking about the article. "Jonathan, America has been a bully to this world for over two-hundred years. And it is all because of our faulty belief system, our 'Founding Principles.'" He used air quotes around the phrase Founding Principles. "The Constitution needs to be flexible, even give way in certain circumstances."

"So we need to amend the Constitution?"

"What we really need to do is rip up the Constitution and start over. Have something in place that is relevant to this century. Let me give you an example. The U.S. is grossly intolerant of religions other than Christianity. It's time to take down the crosses and the Ten Commandments and bury them once and for all. Muslims in this country are offended every time they walk out the door. My current client, Yousef Ibrahim, can't even do his job without being hounded by federal thugs rifling through his file cabinets. And sharia law should be allowed in certain areas of the country. I had a client who had to take off her burqa to get a driver's license. It's outrageous."

"So we need a constitutional convention?"

Brennan thought about it but figured the process would take too long. "What we really need is President Schumacher out of the White House."

CHAPTER 13

Munich, Germany

The U.S. Government Gulfstream G550 carrying the FBI's secret Phantom team touched town in Munich at six p.m. The plane had no markings on it signifying its country of origin. No American flag on the tail, and definitely not the seal of the Federal Bureau of Investigation to which it belonged. The FBI had been working nonstop to find out not only who was committing the shootings in the United States but also who was behind the terror attacks in Europe. Intelligence experts with the CIA, Israel's Mossad, and Great Britain's MI5 had tracked e-mails sent to the United States from a nondescript building in Abuja, Nigeria, a hotbed of shady Internet scam artists and other third-world criminality. After a few busted doors and hacked computers, intel agents found the source of the terrorist planning to be somewhere in Munich, Germany.

And it was the Phantom team's job to root out the origin of the terrorist operation.

Special Agent D.A. "Duke" Schiffer had slept soundly on the seven-hour flight from D.C. He had been accustomed to the travel and the short notice until departure that usually went with it. When Director Stubblefield needed a quick strike force, one that could act in any environment and under any circumstances, he called on the Phantom team. The team included expert snipers, one of whom was Agent Schiffer; two former Navy SEALs; a pilot licensed to fly jets, turboprops, and helicopters; and an explosives expert. Every member was an expert in foreign culture and operations.

Duke Schiffer was forty-two years old, could run a marathon in under three hours, and had been Director Stubblefield's go-to guy for over a decade now. Stubblefield viewed Schiffer as one of the most dangerous weapons the U.S. had in its arsenal. Like the team he led, Schiffer could blend into any environment and strike with lethal accuracy. A martial-arts expert, his hands were as deadly a weapon as a gun. But he rarely went into a hot zone without his baby – his .308

Remington sniper rifle. Just as his sniper sense was second to none, his ability to think on his feet, to improvise on the fly in tense situations, made him an indispensable asset in the war on terror.

Agent Schiffer, along with Agents Olivera, Jenkins, Alvarez, and Guerrero stepped off the Gulfstream and were met on the tarmac by Gunther Frentzen, a member of the *Bundesamt fur Verfassungsschutz*, or BfV, Germany's domestic intelligence agency.

"*Guten abend, Herr* Schiffer," Frentzen said with outstretched hand. He seemed happy to see him like he was an old friend. "We meet again."

"We do indeed," Schiffer said, shaking the man's hand. He didn't smile. Schiffer rarely did when he was on duty.

Frentzen had a head of wavy brown hair that ended just above his shoulders. He looked more like a California surfer than a German intelligence agent. But he spoke good English, which served him well when American law-enforcement came calling.

With his backpack slung over his shoulder, Schiffer wore dark tactical pants and a black hooded sweatshirt with a white Nike Swoosh on the front. The hood was up and covered the sides of his face. The same went for the other members. The Phantom team members didn't like to announce their presence and concealing their identities was an occupational necessity. At the direction of Director Stubblefield, Schiffer and the Phantom team had scouted locations throughout Europe for the past two years, devising emergency evacuation plans in case the President of the United States found himself in harm's way on a trip overseas. The plans were in addition to what the Secret Service already had in their operational manual. But Stubblefield was never satisfied and felt a second layer of security was necessary given the President's standing in the world. The Phantom team's diligence had been rewarded when the Secret Service agents guarding the President were incapacitated in Rome. The Phantom team, shadowing the President's every move, was able to swoop in and rescue the President.

While devising plans in Germany, the BfV's Frentzen had been Schiffer's guide through the streets of Berlin, Frankfort, and Munich. Now, Frentzen had a van ready to take the Phantom team to Munich police headquarters.

"We have a person of interest in custody," Frentzen announced, as they made their way through the rain soaked streets of Munich. The weather had turned cold and the skies were blanketed with a thick layer of gray. "Your CIA is already with him."

"Have they gotten anything out of him?" Schiffer asked.

Frentzen shook his head. "No. He has been very obstinate, cursing and spitting at your CIA man. His name is Zahid Madani, a native of Algeria. We picked him up at the airport after he exited a plane from Brussels. His passport information wasn't matching what we had in our system. So we took him in and started questioning him. A fingerprint examination confirmed he had been using an alias. We think he might have had something to do with the Brussels attack. It is possible he was trying to meet someone here in Munich."

Inside the station's garage, the Phantom team exited the van and followed Frentzen down a back staircase to the basement where CIA agent Aaron Moreno was pacing the floor of a hallway smoking a cigarette. He appeared to be talking to himself, and when he hit the cinder block wall with the bottom of his fist, it was apparent he was not in a good mood. He looked surprised when he saw Frentzen and five others coming toward him.

"Agent Moreno," Frentzen said, pointing his thumb at Schiffer. "Your FBI is here."

Moreno took one last drag before dropping the cigarette to the concrete beneath his feet. He smashed the butt with his boot and kicked it over to the wall. "I didn't expect you until tomorrow morning," he said to Schiffer. He didn't know Schiffer or any of the members of the Phantom team. He had just been told that the FBI was on their way to assist in the investigation and then hunt down the source of the e-mails. He was to extract as much information out of the suspect as he could before they arrived.

Agent Moreno did not shake hands with the members of the Phantom team and there were no other introductions. There didn't need to be. It wasn't a matter of impoliteness. The men simply liked their secrets and they would save their war stories for retirement.

Moreno wore a hooded sweatshirt like the rest of the Phantom team, but it was more because the air conditioner in the room behind him had dropped the temperature to forty-nine degrees. The CIA man Moreno would have liked it colder in hopes of breaking his suspect sooner, a good refrigerated truck would do nicely, but he had to work with what the Germans had available in the basement of the police station.

"The guy's a prick," Moreno said, throwing his thumb over his shoulder indicating the prick was just behind door number one. "I've been going at him for a couple of hours now. He just curses and spits and threatens to kick my ass. He hates Americans. And I can tell he knows something. He definitely knows something. If he was just some punk, I doubt he would be trying so hard not to break. *Herr* Frentzen's comrades are in there now. They don't seem to be having much luck. He doesn't like Krauts either."

"Does he speak English?" Schiffer asked.

"Good enough. He speaks passing German too."

Schiffer had all he needed to know. He wanted to get moving. "Why don't you and I go in," he suggested. "I'll let you and our German friends handle it together, and if you need me to assist I can do that. We'll see if we can squeeze some information out of him."

Moreno thought it couldn't hurt. He was usually better than this but Madani was proving to be a tough nut to crack. Maybe all Moreno needed to get the job done was a little nicotine and the intimidating man in the black hoodie standing behind him. He knocked twice on the door and opened it.

The Germans and Madani were going at it across the table from each other – yelling back and forth and hurling insults at the other. Madani was at a disadvantage given the handcuffs that chained him to the arms of the chair but his spit could reach across the room. He stopped cursing and shouting when he saw Moreno. He had hoped the CIA man wouldn't come back. His eyes then focused on the darkened image of the Phantom Schiffer taking his place in the corner against the wall. Hands clasped behind his back, the hooded Schiffer said nothing, he just zeroed in on the eyes of the man seated at the table. Thinking the worst, Madani could almost feel his testicles shriveling at the sight.

Moreno walked around the table and rested his boot on the chair in front of Madani. "Have you come to your senses yet, Zahid?" he asked. "It's time to stop wasting our time and start talking."

"I will not talk," Madani shot back.

Moreno took the cup of ice water in front of Madani and threw it in the man's face. Madani flinched, thinking the skin on his face was starting to crack into a thousand little pieces. "It's time to start talking, Zahid, or very bad things are going to happen to you." His pointed finger indicated Schiffer was one of those bad things.

Madani kept his focus on Schiffer but lashed out at Moreno. "Let me think for a minute to make sure you Americans understand me. . . Screw you!"

"We know you were in on the terror attack in Brussels, Zahid. We've got surveillance pictures putting you there." Moreno didn't have such pictures but he'd see where his little white lie took him. "We want to know who you are working for."

Madani kept looking at Schiffer.

Moreno slammed the steel table with his fist. "Hey! Zahid, I'm talking to you!" He then slapped Madani across the face. "The 9/11 terrorist attacks were planned in Germany, Zahid. Up north in Hamburg. Remember that? Your terrorist friends who killed themselves that day are probably enjoying their virgins right now. Maybe you'd like to join them."

The cold dead eyes of Madani looked up at Moreno. He did want to join them. "I will see my brothers soon in paradise." He then spit in Moreno's face.

A thoroughly pissed off Moreno stepped back and wiped the spit off his face with the back of his right hand. He then used that hand to slap Madani across the face again, the sting from the cold feeling like it shattered his skin. Moreno had had enough. "I don't think you're going to be enjoying paradise too much, Zahid. Does anybody have a knife?"

The hooded Schiffer had not moved since he took his spot on the wall. Until now. He grabbed a chair from the table and slowly but loudly dragged its steel legs across the concrete floor. Once the chair was against the wall, and with all eyes in the room on him, Schiffer lifted his right leg and placed his boot on the chair. He slowly pulled up the cuff of his tactical pants, each inch showing a little more of the sheathed serrated knife attached to his ankle. He took it out and made sure the light glistened off the steel finish of its four-inch blade.

Matter of factly, Agent Moreno looked at it, liked what he saw, and said to Schiffer, "Yeah, that'll do."

Moreno pushed the table away from Madani so he could stand in front of him. Moreno had a wicked smile on his face, like he was going to enjoy what he was about to do. The man acted like he was demented – eyes bulging more by the minute and a cackling laugh that sounded like he had finally snapped. Maybe it wasn't an act. He reached down to Madani's groin area and started unbuttoning the man's pants.

A suddenly silent and concerned Madani didn't like the way things were shaping up. He didn't like having a man touching him down there. Once Moreno roughly unbuttoned and unzipped the pants, he told the two Germans to hold the man so he could pull them off. With a few forceful tugs, off came the pants and Moreno threw them onto the floor. Now sans pants, Madani sat there in his tighty whiteys with a terrified look on his face. Slaps to the face and sleep deprivation had been part of his jihadist training. They all knew that's what their interrogators would do to them, and they had trained to endure that sort of "torture." But stripping them down to their skivvies was never in the lesson plan.

"Who are you working for, Zahid?" Moreno asked.

Madani's eyes were all over the place – at the two Germans, at Moreno, at Schiffer still holding his glistening knife like he wanted desperately to use it, and then back down to his groin area. The cold steel of the chair was beginning to seep through the cotton layer into his buttocks.

"Last chance, Zahid," Moreno warned.

"I don't work for anybody," Madani blurted out. "I am telling you the truth." He didn't sound very believable.

Moreno knew a liar when he heard one. He turned to Schiffer. "Give me the knife," he demanded.

Schiffer handed the knife over handle first.

"We should have done this a long time ago," Moreno said, smiling. He stood back to take it all in, like a butcher deciding where best to start carving into the side of beef. "Oh this is always my favorite part," he laughed. With the two Germans holding Madani's arms and pushing the chair against the wall to hold the man steady, Moreno dove in. He grabbed Madani's underwear and sliced through with one swipe. He could feel Madani flinch. Moreno then went to the other side and cut through the last stitched fibers holding the underwear together.

"There we go," Moreno said, in haunting fashion.

Madani was now hung out there for all to see. Moreno raised his boot and lowered it onto Madani's thigh. "My, my, my," he said, like he enjoyed what he was seeing. "It is a bit chilly in here, isn't it, Zahid?" With Madani looking at him in fright, Moreno's tongue slowly licked the knife from blade to tip. He turned it over and did the same on the other side. Schiffer started to wonder if the CIA man was half nuts. Of course, he always thought those at Central Intelligence were a different breed. But Moreno seemed to be enjoying the tease way too much. He brought the blade to his lips and kissed it. "Who do you work for, Zahid?"

The nakedness and the frigid air caused Madani to start to shiver.

"Who do you work for?" Moreno said again, slower this time, just in case Madani had not heard him.

"I don't know," Madani quivered.

Moreno lunged in with his left hand against Madani's throat. Madani could not move, could not even spit in the interrogator's face. He could only manage to squirm his head slightly. He prepared himself for the worst.

"Those virgins aren't going to like you when you show up without your manhood, Zahid!" He ran the steel blade up under Madani's penis and started running the dull side back and forth like a saw, long and hard enough for Madani to scream out.

"Time to start carving, Zahid!"

"I don't know the man! I don't know the man!"

"Just like the Butterball at Thanksgiving dinner!" The laugh became more maniacal as the back and forth sawing motion increased. "Yeah, baby! How's that feel!?" Madani's screams in terror could be heard out in the hall. It sounded like Moreno was lopping it off. "Who is he!?"

"I don't know!"

The sawing motion became faster. "I'm going to cut it off and shove it down your throat, Zahid! The virgins won't like that! Who is he!?"

"Please stop!"

Moreno took the point of the knife and started poking at Madani's scrotum. "Where were you going to meet!?" He jabbed the knife with greater force.

"Aaaghh!" Madani thought he could feel the steel knifing his balls. "The yellow brick road!" he blurted out. "The yellow brick road! Please stop!"

Moreno brought the knife up to the man's face and placed the tip under his cheekbone. "The yellow brick road! This ain't the freaking *Wizard of Oz*, you son of a . . .!" Back downstairs the knife went. "I'm going to start cutting right now!"

"No! No! No! I'm telling you the truth! It's near an apartment downtown! I'm supposed to meet someone there! I wasn't told his name! They didn't tell me street names!"

"What apartment!"

"Five! Please stop!"

"You're lying!"

"No, please stop," Madani sobbed. He was fully broken.

Schiffer and Frentzen made eye contact across the room. They had the information they needed and it was time to get moving. Moreno felt a tap to his backside. Schiffer wanted him to end it and get out of there. Moreno took the hint and backhanded the sobbing Madani across the face once again. "I'm coming back for you," he said to Madani while pointing at his crotch. "And when I do, it's coming off."

Back out in the hall, Schiffer informed the Phantom team where they were going and Frentzen called upstairs to ready the van.

"What's up?" Moreno asked. He sounded disappointed he wasn't able to lop off the terrorist's manhood.

"I know where the yellow brick road is," Schiffer said.

"What?" Moreno asked in disbelief.

"We need to get going," Schiffer said. Frentzen was already making calls on his cell phone.

Schiffer turned to walk away before Moreno stopped him. "Agent, your knife?"

"Keep it," Schiffer said, not looking back.

The Phantom team hustled into the garage and took the van while Frentzen and another colleague took the Mercedes sedan with the flashing blue light on the dash. Schiffer told the men to prepare for an entry assault and off came the hoodies. On went the Kevlar vests and helmets. Weapons were passed around and checked.

"Duke," Agent Jenkins said from the back and holding out his hand. "A new knife."

Schiffer smiled. "Thanks," he said, jamming the knife into his ankle sheath.

The rain had stopped and the sun had fully set. The tourists were returning from their Third Reich and Dachau tours – neither the happiest places on earth nor the most enjoyable of experiences given the subject but it provided many with perspective that led them to enjoy life on their return to the "Beer Capital of the World." With no shortage of beer halls and beer gardens, tourists and locals lined the sidewalks with their steins full of German libations and plates full of wienerschnitzel, brats, and large doughy pretzels.

Schiffer got onto the phone with Frentzen. "We're ready to go."

"We are only a couple of minutes away. I have radioed the police and they are closing the roads surrounding the building right now. The apartment building is above some shops but the only entrance to the apartment is on the north side."

Frentzen's Mercedes made a left on *Residenzstrabe* street near the Bavarian State Opera and Agent Olivera followed in behind. The two-vehicle caravan slowed after two blocks, their forward progress slowed by the bollards that let only pedestrians and cyclists go any further.

"It's going to be coming up here on the left," Schiffer said, pointing to the buildings on the north side of the street.

It was hard to imagine that Hitler started the Third Reich on these very streets. He considered Munich the capital of the movement, and although it seemed like ancient history, Der Fuhrer's attempted march toward worldwide domination was not even a hundred years old. During Hitler's reign of terror, Munich citizens were required to salute the shrine to martyrs down at the end of *Residenzstrabe* or they would be in violation of the law. However, many Germans were not sympathetic to Hitler's murderous ways, and some were known to dodge the shrine as a form of silent protest. And those so-called Nazi dodgers turned left down the *Viscardigasse* and its brick-lined alleyway heading north. As the Phantom team van turned left, the headlights illuminated the gold-painted bricks lining the middle of the alley.

The yellow brick road.

"We will park on the corner and go to the left," Frentzen called out.

"Okay, guys," Schiffer said to his team. "Let's make sure we have all our gear."

The Phantom team had loaded the plane they came in on with everything they might need. Battering rams, flash-bang grenades, and a sufficient amount of weaponry to overpower any small force. Now it was time to put it to use.

The team joined up with Frentzen and entered the apartment building. "Fifth floor," Frentzen said, pointing at a diagram. "The fifth apartment on the end."

The Phantom team snaked up the five flights of stairs and came to the landing on the fifth floor. Frentzen, dressed in his slacks and a bulletproof vest covered by his blue blazer, opened the door to the hallway. He spoke German to a woman who stuck her head out of the door of the first apartment.

"*Innerhaulb, innerhaulb,*" he whispered loudly, shooing her back inside. She nodded and closed the door.

The Phantom team reached the end of the hall and Frentzen and two of his men stood ready to assist.

"Jenkins," Schiffer whispered to the Phantom team's tech man. "Video," he ordered.

Jenkins grabbed the video camera out of his backpack and slid the fiber-optic cable under the door. The black and white screen showed nothing but an empty kitchen. Schiffer then pointed in the other direction but the camera caught no movement inside. Jenkins turned the camera up to check the door for booby traps but saw nothing.

"Is there a back way out of this place?" Schiffer whispered to Frentzen.

"No," he responded. "The windows have bars on them."

Schiffer nodded. They would just have to barge their way in. "Olivera. Get this door down." When Olivera stood ready with his battering ram and the others cocked their MP-7 assault rifles, Schiffer gave them one last instruction. "It's *polizei*."

Olivera nodded and with one hard whack the door busted open.

"Polizei! Polizei! Polizei!"

The Phantom team filed in and through the kitchen. "Clear!"

And then the living room and bedroom. "All clear!"

The apartment was empty, but it had definitely been occupied earlier that day. The coffee pot was still warm and a loaf of bread still sat open on the counter. Somebody must have been in a hurry to leave, and the current occupant had no intention of coming back.

Mahmud Basra had been tipped off from a trusted source that Zahid Madani would not be joining him because he had been picked up by German authorities. That meant the police would soon be paying a visit to Basra's apartment. He knew this day would come, and he had planned for it. The terrorist CEO was all about the planning.

"Find anything?" Schiffer asked of Agent Guerrero who had been searching the bedroom. "Male clothing, not much else. No books, no diaries, no papers."

Agent Jenkins had placed the keyboard to the computer in a plastic bag and sealed it for transport. It would soon find its way to the FBI lab in Quantico, Virginia, where any fingerprints found would be matched with any in the Bureau's massive database.

"Can you get into his computer?" Schiffer asked. "Check today's history."

Jenkins pulled out his iPad and hooked it up to the computer's main unit. With a couple of taps on the iPad keyboard, Jenkins brought up the occupant's home page and then the history for that particular day.

"He was reading stories about the shootings in the D.C. area," Jenkins said as he scrolled down the page. "Bingo," he said, stopping the scan. "E-mail to the Nigerian outfit that we raided yesterday. He obviously doesn't know we did that. It's another demand letter – release the Gitmo detainees, death to America, blah, blah, blah."

Schiffer turned to Frentzen. "Well, we're definitely in the right place." He was starting to think of a plan to catch Basra when he returned.

"Wait a minute," Jenkins interrupted Schiffer's train of thought. "Uh oh."

"What is it?"

"Train ticket," Jenkins said, pointing to the screen.

"Crap!" Schiffer exclaimed, slamming the top of the chair with his palm. "What time?"

"Nine o'clock this evening."

Each of the Phantom team members looked at their watches. It was 10:30 p.m.

"Destination?"

"Paris."

Schiffer didn't have to think long. He turned to Frentzen. "We're gonna need a chopper."

CHAPTER 14

Somewhere in Germany

The *Deutsche Bahn* train offered travelers a place to lay their heads overnight while also making time on their journey. In the hotel on rails, tourists looking to make it to the next stop without having to spend half a day in an airport lounge could board the train at nine o'clock and be in bed in one of the sleeping compartments within a half hour. Then, when the following morning greeted the dawn, the next city on the itinerary would be ready and waiting.

Basra had paid for the ticket with one of the bogus credit cards that he was known to have in his possession. He boarded the train and found his compartment. It would be difficult for him to get any sleep. He had a sinking feeling that the authorities were after him, but he thought he was still one step ahead of them. He just needed to get to Paris. The Islamic religion was second only to Roman Catholicism in France, and if he could get to the City of Lights, he could find his brothers in the Crescent Brotherhood and seek sanctuary.

Basra closed the door to the compartment and locked himself in. There were bunk beds in which a person of six feet in length would have trouble fully stretching out. But it would do. There was also a closet that contained the toilet, sink, and shower. With passengers still lined up waiting to get on the train, Basra pulled down the window shade. He had a small suitcase, but it only contained one change of clothes. He would ditch it as soon as he got to Paris. The length of time it took the train to move out of the station began to worry him. *It should not be taking this long*, he told himself. His mind wondered if he should just run. But he had no place to run and hide in Munich. He needed to get out of Germany. Finally, the train began to move, slowly inching its way out of the heart of Munich.

Basra tried to relax. He even let his eyelids close to get some rest. But his heart just about leapt out of his chest when there came a pounding on the door.

Basra froze on the bottom bunk and stared at the door. They had only been moving for a couple of minutes. He had no gun, not even a knife.

Again, the pounding on the door.

He leaned over and cracked the window shade. They were still in the city. If he busted out the window, he might be able to make a run for it and hide in the darkness.

"Entschuldigen sie mich," came a voice from the other side of the door. Excuse me, the tone seemed to say. It was a female's voice. Husky, but female nonetheless. Definitely not a German policeman looking to exercise his authority.

Basra took the chance. He really had no other choice. Not opening the door would raise suspicion. He stood and opened the door a crack. "Yes," he asked, peering out from behind the door.

The tag on the woman's lapel indicated her name was Helga. She was the enforcer on the train, checking tickets and taking orders for when she would serve breakfast tomorrow morning at 7 a.m. sharp, an hour outside of Paris. She must have weighed about two-eighty, and she filled out every inch of her conductor's uniform and black vest.

"You speaka ze English?" she asked of the man behind the door.

Basra could speak three languages – Arabic, German, and English, but he thought it best to go with the tourist English to throw her off. "Yes, English."

Helga was okay with that. She had many American travelers during her time as train enforcer. She pushed her way in the Basra's cramped quarters and nearly squashed him against the bunk. There was hardly any place to move.

"I show you ze room," she said. She then proceeded to show Basra how to work the buttons for the lights and the fan. Then it was into the bathroom to show him how to flush the toilet and turn on the water for the sink and the shower.

"Okay," she said before asking, "you are good?"

"Yes."

As she squeezed out of the compartment, she took out her notepad and readied her pen. "You wanta ze breakfast in ze morning, yes?"

Basra had no desire to ever see Helga the Enforcer again but he nodded yes and tried to shut the door.

But the Enforcer wasn't done. She slammed her meaty fist against the door and held it open. "And you wanta some coffee?"

"No," Basra said, shaking his head. He just wanted to shut the door and go to bed.

Helga, however, was taken aback at the response, like she had never heard of such a thing. "You don't wanta ze coffee?" she asked, shocked beyond all belief.

Basra could see it in her eyes, which were as large as hubcaps. What was wrong with this guy? she seemed to ask. She appeared offended that the man didn't want any coffee with his breakfast. He knew better than to make anyone suspicious. He relented. "Oh, coffee. Yes. Yes."

"Okay," she said, nodding and writing it down. She seemed somewhat relieved that the man wanted her coffee. Basra shut the door, locked it, and breathed a sigh of relief.

Helga the Enforcer told herself to keep an eye on this guy.

Gunther Frentzen had rustled up a chopper within thirty minutes. It sat eight, which was perfect for the five Phantom team members, Frentzen, the pilot, and a seat for the team's gear. They had been flying for an hour when the chopper finally caught up with the train as it snaked its way through the German countryside.

"I can have the conductor stop the train a mile outside of the next station," Frentzen said over the headset.

"That's perfect," Schiffer responded, giving him the thumbs-up. The Phantom team had practiced insertions on yachts, planes, and even a twenty-car train that Amtrak loaned the Government for tactical training. Now it was time to put their training to good use. "Do we know which car he's in?"

Frentzen asked a question of a person on a different channel before turning back to Schiffer. "The conductor believes a man matching the description is in the third car from the end and in the second compartment."

The chopper overtook the train and flew off into the night before landing on the tracks a mile from the station. The Phantom team and Frentzen exited the bird and it took off to provide a light in the sky just in case. The night had turned cold and temperatures hovered in the upper thirties. The team members could feel the vibrations of the rail before the single light cracked the darkness in the distance.

"Jenkins, Guerrero, and Alvarez," Schiffer said, turning on his flashlight. "I want you guys to hike down the tracks and enter the rear of the train. *Herr* Frentzen, Olivera, and I will come in through the front."

He then pointed up. "We have our eye in the sky in case our boy decides to run."

After seeing the flashlight in the distance, the engineer began to deploy the brakes to bring the massive 500-ton beast to a halt. The screeching wheels echoed off the trees lining the surrounding area. Once the train came to a stop, Schiffer waited for the word.

"In position," Jenkins reported. "Preparing to enter the rear of the train."

"Roger that," Schiffer responded. "Let's go."

Schiffer, Olivera, and Frentzen entered the first of ten cars in line and headed toward the end through the small hallway outside the compartments. They came to a stop when they came face to face with Helga the Enforcer at the end of the third car. Given the advanced weaponry they were carrying, she didn't feel the need to ask for their tickets. She also didn't ask them if they wanted coffee. Olivera unzipped a pocket on his Kevlar vest and pulled out a piece of paper. Jenkins had printed it off Basra's computer before they left. He handed the paper over to Schiffer.

"Do you recognize this man?" Schiffer asked her, showing her Basra's engineering firm identification that Jenkins had found on his computer.

Helga nodded. "Yes, that man is in the second compartment," she said pointing. She felt the need to relay to them her suspicions. "He very strange. He did not wanta ze coffee."

Schiffer nodded and then made eye contact with Frentzen, the communication clear that it was time for the German to get the Enforcer out of the way. Frentzen said something in his native tongue and Helga moved off to the side.

"Jenkins, what's your . . . ," Schiffer asked before stopping. He could see the three other members of the team through the window at the other end of the car. "Ready?" he asked looking at his men.

"Ready."

The doors to the car opened at each end and the Phantom team silently filed in. They stopped at the second compartment.

"Jenkins," Schiffer whispered. "Camera."

Jenkins went to work and snaked the fiber-optic camera underneath the door. The lights to the compartment were off and the night vision showed no one in the bunks. The shade was drawn and no movements were detected.

"Is he in the bathroom?" Schiffer whispered.

Jenkins reached his hand down toward the door to try and force the cable in farther. He stopped and put his fingers up against the door. "Duke, there's cold air coming through here."

Schiffer asked Frentzen for the key that he had gotten from Helga. He put it into the knob and turned it. With his German-designed Heckler & Koch MP-7 raised, he looked inside. He walked into the cramped space and checked the bunks. He then told Olivera to open the door to the bathroom. He did, and the end of Schiffer's gun saw nothing. He turned around and pulled up the shade. The window had been busted out.

"Frentzen!" Schiffer shouted out into the hall. "Has your man in the sky seen anything?"

Frentzen spoke several hurried words in German but didn't get what he wanted to hear. "No, he has seen nothing."

Basra had had a change of plans and decided to disembark early.

CHAPTER 15

The White House – Washington, D.C.

Ty Stubblefield was not getting much sleep. As head of America's FBI, the job carried with it an enormous amount of responsibility. While the Bureau was created to "investigate" crimes, the FBI had taken a much more proactive approach after 9/11 to preempt the criminal acts before they happened rather than search for clues afterward. And, thus, a lot was riding on the success of the FBI. He learned of the seventh sniper shooting at 3 a.m. the night before, just twenty minutes after it happened, and he had taken Agent Schiffer's call just after dinner that Mahmud Basra had slipped from their grasp.

The Director was no longer sleeping at home, and it was a mutual decision between him and his wife. They had a wonderful relationship, and Tina Stubblefield had put up with her husband's late night calls into FBI offices for several decades. But the seriousness of the situation required every ounce of the Director's attention. So Stubblefield ate his meals in his office and slept a few hours each night on the couch. He was on duty twenty-four hours a day and he knew he was where he needed to be.

Along with the sniper attacks, one of the myriad FBI investigations greatly disturbed him. And it was getting worse and worse by the day. It could turn out to be a national security nightmare, and something had to be done to stop it. But it was also a political minefield, and the Director knew he had to have ironclad evidence to take his case to the President.

And now, after a few hours of tossing and turning on his office couch, his armored SUV was making its way through the White House gates so he could make his formal presentation.

President Schumacher had arrived in the Oval Office twenty minutes earlier than usual. He couldn't sleep either. The sniper attacks were weighing on his mind. His fellow citizens were dying on the streets of America and he hadn't been able to do anything about it except to tell them their Government was doing everything it could to catch the perpetrators before they killed again.

When the President walked in to the Oval Office from the short walk outside down the Colonnade, he found Wiley Cogdon sprawled out on the couch – one foot on the floor, the other hanging off the side. The President secretly wondered if Cogdon slept in the Oval Office.

Cogdon did not. He had his own bed just north of the White House and used it regularly. But he could function on four hours of sleep at night, and his 4 a.m. wake-up call followed by a can of Red Bull and a cup of coffee jump-started his day and sent him on his way. He had already read four newspapers, scanned his favorite media and political sites on the Internet, and fired off eight e-mails to reporters looking for news. Then, waiting for the President like a son waiting for his father to come home so they could head out to the front yard and play catch, he lounged on the Oval Office couch engrossed in his pocket Constitution like it was as compelling as a Vince Flynn novel.

"Morning, Mr. President," Cogdon said as he rolled off the couch and stood to attention.

"Good morning," the President said, laying his PDB and related paperwork on his desk. He then looked at Cogdon and asked the question he asked of his chief of staff on a daily basis. "What do I need to know?"

"Nothing new since last night, sir," Cogdon said as he put his Constitution in his pocket. "I guess that can be taken as a good thing."

The President nodded. That there hadn't been another shooting was a good thing. Of course, there was no news of a capture either.

The door leading from the desk of the President's secretary was open and the massive body of Ty Stubblefield suddenly filled up the empty frame.

The President's heart sank for a moment at the sight of the FBI Director. Stubblefield was way too early for the national security briefing. This could not be good news. He waved him in. "What's wrong?"

Stubblefield saw the concern and tried to put the President at ease. At least for now. "I don't have anything new on the shootings, Mr. President."

"Okay," the President said with some relief. But the Director wasn't one to show up at this hour. He would normally be hard at work down at the Hoover FBI Building. And the big black briefcase he was carrying was a little out of the ordinary.

"Mr. President, do you mind if I close the door?" he asked.

"Of course not. Go ahead."

The President and Cogdon met Stubblefield in front of the desk. Stubblefield cleared his throat and took a deep breath. Seeing he had their attention, he started his presentation. "Mr. President, I wanted to talk to you before the national security briefing on a matter that has come up. It is matter that you will find greatly disturbing. I want you to know first off that I have considered what I am about to tell you with the greatest seriousness possible without any outside influences whatsoever."

"Well, now you're starting to worry me a bit, Ty," the President said, definitely feeling the seriousness in the Director's voice. "What's this about?"

Stubblefield took another breath. He had gone over what he was going to say several times during the last few days when the pieces of the puzzle were being put together.

"Sir, it's about Art Brennan."

Both the President and Cogdon snorted in contempt. For a second, they both thought the Director must have been joking. The prick Brennan had been a thorn in the President's side for years. Brennan was *persona non grata* in the Oval Office, and few people raised the ire of the President and Cogdon more than he did.

"What's that blowhard said about me now?" the President asked, a smile crossing over his face.

"What a jackass," Cogdon said, breaking the President's rule of no-profanity in the Oval Office. The President let it slide since it dealt with Brennan.

But Director Stubblefield was not laughing. "Sir, if we could sit down I have some things I want to go over with you."

"Sure."

The President took the chair to the left of the fireplace and Cogdon sat on the couch. The Director took the chair opposite the President and opened up his large briefcase. Both the President and Cogdon waited with anticipation, wondering what in the world was so important regarding the loudmouth Brennan.

"Mr. President," the Director started, looking the Commander in Chief in the eye. "Like I said before, I present this to you without any

120

hint of a political bent. I know you don't like Brennan and I personally don't care for him either. But what I am going to lay out to you is based on what I, as Director of the FBI, believe to be concrete evidence of Brennan's criminal activity."

"Criminal activity?" the President asked. "Has he been failing to pay his taxes like his clients?"

Stubblefield shook his head. "No, it's worse than that."

The President thought he was ready for it. "Well, what is it?"

"Treason, sir."

"Treason!" the President exclaimed. A shocked Cogdon almost fell off the couch. "What are you talking about?"

Director Stubblefield expected this reaction. American citizens owe allegiance to the United States, and treason is the most serious offense one can commit against his country. It was not a matter to be thrown around lightly.

Cogdon started flipping through his pocket Constitution, knowing he had the law right at his fingertips. For his benefit as well as the President, he read from Article III, section 3.

Treason against the United States, shall consist only in levying War against them, or in adhering to their Enemies, giving them Aid and Comfort. No Person shall be convicted of Treason unless on the Testimony of two Witnesses to the same overt Act, or on Confession in open Court.

When Cogdon finished, the Director, a lawyer in his pre-FBI days, went to work. "It's the aid and comfort that I think applies, Mr. President."

Given the ease of abuse inflicted upon them by the Crown, the Founding Fathers set forth the specific definition of treason – levying war against the U.S. or adhering to its enemies through the giving of aid and comfort. Considering the severity of the charge and the possible punishments faced by a guilty party, treason would not be an easy conviction for the Government to obtain.

"When was the last time anyone was found guilty of treason?" the President asked.

"It's been since the War."

"The Civil War?"

"No, the second World War."

Only a couple of handfuls of citizens have been convicted of treason since the country was founded. Philip Vigol and John Mitchell were convicted in connection with the Whiskey Rebellion in the 1790s only to be pardoned by President Washington. John Brown and Aaron Stevens were executed for their involvement in the former's eponymous 1856 raid against slavery. Mary Surratt, Lewis Powell, David Herold, and George Atzerodt were hung from the gallows in 1865 for treason and conspiracy in the assassination of President Lincoln. Herbert Haupt and Martin Monti were convicted of treason in the 1940s for their work with the German enemy.

Stubblefield went through the evidence the FBI had collected over the last 18 months. The Director had become concerned with some of Brennan's dealings, and he put together a team of investigators to confirm his suspicions or make him realize he was overreacting. For the first six months, the FBI simply kept watch over Brennan. They didn't bug his phones or open his mail. Everything they did was legal. They kept track of where he went and with whom he met.

But the investigation took a turn after the attempted kidnapping of the President in Rome. The FBI team that rescued the President killed two Russian operatives in the process. They also collected their cell phones as evidence before they high-tailed it out of the Italian Prime Minister's residence. FBI analysts then searched the phones and tracked calls to the Russian Embassy in London. With some help from the NSA and the CIA, it was discovered that the Russian Embassy had contact with Brennan on several occasions prior to the attack in Rome.

"Remember, Mr. President. This was around the time that we caught Roland Barton, the CIA mole, in Baltimore."

"I remember."

The turncoat Barton had been represented *pro bono* by Brennan himself courtesy of the CLA. "Given his clientele, I have always been concerned who he is talking to. There have been more than a fair share of attorneys who have been caught receiving information from their clients in prison and then passing it on to others on the outside."

"So you think Brennan committed treason by having a hand in the attack on the President in Rome?" the lawyer Cogdon wondered.

Stubblefield held up a finger. He wasn't finished. "That was just the start," he said. "It was after learning that information that I wanted to take the investigation to the next level. We increased our surveillance of Brennan and obtained judicial overhears to listen in on his phone calls."

The Director then laid out what the investigation showed in the last couple of weeks. There was a YouTube video of Brennan's speech at Georgetown. Brennan's meeting with Hakim al-Rashid after his lecture was shown to the President in 8x10 glossy photos. There was another meeting between the two as evidenced by the photo taken by the lone patron/FBI agent sitting in the Burger King reading his paper.

"Do we know who this guy is that Brennan is meeting with?" the President asked.

"His name is Hakim al-Rashid and he claimed to be a prospective client."

The President nodded his head. He heard what was said but he was having difficulty putting it all together. "Are you sure this isn't just legal talk between lawyer and client?"

"I thought that was a possibility," Stubblefield said. "The judge that signed off on the warrant said we could listen to everything but privileged communications. Frankly, there wasn't much said over the phone, just where they were going to meet. And we didn't get anything from the meeting at the Burger King."

"So that's it?" the President wondered. He had deep respect for Director Stubblefield, not only for his law-enforcement expertise but his legal ability. But this wasn't hard evidence of treason.

Stubblefield indicated there was still more. He pulled out his FBI iPad and started moving his index finger across the screen.

"But there was a phone call between al-Rashid and Brennan two nights before the sniper attacks started."

The Director tapped his finger on the screen and the Oval Office was filled with the voice of Brennan and al-Rashid as they discussed al-Rashid's plan. Brennan offered his advice and told al-Rashid what he would do to help the cause.

"What you should do is target blacks and Hispanics," Brennan said over the phone. He made no mention of shooting or killing, just targeting blacks and Hispanics. He could have been talking about registering minorities to vote in the next election. "Minorities would be very important in what you are trying to accomplish."

"That is our intent," al-Rashid said in agreement. "We have teams canvassing the areas in D.C. and Baltimore."

While the audio recording played on, the three men took turns looking at each other.

"You think Art Brennan is involved in the sniper attacks?" Cogdon asked. He couldn't believe it.

Stubblefield nodded and then pointed back to the iPad.

"Once your campaign starts," Brennan told al-Rashid, "I'll make sure to get out and tell the world how President Schumacher is failing to respond because he hates minorities, won't lift a finger because it's only blacks and Hispanics. I'll hammer him hard like the Democrats did with Bush after Katrina."

Cogdon practically flew off the couch. "He followed me on *Meet the Press* the other day! He claimed the President wasn't interested in finding the killers because the victims were minorities. That son of a . . . " He stomped around the room mad as hell, cursing silently to himself.

The tape played on. "It will be a double opportunity to take down this President," Brennan said, brimming with confidence. "We might not even have to wait for the next election. He might just resign in disgrace."

Stubblefield could tell the President was still not fully convinced that Brennan was coordinating criminal activity with terrorists. They all knew Brennan was a loose cannon, and he had seemingly become more and more obnoxious over the years. Maybe he thought he could walk a fine line between agreeing with the enemy and aiding the enemy. Or maybe he had finally snapped and sought to wage war on his country.

Stubblefield continued. "We lost track of al-Rashid. Once the sniper attacks started, I pulled off all but a few agents from the Brennan investigation. I still hadn't made the connection between Brennan and al-Rashid. But something interesting happened the day before the first attacks. We had an agent conducting surveillance on Brennan's townhouse in Georgetown. At approximately 5 a.m., a white CLA van backed into his driveway. Brennan opened the garage and was seen talking to four men. Given the hour of the day, the agent was unable to get a good view in the darkness. The men brought boxes out of Brennan's townhouse and placed them in the van. Brennan helped them as well. The men then left, and the agent stayed on Brennan's residence. Brennan left in his Cadillac shortly after 6 a.m. The agent watched the residence and surveillance cameras recorded the perimeter for the rest of the day. Other agents confirmed Brennan arrived at work shortly thereafter."

"Okay," the President said, indicating he was still following.

"When Brennan returned home in the early evening, he called 9-1-1 and reported a break-in."

"A break-in?" Cogdon asked, stopping his pacing. "I thought you said you had cameras and an agent watching the residence."

"We did," Stubblefield said. "Brennan claimed the break-in must have happened after he left that morning. He didn't call the police for thirty minutes after he arrived home that evening. He actually told the police it was the Feds breaking in and ransacking the place." He then looked at the President. "But I don't think there was a break-in. I think it was staged to make it look like there had been a burglary. I got a call from a Sergeant Swanson with the D.C. police, and she stated she became suspicious when she noticed the splintered remains of the door frame were in the garage rather than inside the house. Like someone was trying to break out of the house instead of breaking in. Whatever was being taken out of his townhouse, and I believe it was weapons, Brennan was facilitating the move. To cover his tracks and protect himself, I think Brennan falsely claimed his residence had been burglarized so he could deny any involvement."

The President let out a deep breath and cast his eyes up toward the Oval Office ceiling. The darkness of the early morning had given way to the first rays of sunshine and the light filtered through the eastern and southern windows. The one-time prosecutor was trying to run the evidence through his head.

"You think all of these pieces of evidence show treason on the part of Brennan?" he asked.

"Treason, conspiracy to commit treason, providing material support to a terrorist organization, conspiracy to commit an act of terrorism, conspiracy to commit murder." The Director talked like he could go on with a laundry list of federal criminal violations.

The President stood from his chair and joined Cogdon in pacing the room. They both knew Brennan was a pain in the political rear end. They had grown accustomed to his diatribes, but now he was alleged to have gotten into bed with terrorists. The excrement would most assuredly hit the fan when these explosive details got out. The President probably shouldn't even be discussing the matter with the FBI Director given the political implications. Stubblefield should have gone through his boss, the Attorney General, but given his friendship with President, he had to run it by him first. Now the President didn't know what to do. He didn't have an enemies list, but the Democrats and the press would claim Art Brennan was *numero uno* and try to paint the President as a clone of Richard Nixon.

"So you want to arrest him?" the President asked the Director.

"Yes," Stubblefield responded. There was no hesitation in his voice, no wavering. He had made up his mind that the evidence was sufficient for an arrest.

The political guru Cogdon started running through the ramifications of an arrest. "That would be an absolute bombshell. Arresting an American citizen, an attorney, who has been a sworn enemy of this Administration from day one. It'll look like a political hit job by us. Like we are trying to silence our critics and anyone who doesn't agree with us. We will be raked over the coals by the Democrats."

"Or it might help us put an end to the sniper attacks," Stubblefield said. "Maybe we can cut out the middleman and flush out the terrorists."

Both Stubblefield and Cogdon looked at the President. It was time for him to make the call. He looked at his watch. They had been at it for over an hour and a half, and the national security briefing would start in five minutes.

The President made the decision. "Let's call the Attorney General in on this. We'll run it by her and see what she has to say. Obviously, we are going to have to make sure every 'i' is dotted and 't' is crossed."

Stubblefield agreed. "I'll make the call."

CHAPTER 16

Near Manassas, Virginia

The El Camino pulled onto the off-ramp, leaving Interstate 66 as it made its way around Manassas. Omar Faran was behind the wheel and he dutifully followed the rules of the road by signaling his turn to the right. He came to a complete stop, looked both ways, and made the right turn. From there, he found the frontage road near Manassas National Battlefield Park and started heading the opposite direction he had been going.

In the bed of the El Camino underneath the plywood shelf was Ahmed Yassar lying on a dirty mattress and waiting for Faran to come to a stop and give him the signal. The Yassar/Faran team had four kills under their belt, half of the total loss of life caused by the terrorist snipers. They had yet to be spotted anywhere near the shootings. They made this trip with two suitcases with a couple of days' worth of clothing and other toiletries to make it look like they were traveling. New York was their desired destination if asked. The mattress in the back had been Yassar's idea. A thirty-year-old El Camino was not the most comfortable ride, and if the police stopped them, they could hide the rifle in the floorboard and claim one of the men was napping while the other drove. They would plead poverty and say the El Camino bed was the best accommodations they could afford.

Faran backtracked a mile down the road that hugged the interstate, nearly empty at three in the morning.

"How much further?" Yassar asked through the walkie-talkie. He stopped short of asking, "Are we there yet?" He was beginning to get a cramp in his leg.

"Just another mile or so," Faran reported back. "Kill the brake lights."

Given his proximity to the rear of the vehicle, Yassar pulled the wires to the rear taillights. Once in position, Faran would extinguish the front headlights but leave the car running and in drive. Yassar felt the car slowing and pulling to the right onto the gravel shoulder. There was a short moment of silence as Faran looked for any oncoming traffic and then anything behind him. Confident no one was coming from either direction, he radioed to Yassar.

"Okay. Coast is clear."

Yassar lowered the rope holding the El Camino tailgate in place. He shifted his body on the tiny mattress, better fitting to a baby's crib than a grown man. He peered through the telescopic sight of his Russian-made "Dragon" sniper rifle.

"One of those truckers," Faran said into the walkie-talkie. He didn't identify which one, just anyone Yassar felt was the best target.

Martin Washington stepped out of the brick building of the rest area and waddled down the sidewalk toward his big rig. He had spent the last seven hours asleep in the cab and adhering to federal regulations that he get his mandated rest before he headed back on the road. Now, after relieving himself and splashing some cold water on his face, Washington was ready to head north on Interstate 95 to his final stop in New Jersey so he could drop his load and go home.

His old buddies from his younger days used to call him "PayDay," not because he was always wondering when the checks came in, but because he could pocket a PayDay candy bar from the corner store with the best of them. It was oftentimes a snatch and run type of job, but at the end of the day, Washington would be enjoying his PayDay with a big smile on his face. He had given up his days of petty thievery, now content to pay for his purchases like everybody else. In his big meaty hands, he carried a honey bun, a bear claw, and yes, two PayDays, he bought from the vending machine inside. They would be his last ones, he told himself.

He had a promise to keep.

Washington tipped the scales at a hefty and definitely unhealthy 350 pounds. He had been an over-the-road trucker for twenty years now and the long hours crisscrossing the United States in his Peterbilt did not do wonders for his waistline. He started trucking when he first got married at the age of thirty six. Now in his mid-fifties, his weight and his poor eating habits were taking a toll on his health. His T-shirts were up to XXXL and the overalls were size 54. His wife had nagged him for years to eat better, to lay off the junk food (even the PayDays), and try a little exercise before he turned in for the evening – just a ten-minute walk around the truck stop or the rest area, she told him.

He usually nodded and said he would try. But he'd end up eating three Big Macs, as many large fries, and a gallon of Coke. His cab was littered with fast-food bags and sugary drink bottles. Although he had a stellar driving record, his bosses started noticing his weight and even mentioned their concerns to him. "You sound like my wife" was his usual response. Company policy required him to undergo a yearly physical exam, and with his high blood pressure and diabetes, the doctors told him he didn't have much time left.

"That's okay," he told them. "I'm close enough to retirement to call it a career."

No, they told him. "You don't have much time to live if you keep eating like this."

That visit along with one from his daughter did it for him. She brought her brand new baby girl, Washington's first grandchild, and placed her in his arms. The picture of the event shocked him. The baby looked like a peanut in front of his gigantic frame. He resolved to do better – for himself and for his family.

Now, walking out of the rest area, he slowly stopped in his tracks. He felt like crying. He had stood at the vending machine inside for a good five minutes, trying not to push the buttons, trying not to give in. He had gone for the Diet Mountain Dew, and he told himself his wife would be proud of him. But the packaged honey bun and bear claw were weighing on his mind, and they would most definitely be weighing on his hips in no time. The urge to scarf them down was great, the little fat devil on his shoulder telling him how wonderful they would taste. But the picture of his angel granddaughter shoved the devil away, and he tossed both packages into the trash. Start walking, he told himself. Don't look back. He kept the two PayDays as a sort of compromise. At the next stop, he'd grab a water and something healthy. He smiled to himself. The longest journey starts with one step.

Washington opened the door to his cab and set the bottle of Diet Mountain Dew in the cup holder. He grabbed the handrail and hoisted his large frame onto the step.

Yassar let out a breath and pulled the trigger. From less than a quarter of a mile away, Yassar could tell he got the big man in the stomach. "Shit," he whispered to himself. He didn't usually miss his target like that.

"Did you get him?" Faran asked into the walkie-talkie. He couldn't see what happened. "Do I go?"

"No," Yassar angrily whispered back.

"Go?" Faran asked again. He took his foot off the brake and started pulling away.

Yassar grabbed the walkie-talkie. "Stop! You idiot! Stop!"

Washington had taken the bullet in the stomach and tumbled onto the pavement. Given his fat rolls, it felt like he had been stung in the gut by a hornet. He reached down and could feel something wet coming through his overalls. He was having trouble trying to catch his breath. His spinning mind couldn't even tell his mouth to call for help. He rolled over and tried to push himself up. He looked off into the distance but saw nothing but darkness.

Yassar cycled the bolt on his rifle and put Washington in the crosshairs for a second time. This time he would end it. With the light pole in the parking lot illuminating the side of the Peterbilt, Yassar could see the injured man looking in his direction, his eyes wide and full of fear.

"*Allahu akbar*," he whispered to himself before he squeezed the trigger.

Washington died instantly on the pavement next to his rig, two PayDays still in his hand.

"Now go," Yassar ordered.

Capitol Hill – Washington, D.C.

The Washington metro area awoke to find its ninth sniper victim. One more and the killers will have equaled the carnage of the Beltway snipers in 2002. The news media kept a running tally in the lower left corner of the screen and provided round-the-clock coverage of the shootings. Schools in and around Manassas, Virginia, were closed for the day – administrators too scared to open their doors for fear the snipers were lurking nearby and looking to prey on the children during the daylight hours. Pee-wee football practices were cancelled as well, and cross-country matches were called off.

One local body shop was doing a brisk business "up-armoring" mini-vans in hopes of keeping the occupants safe. Law-enforcement authorities warned people to stay inside. If they had to venture out, they were told to get out of the car and hustle inside. Don't dawdle. People were seen fast-walking it into Wal-Mart, which was hopping with customers, most of them in the sporting-goods section around the gun counter. Little old ladies with blue hair and black canes were checking out the only weaponry left – double barrel shotguns that seemed to weigh more than they did. The aged Virginia biddies weren't going down without a fight, they told the sales clerk, just like their confederate ancestors, most of whom did not appear to be too far up the family tree. Ammunition had been flying off the shelves along with toilet paper and bottled water. People were preparing to hunker down.

Over on Capitol Hill, a press conference was being conducted outside the offices of Michigan Democrat Moeisha Robinson. It was indoors, for safety reasons, of course. Just in case. Surrounding her were selected members of African-American clergy, two other representatives from the Congressional Black Caucus, and Art Brennan.

"Today, we have seen yet another national tragedy," Congresswoman Robinson began. "Another black male was murdered last evening just a few miles from the nation's capital." She didn't mention the man's name. She also made no mention of the ten black gangbangers that were killed by other black gangbangers on the streets of Detroit and Chicago last night. "It is the seventh African-American to be killed in these terrible attacks on our country." She looked closer to her notes before adding quickly. "Two Hispanics have also been killed." Those victims seemed to be an afterthought to her.

Congresswoman Robinson had been representing the inner city of Detroit as a member of the Michigan congressional delegation for over thirty years. During her tenure on Capitol Hill, she spent most of her time deriding Republican efforts to get people out of poverty and into jobs. She thought more people on welfare equaled heartfelt compassion and therefore she worked hard to keep people poor. She once got into a heated exchange on the House floor with then Congressman Anthony Schumacher. She even called him an "inbred honkey," and C-SPAN had never had so many views on YouTube. Republicans usually took the jabs with a shrug of the shoulders – "that's just Congresswoman Robinson." She likes to play politics with race, they would say. Unfortunately, the country was not better off for it.

The faces behind her were grim, and she continued. "I think the current occupant of the Oval Office has failed to act to stop the killings because of the color of the victims' skin. Just like Bushie II after

Hurricane Katrina, he has dithered in the White House while my people die in the streets. I think it is time for that man residing at 1600 Pennsylvania Avenue to resign. If not, I will call for articles of impeachment in order to remove him from office."

She never liked to dignify the President by calling him by his title and the lack of respect showed on a daily basis – on camera and off. She had tried to impeach President Schumacher on three other occasions, usually around election time. It was a surefire way to raise some cash for her campaign coffers.

"Now I would like to turn it over to Mr. Art Brennan," she said, looking to her left. "Art has been a great asset to me over the years and I know he has great concerns with the current occupant of the White House."

Art Brennan had called Congresswoman Robinson after the eighth shooting and told her of his plan to hold a press conference if another victim showed up. He thought it would give him some credibility to have members of Congress and clergy behind him. He had told her to use the Katrina example, even though it didn't have any truth to it. It didn't matter – just saying "Katrina" and the name of a Republican politician in the same sentence could work wonders in her fundraising appeals.

Now it was Brennan's time to shine.

"Thank you, Congresswoman Robinson," he started off. The sincerity in his voice painted her as an American saint. "Where would we be without you?" Many Americans asked that same question.

"I want to echo some of the remarks by Congresswoman Robinson. The President of the United States has failed in his duty to protect the American people. He has done nothing." The crescendo in his voice was beginning to rise. "Absolutely nothing. Why hasn't he arrested that pastor down in Georgia! The terrorists have demanded his arrest to stop the killings! Why does he continue to harass Muslims here and overseas!? He has lost control and must resign for the good of the country!"

Congresswoman Robinson could be seen vigorously nodding her head in the background. Brennan's plot to take down President Schumacher while his terrorist buddies were killing Americans was starting to have an effect. The President's poll numbers had been slipping. His support by African-Americans had dropped ten points in a week. The eastern part of the country lived in fear of the unknown, and law-enforcement agencies seemed unable to do anything about it. Brennan seriously thought he could bring down the President if the current course kept going.

"I hope Congresswoman Robinson will press for an investigation into the President's failure to act. The President must be stopped!"

The White House – Washington, D.C.

The President had just finished the morning national security briefing in the Situation Room. He was tired. The killings and inability to find the terrorists kept him up most nights, and he, like most Americans, wondered whether the morning news shows would bring new images of death.

The President gave the go-ahead for the use of unmanned drones to fly over Virginia and Maryland on a continuous basis once the sun went down. Security cameras were being installed up and down Beltway interstates in hopes of catching sight of every vehicle in the vicinity of a shooting, if and when one occurred. He ordered every asset he had in his arsenal to catch the killers.

And now he had to stand there and watch replays of Art Brennan berating him on every cable news network in America.

"That son of a . . .," Cogdon muttered under his breath.

Once the word was put out that the White House press conference was about to begin, the videos of Brennan paused and live shots of Kimberly Carmi at the podium filled the screen. Carmi, with her dark blue blazer and American flag pin on her lapel, recited the current nature of the investigation and told America that the President of the United States would not rest until the killers had been captured. She stated she could not get into specifics of the actions taken by law-enforcement authorities. She stopped in mid-sentence when the door to her right opened and the members of the press shot to attention.

President Schumacher strode to the microphone with a determined look on his face. He was pissed off about the killings and Art Brennan had now put him in an even worse mood.

Carmi looked at her boss. "Mr. President," she said before stepping away.

"Take your seats," the President said to the press corps. He placed a note card on the podium. "Thank you, Kimberly. Ladies and gentlemen, today we mourn the loss of Martin Washington, a husband, father, grandfather, and American citizen. He was a trucker who traveled this great nation from sea to shining sea as he pursued the American dream. This morning I called his wife Beatrice and offered condolences on behalf of the American people. I know all Americans will keep her and her family in their thoughts today in this their time of need.

I know there are those out there that are fearful right now. They might wonder what their federal, state, and local governments are doing to keep them safe. I can assure you that my administration is doing everything in its power to catch the terrorists who have committed these atrocities."

The President walked out of the briefing room only slightly in a better mood. Telling the American people that he was determined to end the killings was about all he could do short of trolling the streets himself. He noticed Director Stubblefield waiting outside the Oval Office. The Director had missed the security briefing earlier that morning because he wanted to see where Washington was killed firsthand.

"Anything new?" the President called out with hope in his voice.

"No, sir. Nothing yet," the Director said as they walked inside. "Mr. President, I would like to go ahead and move forward with that matter we discussed with the Attorney General the other day. The hard drive we recovered from the apartment of Mahmud Basra indicates he had direct e-mail contact with Art Brennan. While there is no smoking gun in the e-mails, it appears Brennan was passing codes to Hakim al-Rashid. And I believe al-Rashid is the one behind the terrorist attacks in the United States. I want to arrest Brennan right now."

The President didn't need to hear any more. "Do it."

CHAPTER 17

Arlington, Virginia

The Phantom team's raid of Mahmud Basra's apartment in Munich may not have turned up the engineer turned terrorist CEO, but FBI computer technicians found a wealth of information on the hard drive of his computer. Along with detailed plans for the European terror attacks, the information included an e-mail train between Basra and Hakim al-Rashid and then Basra and Art Brennan after Brennan had met with al-Rashid at the Burger King in Arlington. While the messages were in code, it was clear Brennan was passing information on to terrorists to help them implement their killing spree.

The hard drive also showed Basra had been receiving information from a remote outpost outside of Kandahar, Afghanistan for over two years. The information showed al-Qaeda had been training the Crescent Brotherhood's snipers and drivers that were now in the United States as well as the terrorists that had taken part in the European attacks. The men were not named, just referred to by numbers. Once the men had completed their terrorist training, Basra received word that the operation could go forward. It was then that the pieces of the jihadist puzzle were moved to Venice, London, Brussels, Madrid, and the United States for final preparations.

After reviewing all the evidence, Director Stubblefield and Attorney General Claire M. Donovan couldn't wait any longer and simply hope more messages weren't relayed to the terrorists. They decided it was time to take down Art Brennan in hopes it would stop the killings.

The FBI stepped up its surveillance of Brennan and watched him throughout the day. He met with no one outside of his office in downtown D.C., and he left the CLA garage in his black Cadillac at 5 p.m. Two FBI sedans with two agents followed him west on Constitution Avenue before crossing the Memorial Bridge on the way to Arlington. As he approached his townhouse, he noticed the two unmarked cars behind him.

"Foolish Feds," he mumbled to himself. He figured the President wanted the FBI to follow him, maybe scare him into not publicly lambasting the Administration on TV every day. Any attempt at intimidation wouldn't work on Art Brennan. "Fools! You're doing a terrible job of concealing the fact that you're following me, you idiots," he said out loud to himself. He showed his displeasure by flipping the bird to the agents behind him.

When Brennan turned the corner on his street, he noticed the side streets were blocked off with unmarked government vehicles.

"What the . . ?"

A check of his mirror revealed only one car behind him now. The other was blocking the intersection at the end of the block. The FBI was slowly making Art Brennan's world much smaller. Two FBI vehicles were stopped in the middle of the road just past his driveway. There were only two options – stop in the road or turn in. And there was one FBI vehicle parked in front of his garage. The FBI had him surrounded.

Brennan pulled into his driveway and slammed on the brakes. He jammed the shifter into park and the door flew open.

"What the hell is going on here!?" the already red-faced Brennan lashed out. He was approaching full boil. "Get the hell out of my driveway!"

A dozen FBI agents appeared from the side of the house and from across the street. Half of them were heavily armed just in case Brennan decided to make one last stand, a stupid move to say the least.

"Who the hell are you!?" Brennan shot out, charging up the drive. He didn't even wait for a response and lit into the man for being on his property. Neighbors were seen peeking out from behind the drapes at the loudmouthed Brennan shouting to high heaven. "If you don't get off my property right this instant, I am going to call the police to have your asses arrested!" Perhaps he thought the local police would remove the FBI.

"Mr. Brennan, I'm Special Agent Wallace Jones, FBI," he said, his credentials out for Brennan to see. Jones was the same agent who arrested Brennan's client, Yousef Ibrahim, and he was prepared for the verbal onslaught.

"I don't care who you are! If this is about Yousef Ibrahim, I have nothing to say to you here on my front lawn! You can set up an appointment like everyone else, you moronic jack-booted thug!" Never one to be intimidated by authority, he stuck his finger an inch from the agent's face. "Get off of my property right now!"

Agent Jones showed admirable restraint. He figured if he let Brennan rant and rave, he would eventually lose steam and calm down, kind of like a little kid throwing a tantrum in the toy aisle at the grocery store. "Mr. Brennan," Jones said calmly when the irate man in front of him paused to catch his breath. "You're under arrest."

Brennan didn't look shocked, just mad as hell. "Under arrest!? I didn't even touch you! You can't arrest me!"

"Mr. Brennan, I have here a warrant for your arrest."

Brennan scoffed at the paper. "On what charges? It's not against the First Amendment to criticize the President, you pig!"

Agent Jones waited for the shouting to stop. He wanted the place quiet to see Brennan's face when he gave the word.

"Mr. Brennan, you are under arrest on the charge of treason," he said forcefully.

A wide-eyed Brennan took a step back like he had been punched in the chest, a blow that sent shockwaves through his body. His face indicated he had been stunned by the charge. Treason? *It had to be payback by the President*, he thought. Snapping out of his shock, he lit into the agent once again. "This is nothing but a politically motivated hit job by that illegitimate President and his buddy down at the FBI!" He then pointed around the yard. "You are all going down for this!"

"Mr. Brennan, we can do this the easy way or the hard way," Agent Jones said. "It's up to you."

"I don't have to do anything. This is an illegal arrest."

Two agents on the left and right of Agent Jones moved in. They grabbed Brennan by the arms, but he wasn't going easy.

"Take your hands off me!"

Agent Jones stepped forward and raised his voice. He had had enough. "Mr. Brennan, I would advise you not to resist."

"Screw you!" Brennan spewed out trying to wiggle out of the agents' grasp. They spun him around and bent him over the hood of the Cadillac. "I'm going to sue every one you! You all are going down!"

Once the handcuffs were secured behind his back, they stood Brennan up and took him down the driveway to the waiting car. Without a gag, they couldn't muzzle Brennan in his attempt to fire a few more invectives for the crowd that had gathered across the street.

"These bastards are not going to get away with this! This is politically motivated! It is unconstitutional! I'm going to take down that son of a bitch in the White House if it is the last thing that I do!"

The agents shoved the obstinate Brennan into the car and slammed the door shut. Finally some peace. But Brennan was not done. He scooted over to the other side and was seen yelling something about the President to his neighbors hoping they would see the wrong that had undoubtedly been committed upon him. He then started banging his head against the glass, not to break it but to bust his own face. He would try to claim the FBI had abused him during the arrest.

But the FBI was one step ahead of him. They had videotaped the whole arrest just in case Brennan had any ideas. They would also videotape every movement from the street to the detention facility. Agent Jones ordered two agents to get into the backseat on each side of Brennan to keep him from hurting himself. The two agents would most likely get a small bonus for such an assignment as they had to endure the hell-fire rants of the madman Brennan on the way to jail.

It didn't take long for news of Brennan's arrest to hit the airwaves. The *Drudge Report* had red and blue flashing lights with the headline "Art Brennan arrested for treason!" emblazoned across the web site. A picture from a neighbor showed an irate Brennan yelling something as he was stuffed into the FBI vehicle. Cable news shows were on the scene within minutes. One even dispatched their traffic chopper to follow the caravan of black vehicles snaking its way back to Washington.

Above a "Breaking News" banner, the CNN anchor on duty read the sheet that had been thrown in front of her as pictures splashed across the screen.

"We have breaking news to report to you out of Arlington, Virginia, this evening. Art Brennan, the head of the Civil Liberties Alliance based in Washington, D.C., and former attorney for several Gitmo detainees, convicted terrorist Muqtada Abdulla, and CIA mole Roland Barton, has been arrested by the FBI outside his townhouse in Arlington on charges of . . . ," she paused and zeroed in on the words that followed just to make sure she was reading it correctly, "on charges of *treason*," she said practically gasping, "and other related federal crimes in connection with the sniper attacks that have plagued the Maryland and Virginia areas over the past two weeks."

News roundtables quickly commented on the arrest, most commentators hoping it would lead to the capture of the snipers so the

138

locals could get back to their daily lives. Director Stubblefield went live to announce the arrest, noting the severity of the charges and the painstaking investigation that took place before he made the decision. He reminded the American people to be vigilant and stated the hunt for the snipers continued.

Central Detention Facility – Washington, D.C.

Art Brennan actually slept a couple of hours during his first night in jail – mainly because he had worn himself out screaming profanities at the jailers who instructed him to strip off his clothing so they could search every crevice of his body looking for contraband. Once content that Brennan was not hiding drugs in his butt cheeks, they provided him with a jail-issue orange jumpsuit. Thereafter, they placed him in a padded cell just in case he had any ideas of hurting himself. The jail commander also put Brennan on a suicide watch and required deputies to look in on him every fifteen minutes. Per jailhouse regulations, a mental-healthcare worker met with Brennan, clad in his suicide prevention gown, to determine whether he was a danger to himself. After a thirty-minute meeting, the psychologist, in her professional opinion, believed Brennan wasn't crazy or suicidal, just mad as hell at his current predicament and looking to exact revenge on his enemies.

Early the next morning, Brennan was taken under heavy guard to the federal courthouse for his initial appearance before a magistrate judge. At that hearing, the judge informed Brennan of the complaint against him and the laundry list of charges therein, including treason, conspiracy to commit treason, misprision of treason, advocating the overthrow of the government, conspiracy to murder, providing material support to a terrorist organization, conspiracy to commit an act of terrorism, and so on. He was told of his right to retain counsel, his right to a preliminary hearing, and his right to remain silent. He exercised that latter right, only speaking to acknowledge he understood the proceedings.

After the hearing, officers returned him to his solitary cell. The lunch menu was bologna and cheese, a chocolate chip cookie, and a lukewarm cup of coffee. He now began to realize the crap his clients had to endure over the years while they rotted away in jail. At two-thirty in the afternoon, Brennan's army of lawyers arrived from the Civil Liberties Alliance.

It was time to prepare for war.

Laura Vollstad and I. James Blunt arrived in the attorney/client visiting room after having been thoroughly searched and relieved of most of their personal possessions. Cell phones and computers were confiscated, and the only items they could bring in at this stage of the game were a single pen and legal pad each. The three other CLA attorneys who came with them had to wait downstairs – only two at a time with their client, Art Brennan.

After the officer transporting Brennan to the room removed his handcuffs and the door was shut, the two nicely dressed lawyers frowned at their boss, now clad in jailhouse orange. They didn't like what they saw. Brennan took a seat.

"How have those pricks been treating you, Art?" Blunt asked. He wore a gray suit, which matched his hair and his shoes, and he had a concerned look about him.

I. James Blunt, the I stood for Ivan, had worked at the CLA for ten years after cutting his teeth at the Democratic National Committee as deputy legal counsel. A lifelong member of the Sierra Club and PETA, along with an underground membership with the Earth Liberation Front, Blunt thought the DNC was too tame for his tastes and a waste of his energies, and he wanted to go all-in as to changing the way America operated. He fit in perfectly with Art Brennan's anti-U.S. philosophy at the CLA. As Brennan's right-hand man, his dislike for cops, soldiers, and every Republican was a shared trait. He readied his pen for Brennan's response.

Brennan said he was treated well so far, although he did make a comment about how bad the food tasted. Blunt wrote down his complaint and would have a motion filed with the court by tomorrow morning demanding better fare for his client. He had been kept by himself, which he found conducive to marshaling his thoughts and devising a legal strategy to get him the hell out of there and back at the throat of the Schumacher Administration.

"Give me your pen," he ordered to Vollstad. She handed the pen and her yellow legal pad over to him. Brennan then started writing down the notes he made to himself during the night but had no opportunity to jot down because the jailers wouldn't give him a pencil for fear that he would use it to stab his own jugular.

"First of all, I'm going to have to demand better accommodations," he said. "And they can't keep me from having paperwork and something to write with forever."

Vollstad nodded and made a mental note. "We'll file something before the end of the day."

Brennan did not respond as his right hand began to scribble quickly back and forth across the page, the ideas coming out fast and furious. He was halfway down the page before anyone spoke up.

"Your preliminary hearing is tomorrow," Vollstad reminded him.

Laura Vollstad had been with the CLA for only six years but she had rocketed to the top with several fine performances representing some of Brennan's more unsavory clients. Once the terrorist jihadists got over the mental hurdle of being represented by a woman (she did wear a head scarf out of respect for her clients' religion), Vollstad was able to win several motions to suppress evidence based on her argument abilities alone. While the terrorist defendants did not ultimately succeed, Brennan liked her tenacity. She was full of ideas and didn't take no for an answer. She was ready to fight.

"Did you hear me, Art?" she asked, tapping her index finger on the table.

Brennan had almost reached the bottom of the first page of the legal pad. Once he dotted the period at the end of the last sentence, he set the pen down.

"We can file for an extension of time, Art," Blunt said. "We'll continue this until next week and have more time to figure out our strategy."

Brennan shook his head. "No, I want to get the ball rolling tomorrow as soon as possible."

"So what do you want us to file before tomorrow?" Vollstad asked, almost begging Brennan to give her some orders so she could show off her brilliance.

"Nothing. I'm going to go it alone," Brennan said.

Both Vollstad and Blunt scrunched their eyebrows at Brennan like they didn't understand what he was talking about.

"What do you mean 'go it alone?'" Blunt asked. He too was itching to get started. He got paid big bucks to fight like a legal bulldog for his client.

Brennan stopped long enough to suck the air out of the room. He puffed up his chest and sat back in his chair. He looked both of his lawyers in their worried eyes. It was time to drop the first bomb in the case of *United States of America v. Arthur J. Brennan.*

"I am going to represent myself," Brennan said, brimming with confidence. "I am going to take down this Government. Their case is going to go down in flames."

The equally stunned Vollstad and Blunt both looked at each other. They had counseled numerous clients not to go *pro se*. "He who represents himself has a fool for a client" is not just some cute legal maxim. Proceeding to trial without an attorney fighting for you was a recipe for disaster. They had witnessed Brennan almost come to blows with a client who wanted to act as his own lawyer. "That would be suicide! Only an idiot intentionally lets the Government run over them!" he had yelled at the man.

Blunt, who was known for being blunt, didn't hold back. "That's a crazy idea, Art. You need a lawyer."

Brennan shot back. "I am a lawyer! I am the best lawyer in this town! I can take on those pricks in the U.S. Attorney's office."

Vollstad, however, was agreeing with her colleague. "You don't need an attorney, Art," she said to him. "You need five. You need a team of lawyers. Didn't you hear the charges the judge read to you this morning? The Government has thrown everything but the kitchen sink at you. They want to put you to death!"

Brennan slammed the table. "I know that! This is nothing but a political hit job, and I am going to take down this President and his FBI." His stubbornness and exaggerated ego told him he could win anything.

Blunt knew there was no use trying to change Brennan's mind. But he wasn't about to let his boss go it totally alone. "What can we do?"

Brennan passed over the sheet. "I have written some things down. Get out in front of as many TV cameras as you can. Tell the world that my arrest was politically motivated. It's all because of Schumacher, his chief of staff Cogdon, and Stubblefield at the FBI. Tell the people of America that this is what third-world dictators do to people who disagree with them. The Government is quashing free speech and it won't be long before other dissenters are rounded up, thrown in prison, and locked away for good just like me."

Blunt and Vollstad were jotting down their own notes as fast as they could. Brennan had it all planned out. It was a two-pronged attack – one fought in the courtroom and the other in the court of public opinion.

He was going to fight like hell.

CHAPTER 18

Fairfax, Virginia

"Hey sweet baby, what's shakin'," the woman on the street corner said to the officer in the slowing police car. The officer in the front passenger seat took an interest and told his partner to pull over.

The woman's name was Lucinda Gallardo, although on the street she preferred to go by the moniker "Luscious Lucy." She had walked the streets of Fairfax for ten years now, offering her services to any man who had the time and the money. She had been arrested nine times – three for possession of cannabis and the rest for prostitution. She only had two convictions, and the judge took pity on her both times and let her off with probation, a fine, and a stern lecture to clean up her act and fly right.

But Luscious Lucy had no other means to support herself. She had dropped out of high school after becoming pregnant. She gave the baby up for adoption, and the resulting depression led her to the back alleys of Baltimore and Washington, D.C. in search of drugs to fry her brain and erase the bad memories therein.

She used one of her probationary terms to enter a rehab clinic, and for the last two years she had not touched any meth, cocaine, or cannabis. Nicotine was still a problem for her, but she was down to only one pack a day. Still, she needed money. With no education or marketable skills, she sold her body and hoped it was enough to keep her alive. That was if the john paid up.

The police car pulled over to the curb where Lucy was waiting for that night's action. The sky was clear and the warm temps meant Lucy could show off her assets with as few clothes as possible. The officer in the passenger seat lowered the window. "I haven't seen you in a few days, Lucinda," Officer Rich Baker said, calling her by her real name.

Officer Baker had been on the force for twelve years and knew every shopkeeper, business owner, and bar bouncer in this part of town. He was also readily familiar with the druggies, the pimps, the gangbangers, and the women working the streets as prostitutes like Lucy. He had arrested her clients on three occasions. He even placed the cuffs on her once in hopes a ride to the police station and a trip through the criminal-justice system might be what she needed to get cleaned up. It didn't work. She was back on the street in no time. Officer Baker had taken pity on her over the years, realizing she didn't know how to make a living beyond prostitution. He might not be able to change her habits, but at least he could treat her with kindness and respect – something her clients rarely did.

"Baby, I've been around," she said, bending down and resting her arms on the door frame. Her black leather boots were scuffed around the edges from years of use, but her clients didn't seem to mind. They never looked at them anyway. The boots almost reached her knees and the mini-skirt was a good foot above that. She had somehow wrapped her breasts inside of a red leather top that showed a good portion of her stomach, her back, and everything in between. The officers in the car got a full view of Lucy's cleavage as it tried mightily not to bust out of her top.

"You just out for a walk to get some fresh air?" Officer Baker asked.

Lucy smiled at him and took a drag from her cigarette before turning her head and blowing the smoke into the breeze. "Sweetie, I'm just doing my job," she said, "acting as the welcoming committee to the great city of Fairfax, Virginia."

Baker nodded. He tried not to choke on the stench of cigarette smoke coming from Lucy's breath. She had painted on a heavy rouge to cover her pale white skin – her nocturnal hours not being conducive to a good tan. Her eyes had a glazed look, but it was most likely a matter of being tired. She wasn't as young as she used to be. The hooker across the street was ten years younger, and she took away a good portion of Lucinda's business. Body parts were beginning to noticeably droop, and she had no money to lift them back up. Despite her dye job, the gray hairs were becoming more and more noticeable. She didn't know how many more good earning years she had left.

"Had any business lately?"

Lucy sucked some more tar into her lungs. "Here and there," she said. She seemed depressed, and it wasn't clear if it was because of the lack of business or the fact that she had to sell herself night after night to survive.

"How'd you get that black eye?" Officer Baker asked. He was an officer of the law and prostitution was illegal. While some might look down on Lucy for her chosen profession, Officer Baker still had compassion for her and he didn't like it when her clients took advantage of her.

"It's not a black eye," she protested lightly, shaking her head and turning away. The layers of makeup did a poor job covering up the evidence. The glitter didn't even help.

Baker knew she wasn't being straight with him. "Lucinda," he lectured. "Don't lie to me. You didn't have that three days ago when I last saw you."

Lucy shrugged her bare shoulders like it wasn't a big deal. "Sweet baby, it's just an occupational hazard," she said sadly. "It's just part of my life." Through the years, she had suffered plenty of black eyes, swollen lips, and busted noses. Sometimes her clients liked to play rough, while others were simply violent and thought they could have their way with her. That's what they were paying for, they told her, so shut up and take it.

"Lucinda, you can't let them treat you like this," Officer Baker said. "Let me know who did this and I'll take care of it."

Lucy stood up, flicked the cigarette into the gutter, and looked at the empty street in both directions. She bent back down and rested her arms again on the car door. "Sweet baby, why are you so good to me?"

"It's my job," he said with a wink. "Who gave you that black eye?"

The suddenly silent Lucy turned her head to look over the hood of the car. She usually didn't squeal on her clients. Clearing the streets of johns would hurt her bottom line. Sometimes things get out of hand. It was always her fault anyway, she told herself. But she didn't like the guy that did this to her. He was a first-time client with lots of demands on how he wanted things done. Once it was over and Lucy demanded payment, the man became violent, called her an American whore and said it was her duty to satisfy him – no questions asked. Since the guy wasn't one of her regulars, she didn't have any qualms about telling Officer Baker what happened.

"Just some prick that came by last night," she said, shaking her head like she knew she should have walked away from the guy. "To tell you the truth, he kind of scared me."

"Why's that?"

"Just the way he talked to me. Bitch this, bitch that," she recalled. "I get those types every once in awhile. But this guy was different. He kept saying it was my duty to submit to him. I think he was half-drunk. He claimed if I didn't do what he said he would kill me. Said he was some jihadist sent to the United States to kill people and he could kill me if he wanted to. I guess he thought I would do whatever he said. He just kept going on and on about Allah this and Allah that. I just wanted to get it over with and get the heck out of there."

Officer Baker looked over to his partner in the driver's seat. The manhunt for the terrorist snipers was still on and the leads had seemed to dry up. Law-enforcement authorities worried the terrorists had gone back into hiding to wait it out before striking again. Lucy, however, had no clue what was going on. She didn't have a TV and didn't read the newspapers, or care to, on a regular basis. She did wonder, however, what was causing the lack of traffic recently.

Baker took out his notepad. "Can you tell us what he looked like?"

"Oh, he was one of those sand guys."

"Sand guys?"

There was a short silence as the officers waited for a response. Lucy's mind didn't work as well as it used to, taking its own sweet time to connect the dots. The neurons and synapses in her brain were doing war with each other. The drugs had done it to her, and she struggled to find the words. "From the desert," she said, pointing off to the east. Way east. "Middle Eastern!" she exclaimed, finally finding the words in amongst the few brain cells she had left.

"A Middle Eastern male?"

"Yeah. I had never seen him before."

"Did he have a name?"

Lucy looked up into the night sky. There had been so many men over the years. Her clients ranged from twentysomethings enjoying their first go-round all the way up to geriatrics hoping for one last hurrah. And they were multi-national too. She showed no prejudice. There were Americans, Japanese, Italians, Russians, Mexicans, and even one lost soul from Canada looking for a good time. Most, she assumed, didn't tell her their real names lest their wives or significant others find out what they were doing when they claimed to be "working late" or "out with the guys." But she remembered this most recent guy.

"He said his name was Abdel," she said. "Kept telling me he was a

Deputy Commander in some organization. He even made me call him 'Commander Abdel' while we were doing it."

"Did he threaten you with any guns?"

Lucy shook her head back and forth. "I didn't see any." She then remembered something else. "Although he did say he might shoot me if I told anyone about him. Said he could kill me from a mile away without me even knowing he was there."

"Where did you conduct your business with this guy?"

"Oh, it was in his van. It was a white van. He drove by," Lucy said pointing, "just a few blocks down that way. Asked if I was available for a good time. We discussed the financials. He showed me the money so I got in."

"White van?"

"Yeah. I don't remember if it said anything on it. There were a couple of windows in the rear. We pulled off in the park and crawled over the seats into the back."

"What was in the back of the van?"

"Oh, I don't know. I can't remember any tools or anything. All I remember is the floor. It was like wood and, let me tell you, it wasn't very comfortable from my position."

"What happened when it was over?"

"Oh, that's when things started getting out of hand. I got dressed and demanded my money. He had promised to give me two-hundred dollars. When I asked him where the money was, he said I hadn't been good enough, that I didn't satisfy him. And I said, 'Let me tell you something, Commander Abdel,'" she replayed the scene in full sarcastic tones, "'if you don't pay me I'm going to call the cops.' That's when he started hitting me and threatening to kill me. He started choking me." She turned her head and pointed to her neck to show off the exact spot. "I was really getting worried 'cuz he had this weird look in his eyes, like killing was something he did on a regular basis. I thought sure I was going to wind up dumped in a ditch or in some back alley. Finally, I told him if he gave me twenty bucks, I'd keep quiet. He handed it over and kicked me out the back of the van. Then he took off." She stopped to think of the right word to describe the man. "Asshole."

"Can you describe him a little more? Height, age, any identifying marks?" Officer Baker asked.

Lucy thought some more. "Around six feet tall, early thirties. That's all I can remember. The lighting wasn't very good."

"License plate?"

Lucy shook her head. "I don't remember any letters or numbers. It might have been Virginia."

Officer Baker wrote down the last of the information and said something to his partner. He unbuttoned a chest pocket and pulled out a McDonald's gift card. "Why don't you go get yourself a cup of coffee and something to eat, Lucinda." Although he was always concerned with her welfare, he had learned not to give her any spending cash for cigarettes or booze. "If you see that guy again, just call the police. Tell them you want to talk to Sweet Baby Baker about an urgent matter."

"I will," she said, smiling and taking the card. "Thanks, sweet baby."

Five miles away, the van driven by Abdel Ramadi pulled over to the side of the road and slowed to a stop. Red and blue flashing lights filled the side mirrors and lit up the night sky.

"What is going on?" Hassan Jahdari, the sniper in the back, asked in a whisper. He had been covered in a dark blanket ready to zero in on his next victim.

Ramadi slunk down in his seat, trying not to make any furtive gestures that would raise suspicion. "It's just one cop," he said, not taking his eyes off the side mirror. "Just be quiet and I'll get rid of him."

A worried Ramadi started to perspire and his mouth went dry. He had gone out last night all alone on a "scouting" mission to look for possible target areas but it soon became a search for booze and prostitutes. He turned up in a seedy part of Fairfax and decided it was time to reward his successes like he had been doing in Madrid before he was unceremoniously dumped as Deputy Commander. The urge to satisfy his sexual appetite outweighed his quest for jihad, and he was very hungry to indulge in some skanky American fare. So he found Luscious Lucy and satisfied his urges with a romp in the back of the van. He had threatened her not to say anything. There was no way she would have ratted him out to police, he told himself. He had made himself clear.

Ramadi took a deep breath when he saw the officer walking toward the driver's side of the van. The silhouette of the gun holstered on the officer's hip was clearly visible in the glare of the headlights behind him. Ramadi put both hands on the top of the steering wheel, just like he was told to do if he was approached by the cops.

The officer had called his dispatcher and relayed the license plate number and it came back registered to the Islamic Studies Center in Arlington, Virginia. He took a closer look at the sticker on the plate and then slowly approached the window.

"How are you doing tonight, sir?"

"Okay, I guess," Ramadi stammered.

"I'm Trooper Rick Sheridan with the Virginia State Police. Do you know why I pulled you over?"

Ramadi looked at the man in the gray "Smokey Bear" campaign hat with the diamond-shaped emblem in the middle and then the badge on his left breast. The stern look on the trooper's face indicated he wasn't going to put up with any smart-asses tonight.

Ramadi shook his head like he couldn't think of anything he might have done wrong. He was wearing his seat belt and he had obeyed the speed limit just like he was taught. "No, sir, what did I do?" he asked politely and with concern.

Trooper Sheridan reached his left arm into the window and pointed at the three evergreen-shaped air fresheners dangling from the rear-view mirror. "I saw these when you passed me a mile back. You got three of them swaying back and forth obstructing your view. It's a violation of the Virginia Motor Vehicle Code, sir. You can't have anything dangling that might obstruct your view out of the front windshield."

Ramadi looked shocked. He had never heard of such a thing. He hurriedly pulled the strings over the mirror and took down the air fresheners. "I am sorry, officer. I did not know."

"Can you give me your driver's license, registration, and proof of insurance, please?"

Ramadi's heart skipped a beat at the request, and the trickle of sweat sliding down the side of his face felt like a rushing river. His training taught him to avoid handing over his papers if at all possible – that way your name isn't put into the system. He decided to protest, but politely. "Is that really necessary for the air fresheners?"

Trooper Sheridan made sure to get as good a look as he could inside the van. "Yes, sir, it is," he said. "It's standard procedure. If everything checks out, I'll just let you off with a warning and you'll be on your way. Do you have a driver's license, sir?" He wasn't going to ask again.

Ramadi thought he had dodged a bullet. He didn't think his paperwork would raise any red flags (at least not at this time), and the trooper wasn't looking to arrest him. He became profuse in his compliance. "Yes, sir. Yes, sir." He reached over to the passenger seat. "I have my documents right here."

Officer Sheridan took the documents from Ramadi's shaking hands. In the glare of the streetlight he noticed the sweat stain running down the side of the man's face. "Sit tight, sir. I'll be right back."

The trooper walked to the back of the van and stopped when he took a second look at the license plate on the rear door. He thought it was slightly farther out than when he walked by earlier. Thinking little of it, he touched the plate, returned it flush with the door, and got back into his car.

"Dispatch, seventy-four," Trooper Sheridan said into the microphone, straightening the documents in his hands.

"Seventy-four, dispatch. Go ahead."

"Would you send a canine unit to this location?" Considering the driver's heavy perspiration, his shaking hands, and the pulsating carotid artery in his neck, Trooper Sheridan decided to call in the drug dog to make sure there wasn't any illegal contraband in the van.

"Roger that. Anything else?"

"I need you to check the NCIC database on a driver I have here. First name, Abdel – A-B-D-E-L; last name, Ramadi – R-A-M-A-D-I." He then gave the address on the driver's license and the man's date of birth.

As Trooper Sheridan typed the information into a warning ticket for the windshield-obstruction violation, he didn't see the license plate of the van being slowly pushed downward. Jahdari had not made a sound while hiding in the back and he didn't like the way Ramadi handled things. He thought their cover was blown and it was time to get out of there. It was time to run and hide. He got into position and readied his weapon. He could hit a target a mile away, but this one would be no more than fifteen yards. He put the officer in the middle of the crosshairs and exhaled. The index finger on his right hand curled around the trigger.

Jahdari shook when he heard Ramadi from the front of the van.

"There are more of them coming!" Ramadi whispered loudly, turning around in his seat.

Jahdari looked up at Ramadi and then back into his gun sight. He moved the rifle around but saw nothing. The officer in the front seat of the squad car was gone. Three police cars from the Fairfax Police

Department were approaching the scene at a high rate of speed from both the front and rear of the van. Three more from the Virginia State Police were also arriving on the scene and surrounding the van. The sirens were blaring at full song and red and blue lights filled the sky. Officer Baker had heard the dispatch from Trooper Sheridan about a driver named Abdel and made the call. The swarm of officers was either going to find a man who punched a hooker in the face or they were going to find the terrorists who had been waging war on America. Officer Baker had a feeling it would be both.

Jahdari pulled back the license plate. "What's going on?" he demanded to know.

Ramadi didn't know what to do. They couldn't make a run for it now. "What do we do?" he asked the sniper in the back. "What do we do?"

"Driver! Step out of the van!" a voice bellowed from a bullhorn.

Ramadi was inside looking all around. He was beginning to panic. "What do we do? Do we end it? Do we end it?"

Jahdari said nothing. They had no plan to end it. There had never been anything drawn up that they would commit suicide by blowing themselves up if they were close to apprehension. The only weapon they had was the sniper rifle – not the best weapon to use when you are surrounded by gun-toting law-enforcement officers. Jahdari might be able to pick off one cop, but that would be followed by a barrage of bullets heading his direction.

"Driver! Step out of the van! Now!"

Jahdari scrambled up from his prone position. Hidden in the darkness of the rear of the van, he peeked out the front window from behind the driver's seat. It was hopeless. There was no way out. It was either be captured or go down in one last violent blaze of glory. In trying to figure out what to do, he caught sight of the panicked man behind the wheel. Jahdari slowly seethed with rage.

It had been Ramadi who had betrayed him.

Jahdari knew Commander Abdel had gone out the night before, and now it was obvious what he had done. He was not scouting locations, he was screwing around with women. He was just as bad as the American infidels. He had nearly ruined the operation in Madrid and now he had led the police right to him with his sinful ways. He could not be seen as a martyr for the cause. He must rot in jail forever and suffer the wrath of

Allah for his wicked betrayal.

"Do what they say," Jahdari whispered to Ramadi. "I will pick them off one by one."

"I can't do that," Ramadi pleaded. He could not just give himself up. It went against everything he had been trained to do. "I will stay and fight!"

"No! You must get out and sacrifice yourself. Then I will kill these pigs! Do as I say! *Allahu akbar*!"

Ramadi nodded, tears running down his face. He had envisioned the end as being a much grander exit. He would get out so Jahdari could continue the killing. He convinced himself it was the right thing to do. He figured he would get caught in the crossfire and eventually die in glorious fashion.

"*Allahu akbar*," he whispered to Jahdari in the back. He raised his hands and indicated he was ready to follow the officer's orders. He opened the door and stepped out.

"Slowly back away from the van!"

Ramadi did so and then dropped to his knees as he was told. He then put his hands behind his head and complied with the directive not to move. He waited wondering when the bullets were going to come. He could feel the officers ever so slowly approaching him with their guns drawn. He envisioned three or four of them being shot dead within the next ten seconds. He closed his eyes and prepared to die.

As the officer grabbed his hands to cuff him, the first shot rang out.

An officer grabbed Ramadi and dragged him behind a squad car. The other officers took cover and waited. Shouts were exchanged about whether they should open fire on the van. But no more shots came from inside the vehicle. Jahdari had shamed Ramadi in the eyes of his fellow jihadists across the world. The now-handcuffed man had given himself up like a worthless coward.

Jahdari, on the other hand, martyred himself with a bullet to the brain.

FBI Headquarters – Washington, D.C.

At 8:00 a.m. the next morning, Director Stubblefield approached the microphones in the press room of the Hoover FBI Building followed by a host of suits and uniformed officers. Although he was always intense, close friends could tell a heavy weight had been lifted off his shoulders.

He turned to make sure everyone was in place before starting.

"At approximately 9:40 p.m. last evening, uniformed officers from the Fairfax, Virginia Police Department as well as the Virginia State Police, stopped a white van driven by Abdel Ramadi, a citizen of Saudi Arabia, on a traffic violation. It is believed that Ramadi has been involved in the sniper attacks that have taken place in Maryland, Virginia, and the District of Columbia. Ramadi was arrested and has been taken into custody.

Also found in the van was the body of a man with a sniper rifle who we believe also took part in the sniper killings here in the Washington, D.C. metro area. Our investigation has determined the man, a citizen of Afghanistan, went by the name of Hassan Jahdari, which was an alias. His real name was Yaman al-Sahaf and he was wanted by the FBI as well as the United States military for the deaths of ten soldiers. Al-Sahaf died of a self-inflicted gunshot wound to the head."

Director Stubblefield went on to state ballistics tests would be conducted on the rifle in the van to see if they matched with the killings in the area. He also praised the Virginia policemen who conducted the stop and participated in the arrest of the alleged terrorist. He stated the investigation into the shootings would continue and further information would be released when it came available.

CHAPTER 19

E. Barrett Prettyman United States Courthouse – Washington, D.C.

Velma Bourbonnais exited her black Volvo in her designated parking space at the federal courthouse located at Third Street and Constitution Avenue, just a block west of the United States Capitol. She had been a United States magistrate judge for a little over seven years, but it was looking more and more likely she wouldn't be around much longer. She was aware of it, the whisperers and the gossips around the courthouse water cooler had told her what she already knew. The writing was clearly on the wall.

A United States magistrate judge performs the duties assigned by U.S. District Court Judges, the trial judges of the federal court system. The magistrate judge, making over $160,000 per year, signs warrants, conducts initial appearances and preliminary hearings, handles misdemeanor cases, and issues findings and recommendations on motions to suppress to the district court, along with performing other statutory obligations. They are appointed by the district court judges and serve a term of eight years.

And incumbent Magistrate Judge Velma Bourbonnais would not be getting reappointed when her term ended at the end of the year.

Judge Bourbonnais had received subpar grades in her Harvard law classes and had only mediocre success in the legal community. But she did not let her failures dampen her hopes for success. She had a plan, one that didn't require much legal ability, just a little luck. After ten years in the doldrums of small firms and public defender offices, she made the conscious effort to marry into power and trusted she could ride the coattails of any husband to a job of prominence and a life full of grandeur.

She found her man in Gavin LeCocq.

Gavin LeCocq had risen the ladder of political success in the government of the District of Columbia. He had pressed the flesh of constituents and flashed his Democratic credentials to win a seat as a

D.C. Council member. His bright smile and gregarious personality won him great plaudits from like-minded Dems and he ate it all up. He was going somewhere.

And Velma Bourbonnais wanted to go along for the ride.

She latched on to him after a D.C. City Council meeting and wouldn't let go. She handed LeCocq her resume, said she was desperate for a job, and was told he was the mover and shaker in all of D.C. He could make things happen. Batting her eyelashes and leaving the top two buttons of her blouse undone provided the visual aids her resume couldn't project. He liked what he was hearing and seeing. She was forty-one at the time with shoulder length dark hair, and he was ten years older with the first shades of gray starting to make an appearance on his otherwise nicely coiffed head of hair. After a night in the sack discussing her credentials and admiring her assets, LeCocq found her a job. First as legal counsel to the D.C. City Council and then at the Democratic National Committee. Ten years later, Council Chairman LeCocq won his first term as mayor of Washington, D.C. after promising to end the violence in the nation's capital and create new high-paying jobs in the District.

Unfortunately, the only high-paying jobs he was able to obtain were for himself and Mrs. Bourbonnais-LeCocq, and the latter's employment was not without some shady dealings. All the while accepting numerous bribes and kickbacks from contractors within D.C., LeCocq had pressured members of Congress and even two Democratic Presidents that his wife should get a seat on the federal bench. She was not happy just being First Lady of D.C., he told them. She wasn't a housewife content with baking cookies and doing laundry – she wanted to be like Hillary. He was so incessant with his demands that two Senators finally said okay, although neither one of them thought she was qualified for a lifetime appointment to the federal judiciary. But the two Senators owed LeCocq more than one favor and told him they would persuade the federal judges in the D.C. Circuit to give Velma Bourbonnais-LeCocq a position as a magistrate judge. The judges, a majority of whom owed favors to the Senators themselves, reluctantly gave her the position and hoped for the best.

While on the bench, Judge Bourbonnais-LeCocq proved to be a poor administrator of her workload. Hearings would routinely be continued because Judge Bourbonnais-LeCocq was under the weather or had to leave town at a moment's notice, although she made it back in time for that evening's soiree at whatever social function was on the Mayor's schedule. She once told a group of students she liked her job because she could take off whenever she wanted. And she must have liked her job a lot. Work piled up, justice was delayed, and she silently incurred the wrath of the two other magistrate judges who had to try and make up for her slothfulness.

Judge Bourbonnais-LeCocq, like her husband, thought she had the world at her fingertips. On the salary of a D.C. mayor and U.S. magistrate judge, the pair lived in a $5 million townhome in D.C. and drove separate but equally shiny red BMWs. They took lavish vacations, also known as "fact-finding missions" to the Mayor's staff, to such faraway locales like Tahiti, Tuscany, and the French Riviera. All of them on the taxpayers' dime, of course. The District hadn't seen this level of corruption since the Marion Barry days. It didn't take long before the FBI was tipped off to Mayor LeCocq's shenanigans, and the investigation revealed the commission of a host of federal crimes. He was arrested, convicted of taking bribes and kickbacks, and sentenced to a 10-year term as a guest of the federal government at a medium-security prison in Maryland. Only nine more years to go.

The Mayor's downfall meant the end to his wife's life of luxury as well. The swanky townhome was sold, the red Beemers were auctioned, and all of the money went to pay down the Mayor's $10 million fine. She lost everything. The used Volvo she drove had 190,000 miles on it, and she was stretching every dollar to keep her one-bedroom condo. She was barely able to stay afloat, and she knew her job as a magistrate judge was all but over. Even dropping the LeCocq from her name couldn't save her.

According to federal law, the district court is required to empanel a group of citizens to consider whether a magistrate judge should be reappointed to a new eight-year term. The results were not kind to Judge Bourbonnais as most of the informed citizenry found she had little merit and wanted her gone. A magistrate judge can also be removed from the position for incompetency, misconduct, neglect of duty, and/or a physical or mental disability. The district judges on the court thought she qualified for at least two of the grounds, some thought all four, but they decided to just let her tenure expire and save her any further embarrassment. They were just hoping she didn't screw things up in her last remaining months.

Judge Bourbonnais walked into her chambers at the courthouse and sat down at her desk. She had a two-foot-high stack of papers towering on both ends. They were cases that needed resolution but that she had neglected. She would probably just leave it for the next magistrate. She had already begun to pack some of her belongings – the photos of a once-smiling, newly sworn-in judge were in a box somewhere in the closet. The door to her chambers opened and her secretary, Barbara Johns, walked in. She placed another stack of papers in the middle of Judge Bourbonnais' desk.

"Did you hear they caught those shooters?" Johns asked, trying to make small talk.

Bourbonnais shook her head in the negative. She had to cancel her cable package, and she no longer listened to the radio on the way into work for fear she would hear her name dragged through the mud again up and down the AM dial.

"You're scheduled to conduct the preliminary hearings today," Johns said. She hoped the judge would show up so she wouldn't have to explain where her boss had run off to yet again. She added something else that might spark the judge's interest. "You get the preliminary hearing for that guy who has been charged with treason."

Judge Bourbonnais nodded. She had a headache, and the work environment made her feel worse. Her once dark flowing hair, primped and fawned over at pricey salons, had given way to split ends and generic dandruff shampoo. "Get me a cup of coffee, will ya," she ordered. Gone were the days where she had hired help to wait on her hand and foot. Now she just used the secretaries as her personal assistants. The judge picked up the top sheet and took a look at the list of names scheduled to appear before her today.

"Arthur J. Brennan," she mumbled to herself, smiling for the first time in what felt like a year. "Good ol' Art Brennan."

Given her husband's political prowess in D.C. and in Democratic Party circles, Art Brennan was well known to Judge Bourbonnais. He had stopped by at a couple of her holiday shindigs to meet and greet Dem financiers and other assorted pols, bigwigs, and fat cats. Brennan had even offered the support of the CLA's legal team when the Government came after the Mayor. The Judge hadn't read much about Brennan's arrest but heard it said by those friends that still talked to her that he had been jacked up by the FBI. She claimed to know the feeling.

And now he was coming before her court.

Johns entered the office again, placed a Styrofoam cup of coffee on the Judge's desk, and left without saying a word. Judge Bourbonnais took a sip and hopped out of her chair. She grabbed the black robe from the coat rack in the corner and looked at herself in the mirror on the back of the door. The FBI had bugged her phone to gather evidence against the Mayor and followed her around town. With evidence in hand, the U.S. Attorney came after her husband hard and the Mayor and the Judge had lost everything. Now the United States Government wanted to show they had enough evidence to hold Art Brennan for treason and other federal crimes.

Judge Bourbonnais thought she would see about that.

At ten minutes after nine, late as usual, Judge Bourbonnais entered the courtroom to something she hadn't seen since the days when her husband was on trial – a full house. Every seat in the courtroom was taken and most of the spots along the wall as well. The bailiff had already turned the temperature down on the air conditioner because of the heat being generated in the room. News reporters, with pencils at the ready, waited to gather every detail. The lucky few citizens who showed up early to get a spot in the courtroom strained their necks from the back row trying to get their first look at a real live U.S. magistrate judge. The tension was palpable.

"Be seated," Judge Bourbonnais said as she took her chair behind the bench.

"First case today on the preliminary hearing call is *United States of America v. Arthur J. Brennan*," she said, reading off the list. "Would you please bring in the defendant Mr. Brennan."

The side door to the courtroom opened and two Deputy U.S. Marshals entered followed by one holding the arm of the defendant, and two more pulling up the rear. Still dressed in his jailhouse orange, the clanging chains indicated he wouldn't be running away anytime soon. The spectators in the gallery sat hushed and they took in the sight of the first American charged with treason that anyone could remember. The deputies walked Brennan over to the defense table and took up their positions ready to jump him in case he decided to get out of line.

"Deputy, Mr. Brennan is innocent until proven guilty," Judge Bourbonnais lectured from on high. "Remove Mr. Brennan's handcuffs."

The deputy marshal fronted Brennan and unlocked him from his shackles. At the defense table, Brennan took a seat, all by himself. Three attorneys from the CLA sat on the edge of their seats in the front row of the gallery ready to charge into battle when the bugle sounded. All of them had a yellow legal pad on their lap and a pen at the ready. It was still Brennan's show, but they would be working overtime to funnel whatever Brennan needed over the course of the trial proceedings.

"Mr. Brennan, did the judge at your initial appearance admonish you as to your right to counsel?" Judge Bourbonnais wondered.

Brennan stood tall, proud of himself and his abilities. "Yes, Your Honor. I was so admonished, and I have decided to proceed as my own attorney."

She had warned defendants in the past about acting as their own counsel, but if Brennan the lawyer wanted to proceed *pro se* that was his decision. "Very well."

In contrast to Brennan's go-it-alone strategy, the United States of America had its prosecutorial arsenal fully stocked with some of the best legal minds the Government could offer. Assisted by two Assistant United States Attorneys, one Assistant Attorney General, and three other Justice Department attorneys, stood U.S. Attorney Bradley F. Davidson. A Stanford law grad, he had started out as a fresh-faced attorney in the Office of Legal Counsel at the Department of Justice before embarking on a successful career as a deputy solicitor in the Solicitor General's office, where he argued and won nine out of ten cases before the Supreme Court of the United States. Eschewing six-figure salary offers from high-profile D.C. law firms, he jumped at President Schumacher's offer to become United States Attorney for the District of Columbia. He hoped it would someday lead to a lifetime appointment to the federal court of appeals.

Judge Bourbonnais harbored no such dreams, and she didn't particularly like Davidson's seemingly easy climb up the legal ladder. She wouldn't make this easy on him.

"Mr. Davidson," she said, looking down at him over her half-glasses, "it's your case." What are you looking at me for? she seemed to say.

"Your Honor, the United States would call Special Agent Wallace Jones to the witness stand," Davidson said.

Special Agent Wallace Jones strode into the courtroom and swore the testimony he was about to give was the truth, the whole truth, and nothing but the truth.

"Could you state your name and occupation for the record please?" Davidson asked of Jones once he was firmly seated on the stand.

"My name is Wallace Jones, and I am a special agent with the Federal Bureau of Investigation."

"Speak up, Mr. Jones," Judge Bourbonnais barked. It was clear she was not in a good mood. "Pull that microphone closer to you."

Davidson walked Agent Jones through the investigation of Art Brennan. The surveillance videos, the overhears, all of it was set forth in painstaking detail. The FBI had dotted every "i" and crossed every "t" in putting the pieces of the puzzle together. Jones mentioned Brennan's meeting with Hakim al-Rashid and the e-mails from Mahmud Basra.

"And what did Mr. Brennan and Mr. al-Rashid discuss during their last telephone call?" Davidson asked.

Brennan shot up from his seat. He had been quiet too long. It was time to start fighting. "Objection! Your Honor!"

Judge Bourbonnais snapped to attention. "What is the ground for your objection, Mr. Brennan?"

"Attorney-client privilege, Your Honor," Brennan stated. "Hakim al-Rashid is a client of mine, and any evidence obtained by the FBI is in violation of the attorney-client privilege. You must throw it out."

Judge Bourbonnais nodded at the argument. It sounded rational. She turned her eyes on Davidson. "Does the attorney-client privilege mean nothing here, Mr. Davidson?" Are you going to trample on Mr. Brennan's rights? she seemed to ask.

"Your Honor, this is a preliminary hearing. The defendant cannot object to evidence at this stage. If he so desires, he can file a motion to suppress later on."

Judge Bourbonnais had nothing to add. "Objection overruled."

Davidson continued on, the damning evidence starting to pile up. Brennan tried to object but it got him nowhere.

"That is all I have of this witness, Your Honor," Davidson said.

Judge Bourbonnais made a notation on her legal pad before looking toward Brennan. "Mr. Brennan, you may cross-examine if you wish."

This is what Brennan had been waiting for. It was the first time he would be able to make his case to a larger audience than his attorneys. Even though there were no cameras in the courtroom, he had no doubt the press would print his every word and before he knew it the whole world would hear what he had to say.

With intense fire, Brennan lit into Agent Jones on supposed illegal FBI tactics like wiretapping, witness bribery, and spying. He somehow managed to go off on a tangent that the FBI had sanctioned torture. The courtroom sketch artist would later provide TV viewers with an image of the bombastic Brennan, mouth open in full roar, eyes full of rage, and pointing an accusatory finger at the witness on the stand.

"Objection!" Davidson repeated over and over again.

"Sustained. Move on, Mr. Brennan."

Brennan kept at it. This was a preliminary hearing, but it was also his chance to start making his case.

"Agent Jones, you claim you have evidence that terrorists entered my home and walked out with an assortment of firearms that were allegedly used in the sniper attacks."

"Yes, that's correct."

Brennan was ready to pounce. He didn't know all of the evidence the Government had against him, but he knew they couldn't have gotten anything good on him at the house. He was too careful.

At least that's what he thought.

"Didn't I report a break-in to the police, Agent Jones?" He sounded like he had all the answers and once he extracted them from the Government's witness he would undoubtedly be vindicated and set free.

"Yes, you did."

"And I reported that guns had been stolen?" Why would someone looking to provide guns to terrorists want to involve the police? was his tone.

"Yes, you did."

"So were you lying then or lying now?"

"Excuse me?"

"Were you lying when you made the statement ten minutes ago that I provided guns to terrorists?"

"No, I was not."

"How can you say that?"

Agent Jones leaned closer to the microphone so everyone could hear. "Because your townhome wasn't burglarized."

Brennan snorted in contempt. He turned his back on the man and looked with disbelief into the audience. He spun around and shot off the next question. "How can you say that? You just said I reported a break-in."

"Yes, but no one broke into your home."

Brennan was incredulous. He was so involved in his own story that he didn't realize he was leading himself down a road he didn't want to go. A road that would lead him to a place where he would never be able to find his way back. The three CLA attorneys in the front row were squirming in their seats. Vollstad repeatedly cleared her throat to get Brennan's attention and hoped he would sit down and shut up. Some seated behind her thought she was loudly coughing the word "stop" to her boss. He either didn't hear her or chose to ignore the warning. "You must be insane. How can you say no one broke into my home?"

Agent Jones cleared his throat. "Sir, we were watching your home all day long."

The silence was devastating. The only sound came from those in the gallery leaning forward in their seats and gasping in disbelief. Even the motormouth Brennan had been rendered speechless. He looked like he had been punched in the face, stunned at what he had just heard. The Government attorneys just sat back and enjoyed the show.

"We saw you and four other individuals placing boxes into two vans during the early morning hours," Agent Jones said. He would have kept going but he was interrupted.

"Objection!" Brennan blurted out. He just realized he was screwing himself into the ground. An attorney, one who wasn't the defendant on trial, would have known when to have his client exercise his right to remain silent. Brennan knew he was in trouble. "Objection! Your Honor, there's no question pending! I would ask the jury to disregard!"

Judge Bourbonnais had to keep from laughing. Even though she considered Brennan an acquaintance, it was kind of fun for her to see someone's life in greater shambles than her own. And it was clear to her that Brennan was in a heap of trouble.

"Mr. Brennan, there is no jury here," she reminded him. "Just little ol' me. Your objection is overruled."

Brennan seemed flummoxed, something he was not accustomed to in the courtroom. His mind was spinning out of control. "I want to call the President of the United States to the stand!"

"Objection, Your Honor," Davidson interjected.

"Sustained."

"I'm being railroaded, Your Honor! I want to call President Schumacher! And his chief of staff! And the Director of the FBI! They are all in this together!"

"Objection!"

"Unless they are six feet under I want them on this stand!"

"Objection!"

Judge Bourbonnais started banging her gavel on the bench. Brennan was making her headache worse. She was one outburst away from having Brennan removed from the courtroom to save himself from further embarrassment. "Sit down, Mr. Brennan. This is not the time or the place for the calling of defense witnesses or suppression of evidence. You know that."

Brennan felt the marshals closing in from behind. He was out of breath. He didn't know what he had just said. He fell into his seat and had nothing more to say.

Following a brief argument by the U.S. Attorney, Judge Bourbonnais issued her ruling. "Based on the evidence by the United States through the testimony of Special Agent Jones, I find probable cause to believe the offenses in the complaint have been committed and said offenses were committed by the defendant, Mr. Brennan. Thus, finding probable cause, I will refer this matter to the grand jury. It is ordered that Mr. Brennan be held in custody pending any action of the grand jury, and thereafter, on any trial on an indictment."

She then banged her gavel for the final time.

"That is all. Court is adjourned."

CHAPTER 20

The White House – Washington, D.C.

"Shadow and Coyote are on the balcony."

President Schumacher and Wiley Cogdon were trying to enjoy a rare moment of solitude in their hectic fast-paced world of presidential politics. They sat on the Truman Balcony overlooking the South Lawn of the White House, their tiny oasis in the center of the storm, enjoying the fresh air and warm September breezes. Completed in 1948 during the Truman Administration, although not without controversy from architectural purists, the second-floor balcony offered one of the most fabulous vistas in all of the world with unobstructed views of the South Lawn toward the Washington Monument and the Jefferson Memorial.

Although there wasn't much of a view from the President's perch any longer. Security reasons took precedence over the view. Whenever the President wanted some time outside, the Secret Service cleared the gates of all pedestrians and tourists on the south grounds to prevent anyone from taking a shot at the White House. It had happened before, and the Secret Service had no desire to take any chances. Sharpshooters manned the roof and what seemed like a thousand eyes watched over the South Lawn and beyond the White House gates across the Ellipse.

And the Secret Service also rolled out its new taxpayer-funded security wall.

Security agents placed seven-foot-tall bulletproof panels around the perimeter of the balcony. The panels were covered with a scrim that mimicked the architecture of the White House, so only an eagle-eyed tourist with a telephoto lens could tell they were even there. The President, however, didn't like them because they interfered with his view of the monuments. There was no scrim on the back side for his viewing enjoyment, just the black panels. He protested, but in the end, the Secret Service got its wish.

Whenever the President went back inside, the agents would fold up the panels, accordion style, and remove them so tourists could get their pictures of the southern face of the White House sans panels. The Secret Service would only relax when the President's request for fresh air was complete and he was safely inside the fortress that is the White House.

The President and Cogdon sat in two lounge chairs safely behind the bulletproof panels. There they could talk in relative peace – as much peace as can be had with the endless cacophony of police sirens with bigwigs being ferried around Washington or the planes landing and taking off at Reagan National to the southwest. The early September evening brought seventy degrees and clear skies, although a cold front was on its way and expected to drop the temperature into the lower forties by early evening. Tornadoes had touched down in the Midwest earlier in the day and severe thunderstorm watches were in effect for much of the Virginia and Maryland areas. High winds, hail, and deadly cloud-to-ground lightning were forecasted for the better part of the evening. The President and Cogdon thought they had better get their last taste of summer before fall settled in for good.

The two were in relatively good moods considering the state of events in recent days. America had breathed a much-needed sigh of relief after the two alleged terrorists were arrested in Fairfax. Plus, Art Brennan would not be causing any more havoc for the time being as he waited for his pretrial proceedings to take place. Although Director Stubblefield said there could be more terrorist snipers lying in wait, the President felt confident that the FBI would find them and bring them to justice. Since the shootings had stopped, the American people were slowly beginning to get back to their daily lives.

"What are you working on?" the President asked after finishing his read of the FBI report on the jihadist that was arrested and the other that committed suicide.

Cogdon sat scribbling notes down on a yellow legal pad, his pocket Constitution on the small table next to him. "I'm jotting down some notes for your speech in Philadelphia in a couple of weeks."

"The Celebration of the Constitution?" the President asked. It had slipped his mind.

"Yeah. I think you should make mention of Leviticus 25:10 in your speech?"

"Why's that?"

Cogdon stopped his writing. "It's on the Liberty Bell."

"Really?"

Cogdon picked up his notes. "Leviticus, chapter 25, verse 10 states in part, '*Proclaim liberty throughout the land, unto all its inhabitants thereof.*' It's right there on the Bell."

The President was surprised. "I did not know that."

"We should probably make a stop at Independence Hall," Cogdon said, the gears in his historical mind starting to churn. "Did you know the body of Abraham Lincoln was placed in the Assembly Room of Independence Hall?" Cogdon fashioned himself a Lincoln scholar, and the two native Indianans took great pride in the Great Emancipator's early years in their home state. "They had the Liberty Bell placed near his head so the mourners could see it as they passed by the casket."

"I didn't know that either."

While Cogdon went back to scribbling, the President stopped to look at his bald rumpled chief of staff. They had been together so long that the President sometimes forgot how brilliant Cogdon was politically and historically.

"I don't know what I would do without you Wiley Cogdon," the President said with high praise, putting the report on the table next to him.

"I do what I can," Cogdon responded, like his brilliance came naturally to him.

"Have you ever thought about what you want to do after we're finished here at the White House?"

Cogdon stopped his writing, realizing the President was in the mood for conversation, and put pen and legal pad on the table. He had given quite a bit of thought to what he might do when the Schumacher Administration came to a close. Of course, there was still a second-term election to win first. Thereafter, there was the consulting business he would start that would help conservative candidates all across the fruited plain win election after election. He could parlay that into a position as a Fox News contributor and take to the airwaves every week and sell his message. Then, of course, there would be the required memoir of his role in the Schumacher Administration. He imagined a 700-page tome where he would reminisce about how he laid waste to the modern Democratic Party. It would be a glorious read, he told himself.

"What are you going to do with all the money you're going to make from working for me?" the President asked with a laugh, wondering if he would get a cut of the millions.

Cogdon had thought that through as well. It had been in the back of his mind for some time now. "I am going to buy a boat," he said seriously.

"A boat!?" the President blurted out. He could hardly believe it. "You're an Indiana farm boy like me. What are you going to do paddle up and down the Wabash?"

Cogdon shook his head and smiled. It was obvious he had big dreams for his "retirement." "I mean a big boat. A yacht where I can travel the seas in peace and quiet."

The President nodded at the mental picture. "I can see you behind the wheel with your captain's hat on."

Cogdon smiled. He liked that picture.

"You ought to title your book 'At the Helm.'"

Cogdon grabbed his legal pad and wrote it down. He liked that title.

The President raised his arms over his head. He was getting tired. They could hear the wind starting to pick up as it rustled the leaves of the trees on the South Lawn. It wouldn't be too much longer before the line of storms came through to bring a blast of cold air into the region. The President thought they had better discuss one last serious matter before he and Cogdon called it a night.

"Back to the present day," the President said. "I got a call just before dinner from the Vice President. I think she's looking for a good time to exit her post."

Vice President Brenda Jackson was seventy-two years old and had been a steady number two in the Schumacher White House. She was an expert in foreign relations and had represented the country well on her trips overseas.

But she had no desire to be President. If President Schumacher won reelection and served another four years, she would be pushing eighty. Plus, her husband of forty years had just been diagnosed with Alzheimer's and the prognosis for that disease was never good. She had been flying with her husband across the country to see specialists and they all told her the harsh reality that awaited her. She came to the conclusion that she wanted to spend the rest of her husband's days at his side. And being the person one heartbeat away from the Presidency was too much of a responsibility to also act as a competent caregiver. She hoped the President would allow her to resign at a time he thought best for him, the Schumacher Administration, and the country.

The President thanked her for her selfless concern and told her she should spend as much time with her husband as possible. The Administration would be fine, and he knew he could always call her with any questions he might have. The Vice President said she would be available to offer her advice as often as he wanted it.

Now the question became. Who would they get to replace her?

Cogdon had thrown off his captain's hat and put his political one firmly atop his bald head. These were the type of decisions that he was going to get paid big bucks to recount the insights and answers he provided to the President.

After sufficient contemplation, Cogdon gave his thoughts. "Well, your poll numbers are so favorable right now that we don't even have to look at a possible candidate's home state in search of votes. You can pick just about whomever you want. You might be the first President since James Monroe to not even have a reelection opponent so it probably doesn't make much difference who you pick in terms of winning."

It was something Cogdon had mentioned to the President recently, although, in reality, the Democrats would surely put up a sacrificial lamb like McGovern or Mondale or some other token over-the-hill sad sack with the real hope of waiting for President Schumacher to finish his second term and then go with their top-tier candidate.

"So, putting politics aside, you really have to decide who is the best person to take over the job if, God forbid, something happens to you during your term, and, who would be the right person to run for election and succeed you as President."

The President nodded. He had given his successor some thought. He knew Vice President Jackson did not want to be President when she agreed to her current position. So, the President had run names through his mind from time to time. And he always came back to one person. "I think you and I both know who it should be."

Cogdon nodded. "Mr. President, other than you, there is no one right now who Americans trust to lead this country more than Ty Stubblefield. The question then becomes, will he do it?"

The President smiled. That was the question indeed. Director Stubblefield had always said he wanted no part of politics, although he readily agreed with President Schumacher's conservative agenda. But, America didn't need a politician in the White House. The country needed a leader. One who wasn't afraid to take it to the enemy if it meant keeping Americans safe. And Ty Stubblefield was the perfect man for the job.

"I'll think he'll come around once I appeal to his inner patriot."

The discussion was interrupted by a rumble of thunder in the distance.

The President threw his legs off the lounge chair and looked over at Cogdon. "We probably better get inside so the boys can take cover and hunker down for the night," he said, pointing to the Secret Service agents standing guard. "I'll mention it to him the next time we have a private moment. If he tries to say he's not interested, I'll twist his arm a little and tell him it was all your idea."

"Sounds good," Cogdon said. "I'll start thinking about a possible press conference if and when that time comes."

The two men got up from their chairs and prepared to head back inside, the wind starting to whip around the balcony.

"I'll see you tomorrow," the President said as the door to the balcony opened.

Cogdon followed him in. His mind was already working. As they went their separate ways, Cogdon offered one last statement. "Good night, Mr. President."

"Shadow is in the Crown," Special Agent Mac Clark said into his microphone. The call was music to the ears of the Secret Service agents on duty. They could take it down one notch. The President was secure for the night.

"Crap," Cogdon said to himself as he waited on the elevator with his Secret Service agent. He reached into his back pocket and felt nothing but his wallet. "I forgot my Constitution." He couldn't leave without it.

Cogdon retraced his steps and headed back onto the balcony where three agents were folding up the bulletproof screens to get them inside before the storm. A flash of lightning lit up the western sky.

Since the President was safely inside, the Secret Service agents covering the gate at the end of the South Lawn began to scurry for cover and return to their positions inside the perimeter and at the guard houses. No camera-toting tourists were going to be taking pictures any time soon with a downpour on the way.

To the south across the Ellipse, a gray and black El Camino pulled to a quick stop. Then the tailgate was lowered, and the sniper manning the gun exhaled before pulling the trigger.

Ten seconds later, the Secret Service command post began receiving the first emergency transmissions.

"Shots fired. We have shots fired."

CHAPTER 21

The White House – Washington, D.C.

"Sir, we need to get you to the bunker," Agent Clark said to the President, grabbing him by the triceps of his right arm. The President had been five steps from his bedroom door when Agent Clark stopped him in his tracks. There was a sense of urgency behind Clark's statement, and he never made the demand unless there was a problem. And the information coming from the Secret Service command post indicated there was indeed a major problem on the White House grounds. "There have been shots fired on the South Lawn."

Four other agents converged on the President and their pace quickened as they hurriedly escorted him to the bunker. The First Lady's security detail was already on their way with her from the residence. The President did as he was told, they didn't need to carry him, but the grip from Agent Clark became tighter and the pace soon became a quick trot.

The President didn't know what to make of the situation. There had been plenty of cranks who had tried to shoot up the White House over the years. His mind flashed to the sniper shootings and wondered if the terrorists had scurried out of their hole in the ground to strike again.

With the First Lady safe at his side, the President told her he didn't know what was happening outside. They could hear the rumble of thunder even that far beneath the earth. The President turned to Agent Clark. "Mac, get Wiley down here. We'll probably have to work on a statement. As soon as we know what the hell is going on."

The eyes of Agent Clark were getting wider by the second and quick glances were exchanged by him and the other agents near the bunker doors. The distress calls into Clark's earpiece were so loud the President could faintly hear the commotion just standing next to him.

"Mac, did you hear me?" the President asked. "Get Wiley down here."

Agent Clark spoke into his radio. "Horsepower, Clark, can you give me a sit rep on Coyote?"

Why did he need a report on Coyote? the President wondered. Just pick him up and get him downstairs. But it was more frantic calls into Agent Clark's ear. The President could see the concern on the man's face.

"What's going on, Mac?"

"Sir, we have problem," Agent Clark said in a dead serious tone. "Mr. Cogdon has been hit."

The President could feel the blood rush out of his face. "Hit!? What in the hell are you talking about? He wasn't out on the South Lawn. Where is he?"

"Sir, Coyote went back onto the balcony to retrieve something and that's when the shots were fired."

The President looked at the door and made a break for it only to be stopped by Agent Clark. "No, sir. We can't let you go out there."

Three stories above the bunker, chaos had broken out on the White House grounds.

"Horsepower, Roberts! We need an ambulance! Get someone from the medical office up here right now!"

In the pouring rain, an army of Secret Service agents appeared out of nowhere and fanned out across the grounds. Marksmen returned to their positions on the roof and the counter-assault team in their black battle dress uniforms and automatic weapons prepared for war.

"Horsepower, Roberts! We need that ambulance!" Agent Roberts and ten other agents descended on the Truman Balcony where Wiley Cogdon lie face down next to the lounge chair. "Get prepared for departure to the hospital!"

"Roger that, the call has been made." The Secret Service command post had picked up the red phone with the direct line to George Washington Medical Center and told the emergency room to expect a gunshot victim to be arriving in a matter of minutes.

Sirens filled the air of Washington, D.C., and two police helicopters braved the conditions and took to the sky to searching the area south of the White House. Fully lit police cars screeched to stops at intersections in preparation for the ambulance that would be making the short drive from the Executive Mansion up Pennsylvania Avenue to the GW Medical Center.

"Mac, you let me out of this bunker right now!" the President yelled, a pointed finger in his agent's face.

"Mr. President, I can't let you do that. It's too dangerous. We don't know what's going on."

The President would have none of it. He was the "most powerful man in the world" and he wasn't taking no for an answer. "I am going up there! And if you want to fight me then let's have at it! I have to get up there!"

The President strong armed Agent Clark out of the way, who thought it best not to tackle the President of the United States. He made the call. "Horsepower, Clark, Shadow is on the way up."

Four agents led the way followed by the President and Agent Clark and then four more agents pulling up the rear. Behind every door they opened were still more security agents with increasing amounts of heavy weaponry.

"Where is he?" the President asked.

"On the balcony, sir."

Once the President and his security detail got to the second floor, four agents and two EMTs were wheeling the stretcher toward the elevator. The President rushed to the side of his chief of staff.

"Oh God!" he cried out. He couldn't believe what he was seeing. "Wiley! I'm right here!" The President reached out his hand to touch the arm of his chief of staff but there was no response. "Oh God!"

With the elevator full of those helping with Cogdon, the President ran down the stairs with his security detail. "Oh God!" Yelling could be heard on every floor. The President caught up to the stretcher on the ground floor as Wiley was being wheeled to the waiting ambulance.

"Sir, I can't let you go out there!" Agent Clark yelled, grabbing the President by the arm. "It's too dangerous!"

"I'm going to the hospital whether you like it or not! I can either go in the ambulance or you can get the limo but I'm going!"

The President hurried behind the agents with Wiley and helped push the stretcher on the north side of the White House.

"Horsepower, Clark. I need a full package to transport Shadow to GW. Copy?"

The command post issued orders as fast as the requests came in. "Roger that."

The President's limousine roared out of the underground garage along with a decoy and four Suburbans with the counter-assault teams locked and loaded for battle. Shouting could be heard across the North

Lawn as the uniformed officers prepared to open the northwest gate.

"Make sure we secure GW," Agent Clark said into his radio, walking the President toward the limo. "And keep the press back."

"Roger that. We'll send more agents in that direction."

By this time, the reporters still in the White House that evening had taken to the airwaves as the cameras rolled.

"We have breaking news tonight from the White House," the anchor said, looking at the screen and desperately trying to decipher what was being yelled into her ear. "Let's go live to Howard Carson who is at the White House this evening. Howard, what can you tell us?"

With an umbrella trying mightily to keep the driving rain from pounding him in the face, the reporter didn't even look at his notes because he hadn't had time to take any. "I can tell you that there has been a shooting at the White House here tonight. It occurred no more than ten minutes ago. Apparently shots were fired from somewhere beyond the South Lawn. I can tell you the President of the United States has not been hit. I repeat, the President was inside at the time and was not hit. However, I must say it is absolute chaos out here. Someone was apparently hit by one of the bullets, I'm not sure who, maybe a security agent, and as you can see behind me that person is being taken out of the White House by stretcher." The camera then zoomed in to see the grim face of the President. "I can see," the reporter said, squinting through the rain, "I can see the President!" he exclaimed, startled at the sight and then pointing across the way. "The President is right there."

The screen then went blank as a Secret Service agent pulled the plug on the live camera shot. The Secret Service uniformed officers manning the guardhouse dropped the bollards into the ground and opened the gate. Three police squad cars blasted their sirens and led the way for the ambulance and the President's motorcade.

It only took three minutes for the ambulance to reach the George Washington Medical Center, the same hospital where President Reagan was taken after he was shot in 1981. The ambulance doors flew open and the emergency room staff prepared to meet their patient. The President of the United States soon joined them as he helped push the stretcher to the emergency room.

He tried not to look because he knew it was bad. His hands were shaking, and he had to force himself not to let the tears flow. Wiley's shirt was gone and there was a sheet covering the lower half of his body.

The top of his head was wrapped in a white towel that had turned a blood red and the EMT was squeezing the bag to help him breathe through the tube in his throat. The stretcher made it to the emergency room where the medical staff was ready for action.

"Sir," Agent Clark said softly and lightly grabbing the President's arm. He was finally able to stop him. "Why don't we just let them get to work."

The security detail closed off the entire emergency room and kept the President in the next bay. With the curtains pulled, the President couldn't hold back his tears any longer. He choked them back as best he could, but Agent Clark gave him the go ahead and they fell like the rain that was pelting D.C. at that hour.

The First Lady arrived and the President's red eyes told her the news wasn't good. They hugged and wept together. Director Stubblefield rushed in after hearing the news alerts. The President's shake of the head told him there was nothing he could do. Stubblefield left immediately to start the manhunt.

Once the word got out, the press descended on the hospital and took up their positions across the street. The hospital was surrounded by police cars and Secret Service vehicles. Armed agents circled the property and no one was getting inside.

With fresh pictures coming to the newsroom, the anchor reestablished contact with her correspondent on the scene. "Howard, what's the latest?"

Howard Carson had sprinted off the grounds of the White House. Given the chaos, he decided against trying to find his car and simply ran like mad to get to the hospital where a satellite truck had finally made it to the scene. The veteran correspondent was still sucking wind, and with no umbrella, the water dripped off the ball cap his cameraman had given him. He had been able to piece together a few facts.

"I can tell you that at approximately 7:30 p.m. this evening, the President's chief of staff, William Cogdon, was shot once in the head by an unknown gunman while he was on the Truman Balcony on the south side of the White House. As you know, the White House has been the target of shootings over the years, including in 1994, when at least 29 shots were fired on the north side by a gunman, and then again in 2011, when two bullets hit the south side and cracked one of the windows. Like I said, the President's chief of staff was hit, but it is not clear whether he was the intended target. The President was inside the White House at the time. Mr. Cogdon has been rushed to the hospital behind me, and I can tell you the President of the United States arrived via motorcade at approximately the same time. The First Lady has now joined him at the hospital."

The anchor at the news desk tried to interrupt him but Carson stopped her in mid-sentence. "I have just been passed a note from the Associated Press." He turned to a man off camera. "Has this been confirmed?" he asked. The answer was in the affirmative. Carson took a breath. "Mary, we have just received word from the medical staff at George Washington Medical Center. Mr. Cogdon, William Cogdon, the President's chief of staff, has died as a result of his injuries."

He then repeated the message for those who might have just joined in while the pictures on the screen showed the hospital lit up in red and blue flashing lights in the background.

"It is believed to be the first attempt on the life of a Cabinet-level member since April 1865 when Secretary of State William Seward was stabbed by Lewis Powell on the night of President Lincoln's assassination. I can tell you there are a lot of somber faces here, Mary, as we watch members of the President's staff coming in and out of the hospital. You can see the President's spokesperson there, Kimberly Carmi," he said, looking over his shoulder as the camera zoomed in toward the hospital door. "I have also seen Secretary of Defense William Javits walk into the hospital. We do not expect to hear from the President tonight. Obviously, a difficult time for him. Mr. Cogdon was a trusted adviser that the President counted on since their days in Indiana."

Carson gave a similar report at the top of the hour but gave more details on Cogdon's background and his years with the President.

"William Cogdon was 64 years old."

Silver Creek, Indiana

It took nearly three weeks for the body of Abraham Lincoln to make its way from Washington, D.C., with stops in cities like Baltimore, Philadelphia, New York City, Cleveland, Indianapolis, and Chicago, to his final resting place in Springfield, Illinois. Wiley Cogdon would make his final trip home from the nation's capital in less than three hours.

Air Force One banked to the southwest before it dipped its wings over the Indianapolis Motor Speedway, a place cherished by all Hoosiers, including Wiley Cogdon. He had attended forty races during his years, half of them with Anthony Schumacher. Once the President's plane landed in Indianapolis, Cogdon's flag-draped coffin was loaded into a hearse and the slow drive home began.

The hearse, preceded by three motorcycles from the Indianapolis Police Department, and followed by the President's motorcade, took a right on Crawfordsville Road and made its way to 16th and Georgetown in Speedway, Indiana, where thousands had gathered in silence, American flags in one hand and tissues in the other. Pursuant to the special request of the President of the United States, the hearse took a left and down into the tunnel before proceeding to the two-and-a-half mile oval for a final lap for William Cogdon. The Speedway stood silent, save for a lone member of the Gordon Pipers offering a few verses of *Amazing Grace*, as the hearse and the motorcade made its way down the main straightaway and crossed the famed yard of bricks, a lone checkered flag hanging from the starter's stand.

Once outside the Speedway grounds, the motorcade made the hour-long ride west on Interstate 74, where overpasses were crowded with mourners wishing one of their favorite sons goodbye. Approaching the small western central Indiana town of Silver Creek, the crowds grew larger. The American flags were more prevalent and some in the crowd saluted the casket with one hand while holding aloft their own pocket Constitution in the other. The hearse passed by Maple Ridge Farms, where Cogdon stopped every time he came back for the homemade apple pie.

The funeral was held at St. John's Lutheran Church in Silver Creek and was attended by Cabinet members, members of both the House and the Senate, the Governor of Indiana, and a myriad of others who loved and respected William Cogdon. The President sat in the first row next to the First Lady and their three children, all of whom grew up with "Uncle Wiley" being a part of their family. Cogdon had no other family – no brothers or sisters, no kids of his own – just the Schumachers. Julia Ward Howe's *Battle Hymn*, Cogdon's favorite, filled the church followed by the Bible readings and personal remembrances of the President's chief of staff.

After the service, the hearse brought William Cogdon through the streets of Silver Creek for the final time. There was the Cogdon &

Schumacher law office where the two had once practiced law, the Donut Palace where Cogdon arranged town-hall meetings for Congressman Schumacher, and then Silver Creek High School where people voted Cogdon's boss into the White House.

At the Lutheran Cemetery, the flag-draped casket was carried by President Schumacher; Floyd Revson, the third member of the President's "Hoosier Cabinet," as Wiley liked to say; Governor Pence; Secretary of Defense William Javits; Speaker of the House Carlton Spencer, and FBI Director Ty Stubblefield.

The President took his seat with his family in front of the grave. The warm Indiana summer breezes blew some of the leaves off the trees. The President just stared at the flag. The man they would bury had been a mentor, a political guru, and the brains behind his campaigns for Congress and the Presidency. He had believed in Anthony J. Schumacher and spent the second half of his life working to take that man to greater heights for the good of the United States. In the process, he had subjected himself to ridicule for his political ideology, embarrassment for his personal troubles, and even scorn by some for his unwavering belief in the greatness of America.

The President still could not believe he had lost him.

The nineteen gun salute from the howitzers boomed throughout the Wabash River valley. The benediction asked the Lord to keep William Cogdon close and to watch over those who mourned his loss.

"Firing party!" the Marine Commandant ordered. "Fire three volleys!"

"Ready. . . Aim. . . Fire," he ordered. The crackles that followed in the three-volley salute echoed through the trees.

"Ready. . . Aim. . . Fire."

President Schumacher shook with the second round of shots. He would have to move on without his most-trusted political adviser. He could not imagine going forward without Cogdon's brilliant political mind showing him the pros and cons of every situation, instructing him on the finer points of the Constitution, and endlessly feeding him with interesting tidbits of American history.

"Ready. . . Aim. . . Fire."

The military honor guard folded the American flag and presented it to the First Lady, with tears streaming down her face. The President reached to grab hold of her arm. The entire family was crying. The tears continued to flow as the soloist closed the ceremony with Cogdon's other favorite song – a soulful rendition fondly remembering the view of the candlelight through the sycamore trees, the fragrant new mown hay in those local fields he used to roam, and the tranquil moonlight on his beloved Wabash River.

As he was laid to eternal rest, William "Wiley" Cogdon was back home again in Indiana.

CHAPTER 22

Baltimore, Maryland

A nervous Omar Faran paced the floor of the room at the Motel 6 – back and forth he went across the worn carpet biting his nails and worrying up a storm. He peeked out from behind the curtain on every other pass, wondering where his comrades were or if they would ever return. He feared they would be discovered by the police and either arrested or killed. If so, it wouldn't be much longer before the long arm of the law came knocking on room 18.

Faran and the sniper Ahmed Yassar had arrived in Baltimore two days after the shooting of Wiley Cogdon at the White House. The El Camino was no more. It had been stripped of any identifying marks and hid in a storage unit outside of Arlington, Virginia. They would not be going back for it. Whenever in the future the rent wasn't paid, those looking for a bargain at auction would find little more than a rusted hunk of metal and bald tires. The El Camino had done its job though. It had been the vehicle for terrorist jihad and participated in the killing of six Americans.

And the terrorists and their transportation had not been discovered.

Two knocks hit the door and Faran froze in his tracks. He could feel his heart pounding in his chest, the sweat stains in the armpits of his shirt felt like a Brazilian rain forest. *This could be the end*, he thought to himself. There was no back door, no rear window to jump through and make one last dash to save himself. Two more knocks and he flinched in his frozen state. He took a deep breath and hurried to the door. Peeking through the peephole caused him to relax and exhale. He took off the chain, turned the lock, and opened the door.

His brothers had returned safe and sound.

A much relieved Faran whispered, "I was worried you were the cops."

Yassar and Hakim al-Rashid said nothing as they walked inside the room. Faran placed the "Do Not Disturb" sign on the outside handle and closed the door behind them. Yassar carried a plastic bag full of chips, granola bars, and cookies. His other hand held a twelve-pack of bottled water. Al-Rashid carried similar provisions – sustenance to get through the next few days until the final plan could be put into place. They had taken a borrowed Toyota Corolla to the local Wal-Mart to stock up on provisions. The white van in their fleet met the same end as the El Camino. Once Ramadi and Jahdari had been stopped by the Virginia police in their van, it was time for Plan B as to the other team's mode of transportation.

Yassar placed the snacks and the water on the desk in the corner. He then fished out the two newspapers he had picked up at the gas station. It was time to review his handiwork. Five days had passed since the Cogdon assassination, and the coverage still covered multiple pages of the D.C. area as well as national papers. Faran had calmly driven the El Camino out of D.C. on the night of the shooting. He thought Yassar was going to take a few potshots at the White House and they would be on their way. Had he known instantly that the President's right-hand man had been killed, he probably would have panicked, maybe broken the speed limit resulting in their capture. But they made it to Arlington as the manhunt went on behind them. They spent the next three nights at the home of a local Muslim cleric before driving north to Baltimore to meet up with al-Rashid and wait for further instructions.

Yassar sat on the bed and scanned the stories – smiling with pride on the inside all the while. He had taken down a high-ranking official of the United States Government with one shot. The deadly feat would no doubt place him high on the list of celebrated terrorist killers. His countrymen had already taken to the streets to celebrate. He knew his fellow jihadists would praise his name for all eternity.

Faran could not help but peek over his shoulder and glance at the articles. "I still cannot believe you made that shot," he said, gushing at the sniper's skill.

The story included a small-box diagram of the South Lawn of the White House and the Ellipse farther to the south. A solid black line extended from a vehicle icon near the corner of Constitution Avenue and Seventeenth Street to the spot on the Truman Balcony where Cogdon was hit. It was a one-in-a-million shot. Another dashed line showed the path of a shot that hit to the right of the Truman Balcony and lodged in one of the bulletproof windows.

Yassar traced his finger along the solid black line. Inside, he knew he was good, but he was a true believer and could not outwardly take full credit. "I did not make the shot," he said quietly. "Allah made it for me."

The articles pointed out that the killers were still on the loose, still lurking in the shadows and preparing to strike again. The authorities were looking for a dark-colored truck with a bed and/or a white van, both of which were seen in the area at the time of the shooting. The torrential downpour that occurred after Cogdon was shot hindered the view of the security cameras in and around the D.C. area. A couple of vehicles had been stopped within the first thirty minutes after the shooting but no suspects were found. The police had no other leads.

Seated on the other bed, al-Rashid was perusing the other papers with a smile on his face. The U.S. Government was in disarray. Their law-enforcement authorities were looking for a needle in a haystack. The President had not even been heard from since the shooting – the only public appearance he made was at Cogdon's funeral. The American people were also in hiding, afraid to even step outside their homes given that one of their own had been killed outside their country's heavily guarded fortress known as the White House.

"Allah is great," al-Rashid said softly to those in the room while he admired Yassar's lethal handiwork.

The only downer for the group had been the loss of Ramadi and Jahdari. Page three of each paper had passport photos of their sinister-looking faces – defiant poses with their dark steely eyes doing little to mask the jihad in their angry minds – along with the histories of the two men. Jahdari was a great loss to the cause – he had a terrorist resume that most jihadists could only dream of. Also known as Yaman al-Sahaf, he had won great praise for his killing of American soldiers. Now, his FBI Most Wanted picture had a red line with the word "Dead" slashed across his face.

While upset with the death of Jahdari, al-Rashid was even more worried about the Americans' capture of Ramadi. Al-Rashid had been warned on more than one occasion about the careless Ramadi and his rampant drinking and womanizing off-hours, but he could not babysit the man every second of the day. Now, the man's horny urges could come back to haunt them. Al-Rashid just knew the Americans would do everything in their power to get Ramadi to talk.

And he had a feeling that the weak-minded Ramadi would not put up much resistance.

Without a paper to read himself, Faran took to pacing the floor again. He pulled back the curtain ever so slightly and eyed the parking lot outside. The Corolla was still there. The previous night's occupants of the motel had mostly checked out and hit the road. He looked at his watch and it read 10:30 a.m. He knew they couldn't stay here much longer. They had to get moving.

Faran turned away from the window. "What do we do next?" he asked the others. The youngest of the jihadists, Faran's nerves frayed quickly. Over the last five days, he fought a constant urge to vomit. He was a committed terrorist, and he had no fear of dying for the cause, but he wanted to martyr himself on his own schedule, not at the hands of a SWAT team surprising them in the night or the state police on the side of the road. "Hakim?" he asked, now directing his question.

Al-Rashid folded up his paper and threw it over on the bed occupied by Yassar. "We will leave in one hour," he said, heading for the pot of coffee Yassar had made earlier that morning.

The men didn't need to check out. The room had been paid for by a Muslim couple whom al-Rashid had befriended as part of his master plan. He told them little, only saying he might need a favor or two in the near future. He instructed them not to ask questions, and they eagerly complied. They were to return tomorrow and turn in the keys. If anyone asked, they were painting their house and wanted to escape the fumes. And, if asked, they were to claim they had no knowledge of a man named Hakim al-Rashid. Never heard of him. Wouldn't recognize him if he walked right in front of them.

Al-Rashid had shaved his head and ditched his contacts. The glasses were new; he had never worn them before the last three days. Given the arrest of Art Brennan, he knew the FBI probably had photos of him and he needed to change his appearance. Of the three in the room, he was most likely the one with pictures being circulated around police departments, train stations, and airports up and down the eastern seaboard.

He took a sip of coffee and turned on his cell phone. He logged into the e-mail account he shared with Mahmud Basra. The German engineer was hiding in France after jumping the train after he left Munich. Now aware of the news from the United States, he heaped praise on his fellow jihadists and congratulated them on their successful killings. He referred to them by their numbers, no names, and he intentionally left out the number five (Ramadi's number) because of the man's traitorous failures. The coded instructions ended with a salutation of Allah's greatness. After reading the entire e-mail, he logged off and put down his phone. He looked at both Yassar and Faran.

"We are to head to Philadelphia," he told them.

Yassar sat up on the bed, a perplexed look on his face. "Not back to D.C.?" he wondered. He had been wanting to go back so he could bring the nation's capital to a standstill with his sniper rifle. He knew he could do it, and the havoc he could cause would be enormous.

"No," al-Rashid said. "We are not going back to Washington."

"But that is where the President is," Yassar shot back. That was the target he wanted. He suddenly became full of himself and his skill, the cockiness apparent in his voice. "I can take down the President with one shot."

Al-Rashid shook his head back and forth. He had to restrain himself from lecturing Yassar. He would have expected such foolish talk from Faran but not the trained sniper seated in front of him. "We cannot go back to Washington. It is too dangerous. The authorities will be looking for us. They practically have the whole city locked down. We might as well walk into the local police station and give ourselves up."

"But I can bring down the infidels by getting the President!" Yassar yelled.

"Be quiet!" al-Rashid shot back. He looked toward the walls and the door, hoping no other guests heard the outburst. "We are not going back there," he said calmly. "Mahmud wants us to go to Philadelphia. There we are to meet with a man who will help us with the next phase of jihad."

"There we will meet Allah?" Faran asked. He had taken to biting his nails again. He didn't like it when his comrades fought. He just wanted everyone to get along so they could end it as soon as possible on their own terms.

"Yes. The end is near."

CHAPTER 23

The White House – Washington, D.C.

President Schumacher returned to the White House the day after Cogdon's funeral in Silver Creek and a dark gloomy pall hung over the Executive Mansion. Mourners stood silently outside the gate on the north side – the candles they held illuminating their somber faces. A collection of Wile E. Coyote stuffed animals perched on the fence line grew by the day.

The President obviously took the death hard, mentally and physically. He had already lost ten pounds. He had started pacing the floors of the White House in the early mornings or late at night. He would go down to the first floor and slowly walk from the State Dining Room down the Cross Hall to the East Room and back through the Green, Blue, and Red Rooms in a giant rectangle. The Secret Service agents standing guard would see him with his hands clasped behind his back, his head down, tears cascading down his cheeks. Lap after lap he would shake his head, mumble something to himself, and then walk some more. The White House usher secretly worried the President was going to wear a hole in the carpet. The most laps he had ever done was fifty and the only reason he didn't complete any more was he nearly collapsed from exhaustion – the fitful nights of sleep, the lack of all desire to eat, and the loss of his dear friend were taking their toll on the most powerful man in the world.

The mornings when he walked into the Oval Office were the hardest times. He continued to think it was all just a bad dream, a nightmare that would end once he awoke. He kept thinking he would make the turn off the Colonnade and into the Oval Office to find Wiley Cogdon lounging on the couch reading the Constitution and waiting to start the day.

Now when he entered, the silent Oval Office was empty.

The President took his seat behind his desk and sat in the quiet stillness. He had to get back to work. The country needed him. His press secretary had been manning the microphone for the past several days telling the American people about the investigation as well as the President's plans going forward. Defense Secretary Javits and Homeland Security Director Michaelson had also taken a hands-on role, going on the news shows to let everyone know what the Schumacher Administration was doing to catch the killers.

But the Washington whispers were slowly beginning to be heard. The politicians in the capital rarely took time off to grieve. It wasn't in their nature. Campaigns and fundraisers were matters of constant focus, and any day not spent on politics was a day wasted in their minds. So too with the talking heads and print reporters. The left-wing TV media started a clock counting the hours and minutes since President Schumacher was last seen in public – it ticked away in the bottom right-hand corner, a supposed reminder of the President's failure of leadership. Another graphic asked where the Vice President was. One particular blogger said the President was a coward and was probably hiding under his desk. The first editorial showed up lecturing the President on his next course of action.

The Dems weren't much better.

Democratic Party leaders on Capitol Hill took to the airwaves and expressed condolences to the President and offered their full support. But they didn't sound very convincing. None of them liked Cogdon, most of them hated the man, although they didn't say it outwardly. For once however, Congresswoman Robinson was noticeably silent. A few years back, during a particularly contentious fight over reducing welfare and food stamps, she lit into the White House and said she thought William Cogdon, whom she considered to be the brains behind the racist and bigoted idea, would be shot dead in the streets if he ever showed his face in Detroit. Her office refused to comment on the shooting. It was rumored she was hiding somewhere in the Motor City.

But there was a plot afoot. The Democrats had heard it through the rumor mill that Vice President Jackson was on her way out of the Administration to spend more time with her ailing husband. They thought now was the best time to go after President Schumacher. A memo circulated that representatives and senators should get on TV and put doubts in the public's mind about the President's state of mind given that his chief of staff had been killed. Once the campaign to paint President Schumacher as dangerous, half-cocked, and unstable was in full bloom, they would demand that the loose cannon President relinquish control and hand over the reins to Vice President Jackson. Without her heart and mind in it, the public would see the Republicans in the White House needed to be replaced. Otherwise, the President's thirst for revenge would put America in harm's way.

Cogdon would have snuffed out the plan and attacked it before it even developed legs. Two Republican senators caught wind of the plot. Normally, they would have contacted Cogdon. Instead, they told Director Stubblefield. He passed on the information to the President late the previous evening. Once informed about the shenanigans, the fire came back into the President's belly. He took to fast walking the floors again, now fully ticked off. He knew ol' Wiley would have stomped around and cursed and yelled to high heaven. And then he would act. And that's what the President decided to do.

It was time for President Schumacher to take back the helm.

Director Stubblefield decided he would make sure to get to the White House a little earlier than usual, at least a half hour before the morning national security meeting, so he could gauge the President's mood. He knew the man needed to make decisions to keep his mind occupied. Keeping him up to speed on every detail of the investigation would help him get through this dark time.

Stubblefield walked in to the office of the President's secretary and looked through the open door to the Oval Office. The President was seated in his chair behind his desk, alone with his thoughts, as he looked out the windows with the morning sun filtering in. He and Cogdon always liked this time of the morning – peaceful, the new day dawning. Stubblefield knocked softly on the door.

The President turned his head. "Ty, come on in." He swivelled his chair around and pointed to the chair next to his desk. "Have a seat. What do I need to know?"

The big man took a seat and placed his briefcase next to him. Stubblefield thought about asking the President how he was doing but didn't. The redness in the President's eyes was gone, and he was slowly rocking in his chair. He was ready to get to work.

"I thought I would let you know where we are with the investigation."

"Okay."

"We haven't been able to get any information out of Abdel Ramadi, the guy the Virginia State Police caught last week. He is currently being held at the Navy brig in South Carolina. We might need to talk to the Attorney General about declaring Ramadi an enemy combatant."

"Okay, I can do that," the President said, opening up his leather bound pad of paper and jotting down his first notes of the day. "I can transfer him to Gitmo if you want me to do."

Stubblefield nodded. "We have received the ballistics report on the rifle found in the van Ramadi was driving. It was the rifle his cohort used to commit suicide. Our tests have confirmed it was the rifle used in the killing of Joaquin Salazar in Alexandria."

"Okay."

That was all Stubblefield had on that investigation. Obviously, they were still hunting the other killers still on the loose. The Director took a breath, the next subject being a bit more delicate. "Now, sir, about the investigation on Wiley." He stopped to see if the President wanted him to continue.

The President saw the concern. "Go ahead. I want to hear it."

Director Stubblefield showed him the evidence that they had – the diagrams showing the trajectory and where the shots originated. "Sir, the shots came from the southwest beyond the Ellipse," he said, pausing again. "I don't mean to sound flippant about this, Mr. President. But we think the shooter just got lucky. It is highly doubtful he could have targeted Wiley since he wasn't on the Balcony very long at all. The sniper might have picked the first person he could put in the crosshairs. Or he could have just taken a shot in the general vicinity of the Balcony and Wiley was in the wrong place at the wrong time. The second shot was some twenty feet to the right. So we think the shooter fired once, took a second shot, and then got the hell out of there."

"Wrong place at the wrong time?" the President asked, sighing.

The Director nodded. "Yes, sir. I'm afraid so."

The silence of the Oval Office was interrupted by a knock at the door. The President's secretary reminded him the national security meeting was going to start in ten minutes. The President thanked her and began to gather his notes.

"I guess we better head down there," the President said.

Director Stubblefield stood up and grabbed his briefcase. He had one more thing though. "Mr. President," he said, reaching into his suit coat, "I wanted to make sure you had this." He pulled out a pocket Constitution. It was Wiley Cogdon's.

The President took the battered copy, bloodstains splattered on the cover. He flipped through the pages – Cogdon's notes filling the margins, dog ears curling the corner of numerous pages. He closed it and looked at the cover again, running his fingers up and down the face. He then put it in the pocket of his suit coat. "Thank you," he said softly. "Let's get to work."

The national security meeting took place a half hour earlier than usual. The President wanted to get the information he needed and let the people running the various departments get back to work so they could track down the killers. None of the heads asked the President how he was doing, they knew he was hurting. And the best way to help the President was to find the people that committed these acts of terrorism.

The Oval Office meeting was moved to the Situation Room so the President could be in communication with anyone anywhere around the world. CIA Director Parker took the lead with Director Michaelson, Director Stubblefield, and National Security Adviser Harnacke, looking on. Director Javits was on the TV screen on the wall from his office at the Pentagon. Things were ramping up.

"Mr. President, there has been a communication received from the Crescent Brotherhood taking responsibility for the killing of Mr. Cogdon. They are also behind the attacks in Europe and we believe the sniper attacks here at home. They have also called for worldwide jihad."

The President nodded. Same ol' same ol'.

Parker continued. "They have also called for your resignation. They said if you don't resign immediately then the attacks will continue and more Americans will be killed."

The President actually smiled at that one. "Kind of sounds like the Democrats," he said. "What else?"

"Like I said, we have determined the Crescent Brotherhood was behind the attacks in Europe," Parker said. He then turned to the TV screen on the wall. "I think Director Javits can give you more information on that front."

Javits cleared his throat and went to work. "Yes, sir, Mr. President. We have actionable intelligence indicating the Crescent Brotherhood at one time consisted of about six teams that included four to five members per team. We believe four of the teams are out of commission as they were either captured or killed in the attacks across Europe, and, of course, one two-man team was nabbed in Virginia just last week."

"Well," the President said, "that's five teams captured or killed. One to go."

"Yes, sir. Our intelligence sources indicate the sniper teams were trained in Afghanistan at this location." The screen to the left showed an aerial view of the remote outpost where the terrorists lived and trained. The President squinted his eyes at the screen and gave the pictures a good look. "We have solid confirmation that this is the Afghan home for the Crescent Brotherhood."

"You're sure?" the President asked.

"Yes, sir," Director Javits responded. He then paused. Hearing no further questions, he continued. "Mr. President, we believe that there is terrorist training going on at this location as we speak. They might be trying to redouble their efforts given their successes so far. Perhaps another attack in Europe." He paused again. "We have assets in place to take it out if you want. Tomahawk cruise missiles and B-52s ready to go on your command."

The President didn't have to think about it. His mind was clear, and it was time to be decisive. "Have you done everything you can to minimize any civilian casualties?"

"Yes, sir. It's a remote area. Chairman Cummins concurs."

There was no hesitation from the President, no wavering of any sort. "Then level it."

"Yes, sir," Secretary Javits said, taking his cue. He turned to a phone on his desk and made the call. The focus of the meeting then shifted to the FBI Director.

"Mr. President," Director Stubblefield said, "based on information from the CIA and our counterparts overseas we believe the ringleader of the Crescent Brotherhood may be in the Paris area. He was the guy we tracked in Munich but lost him somewhere between there and France. I think if we find him, then maybe we break the case here in the U.S. and find the shooters."

President Schumacher nodded. He liked what he was hearing. He gave his orders.

"Hunt him down," he said before adding, "hunt 'em all down."

CHAPTER 24

Paris, France

The FBI's Phantom team had landed in the dark of night at Charles de Gaulle Airport outside of Paris. Two FBI agents from the Paris legat office brought a van and whisked the team to the U.S. Embassy just off the Champs-Elysees. There the five members of the Phantom team met with the CIA's station chief based in Paris.

Steven Wallard had been with the CIA for twenty-five years. Now at age fifty-five, his life as a spy was on the downhill slide. Retirement was not far off. Gone were the days of sneaking around foreign capitals bugging offices and bedrooms of the rich and powerful. It had been exhilarating work, but Wallard was content to let the younger generation risk their lives in the day-to-day operations of intelligence gathering. He now oversaw the CIA program in Paris, a post he selected more for the food and art the City of Lights had to offer rather than being a hotbed of international terrorism.

But things in Paris were starting to heat up, and thus the reason for the Phantom team showing up in Wallard's office.

Special Agent Schiffer hung up the phone. He had called Director Stubblefield and told him the Phantom team was in Paris and ready to catch their prey. The instructions were to find Mahmud Basra and bring him in. The plan was a simple snatch-and-grab operation – arrest the terrorist and put him on a plane for the United States. Finding Basra could mean cutting off the head of the terrorist snake.

Agent Wallard clicked his computer mouse and a picture of Basra appeared on the screen.

"I will show you the latest e-mail that Basra sent out on behalf of the Crescent Brotherhood," Wallard said, making another click.

The e-mail had been sent last night. It claimed the Crescent Brotherhood was behind the attacks in America and praised the killing of Cogdon, referring to him in the e-mail as "an agent of the devil Schumacher." The e-mail promised to continue the killings in America until the Brotherhood's demands were met, which included Art Brennan's release from custody, the closure of the Guantanamo Bay detention facility, the recognition of sharia law in U.S. courts, and the immediate resignation of President Schumacher.

"Where did this e-mail originate?" Schiffer asked.

"From what we can tell, it came from a computer terminal at an Internet café near the Gare du Nord train station," Wallard said, using his finger to point to the location of the station. "Approximately 9:10 last evening. The surveillance cameras in the area failed to show Basra in or around the area of the café. It's possible he sent someone in there with the password and instructions to send the e-mail."

The meeting was interrupted by a knock on the door. "Sir," the CIA man said to Wallard, "we might have something here."

Wallard waved him inside and got up from his seat. "What is it?"

After the CIA's resident computer geek sat down at the desk and made a few clicks with the mouse, a new window opened on the computer screen. "This just came in." The screen showed the sidewalk in the Strasbourg Saint-Denis area, a well-known Muslim neighborhood in Paris. Men in *keffiyeh* headdresses and Muslim *thawb* robes loitered outside of an eatery selling *halal* food. The man continued. "There is going to be a car showing up at this location shortly."

Just then a black Mercedes with tinted windows pulled to the side of the street. The passenger in the front seat, a large bearded man dressed in a suit and tie, exited and scanned up and down the sidewalk in both directions. He then stepped to the rear door and opened it. A man in all black stepped out. He wore no headdress or cap, nothing to hide his identity. The man didn't make it two steps before those standing outside the eatery erupted in cheers, swarming the man and bestowing on him hugs and kisses.

The tech manning the computer hit pause at the exact right moment. "We believe we have found Mahmud Basra."

The picture showed Basra kissing an elderly man on the cheek. Both men were smiling. Basra turned his face to the south, and the surveillance camera caught the image head-on. The Americans in the room stood in silence, their stomachs churning with anger at the celebration they were watching. There, on the screen, the man being heralded as a hero on the sidewalks of Paris had been the mastermind of the murder of hundreds of innocent men, women, and children all over the world. And he would continue the killings unless he could be stopped.

"Are you sure that's him?" Wallard asked, leaning closer to the screen and comparing the surveillance video with the still photo from Basra's passport. He wanted to be sure.

"Our facial recognition software says it is highly likely that the man is indeed Mahmud Basra."

Now Schiffer had his questions. "Where is this location?"

"It's not too far from the Gare du Nord train station. It's in an area frequented by local Muslims." He then used a laser pointer and circled the area in red light on a large wall map.

"What time was this video taken?" Schiffer asked.

"About forty-five minutes ago?"

"Who's that man Basra is embracing?"

"We don't know," the tech said. "Probably just an acquaintance, maybe an elderly mentor of his."

"Who is that car registered to?"

The computer man felt the collar of his shirt tighten slightly. He knew things were going to get hairy with the information he was about to provide. "The Embassy of the Kingdom of Saudi Arabia."

Schiffer cursed under his breath. It was bad enough the United States had to fight terrorists in every corner of the world but when America's so-called allies were aiding the enemy, it made the fight much more difficult. The Saudis were known to offer assistance to the U.S. with one hand all the while feeding the terrorists with the other. Given the implications on foreign relations, Schiffer immediately thought about calling Director Stubblefield.

But he didn't have time. He had missed Basra in Germany and he didn't want to risk losing him again. His instructions were to find Basra and bring him in. And that's what he intended to do.

"Is that a live feed?" Schiffer asked, pointing at a smaller window on the screen.

"Yes," the tech said, maximizing the picture. "The car is still there, and Basra has not come back outside."

"Somehow we need to keep him out of that car," Schiffer said. "If he gets back to the Saudi Embassy, there's a real good chance we won't be able to get him. Show me where the embassy is located."

Wallard grabbed the laser pointer and circled the spot on the map.

"It's right here. West of the Champs-Elysees on Avenue Hoche."

The tech looked at the video feed again. "Wait a minute," he said. "We might have something going on here."

"What?"

"Another vehicle has arrived," the man said, pointing at the screen. "Looks like more diplomatic plates."

"Saudi?"

The man enhanced the picture and zeroed in on the license plate. "Not Saudi," the man said. "Venezuela."

Schiffer cursed again, not liking what he was hearing. "It just keeps getting better and better." Schiffer knew that if Chavez's boys got hold of Basra, they probably wouldn't be too keen on returning him considering the Venezuelan dictator's dislike for President Schumacher. It looked like the Saudis were trying to cover their asses.

"Oh," the computer tech blurted out, his eyes on the screen. "There he is," he said, pointing to Basra.

Schiffer took a step closer to the screen. It was obvious Basra was saying his goodbyes to his compatriots. He appeared joyous, like he was one step away from guaranteeing his freedom for good. His time on the run would soon be over, and he could enjoy life as a terrorist in hiding. Schiffer saw Basra get into the backseat of the car with the Venezuelan Embassy license plates. There was no more time for surveillance video watching. He turned to his team. "We gotta go," he said. A change of plans was in order. "We're gonna need directions to the Venezuelan Embassy."

The Phantom team hustled to their van and hit the streets of Paris. The CIA man monitoring the surveillance cameras found Basra's vehicle at the Plaza de Charles de Gaulle circling the Arc de Triumph.

"They turned right on Avenue Kleber."

Avenue Kleber is one of twelve spokes, including the Avenue de la Grande Armee and the Champs-Elysees, shooting out of the hub that is the Arc de Triumph.

Schiffer spotted the car and pointed to his right. "We're going to have to cut them off."

Olivera turned on the Avenue Victor Hugo spoke, made a left on Rue de Presbourg, and then a right on Rue Lauriston. Now they were speeding down the street between the Hugo and Kleber spokes.

"They're going to make a right on Rue Copernic," Schiffer said.

As they approached the intersection, Olivera noticed the sign that Rue Copernic was a one-way street. The Venezuelan Embassy was to their left. And they weren't supposed to go left. "Uh, Duke," Olivera said seeing what was ahead. "It's one-way."

Schiffer dismissed it. "The Embassy is just around the corner of the intersection."

Olivera slammed on the brakes as they approached Rue Copernic and wheeled the van into oncoming traffic. It was one lane and packed as far as the eye could see with vehicles. Forward progress was now stopped.

"There's the Embassy!" Schiffer yelled, seeing the yellow, blue, and red flag of Venezuela. Schiffer threw open the van door. He could see the car carrying Basra still down the Rue Copernic. Basra was blocked in by the traffic lining up behind him and his eyes caught a glimpse of Schiffer and two other Phantom team members sprinting in his direction. Basra had to make a decision. He saw Schiffer pick up the pace down the east side of the walk, his gun in his left hand down at his side. Basra was a sitting duck inside the car, and there was no way he could make it to the Embassy now. His only choice was to flee.

"He's on the run!"

Schiffer sprinted down Rue Copernic and came to a halt on the sidewalk on Avenue Kleber. He saw his prey. "He's heading toward the Eiffel Tower!" Schiffer said. "Keep him on this side of the river." Schiffer didn't want Basra to make it to the grounds of the Eiffel Tower and its collection of tourists and armed guards. Who knows what could happen.

Olivera waited for two members of the team to get back into the van. He backed up to Rue Lauriston and gunned the accelerator heading east.

"We'll cut him off," Jenkins radioed.

Schiffer could see he was catching his prey. The marathon runner in him kicked it into high gear. No one was going to outrun or outlast Schiffer. A nearly breathless Basra kept at it though, his lungs burning and his muscles aching. He was running for his life.

"He turned north on Avenue du President Wilson!" Schiffer said before losing sight of Basra.

The Avenue du President Wilson has three lanes each divided by a parking lane and shrouded in trees. Street vendors lined the sidewalk in their tents selling leather purses and other assorted knickknacks.

"We've got traffic!" Olivera reported, the vehicle stopped at a light and boxed in. He turned the van onto the sidewalk until he made it to the Rue Debrousse. It was one way and one lane with cars parked in every available spot. The only way to make it through was to beat anyone coming in the opposite direction so Olivera gunned it.

"He's heading to the Pont de l'Alma bridge!" Schiffer radioed.

The Phantom team made it down the one-way street and screeched to a halt at the intersection. "We're on Avenue de New York!" Jenkins yelled of the avenue lining the Seine River.

"North! North!" Schiffer radioed back.

The van had two lanes of traffic heading south and those cars weren't stopping. Jenkins and Alvarez threw open the doors and set out on the chase. The pursuit was beginning to cause a scene, and Schiffer knew it wouldn't be long before the French authorities would show up and stick their noses in the Phantom team's business.

Basra caught a glimpse of Jenkins and Alvarez about to cut him off to his right. There was no way he could get to the Eiffel Tower and disappear into the crowd. He stopped and turned around, his chest heaving in agony. The *Flamme de la Liberte* sculpture stood between him and the railing keeping pedestrians from the Pont de l'Alma tunnel, the same tunnel where Princess Diana was injured in the car accident. Basra was being boxed in. Schiffer was bearing down on him from the west, gun raised. Basra could not hear Schiffer yelling at him, his hearing drowned out by the pounding of his heart. Jenkins and Alvarez were sprinting from the southwest, and Guerrero had doubled around from the south. Although Basra wouldn't be able to make it to the Eiffel Tower, he had two choices. He could make a mad dash and jump into the River Seine and hope for the best.

Or he could make one last move and end it all.

"Basra! Don't move!" Schiffer yelled at him, now only fifty feet from his catch. He had his gun trained on Basra's chest. "Don't move!"

Basra could barely move in his exhaustion, but he made one last decision. "*Allahu akbar,*" he mumbled to himself. He turned to the south and made the last leap over the railing.

"He's jumped off the overpass into the tunnel!" Guerrero yelled.

Schiffer made it to the railing and looked below to find Basra sprawled out on the asphalt below, a black Mercedes with a dented hood and a busted windshield screeching to a halt. Basra did not move, and the blood pooling under his head indicated he probably wouldn't be going anywhere under his own power.

"Olivera, get to the northbound tunnel," Schiffer said into his radio. "Let's everybody get down there and then get moving."

Schiffer and the Phantom team members on foot hustled down the sidewalk until they could make the jump into the tunnel. The traffic heading south had slowed as the rubberneckers checked out the dead man on the pavement. Schiffer ran up to him before saying something in French to the driver of the car who had gotten out to help. The man returned to the driver's seat and moved his car out of the tunnel and out of the way. The rest of the Phantom team set up a perimeter and motioned for the traffic to keep moving.

"Duke, we have sirens en route," Jenkins said.

Schiffer reached for his phone and took a picture of Basra. He then grabbed Basra's hand and sank the man's palm into his own pool of blood. He fished out the piece of paper with Basra's mug shot, turned it over to the blank side, and laid it on the pavement. He then pressed Basra's bloody palm to the paper.

"Olivera," Schiffer said into his radio. "Where are you?"

"Heading north into the tunnel right now," Olivera said back.

Schiffer stood up and motioned to his team to the northbound lane where Olivera was skidding to a stop. Once the Phantom team was all in, Olivera took off as the emergency responders passed them going in the opposite direction to find the deceased Basra.

"Let's get back to the Embassy," Schiffer said from the front passenger seat, holding Basra's fingerprints in his right hand.

Olivera made a left on the Plaza de Concorde. Traffic was proceeding smoothly but Olivera noticed the flashing blue lights in his side mirrors. Apparently, someone from the Venezuelan Embassy called the police to complain about some armed men in a white van causing trouble. "Duke, we've got company," he said.

Schiffer ducked down slightly and looked into his mirror. *It could never be easy*, he thought to himself.

"Speed it up a bit," he said. He pulled out his phone and punched in the numbers. He held the phone to his ear as Olivera swerved around the stopped cars and gunned it through the yellow light. "This is Agent Schiffer," he said into the phone. "We're on our way to the Embassy and we need the main gate open." He stopped to listen to the response. "Yes, the east entrance. We need it open now."

With the blue lights gaining ground and the French gendarmes outside the U.S. Embassy starting to scurry, Olivera made a quick left, ignored the guards, and made a right into the main gate, which was almost fully opened. The doors to the Phantom team's van shot open and all five hustled toward the gate where two U.S. Marines stood guard and welcomed them to friendly territory.

The sounds of shouting Frenchmen filled the air but Schiffer and the Phantom team ignored them and headed inside.

Schiffer met U.S. Ambassador Hamilton and thanked him for the open-door policy. He told him there might be a need for some diplomacy with the French authorities who probably weren't too happy with the gun-toting Phantom team roaming the streets of a foreign capital.

"I'll handle it," Ambassador Hamilton said with a wink.

"I need a fax machine," Schiffer said.

Ambassador Hamilton extended his hand and showed the Phantom team the way.

Schiffer took out his phone and dialed the number. "Director Stubblefield, please."

It didn't take long for him to respond. "Duke?"

"Director, Mahmud Basra is dead," Schiffer said.

Stubblefield took a second to consider the news. "DOA?"

"Triple six," Schiffer said, using the police code for suicide. "I'm going to e-mail you his picture and fax you his prints so you can make a positive identification."

"How'd you get his prints?"

"A little improvisation."

"Good work," Stubblefield said. Since Schiffer's assignment was complete, he gave him his next order. "I need you and the team to get back here right now."

CHAPTER 25

Camden, New Jersey

The Toyota Corolla was thirty minutes outside of Philadelphia when Ahmed Yassar, Hakim al-Rashid, and Omar Faran started hearing news alerts on the radio. They decided to seek cover before the formal announcement was made. It came over the AM dial, after the reporter at the top of the hour prepared the listener for the statement given by FBI Director Tyrone Stubblefield from Washington, D.C.

"Good afternoon," Director Stubblefield began. "I want to update the American people on the investigation into the recent shootings on the East Coast as well as the terrorist attacks overseas. As you know, one suspect was killed and one was captured last week in Fairfax, Virginia, and it has been confirmed the gun found at the scene of the arrest was the same gun used in the killing in Baltimore. The gun was not used in the Alexandria and Manassas shootings and, obviously, it was not used in the shooting at the White House that killed William Cogdon as that occurred after the Fairfax arrest. We are continuing to look for two or three individuals who might have taken part in the other shootings. One person of interest goes by the name Hakim al-Rashid."

"Oh, no," Faran whispered from the driver's seat of the Corolla. Faran looked over at the man whose name had just been broadcast to the world who was sitting right next to him. Yassar was seated in the backseat, listening intently and keeping an eye on his surroundings. The three terrorists had pulled into a public parking garage just outside of Camden, New Jersey. Al-Rashid said nothing.

"Hakim al-Rashid is an American citizen and was last seen meeting with Art Brennan, who is currently incarcerated while awaiting trial on multiple terrorist-related charges," Director Stubblefield said. For the benefit of those watching on TV, the screen showed a driver's license photo of al-Rashid. The photo was several years old, and the full head of black hair was now gone. The new glasses he was wearing made him barely recognizable.

"They are looking for you," Faran whispered, stating the obvious. He sounded terribly worried that one of the FBI's most wanted men was sitting right next to him.

Al-Rashid only nodded.

Director Stubblefield then recited what the FBI knew about al-Rashid, which wasn't much. Black and white surveillance pictures showed him at various stages of the investigation involving Art Brennan. The FBI thought al-Rashid might be the man behind the American terrorist plot and wanted to find him before he could orchestrate any more killings. Stubblefield warned the public that al-Rashid and any of his acquaintances should be considered armed and very dangerous. Any person seeing al-Rashid was asked to contact their local police agency.

Faran looked over at al-Rashid with wide eyes. His right hand was noticeably shaking.

"Relax," al-Rashid said quietly to him. "Remember, it will all be over soon."

Director Stubblefield's voice continued out of the radio. "I can also report to you that Mahmud Basra, a suspected terrorist with ties to the recent European attacks, was killed last evening in Paris, France."

"Oh, no," Faran whispered, his head falling forward in despair. He was not prepared for that shocking revelation. Faran felt like his world was crashing down on him. Basra had been a mentor to him before he left for the United States. Now it seemed it was only a matter of time before the FBI would find them.

"Law-enforcement authorities had been on the trail of Basra, a Saudi citizen who lived in Munich, Germany, for the past week. Based on evidence collected and interviews conducted, it is believed Basra was the mastermind behind the attacks in Venice, London, Brussels, and Madrid." Director Stubblefield reported, intentionally failing to mention any involvement by the FBI's secret Phantom team.

Al-Rashid reached over to the knob on the dash and turned off the radio. He sat in silence and looked out the front window and through the opening of the parking garage wall.

"What are we going to do now?" Faran asked. He sounded like he was ready to give up.

Al-Rashid took his time finding the right words. A part of him was thrilled to know America's vaunted FBI was after him. He finally felt like he had made something of his life now. But he wasn't done yet.

"It is time to move forward with our final operation," he said.

"But they are looking for you," Faran pleaded. "We will all be captured if they find you."

Al-Rashid shook his head. "No, now is the time."

"Maybe we should hide out for a little while," Faran pleaded.

Yassar reached up from the backseat and slapped Faran upside the head with the back of his hand. He was tired of the young man's whining. There would be no hiding. They were trained killers, and it should be the intention of each of them to kill as many Americans as possible and die as martyrs for the cause. "Grow up, Omar," Yassar scolded. "Have you forgotten your mission?"

Faran squirmed in his seat, bristling at the lecture. He made sure to hold his head high and puff up his chest. "I have not forgotten my mission. I am ready to die for Allah."

"Well, start acting like it," Yassar snapped, his eyes radiating disgust. If he heard any more dissent or questioning of authority, he was likely going to kill Faran himself.

The White House – Washington, D.C.

The President knew his entire focus could not be solely on national security. He had to show the country and the world that America's business was continuing. Despite the loss of his chief of staff and the continuing war on terrorism, the American people expected their President to forge on in difficult times and keep the country moving forward.

"Good morning ladies and gentlemen," the President said, waving the two men and one woman into the Oval Office.

Deputy Chief of Staff Tim Durant entered first followed behind by Assistant to the President Patrick Grim and Deputy Speechwriter Amanda O'Connell. All three of them appeared nervous, O'Connell even awed at being invited into the Oval Office by the President of the United States. It was her first time.

Durant took his place in front of the Resolute Desk and Grim and O'Connell fell in line – all ramrod straight with expressionless looks on their faces. O'Connell could feel her teeth chattering. She feared the President could hear the sound echoing off the walls.

"At ease, folks," the President said with a smile, sensing the tension. "I'm not going to send you to Gitmo or anything like that." The three smiled and breathed a sigh of relief. "Pull up some chairs."

Tim Durant had been Deputy Chief of Staff for two years now. Cogdon had hired him and groomed him as his protégé and possible successor. A graduate of Hillsdale College and a former staff member at the Heritage Foundation, Durant had impressive conservative credentials. And he was just the type of guy Cogdon wanted to fill his shoes in the future.

But it wouldn't be for President Schumacher. As long as he was in the White House, Cogdon's chief of staff position would remain unfilled.

Durant had taken Cogdon's death just as hard as the President had. The dark circles around his eyes indicated he hadn't been getting a good night's sleep. He had kept Cogdon's unhealthy hours since he was hired and rarely saw the light of day. His mind was constantly focused on conservative politics and now he was in charge. Unfortunately, there was no how-to list on how to act in Cogdon's stead. Cogdon had always given him orders and he dutifully followed them. But Cogdon was also a control freak and did things off the cuff. He was also a poor delegator and handled everything from the President's daily schedule to his speeches. Tim Durant couldn't go ten minutes without asking himself, "What would Wiley Cogdon do?"

"Tim, how's everything going?" the President asked.

Durant opened his leather folder and looked at the sheet of upcoming presidential events. Since Cogdon's death, he had been unsure of how to proceed. Was he the President's gatekeeper like Cogdon? Was every legislative or political matter supposed to go through him before it reached the President's desk? He had grabbed hold of Grim in hopes of putting the pieces of the President's schedule together.

"Sir," Durant started. "Today you have the Rose Garden announcement pertaining to the visit by the President of Norway followed by a dinner meeting with congressional leaders."

The President was looking down his own list, asking questions as they went along. O'Connell said she had made the changes suggested by the President on the Norwegian visit to the White House. They went through the next two days of events before the President would spend a quiet weekend at Camp David.

Durant continued. "Then next Tuesday is the Celebration of the Constitution in Philadelphia," he said. He stopped and looked at the President in the eyes. Cogdon had set up the whole event and speakers were lined up. Durant had told those who were invited that the Schumacher Administration was in a holding pattern. He could barely bring himself to ask the President if he wanted to continue with the event.

"Sir, do you want us to cancel the event?" Durant asked. He was sincere, thinking maybe it was too soon for the President.

"Well, hell no," the President said. "The show must go on. Wiley put a lot of effort into this celebration. He would want us to continue. The Constitution has been around for over two-hundred years and it's going to be around long after we're all gone. Wiley's death doesn't mean we must stop everything." The President had made up his mind. It would be a Celebration of the Constitution for the people and a silent tribute to Wiley Cogdon. "It's on."

"Okay," Durant said. "I will make sure everything is in place."

The President nodded and then turned to O'Connell, the one chosen to draft the short speech at the Celebration. "Now, Ms. O'Connell," he said. "How is the speech coming along?"

Amanda O'Connell was thirty-three years old and was recently married. She had not seen much of her husband lately given recent events. The speechwriting office was working overtime to make sure every presidential statement, announcement, and utterance was of the highest quality. On the job for only a year, she had met the President three times but never in the Oval Office. She found him kindhearted and caring. When he would stop by the speechwriting office just to the west of the White House in the Old Executive Office Building, he seemed to take great interest in her work. A graduate of Illinois State University with dual degrees in journalism and political science, she had grown up an hour south in Springfield where she worked as a docent during the summers at the Abraham Lincoln Presidential Library. She was well-versed in Lincoln lore and sprinkled her early drafts with anecdotes and quotes from the Prairie Lawyer. Cogdon liked her work and directed her boss to give her more assignments.

Durant had told her the day before that she would be making a visit to the Oval Office to discuss the President's speech. She could hardly sleep. She wore a black skirt and a white blouse. Her dark hair was made up like she was going to the prom. The only thing she tinkered with more was the draft of the President's speech in her leather folder.

"Sir," she said before clearing her throat of her nervousness. "Sir, have you read the fourth draft?"

"Yes, I liked it," the President said, himself looking over the draft in front of him. "I just have a few thoughts. Since we are going to be near Independence Hall, I think we can work in a mention or two about the Declaration of Independence as well as the Constitution. And let's make sure we mention the verse from Leviticus that is on the Liberty Bell." The President was starting to sound like Cogdon with all his directives. "And don't be afraid to mention Lincoln either. He went to Independence Hall prior to his inauguration and then for one final time as his funeral procession wound its way back west to your home town of Springfield."

O'Connell smiled. The President had remembered where she was from.

"Wiley would like that," the President added.

"I will get right to work on it and have it for you by the weekend to look over once again."

"Good," the President said before he was distracted by the appearance of two men at the door to the Oval Office. *Uh oh*, he thought to himself.

Secret Service Director Allen Defoe and Director Stubblefield were standing at the door with stern looks on their faces.

"Is there a problem?" the President asked, waving them in.

"No," Director Stubblefield said. At least nothing imminent that he could speak of.

The President's schedulers and speechwriter took their cue and started grabbing their materials to get back to work.

"We were just discussing the upcoming Celebration of the Constitution in Philadelphia," the President said.

Director Defoe cleared his throat and spoke up first. "About the event in Philadelphia, sir," he said slowly, stopping the President's deputies in their tracks. They all wondered if they needed to hear what the head of presidential security had to say.

"Yes?" the President asked, sounding like he didn't want to hear what Director Defoe had to offer.

"Mr. President, I think you should reconsider attending the celebration," Defoe said in all seriousness.

The President started shaking his head back and forth. "Allen," he said, "I'm not going to cancel the Celebration of the Constitution. How would that look?"

"Sir, I am worried about your security."

The President wasn't sure if he should laugh at the statement or not. "Yeah, I know that, Allen. That's your job."

Director Defoe expected some presidential blowback. If the Secret Service had its way, the President would never leave the secure bubble of the White House. Given Cogdon's assassination just across the way, Defoe preferred the White House bunker.

"Sir, we have some intelligence reports that terrorists are looking for another score," Defoe said. "And you are tops on their list."

"Allen, I am the President of the United States. I'm always a target. But that doesn't mean I'm going to hide in the bunker."

Defoe nodded like he understood, but he worried about the President's safety every minute of the day. "Sir, it's a huge public event. It's been well-advertised. I'm just worried that the terrorists might want to use the celebration as a target."

"Ty, what do you think?" the President asked.

Director Stubblefield looked at Defoe and then back at the President. He was conflicted. He, as a lawman, knew the predicament Director Defoe was in. Defoe and his agents had to be successful one-hundred percent of the time, but the terrorists only had to succeed once to inflict serious damage on the psyche of the country.

"Sir, I think Director Defoe has some valid concerns," Stubblefield said. He tried to tread lightly because he knew the President wouldn't cancel the event easily. "Given what happened to Wiley, it might be appropriate to be a little extra cautious."

The President decided to end the matter right then and there. "I understand your concern," he said. "Both of you. And I have full confidence in the Secret Service. But we are going forward with the Celebration. Take the precautions that you need, Allen, but prepare for the event to take place."

"Yes, sir," Director Defoe said. He had addressed his concerns, and now he had his orders.

As everyone started to exit the Oval Office, the President made one last comment. "I don't have anything to worry about anyway," he said. "Ty's going to be there with me reading the Second Amendment, right?"

"Yes, sir," Stubblefield said. "I'll be there."

CHAPTER 26

Philadelphia, Pennsylvania

Pastor Carson Levitt took to the microphone a block and a half from Independence Hall. Camera shots could just barely see the top of the former Pennsylvania State House and that was all the closer Levitt was going to get to the place where the Declaration of Independence had been signed and the Constitution had been drafted. The Secret Service had already taken over the area surrounding Independence Hall and the Liberty Bell for the President's speech tomorrow – the barricades were up and the metal-detectors were being installed.

So, Pastor Levitt had to take his hate-filled road show down the street.

Given that the President wasn't due until tomorrow morning, the press had nothing better to do than to give Levitt a microphone. The ten reporters and as many camera operators huddled together as Pastor Levitt straightened his tie.

"Is everybody ready?" he asked, sounding like he would be willing to wait if anyone needed to have another sip of latte.

The cameramen stepped forward, their dominant eye peering through the viewfinder, and then the red lights came on.

"Good morning," Levitt started. "Thank you all for coming. It is great to be with you today in the City of Brotherly Love. The place where our First Amendment was proposed, debated, and adopted."

Levitt was calm, almost professorial, like he was a tour guide preparing tourists for what they were about to see when they walked down the street. But it didn't take long before the hell-fire burning inside him spewed forth out of his mouth. He railed against the Muslim people, claiming they were the dogs of the world and should be kicked out of the country and back to their "primitive 7th century caves and other holes in the ground!"

He called on the U.S. Government to start racial profiling and forcibly remove Muslims from their homes "because we all know they are in bed with the terrorists!" The reporters were rolling their eyes at the histrionics; some had even stopped taking notes because they had no intention of writing a story on this nut case.

Pastor Levitt then reached into his briefcase, pulled out a book, and held it high over his head. "Tomorrow, I invite every freedom loving American to meet me in Philadelphia! Together we will show those Muslims what we think about their holy book! When the President speaks, we shall meet in Independence Mall Park and show what leadership is all about!"

Federal law-enforcement authorities were well aware of Pastor Levitt's planned protest and cordoned off an area to the southwest of Independence Hall at Washington Square, a tree-shrouded green space that included the Tomb of the Unknown Revolutionary Soldier. The barricades were up so Levitt and his band of haters could exercise their free-speech rights and howl at the moon without disrupting the Celebration of the Constitution. The local police chief said it was going to be a zoo in downtown Philly tomorrow.

And that's just what Pastor Levitt wanted.

Seven blocks away, Hakim al-Rashid, Omar Faran, and Ahmed Yassar were seated on the floor of a one-bedroom apartment above "Mr. Egg Roll," a rundown eatery in a particularly seedy section of Chinatown. The trio had crossed the Delaware River via the Ben Franklin Bridge from Camden, New Jersey, late last night and under the cover of darkness.

A friend of al-Rashid had rented the apartment a week ago once it became known the plan called for operations in Philadelphia. The paint on the walls of the apartment was peeling, and the water stains on the ceiling indicated a leak had been going on for some time. The threadbare carpet, its original color could no longer be determined, looked like it had been installed during the time of Chairman Mao. The place came sparsely furnished, which did not matter to al-Rashid and his cohorts. They wouldn't be staying very long anyway. But the apartment did have running water, electricity, and a gas stove. Just enough to allow the men to implement their plan of terror.

Moreover, it gave them a place to plot in the shadows without worrying about being discovered. Most of the employees of Mr. Egg Roll spoke only Chinese, and the few that were conversant in English usually cursed the local authorities for towing their customers' vehicles, not picking up the garbage, or citing the restaurant for health-code violations. Philly police spent their time in other parts of the city, sometimes taking twenty minutes to respond to emergency calls in this part of town. The locals tried to ignore the crime, hoping to keep the inspectors from showing up and closing down their businesses. They kept their heads down and their mouths shut. It was a perfect spot for al-Rashid and his men to hide out.

"We need to scout out our location this afternoon," al-Rashid said to Yassar and Faran, both of whom were sitting on the floor. The smell of roasted duck and sweet and sour pork started filtering through the ceiling as Mr. Egg Roll prepared for lunch. "Get a good lay of the land before tomorrow."

Yassar had his sniper rifle ready to go. The two backpacks full of explosives were sitting in the corner. There was little else to do but execute the plan.

"Will you be coming with us?" Faran asked. The worrywart in him was starting to show again.

"No," al-Rashid said. "I cannot go downtown today. It is too dangerous. Law-enforcement officers might have pictures of me and, if they find me, it could blow the whole operation. Plus, I will meet with the boss while you are doing that."

The other two men had never met "the boss," and only vaguely knew about how the operation was going to take place.

"Ahmed, you will need to find a high place for your firing position," al-Rashid instructed. He pointed to a spot on a tourist map that his friend had left in the apartment. "Somewhere in here."

"Okay," Yassar said, taking a closer look at the streets and the surroundings.

"Don't find your position today, though. Just pick a spot and you'll get up there tomorrow."

Yassar nodded. He didn't need to be told but said nothing.

"Now, Omar," al-Rashid said, turning his eyes to Faran. "Today, you are just going to be acting like a tourist. Keep your sunglasses and your hat on. Take a few pictures with your cell phone and look for choke points where the crowds will be tomorrow."

"Okay," Faran stated. He was glad that the preparation for the attack was finally taking place. It took his mind off the worrying. "Do we need to scout out your location for tomorrow?"

"No," al-Rashid said. "I'll be near the boss."

Al-Rashid looked at his watch. "You guys better get going. There will still be plenty of tourists out there this afternoon. Just try to blend in. Don't do anything suspicious. And keep a good distance apart. You can communicate over the phones but say little. I have to get ready to meet the boss. He should be here in about twenty minutes."

CHAPTER 27

Philadelphia, Pennsylvania

Director Stubblefield had ordered the Phantom team to head to Philadelphia yesterday evening in preparation for President Schumacher's speech and the Celebration of the Constitution. Now it was the morning of the event and it was all hands on deck. The Celebration would bring together some of the most powerful people in the federal government. It would be like a State of the Union address at the Capitol with the President, the Vice President, Cabinet members, Supreme Court Justices, Congressman and Senators, and military leaders all congregated together in one spot. But instead of the familiar surroundings of the House of Representatives, the Celebration was outdoors in the middle of downtown Philadelphia.

The Secret Service had called in agents from as far away as Chicago to help with the event. Rooftops were manned 24 hours a day, manhole covers were welded shut, mailboxes and newspaper racks were removed. Traffic on the Delaware River was closely watched and the bridges had a marked police car parked on both sides. Sensors were installed at multiple locations within a mile of Independence Hall and sniffed the air for chemical or biological agents. Surveillance cameras kept watch of every tourist and local that walked in the vicinity. Security tents were going up and the magnetometers were ready to scan what was expected to be twenty thousand people the following day. Bomb-sniffing dogs patrolled the grounds. Signs told those wanting to watch the festivities that they could not bring in any backpacks, large purses, glass bottles, or any liquid containers over sixteen ounces. Just below it were pictures of a handgun and a knife in a red circle with a line through them just in case someone thought they needed to bring a weapon into the event. In the mid-September warmth, the sound of car horns filled the air. The locals had been warned about the traffic jams that were starting because of today's road closures, but the angry drivers in their idling vehicles couldn't help but pound the steering wheels and let the profanities fly at the inconvenience.

Together with the Secret Service and the FBI, the Department of Homeland Security, ICE, ATF, the U.S. Marshals Service, along with the Pennsylvania State Police and the Philadelphia Police Department had mobile command units ready to offer assistance wherever needed. Uniformed officers and agents in plain clothes patrolled the streets looking for a needle in a haystack.

At the corner of Chestnut and 5th Street, just to the east of Independence Hall, the FBI's modified conversion bus sat fully powered and staffed. The bus had a wall full of TV screens showing surveillance videos from around the city and beamed to its roof full of satellite dishes.

An antsy Agent Schiffer paced behind the FBI agents monitoring the screens. He didn't like to be cooped up inside watching TV. He needed to get out amongst the people. Director Stubblefield was due to land in Philadelphia within the next hour. The President was scheduled to arrive in three hours and give his speech at high noon.

But Agent Schiffer couldn't wait that long. He motioned to the other four members of the Phantom team to meet him at the driver's end of the bus.

"We need to get outside and start scouting locations and scanning the crowd," Schiffer told them. "We aren't much help in here. Let's split up into two-man teams. Guerrero and Alvarez will take the grounds north of Independence Hall. Jenkins and Olivera will take the south side. I'll take the east and west sides. Keep in contact with each other."

Schiffer reached into his pocket and pulled out photos of Hakim al-Rashid from his shirt pocket underneath his dark pullover. It was a driver's license photo from two years ago. The beard and dark hair were in full bloom, and al-Rashid had no glasses on. It was the best head shot the FBI had to go on. Schiffer gave each team member a photo and told them to be alert.

The Phantom team exited the bus and headed to their locations. Schiffer, dressed in khakis and the plain pullover, walked down the brick-lined street in front of Independence Hall. The staging area was being prepared on the grassy area to the north of the former Pennsylvania State House. The tents were up behind the stage. The lucky tourists who had been allowed to view the interior of the Hall prior to its closing were lined up around the corner and straining to hear the rangers from the National Park Service in all the activity and noise. The American flag was flying high toward the south and the sunshine helped warm the temperature when it peeked out from behind the puffy white clouds. A portly Ben Franklin impersonator, complete with brown waist coat, knee breeches, and tri-cornered hat, entertained children with his kite and key and posed for photos with the tourists. Schiffer gave a quick glance at a family having their picture taken in front of the statue of George Washington standing outside the Hall's front door before moving on.

Schiffer walked to the corner of Chestnut and 6th Street at the west side of Independence Mall. He noticed a food cart across the street. Two men in suits were talking to the proprietor selling hot dogs, giant pretzels, and cheese steak sandwiches to anyone who might have skipped breakfast. The security sweep was already clearing people out of the way. Two Secret Service agents were telling the man that it was time to take down the umbrella and pack up. He was told he could return to the spot and open up one hour after the President leaves. He did not object. He would just move farther west and sell his wares until he had no more. He expected big business today. The horse-drawn carriages were headed for the barn until the late afternoon.

Schiffer's phone buzzed on his hip. "Schiffer," he said, holding the phone to his ear.

"It's Olivera."

"Yeah, go ahead."

"All is clear on the south side."

"Ten-four," Schiffer responded. He was about to say something when a man caught his eye. Something out of the ordinary. "I'll call you back." He hung up the phone.

The man had been standing at the corner of Chestnut and 6th Street. He had raised his cell phone and taken a picture of the north side of Independence Hall. With a cloud overhead shading his view through his sunglasses, the man took them off, placed them on the bill of his Phillies cap, and then tapped his phone to take the picture.

The eagle-eyed Schiffer had seen those eyes before.

But he couldn't remember where. Schiffer had been all around the country and the world for the FBI training law-enforcement agencies and catching criminals. He had perused countless mug shots looking at the all-important eyes of wanted men hoping he would see those eyes some day and give away his prey.

The man on the corner looked familiar. He wore jeans and a black button-down dress shirt. The red Phillies cap looked like it covered a closely cropped head of dark hair. The man was roughly six-feet tall and had a slender athletic build, much like Schiffer.

The man had taken the picture of Independence Hall and proceeded north on the sidewalk bustling with tourists and hired hands preparing the grounds for tomorrow. It appeared to Schiffer that the man was alone. He kept glancing to his left and then his right. Maybe he was undercover for another agency. Schiffer kept an eye on the man from about fifty feet.

When the man stopped at the corner to take a phone call, Schiffer now knew he had seen the guy before. As the man raised the phone in his right hand to his ear, Schiffer noticed the tattoo of a crescent moon on the back of the man's hand.

The eyes, the tattoo. Now Schiffer was positive he knew the man.

He had trained him.

The man finished the call and crossed the street. Schiffer kept following behind and punched in the number on his phone.

"Stubblefield," the Director said, taking the call from the backseat of an FBI Suburban en route to Independence Hall. "What's going on Duke?" The tone indicated Stubblefield knew there had to be a problem.

"Where are you?" Schiffer asked.

"I just landed. I'll be downtown within a half hour depending on the traffic. What's going on?"

Schiffer thought he would give the Director a report. "I split the team into two and we are patrolling the area." He then stopped talking as the man turned the corner. "I am on foot. I spotted someone we might have an issue with."

The Director didn't like the sound of that. "Who?"

"A couple of years ago, the FBI sent me to Saudi Arabia to train several members of their police sniper teams."

"Yes, I remember."

"One of the men had a crescent tattoo on the back of his hand," Schiffer said, rounding the corner and catching sight of the man again. "I can't remember his name but I think he had connections with the Saudi royal family and acted as a security agent on a trip to the U.S."

"Okay," the Director said, jotting down the specifics on a note pad.

"Are there going to be any foreign dignitaries here today?"

"No," Stubblefield responded. It was strictly an American

celebration. The Saudis had no reason to send a representative.

As the man and Schiffer walked away from the Independence Hall area, the crowds started to thin. Schiffer caught himself twice to make sure he wasn't letting the man know he was being followed.

"You remember a name?" Stubblefield asked.

"No, not off the top of my head," Schiffer said. His mind was running through the training sessions he had given. He could see the man in his mind along with where they had trained. But he could not remember the name.

"Who do I need to contact to find out?" Stubblefield asked, trying to help.

Schiffer said nothing in response. When the man stopped at the corner ahead, Schiffer pulled to a quick stop outside of a jewelry store and did some window shopping. When he saw a woman approaching the door, he turned his back to the man down the street, opened the door, and used the glass to check the reflection behind him.

It was then that Schiffer saw the man had met a friend.

"Duke, are you there?"

Schiffer put the phone back to his ear. "Let me call you back, Director."

"Is everything okay?"

Schiffer turned to see the two men crossing the street together. Schiffer started moving again. "I'll keep you posted."

Ahmed Yassar and Omar Faran said little as they walked down the sidewalk on their way back to their Chinatown hideout. They had made one last scouting mission and it was about time to get into position. There would only be one last meeting and final prayers with Hakim al-Rashid before they would unleash a bloodbath on the American people.

Schiffer kept a close watch on the two men, who were now well removed from the tourists and historical sites. The smell of roasted duck in the air was so thick a blind man would know his whereabouts. Schiffer could not think of any legitimate business the man in the Phillies hat might have in these parts. If the man was involved with Saudi security, he should have been heading in the direction of downtown. Maybe the men were hungry for Chinese, but Schiffer doubted it.

The local shop owners were getting ready for the upcoming lunch hour. Unlike some of the businesses near Independence Hall, the Panda

Buffet, Lady Huan's Wok, and Chopsticks Emporium would be open and ready for customers. Two Chinese men in aprons were hosing down the crumbling sidewalks blackened with years of foot traffic, discarded food, and garbage. The gates on the doors were pushed back but the bars on the windows would remain tight. The Chinese men made no eye contact with Schiffer as he walked by.

The two men Schiffer was following turned the corner and left his sight line. He reached over to make sure his handgun was holstered on his left hip. He also had a .38 Smith & Wesson J-frame revolver strapped to his right ankle. He stopped behind the front facade of the building on the corner and took a quick peek around the side.

The two men were stopped outside of Mr. Egg Roll talking to a white man. Schiffer kept his body behind the wall, but his eyes could barely believe what they were seeing. The two men had removed their caps and sunglasses. They were clearly Middle Eastern. But now it was the white man that caused Schiffer's jaw to drop.

The two Middle Eastern men were talking with Pastor Carson Levitt.

"What the hell?" Schiffer whispered to himself. He had trouble believing what he was seeing.

The three men were talking like they were friends, but how could that be. Maybe the two Middle Eastern men weren't Muslim, maybe they practiced whatever religion Pastor Levitt claimed to represent. But that was highly doubtful. The Saudi security man could never show his face in his home country again if he was associating with Levitt.

Schiffer knew he had a problem on his hands. He reached down to his right hip and unholstered his cell phone. He punched in the number for Director Stubblefield.

But the call never went through. The stun baton zapped Schiffer's body with a high-voltage current and dropped him to the pavement.

CHAPTER 28

Near Independence Hall – Philadelphia, Pennsylvania

Director Stubblefield entered the FBI's mobile command unit on 5th Street to the east of Independence Hall and received a five-minute briefing. Two hours to go until the President's arrival. The roadways the presidential motorcade would take from the airport to Independence Hall would be closed in one hour. The crowd had swelled with the warm weather and little chance of rain. Stubblefield looked over the monitors and everything appeared to be proceeding in an orderly fashion.

"Has the Secret Service voiced any concerns?" Stubblefield asked to his deputy.

"No, nothing," the man said. "All systems are go. They have the whole area locked down tight. Choppers are in the air."

Stubblefield nodded. He had great respect for the Secret Service, but it only took one crazed loner to create a panic.

"What about down the street at that idiot's protest?" Stubblefield asked. The Levitt Koran burning had received a fair amount of coverage, not enough to upstage the President, but enough that thousands of people were expected to support or curse his actions.

Stubblefield's deputy pointed to the screen on the far right. "The Secret Service has blocked off any access from the park two blocks south of Independence Hall. No one is allowed access from the south side. So they don't expect any spillover into the President's event."

"Which way is the wind blowing?" Stubblefield asked.

"North to south."

Stubblefield nodded. That was good for several reasons. Any type of biological device would be blown away from the Celebration. And if the protesters at Levitt's event got rowdy, the tear gas would move downwind of the President.

The door to the mobile command unit opened and the Phantom team's Agent Olivera stepped inside. He made quick eye contact with Director Stubblefield. He didn't have to point to him or wave him over.

Director Stubblefield took two steps toward Olivera. "What's wrong?" Stubblefield could see it in his eyes.

Agent Olivera walked to the Director's side and whispered in his ear. "We have lost contact with Agent Schiffer."

The six-foot-four Stubblefield looked down on the six-foot Olivera and glared at him with his dark eyes. "What do you mean lost contact with him? I just talked to him a half hour ago."

Olivera spoke softly but clearly. "We split up into two man teams."

Stubblefield nodded. "Yeah, I know, he told me that."

"We were supposed to check in every ten minutes," Olivera said, the concern evident in his tone of voice. "He's not answering his phone."

"Maybe he has a reason to be quiet," Stubblefield offered.

Olivera was aware of that. "But we send a ping on the phone to indicate the communication was received even if we cannot answer the phone."

Stubblefield was trying to run through the possibilities. Schiffer was one of the greatest assets U.S. law-enforcement had at its disposal. He could also take care of himself, had proved it time and time again, but it was not like him to go dark. Especially on a day like this when he knew the Director would want him available at all times. "He told me on the phone he was following somebody."

The three other agents of the Phantom team entered the mobile command unit.

"Anything?" Agent Olivera asked, looking at each one.

"No," Agent Jenkins responded, shaking his head back and forth. "No word from Duke."

Stubblefield placed both of his hands on his hips. Something was wrong, and he had to make a decision. He clapped his hands together to get the attention of the agents manning the controls. "All right, everybody listen up," he said forcefully. He now had everybody's attention. "We have lost contact with Agent Schiffer and I need to find him ASAP. Last known location was . . .?" he asked, looking at Olivera.

"West side of Independence Hall," Olivera reported.

"West side of Independence Hall," Stubblefield said again. "He told me he was tailing a suspicious male, possibly a Saudi security agent. I want surveillance videos checked for the past forty-five minutes. I also want to find out where his phone is. It has a locator device in it. Go find his phone." He then stopped to think if he needed to add any other directives. He had only one.

"And find Agent Schiffer."

Chinatown – Philadelphia, Pennsylvania

"You fools!" Hakim al-Rashid shouted at Ahmed Yassar and Omar Faran. He could not remember when he had been this irate. He slapped Faran across the face to show his anger. He wanted to do the same to Yassar but he thought better of it. "You almost blew the entire operation!"

Al-Rashid stalked around the apartment above Mr. Egg Roll, lecturing the two men on how they had led a U.S. lawman to their location.

He pointed over to Yassar. "I cannot believe you were so careless!" he yelled at the former Saudi security man. "You know better than that!"

The terrorist plot had almost been blown. Al-Rashid had just finished his last meeting with "the boss," Pastor Carson Levitt, who was a close personal friend of al-Rashid. Levitt was no pastor of the Christian faith. He was a Muslim convert, and he was fully committed to the call for jihad. Al-Rashid had come up with the plan – have Pastor Levitt threaten to burn the Koran to raise the ire of militant Muslims around the world.

And it had worked. The planned Koran burning near Atlanta was the signal for the European terror attacks to commence. And the one scheduled for later that day would be the continuation of the worldwide war here in America. Pastor Levitt's ability to draw huge crowds ensured mass carnage. The whole world would witness the horror on TV.

And it was almost stopped before it could happen.

Once al-Rashid received the call that Yassar and Faran were on their way back to the apartment, he said his goodbyes to Pastor Levitt, told him he would see him later, and went outside to make sure nobody followed his two compatriots back to their base of operations.

He was glad he did. While hiding in the vestibule of the Golden Dragon restaurant, al-Rashid noticed Agent Schiffer – who obviously had the look of a lawman, just like Yassar – from a block and a half away. While pretending to peruse the day's lunch menu, al-Rashid watched Schiffer walk by and knew from the quick pace in Schiffer's steps that he was on to the two terrorists he was following. Al-Rashid had planned for this eventuality. He knew something would come up and he came prepared. He placed the menu back in the rack and tapped his stun baton walking cane on the floor. With a fake limp, he walked outside leaning on his faux cane, turned right, and hobbled to catch up with his prey. When Schiffer was distracted with making his phone call, al-Rashid raised the cane and gave Schiffer a high-voltage shock to the neck. Schiffer only heard the snap, crackle, and pop of the electrical arc heading toward his head before he lost all sense of balance and control of his muscles. With a helpless Schiffer slumped up against the side of the building, al-Rashid yelled for his cohorts to help him get Schiffer up to the apartment. None of the locals saw or heard anything. Or if they did, they didn't care about the outsiders in their midst to do anything about it.

Now Agent Schiffer was bound at the ankles and wrists with plastic flex cuffs, a handkerchief acting as a gag. They had relieved him of his two weapons and his phone and frisked him to make sure he didn't have any locator devices on him.

Now that the lecture was over, Yassar thought he would find out what their catch was all about. Yassar took great interest in Schiffer's FBI badge. He had Faran roll Schiffer over and up to his knees so he could get a better look into his eyes. He had come to after the jolt from the stun baton.

"Well, well, well," Yassar said smugly. "If it isn't Special Agent D.A. Schiffer from America's famed FBI." He patted the badge in his hand. "We meet again."

A groggy Schiffer blinked his eyes twice to clear the cobwebs. He now remembered who Yassar was. Unable to speak because of the gag, he nodded.

"You know him?" Faran asked, standing behind Schiffer.

"Yeah," Yassar said with a smile. "Agent Schiffer here provided some great instruction to me and my fellow countrymen several years back when he and the FBI worked with the Saudi police force." Yassar then slapped Schiffer across the face with the back of his hand in appreciation. Schiffer flinched but held firm on his knees.

"Agent Schiffer is one of the best sharpshooters in all of the world," Yassar said, tapping Schiffer's badge in his hand as he paced back and forth in front of his prisoner. "He provided us with some very good tips on how to kill people without them even knowing what happened." He then stopped in front of Schiffer and looked into his eyes. "And I intend to put that instruction to good use today, my friend."

He gave Schiffer another hard slap to his face. Faran thought he would get in on the fun and backhanded Schiffer across the head from behind.

Hakim al-Rashid came out of the bedroom. He smiled at his two comrades, knowing they were having a little fun before they dumped Agent Schiffer out with the rest of the trash. He finished buttoning his white dress shirt, two sizes larger to cover the suicide vest wrapped around his midsection. He buttoned up and stopped in front of the mirror on the wall to work on his tie. He looked at Agent Schiffer in the reflection.

"Agent Schiffer?" he asked, putting the black tie into a knot. "I'm afraid I don't know that name."

Yassar tried to fill him in. "He's a decorated sniper and a SWAT team member." That was all Yassar remembered. "But I haven't heard much about him recently. Maybe he has fallen off the radar at the FBI."

Faran backhanded Schiffer again as he headed toward the kitchen to start in on the cheese ball and crackers for lunch. He knifed off a healthy portion and placed it on the Ritz. He stuffed it in his mouth and put the knife back in the cheese ball. He then went over to the sink and filled a teapot full of water. Once full, he took it to the stove and fired up the burner.

Now finished with his tie, al-Rashid thought it was his turn on the prisoner.

"What are we going to do with you?" he asked Schiffer, punching Schiffer in the mouth and drawing blood. He then turned to Yassar, who was opening up a bottle of water. "Maybe we ought to ask him some questions to see what he might know."

Yassar took another swig of water while Faran had another cracker. Al-Rashid waved Yassar over. "I want you to take his gag out," he said to Yassar before turning to Schiffer. "But if he yells out, I want you to shoot him."

Yassar nodded like he hoped he could. He pulled out his nine-millimeter and put it up against Schiffer's head before loosening the gag.

Once free of the gag, Schiffer licked his lips and spit out the blood onto the floor. Al-Rashid brought over a bottle of water and poured a couple of ounces over Schiffer's lips.

"Can I get you something else Agent Schiffer?" al-Rashid asked sarcastically, like he was intent on granting his guest's every wish.

Schiffer gave another light spit of blood onto the floor before returning his eyes back up to al-Rashid. "How about some kung pao chicken and a side of rice?" he asked with a hoarse voice. The gag had dried out his throat and the blood didn't offer much relief.

Al-Rashid and Yassar got a laugh out of it.

Al-Rashid pulled up a chair and turned it around before taking a seat. "I'm afraid our cook doesn't do much other than cheese, crackers, and a cup of tea," he said pointing over his shoulder to Faran in the kitchen.

Faran raised his arms like it wasn't his fault. He was a jihadist not a chef.

"Who were you looking for earlier on?" al-Rashid asked.

Schiffer nodded his head to his left in the direction of the man holding the gun on him.

"Mr. Yassar?"

Schiffer nodded.

Al-Rashid smiled. "Well, Ahmed," he said to his comrade. "It appears you made a lasting impression on Agent Schiffer when you met him all those years ago. He remembered you and wanted to say hello."

"Isn't that nice," Yassar responded.

Schiffer licked his lips. "What do you guys have planned for us today?"

Al-Rashid smiled. He looked over to his left at the TV up against the wall. It was a color model but it was so old it didn't have a remote control or a mute button. The sound had been manually turned down. Al-Rashid pointed over to the screen. A local affiliate was on the scene and prepping the viewers about the President's visit at Independence Hall as well as Pastor Levitt's event just a couple of blocks to the south.

"We are going to head downtown and have some fun," he said.

"Sounds good," Schiffer said. "We should probably get going then."

Al-Rashid laughed. If only Agent Schiffer knew what was going to happen to him and his fellow Americans in just a short while.

"Your President has called for a Celebration of the Constitution," al-Rashid said beginning his lecture. "But today is the last day you Americans will celebrate the Constitution that has brought sin and evil to this part of the world and beyond. Today, in the city where the Founding Documents were born, those documents will meet their death. Today begins a new world revolution that will finally bring sharia law to your homeland. You infidels will sully this earth no more. And we're going to have a front row seat."

"Do you have an extra ticket for me?" Schiffer asked.

Al-Rashid smiled again. He liked the man's spunk in spite of the obvious demise staring him in the face. "You, my friend, won't be joining us this afternoon."

"Too bad," Yassar said with a smile on his face. "He won't get to see me use the skills that he taught me."

"Too bad, indeed," al-Rashid said.

"Of course, he has probably been reading about it in the papers for the past several weeks," Yassar said.

Schiffer glared at the man, a man he had trained for good not evil. "You were the other sniper," Schiffer said.

Yassar nodded, a smile of pride crossing his face. "Let's see, there was that Hispanic man at the gas station in Alexandria. I dropped him with one shot. And then there was that fat man at the rest area near Manassas," he said, counting to two on his fingers. "And then, of course," he said before stopping for dramatic effect, "there was the coup de grace, the President's very own Mr. Cogdon." He pronounced it "Cog-doan."

"You killed Cogdon?"

Yassar smiled again and nodded, basking in his own lethal glory. He bowed his head slightly. "Guilty as charged."

"Man, that was a hell of a shot," al-Rashid added in admiration. "Only a man with the talent of Ahmed Yassar could pull that off."

Yassar smiled. "It's a shame Agent Schiffer won't be able to see me in action one more time," he said.

Al-Rashid rose from his chair. "I hadn't thought about that, Ahmed." He sounded concerned about the slight. He paced back and forth across the room in thought. "It would be rude to invite Agent Schiffer in and not let him see your handiwork." He then stopped in front of Schiffer. "I'll tell you what I am going to do. I'm going to leave Mr. Faran here to keep you company."

Faran bolted in from the kitchen unsure of what he just heard. "What? I'm staying here? I thought I was going downtown?"

Al-Rashid held up his hand at the young man. He had a slight change of plans. Faran was too jumpy, and he was getting too cocky for his own good. He was liable to tip off the authorities and blow the whole operation. "I want you to stay here and watch over Agent Schiffer. Put him in front of the TV so he can watch the slaughter of thousands of Americans today. Once the killing begins and the bodies of dead Americans fill his crying eyes, then you can put a bullet in his brain and join us downtown. There will be such great panic that you will cause even more damage with your suicide vest when you meet the people as they cowardly run away."

Faran was not happy with the change of plans. He wanted to be in the center of action when it began. He tried to protest but al-Rashid would have none of it. Al-Rashid grabbed his suit coat and put it on. He then looked himself over in the mirror one last time.

"Agent Schiffer," he said. "Your good friend, Mr. Yassar, and I are going to leave now. Unfortunately, we won't be able to meet again, but it was a pleasure getting to know you this morning. Sorry about the stun gun." He stopped one last time in front of his prisoner and gave him a final parting shot with the back of his hand. "No hard feelings?"

Yassar waited for his turn to say his goodbyes. "It was nice seeing you again, Agent Schiffer," he said. "Thanks for all the tips." He then punched Schiffer in the mouth.

Al-Rashid grabbed his Koran and waited at the door for Yassar. He then turned to Faran. "Once you see us on stage, kill him and get downtown."

CHAPTER 29

Near Independence Hall – Philadelphia, Pennsylvania

"Where is he?" Director Stubblefield barked inside the FBI mobile command unit. He had asked that very question every five minutes, but he still wasn't getting an answer.

Olivera shook his head. "Still nothing, sir."

Stubblefield didn't like the answer. Schiffer had been off the radio for over an hour now, and with every minute of silence Stubblefield grew more worried.

One of the agents manning the screen spoke up. "Sir, the President is en route to Independence Hall."

The Director nodded. He had to think fast. With Agent Schiffer missing and the President on his way, he just knew something unexpected was about to happen.

"Anything from the Secret Service?" he asked the computer man.

"No, nothing," the man responded. "The radio traffic indicates all systems are normal."

"Yeah," Stubblefield responded. "As normal as you can get with the most powerful man in the world on his way." He started tapping his right index finger on the headrest of the chair.

"Sir, we might have something here," Agent Olivera said, looking over the shoulder of another computer technician.

Stubblefield hurried down the line. "What is it?"

"We got a ping on Agent Schiffer's phone," Olivera said. "The phone sends out a ping every hour. Either he did it or the phone did it automatically."

"Where is he?"

Olivera tapped the computer technician on the shoulder. With a few taps on the keyboard, he had the answer. "The ping came from the Chinatown area."

Stubblefield swatted his massive hand at the equally large biceps of Agent Olivera. "Get the Phantom team ready to move."

"Yes, sir," Olivera said, hustling out of the mobile command unit.

"Can you try to home in on that ping?" Stubblefield asked.

The computer technician shook his head. "I need another ping to do that."

"Call Schiffer's number."

The technician punched in the number and heard three rings. He then shook his head. "Voice mail, sir."

Director Stubblefield's phone buzzed on his hip. He looked at the number and saw it was Olivera. "Yeah, go ahead."

"Sir, we are ready," Olivera said, now in the driver's seat of the Phantom team's Econoline cargo van.

"Get to the Chinatown area," Stubblefield ordered. He had to restrain himself to keep from telling them to wait for him.

Olivera and the Phantom team hauled ass through the empty and blocked off streets leading away from Independence Hall. He knew how to get to Chinatown but he didn't know where he was going once the team got there.

"Sir, we got something!" the computer technician blurted out. "We got another ping!"

"Where is it?"

The computer tech pecked away at the keyboard, much too slow for the Director.

"Come on, come on," Stubblefield barked. He put the phone back up to his ear. "Standby guys, we might have something here."

"The phone is on the move," the techie said.

"Show me on the map."

The computer tech punched in a few keys and a street map of Philadelphia appeared on the screen. He zoomed in on the Chinatown area and the blinking red dot indicating Agent Schiffer's phone.

"It's on Race Street," the man said.

"Race Street," Stubblefield announced over the phone.

"We're on Race Street," Agent Jenkins said, taking over the phone while Olivera drove.

The street was one-way and since other streets had been blocked off for emergency vehicles, it seemed every local was using the street to get around the congestion. Olivera swerved from lane to lane and laid on his horn.

"Give us a cross street, Director," Jenkins said, as the Chinese restaurants flew by.

"He's turned north on 11th Street," the computer technician said.

"North on 11th Street," Director Stubblefield announced. He looked closer at the screen. "There's a police station up on 11th Street before you get to the expressway." Stubblefield allowed himself to breathe a sigh of relief. Maybe Schiffer was hightailing it to the police station to get a ride back.

"We're on 11th," Jenkins announced. "Where is he?"

"He's stopped on the corner of 11th and Spring," the computer technician said. "There's a Chinese restaurant on the corner."

The Phantom team roared to a stop in the middle of the intersection behind a garbage truck picking up a load. "We are at the location," Jenkins said, grabbing his MP-7 rifle. "Hold on, Director."

A young Chinese man standing next to a pay phone looked at the four heavily armed men hustling out of the van. Deciding he didn't want any part of the Phantom team, he took off down the alley. Agent Jenkins took the lead and focused in on the Bamboo Garden restaurant.

"Olivera and Guerrero will take the front door," he said. "Alvarez and I will cover the alley and the back. Director, stand by, we are preparing to enter the restaurant."

Once everyone was in position, Olivera motioned to the two men in the garbage truck to move on down the road so he and Alvarez could see if anyone was coming from the other side of the street.

"We're going in," Olivera radioed.

With his gun raised, Olivera pushed open the door and entered the restaurant followed by Agent Alvarez. The lunch crowd ceased talking until they realized the Kevlar-clad men had automatic weapons. The whole restaurant erupted in screams of horror. Tables were overturned, plates of General Tso's chicken and szechuan shrimp flew through the air and crashed onto the floor.

"What's going on?" Stubblefield asked over the radio. He could hear the commotion and hated not being there. "Guys, what's going on?"

Olivera and Alvarez lowered their weapons and raised the badges trying to calm the stunned crowd, some of whom were trying to escape by crawling toward the kitchen. Olivera tried asking the frightened old man if he saw a white male come in the restaurant, but the Chinese man either didn't understand English or he was unleashing a furious barrage of epithets while shaking his head back and forth. The woman running the cash register grabbed a handful of bills and threw them at the two FBI agents thinking they were robbing the joint.

"Sir, the phone is on the move," the computer technician said

"What!?" a surprised Stubblefield asked.

The tech pointed at the screen. The red dot was moving north on 11th Street.

Stubblefield grabbed his radio. "All units, the phone is on the move north on 11th Street. Copy?" He made eye contact with one of his assistants. "Get a car and a driver ready for me," he ordered. He couldn't take it any longer.

Olivera and Alvarez looked at each other and then got the hell out of there. When they exited the restaurant, Jenkins and Guerrero were coming around the corner from the alley to meet them.

"He's stopped in front of the police station!" Director Stubblefield radioed. He then told another man to get on the horn to that police station to let them know the FBI was in the area.

The four Phantom team members all saw the same thing just up the block. The garbage truck had stopped in front of the police station and one of the garbage men on foot was directing the beast of a machine as it backed into the parking lot to unload the Dumpster.

The Phantom team took off with guns raised. "Don't move!" Olivera shouted at the garbage man on foot. "Get your hands in the air!"

Agent Guerrero opened the driver's side door and yanked the driver out of his seat and onto the pavement. "Don't move!"

Jenkins grabbed the man on foot and pushed him up against the truck. Two police officers suddenly appeared at the front door of the station.

"FBI!" Alvarez yelled at them before pointing behind him. "Block off the street! Don't let anyone in!"

"Cab's clear!" Agent Guerrero yelled.

Jenkins was starting to get a bad feeling in his stomach. He wondered what was in the belly of the beast. "You pick up any large articles today?" he asked of the frightened garbage man with hands raised over his head.

The man couldn't speak. He just shook his head back and forth. He couldn't think of anything other than the normal trash pickups.

Back in the mobile command unit, Stubblefield told the technician to call Schiffer's phone again.

"We got a cell-phone beacon coming from your truck," Jenkins said into the man's face. "A cell phone that doesn't belong to you. We're gonna need you to release the compactor."

The wide-eyed man looked at the back of the garbage truck and tried to put two and two together. He hadn't even stolen anything. When the pocket of his jacket started vibrating, his eyes drifted downward. One of his hands came down and reached into his pocket. "You mean this phone?"

With his left hand in the man's chest, Jenkins grabbed the phone with his right. It was turned on and the screen showed the FBI seal. "Shit," he said. He then turned back to the man. "Where did you get this phone?" His tone indicated the man better have a clear and definitive answer or there was going to be serious repercussions.

"It's not mine," the man protested.

"I know it's not your phone, dickhead," Jenkins said, jabbing the man in the chest with his fist. He tried again. "I want you to tell me where you got this phone right now."

"On Race Street," the man whimpered. "Just about thirty minutes ago. I think somebody threw it in the back when we were inside taking a leak. It looked nice so I was going to keep it."

"Sir, we have Agent Schiffer's phone," Jenkins radioed to the Director with the good news before telling him the bad. "No Schiffer though. The garbage man here says someone must have thrown it into the truck on Race Street."

"Ask him where," Stubblefield said.

Jenkins asked the man where he stopped to take a leak. "You are going to show us," Jenkins said. It wasn't a request. He grabbed the man by the arm and hurried him down the street to the Phantom team van. "He's going to take us where he thinks the phone was put into the truck," Jenkins told the Director.

"Ten-four," Stubblefield said. "I'm heading that way."

CHAPTER 30

Near Independence Hall – Philadelphia, Pennsylvania

"Director, the President is on site," one of the FBI agents manning the computers reported.

Stubblefield figured as much, what with the wailing sirens announcing the arrival of the President's motorcade.

The President and the First Lady arrived thirty minutes early to meet with the assembled dignitaries. Given the patriotic festivities, the First Lady wore a red dress, and the President went with the blue suit, white dress shirt, and red tie.

"Mr. President," Secret Service Agent Mac Clark said from the front seat. "We will be exiting under the tent."

The President nodded. He liked exiting the limo and waving to the crowd but he relented to the wishes of the Secret Service.

"All units," Clark announced into his wrist microphone. "Stagecoach is stopping."

Once Clark received the all-clear from the phalanx of Secret Service agents in and around Independence Hall, he stepped out of the front seat and opened the rear door to the limo. The President stepped out and offered a hand to the First Lady. They then proceeded through a side door into Independence Hall where a line of well-wishers was waiting for a handshake with the President. The First Couple moved quickly, wanting to stay on schedule. They made it to the other side of Independence Hall where they exited and walked through another tent to the Liberty Bell Visitor's Center.

The White House photographer took pictures of the President and the First Lady admiring the 2,000 pound Bell with its distinctive crack. Although people were once allowed to touch it, the custodians of the Liberty Bell had moved it out of arm's reach after some nut job took a hammer to it back in 2001. Still, the inscriptions on the Bell were clear.

"There it is. Leviticus, chapter 25, verse 10," the President pointed out the words to his wife just under the Bell's American Elm yoke. "I didn't even know about that until Wiley told me."

The First Lady nodded. Mentions of Cogdon still brought tears to her eyes. She tried to keep it together. They held hands and moved on when they saw Director Stubblefield approach.

"Where have you been hiding?" the President asked his friend. "Are you ready for your Second Amendment reading?"

The big man wore no smile, and a look of deep concern was etched on his face. He did allow himself to accept a hug from the First Lady. He then asked for a private moment with the President. When they were alone, he said. "Sir, we've got a problem."

The President's heart sank. *When isn't there a problem*, he thought to himself. "What's wrong?"

"I've lost contact with Agent Schiffer."

The President was well aware of Agent Schiffer's heroic exploits. He had privately bestowed several law-enforcement medals on Schiffer on behalf of the United States of America for his bravery and actions above and beyond the call of duty. The President understood the Director's worry.

"For how long?"

"Going on over an hour now," the Director reported. "Schiffer had reported he was following what he thought was a member of the Saudi police force. He went dark shortly after that. My guys just found his phone in the possession of a garbage man in the Chinatown area. Apparently the phone had been thrown into the back."

The President wasn't sure of what he could do. He knew Director Stubblefield would not rest until the FBI found his man.

Stubblefield took a deep breath. He had been running the possibilities through his head for the last half hour and he knew something was very wrong. He just didn't know how widespread the problem was.

"Sir, I think you should postpone the event," he told the President, knowing full well the backlash that would soon follow.

"Ty, I am not going to cancel the Celebration of the Constitution," the President said in no uncertain terms.

"Sir, I am concerned for your safety," Ty pleaded. "And the safety of every other government official and American citizen who is on site today."

The President started shaking his head. "Ty, the Secret Service tells me they have locked this place down like Fort Knox. Everybody's been checked coming in. I have no concerns at all about my safety or the safety of everyone else out there."

The Director knew better than to argue with the President. The show was going to go on. "I understand, sir." He then started to back away like he was leaving.

"Where do you think you're going?" the President asked, stopping Stubblefield in his tracks.

"Sir, I have to go find Schiffer," the Director said.

"Oh no," the President said, taking a step forward. "You are not going out there, Ty."

The Director held up his hands, palms out, like it was his decision to make. "Sir."

The six-foot-two President stood toe-to-toe with the six-foot-four Stubblefield. "No," the President barked, jabbing his right index finger in the big man's chest. "You are staying right here. I already lost one friend in the last two weeks and I am not going to lose another one." The President had raised his voice enough that the First Lady was making her way over to see what the commotion was all about.

"Sir, I need to be out there."

"No," the President thundered again. "You've got your agents out there to do that."

The First Lady heard the continued discussion and looked at Stubblefield with her beautiful brown eyes full of concern. She didn't want Stubblefield to go out there either.

"You're staying right here," the President demanded. "And that's an order!"

Director Stubblefield raised his hands in defeat. The President looked like he was one step away from handcuffing the Director to him, so he relented. "Okay. Just let me make two phone calls and take a restroom break and I'll meet you out there."

"Okay, that's better" the President said, relieved that his friend finally saw it his way. He looked around Stubblefield at the Director's bodyguards and pointed at them, as if ordering them that they had better keep an eye on their boss. He then turned back to Stubblefield. "I'll see you out there."

Chinatown – Philadelphia, Pennsylvania

With Hakim al-Rashid and Ahmed Yassar on their way to Washington Square and Pastor Levitt's protest, it was just Omar Faran in the apartment with Agent Schiffer. He was pissed off at the change of plans and decided to exact his own measure of revenge on the captured FBI man. Without any higher-ups in the vicinity, Faran took it upon himself to show Schiffer that he was now in charge.

"Agent Schiffer," Faran mocked, like a defense lawyer looking to work over a dirty cop on the witness stand. "You don't seem so tough." He backhanded him across the face once again, the smack of skin echoing in the near empty apartment.

He put his cell phone on the table and grabbed Schiffer's FBI badge. He pretended to admire it, rubbing his fingers over the shield. Somehow, he wanted to use it against his prisoner. He decided to hold it in the palm of his hand and whack Agent Schiffer across the cheek. The jolt toppled Schiffer to the floor. The flex cuffs on his wrists and ankles indicated he could offer no defense.

"Here, let me help you there," Faran offered, helping Schiffer back onto his knees. Once upright, Faran kicked Schiffer in the stomach, toppling him over once again.

Faran laughed. "You are such a weak man."

Faran tapped the badge in his hand and walked back to the kitchen. He grabbed the knife from the cheese ball and thought about his next plan of attack.

He went back to Agent Schiffer and waved the knife in front of his face. "Maybe I should gut the American infidel right now and send him on his way to hell," he announced to the walls. He then looked down at Schiffer before helping him up again. "Wouldn't that be nice? You would slowly bleed to death, suffering the agony for being an agent of the devil."

Faran walked back to the kitchen, jammed the knife in the cheese ball, and lathered up a cracker for a quick snack. He jammed the knife back in and grabbed the badge again. He then looked at the stove. Now he had another bright idea.

He turned on one of the front burners and then looked over at Agent Schiffer with a demented smile on his face. His jihadist mind was practically giddy with evil. He held the badge over the fire until he could stand the heat no more. He then hurried over to Schiffer and jammed the scalding hot badge into the agent's neck.

"Aaaghh!" Schiffer cried as the hot badge seared the side of his neck. He toppled over to end the branding.

Faran grabbed Schiffer by the neck and brought him to his knees again. He was having so much fun he was losing track of time. He thought he might just stay in the apartment and torture his prisoner for the rest of the afternoon. Although if al-Rashid and Yassar knew what he was doing instead of preparing for his role in the terror operation, they would not be pleased.

Schiffer was aching inside. One of his ribs might have been broken, and another good punch to the face could do some lasting damage. He worried his right eye was going to swell shut. And the cavalry wasn't coming because nobody knew where he was. He had to do something.

"Could I get some water?" Schiffer croaked.

Faran laughed at him once more. *What a weak man*, he thought to himself. And he calls himself an FBI agent. Faran walked over to the table and opened a bottle of water. He walked back over with that torturer's grin on his face. He jammed the neck of the bottle into Schiffer's mouth and tilted his head back. He then poured and poured and poured until Schiffer finally could take no more and threw up and fell forward.

Faran laughed maniacally. "Was that good?" he asked. "Want some more? Poor little baby can't even hold his water."

He pulled Schiffer back up to his knees and slapped him across the face again.

Faran grabbed Schiffer's confiscated five-shot ankle revolver and spun the cylinder round and round. He popped out the cylinder and looked at the five bullets waiting to be fired. He spun the cylinder again before getting another idea. He turned the gun over and poured out the bullets, each one clanking onto the table. He looked at Schiffer and smiled. He grabbed one bullet and placed it into one of the cylinder's chambers. He clicked the cylinder into place and spun it around twice.

"I'm supposed to kill you before I leave, Agent Schiffer," Faran announced. "It looks like I only have one shot at it," he said holding up the gun. "I hear the Russians like to play this game."

Faran walked over to Schiffer and put the gun to the agent's head. "So long, Agent Schiffer."

Faran pulled the trigger. "Boom!" he shouted after nothing but a click was heard from the gun. He laughed again as Schiffer flinched.

Schiffer had no desire to give Faran a second chance.

"Shouldn't you be getting ready to blow yourself up?" he managed to ask. He nodded his head over to the TV.

Faran had indeed lost track of time. He needed to get dressed. Before that, he had to go through his ritual washing and then offer his final prayers to Allah. He knew he had to follow the jihadist protocol if he wanted to meet his virgins right away this afternoon or early evening.

Faran didn't tell Agent Schiffer that he was right, that he did need to get a move on if he wanted to get downtown in time for the festivities. He slapped Schiffer across the right side of his face to thank him.

Schiffer could hear the shower faucet come on in the bathroom. He didn't know how many minutes it would take Faran to shower but he figured it wouldn't be long.

Schiffer managed to push himself off his knees and onto his feet. His knees were aching after kneeling for the better part of an hour. He had his eyes on the phone on the table. With his boots on and his ankles tied together with the flex cuffs, he bunny-hopped it across the living room into the kitchen as silently as possible. With his cuffed hands behind his back, he grabbed Faran's phone with the tips of his fingers. He flipped it open and ran his thumbs over the numbers. He was thankful the cheap throw-away phone wasn't an iPhone with a flat screen he wouldn't be able to see. He thought he might only get one shot at this considering he couldn't tell what he was doing behind his back. He found the "1" on the keypad and set out tapping in the ten-digit number for Director Stubblefield. With the water being turned off in the bathroom, he didn't have much time.

He put the phone back on the table and leaned in. Given the unknown number, the Director probably would just let it go to voice mail.

"It's Schiffer," he whispered. "Chinatown. Second floor." That was the best information he could give the Director at that time. When al-Rashid and Yassar had left, Schiffer heard their footfalls go down five steps to a landing and then down another five steps before a door to the street opened. Message given, he turned around and snapped the phone shut. He hopped back over to the living room and dropped to his knees.

Faran came out of the bathroom wiping the water off his bare chest with a towel. He looked at the TV and then at his prisoner. He twirled the wet towel around and whipped Schiffer across the head.

"You had better start saying your prayers," Faran smirked. "You are not long for this world."

CHAPTER 31

Independence Hall – Philadelphia, Pennsylvania

Director Stubblefield was standing in the corner of the Assembly Room where the Declaration and the Constitution had been drafted, debated, and signed. His bodyguards were out in the hall since the Secret Service had the room and the entire building locked down. The dignitaries were milling about waiting for their introduction onto the stage before the President's speech and then the ceremonial reading of the Constitution. The President was working the room like the good politician he was and thanking those that came for agreeing to take part in the Celebration.

Director Stubblefield, however, was not glad-handing anyone. He was still distracted with the Schiffer matter and he waited in the corner for any type of notification from the Phantom team. Attorney General Claire Donovan came over to say hello when the phone on Stubblefield's hip starting buzzing.

"Excuse me, Claire," he said to the Attorney General, holding up his right hand. "I need to take this."

He had directed every call to his voice mail, and he wasn't sure of the number of the caller. But he was going to take every call that came in to him today. He dialed his voice mail and moved farther into the corner of the room. With the amount of talking going on, he put his left index finger in his ear so he could hear.

"It's Schiffer," the recorded voice whispered. "Chinatown. Second floor."

Stubblefield looked at the number again. The number didn't come from a Phantom team member, and it wasn't one programmed into his phone. He played the message again.

"It's Schiffer. Chinatown. Second floor."

Stubblefield strained to hear the words as he played the message one more time. He turned around and spotted the President across the way. He tried not to give it away that something important had come up.

Something that needed his immediate hands-on attention. He knew the President wouldn't like it but he was going to disobey orders. He couldn't leave one of his men out there.

"Hey, Claire," Stubblefield said to the Attorney General, stopping her as she walked by again. "If the President asks, I'm going to use the restroom."

The Attorney General smiled, finding it somewhat odd that the Director of the FBI would ask her to vouch for his whereabouts to the President of the United States. She wasn't sure what Stubblefield was doing or what he was up to, but she said okay.

As best he could do given his size, the Director ducked out of the Assembly Room without anyone noticing. He then ditched his bodyguards and picked up the pace as he hustled out of Independence Hall. He called his assistant. "Where's my car and driver?"

"East side by the mobile command unit," the man responded.

"I'm on my way," Stubblefield said, breaking into a run. "I want you to trace the call that just came to my voice-mail account. I think it came from somewhere in Chinatown."

"I'll get right on it," the man said.

The Director hung up and dialed Agent Jenkins. "Where are you?"

"We're still in Chinatown," Jenkins said.

"Hold fast. I just got a voice mail from Schiffer. I think he's somewhere in Chinatown. As soon as I find out, I'll tell you where."

In his business suit, Stubblefield ran down past the President's limo still idling at the ready. He saw the FBI sedan next to the mobile command unit.

"Chinatown!" he yelled to the driver as he strapped himself into the front passenger seat. "Move it!"

The squealing tires left a waft of rubber smoke floating through the air. The red and blue flashing lights in the car's grille lit up and the siren squawked as the car proceeded through the empty intersections.

Stubblefield jammed his hand into his suit coat and grabbed the nine-millimeter Glock 17 housed in his shoulder holster. He took it out, chambered a round, and jammed it back into the holster. He was readying for battle. He then grabbed his phone again and called the mobile command unit.

"Where are we going?" he asked the man on the other end.

"Race Street and Hutchinson!"

The Director hung up and dialed Agent Jenkins. "Race Street and Hutchinson!"

"Roger that," Jenkins said. "We're just a couple blocks away."

"Do whatever you have to do to get him back!" Stubblefield ordered.

Chinatown – Philadelphia, Pennsylvania

Omar Faran had finished his prayers and checked on Agent Schiffer again. He was having a great deal of fun torturing his prisoner. He kicked Schiffer in the stomach and yelled at him to get up. "Get on your knees!"

Schiffer was lying on his side, his ribs aching. Faran uprighted Schiffer and turned him so he could see the television. The Celebration of the Constitution and Pastor Levitt's Koran burning were about to start. And it was about time for Faran to get moving.

"Soon your countrymen will be getting what they deserve," Faran lectured to him. "Just like on 9/11." He wrapped his right hand around the back of Schiffer's neck and squeezed. "Look at that TV screen, you American devil. You and the infidels will soon be on your way to hell," he growled in anger. His tone then softened. "And I will be joining my comrades in paradise." He let go of his grip. "Do you have any last requests?"

Schiffer licked his dry lips. He wasn't going to ask for another drink. "Maybe you could turn up the volume so I can hear my countrymen read the Constitution one last time."

Faran scoffed at the request. That was it? No plea for mercy? No begging to spare his life? It was such an innocent request that Faran couldn't help but take pity on his prisoner. "Sure," he said, walking over to the TV and turning the volume knob. "I can do that. I wouldn't want you to miss out on your fellow citizens screaming in horror as they get slaughtered in the streets of Philadelphia."

Faran gave Schiffer another good slap and laughed. He walked back into the bedroom to put on his suicide vest and the clothes that would conceal it. The jihadist's preparation was almost complete.

Schiffer decided it was time to make his move.

Outside at ground level, the Phantom team van and Director Stubblefield's sedan were roaring to a stop. Agent Guerrero opened the rear doors of the van and hopped out carrying a bulletproof vest. He handed it over to Director Stubblefield.

"Which one?" Agent Jenkins asked, looking around at the buildings lining the street.

The Director didn't have any better coordinates than Race Street and Hutchinson, and the block was littered with Chinese restaurants of every color and dish. But the closest one to the intersection with a second floor was Mr. Egg Roll to their west.

"Let's try that one," the Director said, pointing at the restaurant. It was three stories and the attached building to its right was barely one and a half. "Olivera, get the van up against the wall and see if you and Jenkins can use the ladder and climb onto the roof. Take some flash-bangs with you."

Restaurant doors in the area were closing up and down the block, and the locals were scurrying to hide behind their bar-covered windows. Mandarin Chinese could be heard as men yelled at their wives and children to take cover.

The Director closed the Velcro on his bulletproof vest and gave his final order. "Let's go get him back."

Upstairs on the second floor, Schiffer stood up from his knees and hopped as quietly as he could into the kitchen. The volume on the TV muffled his thumping boots.

He skipped the phone on the table this time and went straight for the stove. He turned around, spun the burner knob with his cuffed hands, and waited for the fire to light. Sweat was rolling down his face, and he could hear Faran closing a closet door in the next room. He held his wrists over the flames and kept them there as long as it took.

"Aaaghh," he grunted under his breath. The blue flames were lapping at his wrist. He could feel the hairs on his arms and then his skin starting to burn but the plastic flex cuffs finally melted away.

He broke free of his plastic chains and hopped to the table kicking a chair over in the process. With the noise, he had just outed himself to Faran.

"Schiffer! Schiffer!" the Phantom team yelled from the street and up the apartment stairwell. They still had no idea where he was.

A startled Faran came running out of the bedroom to see what was happening when Schiffer grabbed the knife out of the cheese ball, sliced through the plastic flex cuffs around his ankles, and broke free.

"Hey!" the wide-eyed Faran yelled, going for his waistband and Schiffer's revolver.

Schiffer lunged at him and with his left hand jammed the knife into the left side of Faran's neck. Faran clutched his throat in agony as blood squirted out of his neck. He grabbed his gun with his left hand and pulled the trigger but the chamber was empty. Schiffer forced the gun toward the ceiling and Faran's next pull of the trigger blasted a shot into the ceiling raining plaster onto the men. Schiffer grabbed Faran's left wrist with his right hand and knocked it against Faran's head, causing him to drop the gun.

The Phantom team members in the hall could hear a struggle. They bounded up the stairs. "Schiffer! Schiffer!"

The now disarmed Faran backed into the living room, gurgling in his own blood, trying to take the knife out of his neck with his free right hand. Schiffer grabbed him by both wrists and thrust his boot into Faran's stomach sending the jihadist crashing through the second-story window and out onto the street below.

The door to the apartment blew off its hinges. Agents Guerrero and Alvarez entered, guns raised and ready to fire, followed by Director Stubblefield.

"Duke!" Stubblefield yelled, his own gun aimed to fire.

The Phantom team found Agent Schiffer, standing alone at the window looking down to the street below.

Agents Olivera and Alvarez were already off the roof and onto the ground. Faran lay sprawled on the cement sidewalk, blood pooling around his neck and draining into the gutter. Olivera motioned that the man with the knife still sticking out of his neck was dead.

Schiffer finally took a breath.

While Guerrero and Jenkins checked and secured the apartment, Director Stubblefield hurried over to Schiffer and looked over the battered and bruised man. "We're gonna need an ambulance," he radioed downstairs.

"No, I'm all right," Schiffer responded, bending over at the waist and placing his hands on his knees. His chest was still heaving and the exhales were still coming on fast. "Just give me a minute."

Director Stubblefield put his arm on Schiffer's back. "Man, you scared me there for a second," he said, shaking his head. "I thought I had lost you for good."

Schiffer was finally starting to catch his breath, the adrenaline still coursing through his veins. "Thanks for coming." He then straightened up and looked the Director in the eye. "We need to get back downtown."

Director Stubblefield tried to reassure him. "Duke, the President is going to be fine. The Secret Service has that place locked down tight."

Schiffer shook his head. "It's not the President they're after. It's the protest to the south of Independence Hall."

"What?"

"It's the Pastor. He's in on it. That man I was following is Ahmed Yassar. I helped train him as a Saudi police sniper. He killed Cogdon. That client of Art Brennan is also involved."

Director Stubblefield raised his radio. "Phantom team. We're moving."

CHAPTER 32

Philadelphia, Pennsylvania

Agent Olivera hustled the Phantom team van back toward the Independence Hall area through the empty streets of Philadelphia closed to public traffic.

"Go south," the Director said. "You're going to have to come from the southwest. The Secret Service has the area around Independence Hall shut down."

Stubblefield reached for his phone and dialed in the number to the Secret Service command post but got nothing. He looked at the phone again and saw he had no cellular service. Once the President was set to speak, the Secret Service jammed all cellular service within a three-square-block area to prevent cell phones being used as bomb detonators. He couldn't call in the cavalry, so the Phantom team would have to go it alone.

Director Stubblefield looked over at Schiffer, who was rubbing his wrists. The skin was bright red.

"What happened to your wrists?" the Director asked.

Schiffer kept rubbing them. They hurt like hell but he shrugged it off. "Cooking accident," he said.

"You need some ice?"

Schiffer shook his head. "No, I need my Remington."

Agent Guerrero responded from the backseat. "Here you go, Duke," he said, handing up the sniper rifle. Guerrero also handed him a Glock 17, a radio, and an earpiece.

Stubblefield pulled out a map of Washington Square and showed it to those seated in the back of the van.

"The north and northeast entrances are all closed off," he said, pointing at the map. "That way nobody can make their way to the area around Independence Hall. So we're looking at the south and west sides."

Schiffer pointed his finger at the southwest corner. "It's a bottleneck right there with those buildings," he said. "It'll be a killing field if we don't get there in time."

"Duke, you need to find a nice high place to do your work," Stubblefield told the sniper. He then looked over at the man, whose right eye looked like it might swell shut with the beating he had taken. "Do you need to take Jenkins or Alvarez with you to act as a spotter?"

Schiffer kept studying the map while shaking his head. "No," he said.

"Duke?" Stubblefield asked again. "Are you sure?"

Schiffer put the Director's concerns to rest. "I'm fine. You need the team on the ground." He then looked the Director in the eye. "I'll take care of Yassar myself."

Washington Square – Philadelphia, Pennsylvania

Although thirty thousand flag-waving people had showed up to see the President and hear the reading of the Constitution, two thousand people decided they would attend the circus down the street at Washington Square. About half were there to see what the nut of a pastor was going to do, while the other half came to curse and swear at him for being an idiot. Whatever their reason for attending, Pastor Levitt and Hakim al-Rashid were happy with the turnout – *plenty of victims*, they thought. Plus, the live TV cameras would provide an audience of the massacre all across the globe.

Just after the noon hour, Pastor Levitt and al-Rashid prepared to leave their tent and make their way to the stage. Al-Rashid had put the whole plan together. He had promised Levitt that the production would rival any drama seen on any New York City stage. But instead of Broadway, this was al-Rashid's Ford's Theatre. This was his moment to make the leap to the stage.

The two men walked out of the tent, al-Rashid allowing Pastor Levitt to go first to give the man his proper due. Levitt carried a book with him, presumably the Koran he planned to torch, and the torrent of epithets came rushing from the crowd behind the steel gates keeping them from charging the loathsome man.

The Phantom team van screeched to a stop behind the barricades one block to the west of Washington Square. Director Stubblefield and Agents Olivera, Jenkins, Alvarez, and Guerrero took off on foot down Locust Street, while Agent Schiffer and his Remington sought out higher ground.

"Get as many people out of here as you can!" Stubblefield yelled to the Phantom team members. "And get to the stage and take out al-Rashid and Levitt!"

The Philadelphia police had screened everyone walking into Washington Square to make sure they didn't have any weapons or explosives in their backpacks or purses. But they didn't check the two men in suits walking on to the stage in the middle of the square. No one had frisked Pastor Levitt or Hakim al-Rashid – security guards don't search the entertainment – and only the two men knew what they were carrying on them.

Pastor Levitt and al-Rashid wore wireless microphones to keep their hands free, and Levitt's voice carried nicely on the sound system speakers.

"Thank you very much for coming!" Pastor Levitt bellowed. The welcome was followed by a smattering of applause and even more boos and hisses. "I have come here today to exercise my constitutional right to express myself!" he thundered. "And to burn this here Koran for all the world to see!" he said, raising the book high in the air.

Ahmed Yassar readied himself at the corner of South and West Washington Square Streets. On the roof of a five-floor townhouse, he had climbed the rear fire escape without a second look from anyone. The occupants were either hunkering down inside, or more likely, down the street watching the President. Yassar placed his Dragon sniper rifle on the edge of the flat white roof. He snapped a ten-round magazine into place and positioned four more on the ledge.

"It is time to set fire to the words of the false prophet!" Levitt shouted, pulling a lighter out of his pocket. Shouts rang out from the crowd, and the pushing and shoving between protesters started.

Agent Schiffer had run up eleven flights of stairs to the top floor of a condo building across the street from Washington Square. There were buildings with higher perches to his north but his current position would have to do. He had no more time to search for higher ground. His ribs were aching, and every labored breath felt like a knife was stabbing him in the side.

Hakim al-Rashid moved in from the corner of the stage. This was his moment. "You will do no such thing!" he yelled to Pastor Levitt. The near riotous crowd suddenly went silent, wondering what was going on. He grabbed the lighter away from Pastor Levitt, who backed away like he didn't know what was going on. Al-Rashid then reached into his suit coat.

"This is really what you should be burning!" he yelled, pulling out a souvenir parchment copy of the Constitution. "Your Constitution shall burn in hell!" he shouted, pointing into the crowd as he lit the parchment aflame. The two men went to opposite corners of the stage to maximize the carnage.

"Get back!" Director Stubblefield yelled as he charged through the crowd like a linebacker. He and the Phantom team were nowhere near the stage, but he and the agents waved their arms and shouted at the top of their lungs over the sound system. "Everybody run! Get back! Get away from here!"

Ahmed Yassar readied his Dragon rifle on the roof line. He had no view of the center of Washington Square given the mature trees impeding his view, but he could faintly hear the strong voice of al-Rashid. He looked through his scope and waited for the stream of screaming people soon to appear in his killing zone. He would take them out one by one.

"And not only should your evil Constitution go up in flames!" al-Rashid yelled as he let go of the last burning remnants of the Constitution from his hand. "So too shall you infidels burn in hell!"

It was then that al-Rashid and Pastor Levitt opened their suit coats revealing the suicide vests underneath. "Soon all of America will be destroyed!"

"Everybody get down!" Director Stubblefield yelled. "Everybody get down!" He pushed his way through the crowd and even threw one man out of the way. He finally had a clear shot. Pointing his Glock 17 at al-Rashid, Director Stubblefield fired off one shot, striking the terrorist in the upper chest.

Agent Jenkins anchored his first shot into Levitt's chest, and the pastor stumbled backward off the stage. Then the pandemonium started. The panicked crowd took off running for their lives, some trampling those who had fallen in the melee. Ahmed Yassar raised his head from behind his rifle scope. He could feel a spike in his adrenaline, which his sniper training quickly tamped down. He could hear the screaming, and he could feel the stampede heading his way. But there should have been a blast. The ground should have shook and the middle of Washington Square should have been on fire by now.

He looked down below once more before his head twitched to the top of the building to the north of his position. He didn't know why he turned. Maybe it was a noise that he heard, or maybe it was a glimmer of light that caught his eye. Whatever it was, he saw something. Looking up, he could see a lone man on the roof, the distinctive silhouette of a sniper looking down at him. He had seen the sniper before. He even recognized the man's left-handed shooting position.

Didn't Agent Schiffer teach his sniper trainee to get to the highest position possible? Wasn't the sniper then to conceal himself from his prey? Those thoughts flashed across Yassar's mind in a split second. He remembered the training, but he thought he would be the hunter on this day. He never thought Agent Schiffer would be hunting him. Yassar could feel the hair on the back of his neck standing on edge. He could not move.

He knew he was a dead man.

Agent Schiffer didn't have to close his right eye much. Yassar and Faran had done most of that for him with their beatings. He exhaled one last time as his left index finger feathered the trigger on his Remington.

"This one is for Wiley Cogdon."

Schiffer squeezed the trigger and then cycled the bolt on his Remington for a second shot. None would be needed.

Outside Independence Hall – Philadelphia, Pennsylvania

The President rose from his seat and took his place behind the podium with the presidential seal. He looked out over the gathered throng. Wiley Cogdon would have been smiling from ear to ear at his grand celebration.

"Thank you, Mr. Mayor," he said in appreciation of the introduction. He also thanked the dignitaries who had come to the Celebration as well as the thousands of Americans outside Independence Hall and the millions more watching on television.

"We gather here today in the Cradle of Liberty, just steps away from where in 1776 our Founding Fathers pledged their lives, their fortunes, and their sacred honor in direct defiance of King George III. There, inside Independence Hall, our Founders in the Declaration boldly proclaimed for all the world to see the bedrock of this infant nation's republican form of government that 'all men are created equal' and 'they are endowed by their Creator with certain unalienable Rights, that among these are Life, Liberty, and the pursuit of Happiness.' To implement that way of governing and protect the rights of the people, the Framers of the Constitution sought to limit government and to "secure the blessings of liberty" granted to us by our God above for generations to come.

"Throughout the more than ten score years since the Declaration was signed and the Constitution was adopted, the United States has weathered the storm of division in the Civil War, the tumultuous fight for civil rights, and the evil reach of tyrannical regimes throughout the world. Ever since that seventeenth day of September in 1787, the Constitution has remained the fabric that has held this country together through trial and tribulation. With the separation of powers, checks and balances, the Bill of Rights, and the amendment process, 'the supreme Law of the Land' has been the source of law to protect the rights to life, liberty, and the pursuit of happiness of every man, woman, and child of every race, creed, and religion.

"The Celebration of the Constitution is a celebration of liberty, of freedom. And today, we reaffirm that most treasured document as well as remember the continuing and constant need to ensure its survival. It is our duty as Americans, as free people, to teach the Constitution to our children so they too may appreciate the freedoms the document seeks to protect. We must also remind those who come after us about the bravery of those who came before us – those intrepid Americans who fought to secure our freedom at Lexington and Concord and those who struggled to preserve it at Gettysburg, at Normandy, and in Afghanistan – as well as pray that God may guide those in the present day who have sworn to preserve, protect, and defend the Constitution of the United States. As Daniel Webster once said,

> *'Hold on, my friends, to the Constitution of the United States of America and to the republic for which it stands. Miracles do not cluster. What has happened once in six thousand years may never happen again. Hold on to your Constitution, for if the Constitution shall fail, there will be anarchy around the world.'*

"So today, as we celebrate our Constitution, let us renew our love of liberty. Let us rekindle that spirit in our minds. That spirit which Lincoln said 'prizes liberty as the heritage of all men, in all lands, everywhere.' Let us plant the seeds of liberty in the hearts of all children so that we may preserve our God-given rights for future generations, and as the Liberty Bell so boldly states, let us 'proclaim liberty throughout all the land unto all the inhabitants thereof.'"

Once the President concluded his remarks, he closed the binder holding his speech and waited for the applause to subside. He then reached into his suit coat and pulled out a pocket-sized copy of the Constitution. Wiley's very own copy. He ran his fingers over the bloodstained cover. He could almost envision Cogdon hiding off to the side of the stage, pacing back and forth, worrying that the President might screw it up. The thought brought a smile to his face. He turned to the Preamble and looked out over the crowd.

"'We the People,'" the President began, "'of the United States, in Order to form a more perfect Union, establish Justice, insure domestic Tranquility, provide for the common defense, promote the general Welfare, and secure the Blessings of Liberty to ourselves and our Posterity, do ordain and establish this Constitution for the United States of America.'"

As the Speaker of the House strode to the podium to read Article I, the President found his seat and saw Director Stubblefield returning to his spot in the row behind. He looked out of breath as he toweled off his head with a handkerchief.

"Everything okay?" the President asked. He thought the Director must have been in the restroom an awfully long time.

Stubblefield smiled and gave the President a wink. "Everything is fine, Mr. President. Everything is just fine."

CHAPTER 33

Silver Creek, Indiana

President Schumacher bent down and brushed away a few dried leaves that had collected in front of Wiley Cogdon's tombstone. The engraver had done a nice job on the marker. It was simple, just the way Cogdon would have liked it. The first line read: William "Wiley" Cogdon, while the second simply said "American." There was an American flag etched on the left and a copy of the Constitution with the "We the People" on the right.

The President had come to the cemetery to pay his respects now that the latest fire confronting America had been put out. All of the terrorist snipers had been captured or killed, much to the relief of the American people. Abdel Ramadi was indicted on terrorism charges and was beginning his slow rot in jail. Art Brennan was doing the same – his trial was set for the middle of next year and he still intended to represent himself. It was sure to be a show. People were still shaking their heads at the fraud that was Pastor Levitt and how he had converted to Islam to start jihad here in America. Most people also could not comprehend how he and al-Rashid intended to martyr themselves (and take thousands of lives with them) in Philadelphia.

Joined at the grave by FBI Director Stubblefield, the President placed a plush Wile E. Coyote stuffed toy in front of Cogdon's marker and closed his eyes in prayer. He would never forget the man, and his chief of staff's words of wisdom and love of the United States Constitution would remain forever in his heart and mind. What's more, the Celebration of the Constitution had been such a success that plans were already underway to expand the celebration all across the country next year. It would be Wiley's lasting legacy for America. He would be very proud.

Although the American people were trying to catch their breath after the latest terrorist episode, there was one other bombshell that was set to go off in the coming days in Washington. Vice President Jackson was going to make it official. It was time for her to resign to spend time with her husband. America was going to need a new Vice President.

After the President straightened the red, white, and blue carnations one final time, he and Director Stubblefield made their way back to the President's limousine.

"You know Vice President Jackson is going to resign next Monday, don't you?" the President asked his longtime friend.

Stubblefield looked over at the President. "I have heard that rumor," he said, not sure where the President was going with the topic.

The President turned his head and put his hand on the Director's shoulder. "I think you and I need to have a little talk."

THE END

For Those Who Might Be Interested

Pursuant to 36 United States Code §106 (36 U.S.C. §106), September 17th has been designated as Constitution Day and Citizenship Day with the purpose to "commemorate the formation and signing on September 17th, 1787, of the Constitution and recognize all who, by coming of age or by naturalization, have become citizens."

James Madison (1751-1836), a Virginia delegate to the Constitutional Convention of 1787, is known as the "Father of the Constitution" for his work in drafting the Constitution and the Bill of Rights.

Gouverneur Morris (1752-1816), a Pennsylvania delegate to the Constitutional Convention of 1787, has been called the "Penman of the Constitution" and is said to have drafted the Preamble.

Daniel Webster (1782-1852), United States Representative, Senator, and Secretary of State, has been called the "Expounder of the Constitution" for his scholarship and oratorical interpretations of the Constitution.

Six men signed the Declaration of Independence and the Constitution: George Read, George Clymer, Robert Morris, James Wilson, Roger Sherman, and Benjamin Franklin.

Rob Shumaker is an attorney living in Illinois. *Manhunt in the Capital* is his fifth novel. He is also the author of *Thunder in the Capital, Showdown in the Capital, Chaos in the Capital, D-Day in the Capital, Fallout in the Capital, Phantom in the Capital, Blackout in the Capital,* and *The Way Out.*

To read more about the
Capital Series novels, go to

www.USAnovels.com

••• •••• ••—